Advance Praise for *Perfect Enemy*

"Dystopian science meets utopian politics as competing visions for the future of the Middle East unfold across Israel's brittle political landscape. From the gossip-laden corridors of the Knesset to the high-tech labs of Tel Aviv and the rugged hillsides of the biblical West Bank, Sinclair draws on his deep familiarity with local politics, customs and social cues to keep the action thundering toward a startling, thought-provoking payoff."
Matthew Kalman, author of *The Murder of Yasser Arafat* and *Psychobibi*

"A blood-splattered room littered with the corpses of Arab terrorists and Israeli settlers... The perfect setting for a Middle Eastern love story. Hold on for a harrowing ride full of twists and turns. A page-turner!"
Rabbi Burt Visotzky, Appleman Professor of Midrash and Interreligious Studies Emeritus, author of *A Delightful Compendium of Consolation: A Novel*

"I couldn't put the book down!! Engaging and intelligent."
Paula Weiman-Kelman, filmmaker and director of *Eyes Wide Open* and *Fringes*

"A compelling read which drew me in and kept me involved throughout. It evokes the people and places of contemporary Israel skillfully and authentically and I found myself engaged with the characters and eager to know how the story would end. It's an intelligent thriller that gets the reader thinking about issues in Israeli society and politics that are all too relevant today."
Alan Hoffmann, former Director-General and CEO of the Jewish Agency for Israel

A Note from the Author

This book was written and completed many months before the 2023 Simchat Torah massacre by Hamas and the subsequent war.

The themes of the book – Jewish trauma, the desire for revenge against those who have caused us harm, the persistent hopes for peace, and the brutal realities of this region – are perhaps even more relevant now than before. I hope that this novel will add its voice to the conversations, issues and questions that this period has brought forth, perhaps shedding a different, more textured, kind of light. Fiction, ironically, can sometimes provide a depth of understanding that fact cannot.

Parts of the book, starting as early as the TV interview in chapter 2, might read like they were written after October 7th, but they were in fact written months or even years ago. So were the scenes from the final pages of the novel, which – without giving away any spoilers – may bring to mind some of the worst moments of October 7th. Prescient foreshadows have become painful echoes.

The book is probably harder to read now than it would have been on October 6th, but I hope that it will still be a compelling, suspenseful, exciting read, offering some respite from the despair that hangs over us. It even contains moments of humor, and despite everything, I hope those will make you smile. We still need that.

Thank you for reading *Perfect Enemy* and thereby taking the plunge into this messy, painful, traumatized, but still beautiful, part of the world.

PERFECT ENEMY

Alex J Sinclair

First printing, 2023.
ISBN 978-965-93101-0-4
Different Angle Books
DifferentAngleBooks@gmail.com

"The past is never dead. It's not even past."
William Faulkner, *Requiem for a Nun*

Chapter 1

The newborn baby cried, but the doctor made no attempt to calm him. She cleaned up the baby, weighed him, and diapered him. The baby began to quiet down for a moment, and seeing this, the doctor took a metal clip from the medical chart on the table in front of her, and carefully attached it to the baby's right arm. The clip pinched the baby's flesh and dug into his skin, causing the baby to shriek at this new source of pain. The doctor watched as the skin between the teeth of the clip got redder, and the baby wailed harder.

"That's right," she said. "Hurts, doesn't it? That's for my great-aunt Frida. Frida Eisenbaum and her three children. Treblinka, 1943. Cry, you little shit. There's plenty more where that came from."

The medical facility was private, gleaming, state of the art, but small: just this one birthing room, set off from a slightly larger space of laboratory rooms and sterile refrigerated storage units. The facility was five levels underground; far above, the noise, fumes and humidity of Tel Aviv jostled for space in its clogged rush hour streets. But down here, all was calm. The procedure had been a C-section, with the mother sedated under general anesthetic, as per the plan. Apart from the mother and the baby, the room contained just two women. The first woman, the project's anesthesiologist, removed the clip that she'd clamped on the baby's skin and put it back on the clipboard, and the second, the ob-gyn surgeon, having cut the umbilical cord only moments ago, got to work suturing the mother's womb.

The anesthesiologist put the baby in the incubator, took out her pen, and began to fill in the paperwork on the clipboard. The baby continued to whimper, and the sound suddenly transported her back to that night: pinned against the seat by the airbag, windscreen cracked with bullet holes, her husband's blood splattered on her face, her own baby girl crying out in agony in the seat behind her before the wails dwindled into that awful silence. *Never again*, she whispered to herself.

She attached a tag to the baby's wrist, giving its forearm another hard pinch as she did it. The baby cried out in pain again, and the doctor nodded grimly, blinking away a tear.

Never again.

Chapter 2

Twenty minutes later, the surgeon, out of her scrubs, knocked on the door of Akiva Cohen's office. Cohen had been running the project for over a decade, and she had worked with him for most of that time. She'd trained as a midwife and an ob-gyn, done residency at the Hadassah Ein Kerem hospital at the outskirts of Jerusalem, and spent years delivering hundreds of babies with the sole purpose of preparing for this delivery. Her last delivery.

She heard a muffled "come in," opened the door, and walked up to Cohen's desk.

"Nu?"

"All went as planned. Birthweight 3.1 kilos. Apgar 9. Looks and sounds like a regular baby boy."

Akiva took a deep breath. A tight smile. "You could have told me on the phone, you know. Or passed on a message via Neta."

The surgeon shook her head. The tired wrinkles around her eyes creased briefly with kindness. "Had to tell you myself. Had to see your face when I told you."

Akiva tilted his head in acknowledgement. His smile loosened just a little. "Yup. I guess you did. Thank you, Shira. I'm glad you came."

Akiva's fists clenched themselves involuntarily, looking for air to punch in joy; his stomach lurched with terror.

There's no turning back now...

He fished out a paperclip from a mesh metal tray in the corner of his desk.

Fingers shaking slightly, he began twisting and bending it out of shape, balancing it on the desk. His forehead prickled as it sensed Shira's gaze still upon him.

"Anyway..." she said. "Can't stay... have to go back down there to finish up."

But she remained motionless, looking at Akiva, patiently watching. Waiting.

Akiva's fingers scrambled for another paperclip from the pile. "How is Sivan doing?" he murmured, still not looking up.

"She's keeping the mother under sedation for the time being. But she's fine. Tired. Happy. Scared. Not quite sure what to think. Like me."

Akiva finally met her gaze. "I know. This is where it gets complicated."

Shira closed her eyes for a moment too long to be just a blink. "Anyway – I'd better go get started on that cleaning up." She gave a brief, tired smile, gathered her things and walked out of the office.

Akiva's office door was labeled:

Dr Akiva Cohen
Director, GeneLight Corporation

GeneLight's offices were on the twentieth floor of a shiny Tel Aviv skyscraper overlooking the Mediterranean. Around, above and below them were lawyers, accountants, insurance firms, a couple of hi-tech startups – all the usual accoutrements of Tel Aviv's swanky office buildings. To the outside world, GeneLight looked like just another faceless biotech company, like dozens of others in Israel's "startup nation." Shira walked out of the suite, past the bank of public elevators that led to the lobby, to a single elevator at the end of the corridor. Using a combination of thumbprint and iris recognition, she called GeneLight's secure elevator, which gave direct and swift access to their laboratory facility twenty five floors below. Until today, a total of four people had ever set foot in that underground facility. The mother had been the fifth. The baby was the sixth.

Akiva leaned back in his chair and closed his eyes in relief. The first phase of the project, the Scientific Phase, had now come to completion.

But his chest tightened with a pang of nervousness. Phase 1 was over, but Phase 3 – the Public Phase – was still another nineteen or twenty years away, at least. Phase 2 was now beginning, and there was still a long way to go.

Akiva opened his laptop and went into his email. He selected a few pieces of junk to trash, and then opened up an incognito window, ran a separate program, and clicked on the message from the other day. He began reading it, for the umpteenth time. He didn't believe in God anymore, but this reminded him of the days in which he used to pray. Reading the same text over and over again, each time feeling a new sense of elation from the familiar words:

> From: jondoherty@newstartbayarea.com
> To: akivacohen@privatemail.co.il
> Subject: follow up on your request
>
> Dear Dr Cohen,
> I'm following up on our conversation a few weeks ago
> and your subsequent email with further details –

Suddenly, though, before Akiva could get to the end of the email, there was another knock at the door. Akiva hastily closed the email, re-encrypted it, and shut his laptop.

"Come in."

This time a man entered. Taller and slimmer than Akiva, sun-tanned, buff. Akiva led the life of a scientist: sedentary, inactive, brain always on the move but seldom body. His body had paid the price, with high blood pressure and a bulging waistline. He was in his 40s, but looked older, grey hair frizzing unkemptly, Ben-Gurion-like, over a bald patch. The man who had entered was a couple of years older, but somehow looked ten years younger. Yoav Schindler,

Akiva's collaborator and partner. And funder.

The two men hugged. Not the usual half-hearted, don't-worry-we're-heterosexual, man-hug used on birthdays, religious holidays, or family celebrations, but a real, full-blown, body hug. The kind of hug reserved for once in a lifetime breakthroughs.

They broke apart, but still held each other by the shoulders.

"Akiva, mazal tov." Yoav shook Akiva excitedly. "You've done it. The sacrifices, the secrecy, the pain... but you've done it."

"*We've* done it. I couldn't have succeeded without you." Akiva dropped his hands from Yoav's shoulders, and they flapped uselessly by his side. He put them in his pockets for a moment, but then took them out and put them back awkwardly on Yoav's shoulders.

"Enough with the modesty," said Yoav. "I'm just the money guy. This is your achievement. You own this."

"Thank you," said Akiva. "Thank you for believing in me all these years."

Akiva tried to move back a step, but Yoav kept his arms firmly on Akiva's shoulders, his eyes locked on Akiva's, a look of quiet satisfaction on his face. "I knew you would succeed," he said. "Always knew it, thank God."

Finally, Yoav broke off, and looked around the room. "Look, the Blonde Bitch is on TV again," he sneered, gesturing with his head.

A flat screen TV, permanently set to the news channel, hung on the side wall of the office. Most of the time it was set to mute.

"It's a really unpleasant nickname," muttered Akiva. "You shouldn't call her that." He moved back toward his desk and randomly shuffled a few piles of paper around.

"Why not? Everyone else does." Yoav looked at the screen, unbuttoning his cuffs and rolling up his sleeves as if challenging the two-dimensional image to a fight. "All the liberal crap that comes out of her mouth, she deserves it. Turn it up and let's listen for a minute. It's good to keep abreast of how the enemy thinks."

"Seriously...? Let's not waste our time on–"

"Turn it up," repeated Yoav. Akiva did not protest further. He opened a drawer in his desk, pulled out the remote, unmuted the TV, and sat back in his desk armchair, pretending to watch. The "Blonde Bitch" was Hadas Levinson, a young, up-and-coming politician of the left-wing Labor party. The right-wing bloc led by the Likud and its uncompromising leader had won the previous elections, but Levinson, elected to a high position on the Labor party's list through its primaries after this defeat, had begun to lead a movement to push out many of the old guard and put together a slate of young, fresh faces. She was already being spoken about as the future leader of the opposition and maybe even a future Prime Minister.

"...of the current government's position." The volume went up as Levinson was being interviewed on one of the early evening news shows. "These policies have been leading Israel towards an abyss for the past two decades, and we have to wake up before we fall into that abyss. We can no longer control another people and expect them and the world to be okay with that. The Prime Minister and his coalition continue to lead us in the delusion that long-term peace is possible without first solving the Palestinian question. It's criminal that they still hold to this delusion."

"Criminal?" The interviewer interrupted. "That's a strong word. Do you really mean it?"

"You know what – yes, I do," replied Levinson. "A criminal is someone who endangers the life and property of another person. And that is exactly what this Prime Minister is doing. He is therefore, by definition, a criminal."

"Turn it off," spat Yoav, turning away in disgust and waving his hand dismissively at the television. "I can't take it any longer. The chutzpah of this... girl... this child... this fucking bitch who's barely out of diapers... to call one of our country's greatest leaders a criminal..."

"You wanted to listen," mumbled Akiva, half under his breath, pressing the mute button and returning the remote to its drawer.

"I must be some kind of masochist," snorted Yoav. "You know the hardest thing about our work? It's the patience. To think that we have to wait twenty more years before we can wipe the smug smile off people like Levinson's faces..."

"Patience is the name of the game now," sighed Akiva, almost to himself. He swiveled his chair away from his desk and looked out at the silent bustle of Tel Aviv with the twinkling sea beyond, inhaling the calm hum of the air conditioner. The constant lies lay congealed beneath the surface of his skin, blocking his pores. His whole being ached to break free. *Not yet, Akiva, not yet. Soon.*

Yoav drew closer to Akiva, turned his chair back to face him, and put an avuncular hand on his shoulder again. "Anyway. Akiva, I'd like us to call the staff together. Bring everyone in. Let everyone share this moment of success. Now is the time for recognition: I want to personally honor everyone who knows the truth about the project."

"But we've–" Akiva tried to protest.

"Who needs to be here?" pressed on Yoav, ignoring him. "Obviously Shira and Sivan. But who else?"

Akiva looked around the room, trying not to make eye contact. Sandpaper grated in his mouth. There was a carafe of water on his desk. He looked at it but didn't reach for it. Didn't trust himself to pour it without shaking. "Yoav... you know that the success of this project has always depended on secrecy. On nobody, not even you, knowing who else knows."

"Today is different," said Yoav. "Today we finished Phase 1. It's taken us years. Years of my life as well as yours. We have a long journey still ahead of us. But first we must celebrate."

Akiva's eyes were drawn back toward Yoav's as if in a tractor beam. He took a deep breath and exhaled. "Fine. You're right."

"I'm always right, Akiva, don't you know that by now?" said Yoav, with a winning grin, pulling off the illusion of self-deprecation along with impossible, unbreakable self-confidence. "So? Who?" He leaned up from Akiva's chair and stood expectantly above him.

Akiva rubbed his hands uneasily on the tops of his trouser legs. The sweat from his palms left a slight imprint. He inched the chair closer to the desk, keeping his legs out of Yoav's line of sight.

Calm, Akiva. You're so close. Tell him what he wants to know. As usual.

"I've kept the insides of the project a closely guarded secret," he said. "As we have always agreed. There's the four of us here, of course – you, me, Shira and Sivan – and, well, it's the five of us actually, because Neta's in the loop too."

"Neta? Seriously? I thought she just answered the phones up here, I thought you'd kept her away from compromising information."

"She's... um... never been down to the lab itself," said Akiva. "But at some point, she got suspicious, and I had to bring her into the circle. It wasn't easy. She almost ran out of here screaming. But she came around, and I have no doubts about her loyalty to the project." He looked up at Yoav briefly, almost daring Yoav to question him, but then backed down.

Yoav clicked his tongue five times, as if writing to hard disk the information that Akiva had just given him. He took a leisurely glance round at the TV on the wall. The day's headlines were scrolling through a bar at the bottom of the screen. Yoav scrutinized them for a few moments, muttering a private commentary on each headline as it rolled past. "Good... Interesting... *Idiots*... Must talk to him about that..."

In due course he sniffed languorously and turned back to Akiva. "So that's the entire staff here at GeneLight. Who knows apart from this group?"

Akiva paused. Yoav wasn't going to like this. "Tomer knows too."

"Tomer Kleinberg? Shit. That is such a mistake. Why him?"

Akiva licked his lips, trying in vain to bring some moisture to his throat. "I had to tell him, Yoav. He's my lawyer, and I'm engaged in a complex business here that is only going to get more complex as the years go by. I need protection. I'm not like you. You have... connections, you'd be fine if something went wrong, if we got found out. But I need to feel... safe."

Yoav sighed. "Who else?"

Akiva forced his shoulders back, his neck up, his head straight. *You're better than him.* "That's it. That's everyone. Six people."

"Six days of creation," said Yoav, leaning in toward Akiva again, giving him another squeeze on the arm. "A fitting number for the new being that we have created here. Call Tomer. Tell him to come over here tomorrow evening for a *L'chaim.*" He pulled out his wallet and, like a card sharp playing a trick, nimbly extricated two 200-shekel bills and magicked them onto the desk in front of Akiva. "Buy a good bottle of whiskey for us all."

Akiva made as if to argue for a moment but stopped himself and let Yoav leave. As the door shut, he grabbed the carafe of water with both hands, poured himself a glass, and brought it unsteadily to his lips.

It's going to be worth it. It has *to be worth it.*

He looked at the money that Yoav had left on the table and picked it up stoically. He held the notes by their corners, rubbing them softly between his thumb and his forefinger, glancing at the office door where Yoav had just left, then looking down again at the money. He stuffed the notes into his trouser pocket, and then wiped his hands on his shirt.

Just a few more weeks. Then it'll be too late for Yoav to stop me. For anyone to stop me.

Chapter 3

O ver the past couple of years, Hadas Levinson had become a household name – or rather, household nickname: she was aware that half the population of the country called her "the Blonde Bitch." She happily accepted this nickname for two reasons: firstly, because it didn't hurt her political ambitions to be portrayed with such hate by the right wing. It just made her a stronger candidate amongst her own base. Secondly, the association that everyone had with her free-flowing blonde hair made it easy for her to disguise herself. Before leaving the Knesset, she would go into a bathroom, put on a brunette wig and dark sunglasses, and walk out. She'd never once been recognized. The wig made her whole head incredibly hot – *how the hell did Ultra-Orthodox women cope with these things all day long*, she often wondered – but she was prepared to pay a bit of *schvitz* as the price of anonymity.

After her TV interview, she walked out of the Knesset's front gates and turned left, heading downhill toward the Israel Museum. She was always amazed by how small the city was. For all that the right wing blustered about Greater Jerusalem and its Arab neighborhoods being part of Israel's "eternal, undivided capital," the parts of Jerusalem that most Israeli Jews were familiar with were all within walking distance.

She crossed Ruppin Street and took one of the paths that led into the Valley of the Cross. The Valley was a collection of footpaths and half-footpaths through hills, rocks, and grass, that formed a natural barrier between the Knesset, the Supreme Court, and the Israel Museum on one side and the beginning of downtown Jerusalem on the other. It was owned by the Greek Orthodox Church, and an age-old contract forbad it in perpetuity from being developed. It was one of Jerusalem's lesser-known gems: in the middle of everything, literally steps from the centers of power, it was a green space away from the crowds. A place where one could be anonymous out in the open.

Walking toward her was a man in a white shirt that would be worn only a handful of times and then discarded, a pair of designer jeans, and some kind of Italian import crocodile- or snake-skin shoes. His skin was the light olive shade that could easily have been either Sephardic Jew or Palestinian Arab. He, like Hadas, wore sunglasses, but his, she was sure, must have cost five times as much as hers.

"*Salaam aleikum*," she said to him as they drew together, and gave him a brief but warm hug.

"And *shalom aleichem* to you, my dear," he replied. "I would say that it's been too long since I last saw you, but you're on my TV screen pretty much every day. What an interesting job you have!"

Hadas shrugged. "Beats poisoning teenagers for a living."

"My dear, you underestimate me," said the man, shaking his head in faux disappointment. "My company sells cigarettes to young people, old people, men and women, Jew and Arab – we are an equal opportunity poisoner!"

The man was Omar Suleiman, and he was a member of the elite club, small in number but large in cultural importance, of wealthy East Jerusalemite Palestinians. He'd inherited his father's company, a mid-size importer and distributor of cigarettes, and turned it into one of the Middle East's largest.

"You know," retorted Hadas, "If an Israeli called me 'My dear,' I'd immediately have him sprawled across the papers for sexual harassment."

Omar smiled. "My dear," he repeated, lifting his sunglasses momentarily to reveal a trademark raised eyebrow, "You can take the boy out of Harrow, but you can't take Harrow out of the boy." Omar's father had been invited by the PLO in the late 1990s, during the heady days after the Oslo peace process, to spend two years in London as the PLO's business attaché, and the impressionable early-teenage Omar had spent those years in one of London's most prestigious public schools.

"I thought that the Palestinians have never forgiven the Brits for the Balfour Declaration?" said Hadas with a grin.

"Well, my dear, it's true that the Balfour Declaration was one of the greatest diplomatic disasters ever to befall the Arab world, and that the actions of the British led to the stillbirth of the Palestinian national movement, the radicalization of Islam, and the schisms of the Middle East as we know it." Omar paused for a perfectly timed beat. "But on the other hand, a good strong cup of PG Tips with a nice chocolate biscuit does lead one to feel rather forgiving of the chaps, doesn't it?"

Hadas giggled in loving exasperation. "OK, I give up... as usual..." she said. She sat down on a bench by the side of the footpath.

"That's the spirit," preened Omar. "Now if only your army would have the same attitude once in a while..."

He sat down next to her, and she gave him a playful kick. Their banter was part of their relationship, and had been from day one. Hadas wasn't like this with anyone else – she was business-like, steel-willed, no bullshit, no messing around. But with Omar she found herself taking part in extended comedy routines like some kind of high-end BBC sitcom. She knew that Omar played up the whole British schoolboy thing for her – he also wasn't like this with anyone else – but she loved it.

They sat next to each other in silence. The evening sun reflected brightly off the sandstone footpath. The hum of crickets came from a nearby shrub, and birds chirped overhead. In the distance, the rumble of Jerusalem traffic, the occasional car horn.

Omar reached his hand across and began entwining it in Hadas's fingers.

She pulled her hand away. "Omar, we can't. It's too public. Even with my wig on. I can't risk it."

Omar sighed: "*There is a comfort in the strength of love; 'Twill make a thing endurable, which else would overset the brain, or break the heart.*"

Hadas looked at him with the kind of frustrated patience that is reserved only for those we really love. "OK, showoff. Keats?"

"Wordsworth, actually." Omar smiled.

"You know, some men use comedy as a deflective shield. For you, it's melodramatic poetry."

"I shall polish up my Mel Brooks impression for next time, my dear."

A pause. They looked at each other in silence. Hadas reached over and took off Omar's sunglasses. He squinted at the light, but his eyes were dry. For all his sensitivity, he was still a mix of stiff-upper-lipped Brit, dignified patriarchal Palestinian, and tough guy Israeli, and none of those character traits would have permitted his eyes to tear up. "If only you'd spent some time in America," she had once told him. "Then maybe you'd have feelings."

"Feelings, my dear, in my family," he'd answered, "are what happens when you stub your toe on the table leg. *Those* are feelings."

Omar reached across to take off Hadas's sunglasses too. She raised her hand and stopped him.

"Can't do it. Unlike you, my eyes *are* showing my emotions right now."

"I know. I will just have to imagine them, then."

A pause again. The tranquility of the setting was calming, almost hypnotizing. Hadas composed herself.

"Omar, I don't have much time. There's a vote I have to be at in half an hour."

"How tiresome. I was so looking forward to sharing my thoughts at length with you about Middlesex's latest follies." Hadas gave him another of those looks of frustrated loving patience. "Cricket, my dear, cricket."

"Again with the cricket," muttered Hadas, rolling her eyes.

Omar sighed. "Fine, fine, fine, I'll stop," he said, and switched into serious mode. "I heard they're going to close the case against those settlers in East Jerusalem?" he asked, leaning against the back of the bench, hands behind his head, stretching his feet out. He breathed in deeply, inhaling the light scent of jasmine from a nearby tree. To those who did not know Omar, this would have looked like listlessness; Hadas knew that this was his pose when his brain was at its most attentive.

"I heard so too. Annoying, but not surprising."

"Such myopia," groaned Omar. "There's a real strategic opportunity here to address residency and nationality issues for East Jerusalem Palestinians. Might write something about it tomorrow. The editor of *Al-Quds* has been pestering me for another piece."

It was almost like a metamorphosis, Hadas thought, how he did that. One minute Omar was this ironic, self-knowing caricature of an Englishman abroad; the next minute, he was back to Omar the Palestinian nationalist, a unique "connector" who had ties to everyone, but *everyone*, in the Palestinian business and political community. His outspoken op-eds in the international media made him a thorn in the side of the Israeli establishment, but his political activism in collaboration with Jewish Israelis made him something of an *enfant terrible* in the Palestinian community too. He received the occasional death threat both from right-wing Jewish settlers and radical Islamic terrorists who believed that he had "sold out to the Zionists." *Sometimes,* he had once joked with Hadas, although it wasn't really a joke, *I think that I'm the one who needs a brunette wig.*

"*Yalla, habibti.*" So, my love. "What shall we talk about?" said Omar. "Is this always how it's going to be? A few moments snatched here and there?" He put his sunglasses back on again.

"I hate it too, Omar," said Hadas. "But you know it's the only way. For both of us."

"You're right, I know," sighed Omar. "I can see the headlines now. 'New survey finds that most Israelis would be perfectly okay with their future Prime Minister's husband being Palestinian.' Hmm. I think not."

"Ah, we're playing Israeli-Palestinian conflict poker, are we?" grinned Hadas.

"I'll see your 'new Israeli survey' and raise you. You think that you could breeze in and out of Jenin for your business meetings with Hamasniks with your Blonde Bitch Israeli wife in tow?"

"Touché," beamed Omar, doffing an imaginary cap in Hadas's direction.

They both sat in thought for a few moments.

"You realize this is the first time we've used those... um... words... to describe our future?" murmured Hadas.

"Yes, I was just thinking the same thing," said Omar. He paused. "I like it." He cleared his throat and made a gesture as if to introduce the empty footpath in front of them to Hadas. "'My *wife* Hadas Suleiman.' It has a nice ring to it."

"I think I'll be keeping my name," smiled Hadas, leaning over to give him an elbow to the stomach, "you old-fashioned patriarchal oaf. But I like the sound of it too... 'my husband Omar'..."

They sat in quiet shared rumination, enjoying the fantasy but weighed down by its impossibility.

"In another universe, maybe," said Hadas.

"Or in this universe, if we both give up everything else in our lives," said Omar.

Hadas gave a nervous laugh, but then realized that Omar hadn't made a joke. "You're serious?" she asked. "You'd give up your business, your position in Palestinian society, your reputation, everything that makes you who you are... for me?"

Omar shrugged. "I don't know. It's a hypothetical question, isn't it? Because you're never going to give up your political career for me. And you shouldn't. You are an amazing person and someone who might actually bring some change to this pathetic region, and a little thing like the love of your life shouldn't come in the way of that."

Hadas looked at the ground. "I can never tell when you're being ironic and when you really mean it," she said.

He took off his sunglasses once more and studied her carefully. "I'm being serious, Hadas. I love you. You are the love of my life. I've never felt this way about anyone before. I wish you could be my wife. In another time, another place, I would want to marry you and have children with you and live happily ever after. But we live here, in this place, in this time. And both of us are addicted to this place and this time. Both of us, each in our own way."

Hadas turned her eyes to the ground again. A shiver of reality passed through her body. "We could elope and move to New Zealand together."

"Hmm," said Omar. "They do a rather lovely *Sauvignon Blanc* down there, I'll give you that. But my dear, after two weeks of gazing at the sheep we would both find it terribly boring. We would long to be right back here in this swamp. Back with the shitty highs we get from this shitty part of the world."

"You're right," said Hadas. "A girl can dream, though." She looked up from the ground at Omar's face again. "You're the love of my life, too. I also wish... wish we could be together, wish we could be normal... but you're right, I also want to do things here, for this country, for both of our peoples..."

"And if our relationship was public, that would be impossible," concluded Omar. "That's just how it is. And so, for the time being, at least, we must stick to these secret meetings. On the bright side, we're getting to know so many hotel rooms around this city that we could open up quite a definitive travel review website!"

Hadas gave a kind of gurgle that was a laugh and a cry at the same time. She elbowed Omar in the ribs again.

Another pause, as they both reveled in that moment when two people have told each other how they feel about the other, when each knows that, quite amazingly, quite insanely, quite impossibly, the other person feels the exact same way. Hadas sighed. "I have to get back. It's a vote on this new environmental legislation that I'm co-sponsoring. Got to be there."

Omar patted her on the hand. "Ever the crusader for all that is good and right in the world. Go get 'em, my love. My parallel universe wife..."

Hadas smiled. "I can live with that for now. Goodbye, my parallel universe husband. I'll see you tomorrow night?"

"Yup," said Omar. "I'll pick a hotel and text you. But wait, give your eyes a little wipe first." He held out a tissue.

"So thoughtful, my parallel universe husband is," sniffed Hadas. She took the tissue and wiped a couple of tears from the corner of her eyes. Then she stood up and, without looking back, walked back up the hill in the direction of the Knesset.

Omar waited a few minutes and sighed a deep, pained sigh. Then he got up and headed off in the other direction, toward where he'd parked his car, ready to head back to East Jerusalem.

Chapter 4

Akiva slumped back in his chair and blew out his cheeks. After waiting a minute or so to make sure that Yoav wasn't coming back, he pulled open a drawer in his desk; the same drawer where he kept the TV remote. In it was an eye mask and a box of disposable earplugs. There was a sofa on the wall of the office, opposite the TV, the kind that might be used for informal meetings with business associates when "across the desk" wasn't the right vibe. But Akiva didn't have any business associates. The sofa served a different purpose. He gingerly walked over to it, sat down, and carefully rolled the earplugs into small tubes before placing them into his ears. He then put on the eye mask and curled up on the sofa with his back to the TV, stuffing his face into the crease of the cushions. Slowly the earplug tubes expanded in his ear canal, blocking out the faint sounds of the street below. Between the earplugs and the face mask, Akiva found himself in total sensory deprivation, and that was what he wanted right now. What he needed.

There were no lies in the silent blackness that enveloped him. In the blackness he saw his future, the world's future, the future that he alone would create. In the blackness there was light. Just for a few minutes.

He'd first met Yoav many years ago, when he was a graduate student. It was the height of the Second Intifada: bus bombs, explosions in cafes and nightclubs, deadly gunfire on cars traveling near Palestinian villages. Barely a day went by without further terrorist attacks and casualties. Two weeks ago, a Palestinian terrorist had blown himself up along with thirty men, women and children celebrating the Passover seder at a hotel in Netanya. The whole country was in shock; the IDF was in the middle of a massive and bloody operation in Jenin in an attempt to destroy the Hamas network responsible for the waves of suicide bombings; and in Jerusalem, Tel Aviv, and Haifa, the cafes and pubs were empty. A pall of death hung over the whole country. A nervousness infested every conversation. People jumped at any loud noise, any ambulance siren, any traffic jam.

Inside the Hebrew University of Jerusalem's Givat Ram campus, though, an air of normalcy remained. Security at the entrance had been tightened, so once inside, you could relax. It was a beautiful, warm spring day, and the campus was buzzing with activity. Akiva sat on the grass in the middle of a large central lawn, reading the copy of *Scientific American* magazine that he'd just bought. It took the foreign newspapers and magazines a few days to make it to the shops in Jerusalem, and he'd been waiting for this one to arrive. There was a long-read piece in it with updates on the life of Dolly the Sheep, the first mammal to have been cloned from another animal. Dolly had been created by a team from the University of Edinburgh a few years ago, but, so it was reported, was now suffering from premature arthritis and other early onset health problems, raising many questions about the process's success.

Givat Ram was the home of Hebrew University's science faculties. The more famous Mount Scopus campus, in the far north of the city, was where the humanities departments sat, and that was the image that was usually conjured up in most people's minds when they heard "Hebrew U." Givat Ram was the lesser-known, less glamorous campus, with student dormitories that were falling to pieces and an array of squat, functional department buildings that would win no architecture prizes. But it lay in the center of the city, near the Knesset and the Supreme Court. Near the centers of power.

Cross-legged, leaning against his book-stuffed backpack behind him, Akiva began reading the magazine. After a while, he became aware of someone standing over him.

"You too, huh?" The figure stood between him and the sun, so all Akiva could make out was a tall silhouette. But he could see that the silhouette was holding the same *Scientific American* as he was.

Akiva squinted, and made out the features of a fellow student whom he knew by face, but not by name.

The tall student sat down on the grass opposite Akiva. Like Akiva, he wore a small knitted *kippah* on his head, signifying membership in the Religious Zionist community. He tapped his magazine on Akiva's, as if clinking wine glasses together. "Yoav Schindler," he said. "I've seen you around. Akiva, isn't it? Akiva Cohen? You're the lead doctoral student in Farbstein's research team, right? Everyone says you're his great prodigy. His anointed successor."

Akiva shrugged, his cheeks flushing with fleeting redness. "I don't know. There's a lot of smart people around here. Which of us will end up succeeding Farbstein – a lot of that's down to luck, I think. But yeah, I'm on the team."

"I hear Farbstein's been enjoying some serious *Schadenfreude* these past few weeks because of this Dolly setback," said Yoav. "That Edinburgh team are your chief rivals, right?"

Akiva hesitated. He looked back down at his magazine, debating whether to respond. Conversations like this, interactions with new people, drained him. He'd learned how to engage with people when he had to, how to make small talk, how to joke, even, but it sapped his emotional energy. There was something about this Yoav, though, that demanded response. Something insistent, something compelling.

Akiva folded over the corner of the page he was reading and closed the magazine with resignation, placing it on the grass in front of him. "Yeah, he's quite a competitive sort, loves winning, hates losing," he said. "You'll find that out soon enough, I guess. You've just started here, right? I've seen you around

21

campus, but not in lab or class. What program are you in?"

Yoav nodded but continued to press Akiva, moving imperceptibly closer to him with each question. "So: what do you think? First sheep, next humans? That's Farbstein's end goal, isn't it? Isn't that what you're researching too?"

Akiva nodded back. The back of his shirt felt damp, clinging to his skin. He pulled it up, trying to shake some air through it, and lifted his collar over his neck, which suddenly simmered with heat from the spring sun behind him. He had the uncomfortable feeling that he was being tested. By whom and for what purpose, he wasn't sure. "Humans... yes, eventually. Still a ways to go before we get there. Is that what you're thinking of focusing on too?"

"I'm focusing on saving the Jewish people," said Yoav.

Akiva gave a short laugh, but then realized that Yoav wasn't joking.

"So what about this British team?" Yoav continued. "How far ahead of us are they?"

"In some ways they're ahead of us," reflected Akiva. "They've certainly got the headlines, and of course they birthed a live mammalian clone, which we haven't yet. But I think there are other ways in which our work is superior. This setback for them" – here he tapped his magazine and shrugged his shoulders – "makes it pretty clear that in the long game, we're not far behind them, and maybe even ahead of them."

Yoav smiled. In one smooth, graceful movement, he sat down on the grass, tossed his magazine to the side, and leaned back next to Akiva, stretching his legs out and resting on his arms. "Good to hear," he said. "Good to hear."

Akiva remained cross-legged. He wiggled his shoulders to relieve the nervous tension that Yoav's nonchalant self-assurance had saturated into them. He could sense him still watching him. *Why did other people have to be so damn confident? How do they do that?*

Yoav said nothing. He examined Akiva pensively.

With his right hand Akiva started brushing a patch of grass to and fro, like stroking a cat's belly, enjoying the soft feeling of the blades as they gently tickled his fingers. He looked up to see Yoav still watching him and finally grasped at something to say. "So... what... what exactly are you studying here?"

"I'm kind of a non-matric for now," drawled Yoav. "Investigating a few different... options." He turned onto his side, chin resting on hand, with a cool ease that made Akiva's skin tingle with both envy and agony. "Tell me, what do you make of the government's response to all the terrorism we're experiencing?"

Akiva was momentarily thrown. "Um... fine, I guess," he mumbled.

"Come on, you can do better than that," said Yoav, punching Akiva playfully on the arm. But then Yoav became serious, leaned toward him, and spoke more quietly. "Akiva: I know who you are. I know where you come from. As far as I'm concerned, you're Likud royalty. Your opinion matters to me."

"I think you have me mixed up with someone else," said Akiva, looking down at his shoes.

"Naftali Cohen. One of the architects of Begin's first electoral victory in 1977. Brilliant young political thinker and strategist, practically wrote the book on campaigning from the center-right in Israel. Rumor has it that Begin saw him as a future cabinet minister, was grooming him to run for office. Forgotten today, because he tragically died before his time in–"

"I know when my father died," cut in Akiva.

"Sorry," said Yoav. "I didn't mean to... you know... hurt you... it's just that... well, I'm one of those who hasn't forgotten him. I've studied him. Look, you've probably already guessed this, but I'm not–"

"You're not a scientist," Akiva cut in again.

"Right." Yoav smiled. "I must stick out like a sore thumb here."

"Well," sighed Akiva, shifting a bit and maneuvering himself onto his knees, looking Yoav up and down, somehow tapping into Yoav's confidence and drawing on it for himself, "Let's see. We have the designer shades, exhibit number 1. The designer haircut, exhibit number 2. But the clincher is the designer linen jacket that a) I could never afford and b) I could never pull off even if I could afford it... so yes, I think you're just a little too cool and confident for this campus. We're all science nerds here. We're the ones who got beaten up at school for being too smart."

"Ouch," said Yoav. He paused and snapped into a serious tone again. "But lest you misunderstand me: I was also smart at school. In other ways."

Akiva's stomach twisted with a brief pang of something that he couldn't quite explain: like the moment of zero G-force on a rollercoaster, adrenaline and excitement mixed with primeval fear.

"I don't doubt it for a minute," he said. "So. You're smart. And you're not a scientist. But you've been milling around Givat Ram for weeks, and now you're quizzing me about biogenetics and cloning. So, Yoav Schindler, what are you? Who are you?"

Yoav reached over for his magazine, straightened it out on the grass between the two of them, and placed it delicately on top of Akiva's copy, adjusting it so that the two magazines stacked together precisely. He took off his sunglasses and looked at Akiva. Yoav's eyes were shining, mesmerizing. His smile was infectious.

"I work for a small, rather secretive, but very well-funded thinktank," said Yoav. "Our mission is to identify the best and brightest young doctoral students whose work we believe could benefit the State of Israel in some way in the future and... support them. Help them become scientists who are truly working for the good of the Jewish people, rather than slaving away in the academic rat race to get another paper published in a minor journal."

"And... what does one have to do in order to receive this support? Is there an application process?"

"Application process? No," said Yoav. "We are – how can I put it – 'proactive' in our search for those who we think meet our criteria."

"Well, I'm flattered," said Akiva. "So what's next? Is there some kind of interview?"

Yoav smiled warmly, his magnetic eyes still laser-locked on Akiva's. "You just passed it."

Minutes went by. Akiva's breathing was slowing, his nerve endings finally feeling less singed and raw. The future soothed his muscles, relieved the tension in his shoulders. He took a deep breath and resurfaced. He blinked as the fading light from the Tel Aviv beachfront entered his world again. He turned over and saw Shira standing above him.

"How long have you been standing there?" he asked.

"Only a minute or so. I've finished up the urgent stuff down there. Yoav came down to the lab and told us that he'd just been in with you. I wanted to see how you were doing but I know better than to disturb you when you're in recharge mode."

Akiva swung his legs onto the floor and sat back on the sofa. Shira sat down on the sofa too, not quite next to him, but not quite business-like distance apart either.

"Are you okay?" she said. She took a couple of the sofa cushions that Akiva's face had scrunched up, and started fluffing them out. She looked carefully at him. "Do you need more time? Do you need me to go?"

"No, it's fine," said Akiva. "I'm happy you're here. You're the only person in the world who knows that I do this."

"I'm the only person who knows lots of things about you, Akiva," smiled Shira. She moved across the sofa and hugged him chastely. "I'm happy to be here. I can't believe we've made it to this moment. I'm so proud of you, Akiva." She held on to the hug and her hand moved less chastely up to the back of Akiva's neck.

Akiva drew away. "I can't, Shira. You know I can't."

Shira took a deep breath. "I thought that... now that you've succeeded... now that we've made it to this point... maybe we could be free, be able to... We could be a project too. We once were. We could be again."

Akiva turned toward Shira and reached out for her hand. It was the first time in years that he had held it. For a brief moment, it awakened memories in him, and suppressed emotions bubbled to the surface. Visions of family, warmth, happiness, Shira at his side over the next twenty years. He could tell Shira the truth. She could come with him. They could carry out his mission together.

But as he turned her hand over in his, he hit reality again. On the inside of Shira's arm was a row of numbers. 140602. Her grandmother's Auschwitz number. Akiva winced, staring at the number, unable to get past it, eyes drawn to it like a car crash. She'd had it tattooed there some years ago – it was a "thing" among many young Israelis. Akiva had been appalled when Shira had first shown it to him. *It's such a burden to have that on your skin, to see it every day,* he'd said. *No,* Shira had replied, *it's not a burden. It's a reminder. A reminder of our past. And our present. So that we never forget.*

Shira's tattoo had convinced him that he could never be with her in the long term, never tell her the truth about his real plan, about his dream, about his future. But now, as he intertwined his fingers with hers for the first time in years, with his other hand he caressed her skin under the tattoo, wondering...

"I don't know," he said. "There are things... things about me... things that you don't know..."

"What are you talking about, Akiva? I know pretty much everything about you," said Shira, keeping hold of Akiva's hand, her smile fading slightly.

Akiva continued tracing his finger slowly through the numbers:

1-4-0-6-0-2...

And back again... 2-0-6-0-4-1...

1-4-0-6-0-2...

"You don't..." murmured Akiva. "There are... there are things I've been hiding from you. Things that might make you hate me."

"Nothing could make me hate you," said Shira, a warm smile back on her face, her fingers squeezing his.

Akiva leaned forward and kissed her softly but briefly on the lips. "If you still feel that way in a few weeks' time, ask me again then."

Shira furrowed her brow in puzzlement. "I don't understand..."

"I... I promise – I'll tell you more when I can. Go home and get some rest. I'll help Sivan finish up downstairs. You can come back later and relieve her for the night shift." Akiva paused and put his hand on her arm. "And please don't mention any of this to Yoav."

Shira crinkled her lips into a trembling smile and kissed Akiva gently on the cheek. She nuzzled herself briefly against his ear. "You dork," she whispered to him. "You're a silly, closed-in, dork. But you're a good dork. A good man. I just wish you'd let me in."

Akiva looked down at his hand, still entwined in Shira's. "It's... it's so complicated... I just can't..."

Shira disentangled her hand and stood up. She sniffed a little but took a breath and dusted herself off. "It's fine, Akiva," she said, forcing another smile onto her face. "I've trusted you every step of the way, you know that. What's another few weeks?"

Akiva looked at her in silence for another long moment. He opened his mouth as if to say something. But before he could, Shira turned, opened the door, and left.

Akiva stood still, nodding softly to himself, looking at the closed door in front of him. A few more weeks. *Maybe.*

Chapter 5

T he sun began to set. The mother, a non-Jewish Romanian mi-
grant-worker-turned-prostitute, was resting. In two days' time, on Friday, she would be paid handsomely and released, believing that she had carried
a baby as a surrogate for a pair of rich North Tel Aviv yuppies. GeneLight's
lawyer, Tomer Kleinberg, had drafted an iron-clad contract with her so that she
would have no further claim on the child. In fact, she wouldn't even know how
to begin looking for the child, or even for the facility: the contract had used a
shell company, set up for this transaction and then immediately disbanded, with
a PO box address that had been rented by another temporary shell company.
When the time had come for the scheduled C-section, the mother had been
sedated elsewhere by Sivan, brought in to the GeneLight laboratory under cover
of darkness, and would be returned to her home that way too. Nothing had been
left to chance; there were no tracks leading back to Akiva or GeneLight.

The whole project had layers upon layers of secrecy, sleights of hand, shell
companies, misdirections of colleagues and friends, legal and semi-legal protec-
tions. Only a few people actually knew the baby's true identity, but there had
been dozens of unwitting collaborators over the years; the Romanian prostitute
was only the most recent.

Akiva walked out of his office, down the corridor, and took the secure elevator down to the lab. The GeneLight laboratory consisted of several rooms, all
shining with white walls and metal surfaces, most of which looked like typical
biogenetic laboratory environments. Akiva walked in with a self-satisfied grunt,

immediately buoyed by the familiar smell of disinfectant, by the clean, gleaming counters, by the soft whirr of the various machines in the background. He put his hands in his pockets and strolled around, tapping a hand on a metal table, peering at a setting on a refrigeration unit, adjusting a knob on one of the machines. Here he was a different person. Here self-confidence flowed through his veins. Here was his home, his castle.

At the far end of the lab was a door leading to a very different room: the operating theater for the birth, which had been fully equipped with everything you would expect at a first-class modern surgical facility.

Akiva breezed in. The mother had been removed to a separate, smaller, recovery room; the baby was in an incubator, asleep; and Sivan, the anesthesiologist, who doubled as GeneLight's Operations Manager, one rung below Akiva and Yoav, was clearing up some of the equipment from the birth and tidying the room.

"Shalom Akiva, mazal tov!" said Sivan, walking over to him to give him a hug. "I know how long you've waited for this, how hard you've worked."

Akiva glared at her. "*Du vergisst die Vorschriften!*" *You are forgetting the regulations!* He continued his reply in fluent German. "Remember: no Hebrew is to be spoken in the child's presence at any stage! The child must grow up hearing only German and speaking only German. This is *crucial* to the project's success."

"But Akiva, it's just a baby, and it's fast asleep," protested Sivan, still speaking Hebrew. "It doesn't matter yet at this stage..."

"It *does* matter, and we have to start now, right now," fumed Akiva in German. "Research shows that even newborn babies pick up the speech patterns of different languages. We need to begin the all-German environment from day one. This child must grow up as a German, hearing only German, imbibing only German culture, speaking only German. His genes will take care of the optics. We need to make sure that he sounds the part too."

"*Es tut mir Leid.*" *I'm sorry*, Sivan mumbled, this time in German. She got back to work, tidying up medical implements and seeing to the various instruments around the baby's incubator. The staff of GeneLight had spent endless hours learning German. They had perfected their accents, worked on their fluency day after day, evening after evening. Akiva had stressed that this piece of the project's puzzle was no less important than the science.

Akiva sat down by the incubator looking at the sleeping baby, and Sivan peered over his shoulder.

"It looks a bit like my Meirav did when she was born," said Sivan, speaking softly now in German. "Is that a terrible thing to say?"

Akiva continued to gaze at the infant. "I don't think so. A lot of newborn babies look alike."

"I've been having more flashbacks since the birth," said Sivan quietly. "To the night they were murdered."

Akiva didn't respond.

"What we're going to do to this child..." said Sivan, "to this child, and to all the other ones afterwards, this will bring us redemption. No more Yosefs. No more Meiravs. No more Jews who will go through the pain that I went through. Right, Akiva? No more pain. No more murders. Never again."

Akiva swiveled around and looked deeply into Sivan's eyes. He put his hand on Sivan's arm, squeezed it gently and warmly, gave a brief nod. "That's right. *Never again*. No more pain." *And that, Sivan, is the truth.*

The two of them sat there in silence for a few more moments, gazing at the baby.

"Sivan," said Akiva, still in German. "Would you do me a favor and get me my notebook from the other room? Sorry, I just wanted to write down a few observations, but I think I left it over by the elevator."

"Of course," said Sivan. As she left the room, the door swung shut and she disappeared from view. Akiva craned his neck to make sure that Sivan was out of sight. Then, leaning down into the incubator, he kissed the baby's forehead, lovingly keeping his lips pressed to the child's warm skin for a moment as he breathed in its newborn smell, stroking its soft wispy hair.

"*Mein schönes Baby*," he whispered. *My beautiful baby.* "*Ich werde immer auf dich aufpassen.*" *I will always take care of you.*

Never again, Akiva repeated to himself. *That's exactly right.* Things might not turn out quite the way Sivan and Yoav thought they would, but on this, at least, they agreed. This child would bring redemption.

Chapter 6

The Jerusalem morning sun brightened the Knesset entrance courtyard as Hadas Levinson walked through its front gates the next day. As a backbench Member of Knesset, she had a small office of her own, but its claustrophobic sterility drove her crazy. She preferred the vibe of the shared space for parliamentary aides, elsewhere in the building, with its gray cubicles, battered desks and fabric-ripped chairs whose up-down mechanisms no longer worked; kind of like her old newsroom days. Hadas walked into the shared office and picked her way through an obstacle course of desks, chairs, and filing cabinets. The faint smell of stale tobacco hung in the air, despite the building's no-smoking policy. She made it over to one particular cubicle and tapped the woman sitting there on the shoulder. "No matter how early I get here, you're always here before me, huh?"

"Morning, Hadas." The aide swung her legs around and gestured back at her laptop. "Just working on the budget for the child benefits bill."

Hadas perched on a nearby chair and slung her briefcase on the floor. "Excellent. One step ahead of me as usual."

"How did the speech go yesterday?" asked Tzehainish. Tzehainish, an Ethiopian Jew whose family had been airlifted to Israel during the legendary Operation Solomon of the 1990s, had been Hadas's aide almost from day one.

"The speech? Grand total of nine MKs present in the chamber to hear it," replied Hadas, spreading nine manicured fingers in front of Tzehainish's face. "The coalition organized a boycott. All walked out before I even started speaking."

"Three guesses who was behind it," said Tzehainish.

"I don't even need to guess," fumed Hadas. "I know it was Navon. One of his henchmen from the Ultra-Orthodox caucus walked up to me afterwards and bragged about it. 'Message from Shmuel,' he said to me. 'This is what happens when you try to mess with us.'"

Tzehainish sighed. "He's not your biggest fan, is he..."

"Well," said Hadas, rubbing her hands together in devious irony, "I'm destroying the Jewish people, and all that."

Tzehainish pretended to tear out her hair: a fantastic explosion of deep black curls which seemed to defy the laws of gravity. "Aargh... makes no sense!" she wailed melodramatically.

"Since when did you start looking for sense and logic in this building?" smiled Hadas.

A man walked into the office. He was in his early sixties, with graying temples and a loud tie. "I see that Ebony and Ivory are still plotting to change the world, then?" he announced.

"You know that if I ever want to destroy your career, I'll just tell the press that you use those nicknames for us, don't you, Benny?"

Benny Shoham laughed. He was one of the Labor party's veteran politicians, one of Hadas's mentors and favorite senior colleagues, with a second-to-none track record of anti-racism legislative work and political activism toward equal rights. But he also had a terrible sense of humor.

"See, Hadas, you're making three serious mistakes in that statement," he replied, wheeling over the biggest chair he could find, sitting grandly in it and putting his feet up on a nearby desk. "First of all, you assume that I have any career worthy of the name that is left to destroy. *Strike one*, as the Americans say. Secondly, they are not nicknames, they are terms of affection and endearment, the use of which to describe you makes literary allusion to the classic song by Paul McCartney and Stevie Wonder that talks of perfect harmony, which is clearly your political and spiritual goal, and an admirable goal at that, in my humble opinion. *Strike two!* And thirdly," he trumpeted, producing as if from nowhere that day's newspaper, "There's no such thing as the press any more. Our work is reported on by sweaty-palmed teenagers tweeting away in their bedrooms – they are our real masters." He crumbled the paper between his hands and threw it theatrically over his shoulder. "So *strike three,* and we all lose!"

Hadas turned to Tzehainish. "See what I have to put up with? And you want to become a politician too? Are you nuts?"

Tzehainish nodded. "And he's one of the good guys. God help us."

Benny wagged a finger at Tzehainish with a comical *tsk-tsk.* "You see, that's the problem with you traditionalists. Enough already with the belief in God!"

Tzehainish folded her arms and shook her head. "You know, Benny, it *is* possible to believe in God and still be a left-winger. If the Left wasn't so condescending to traditional communities about their beliefs, more of them might vote for us."

Benny raised his hands in mock surrender. "Do you think that the senators' aides on Capitol Hill talk to them like this? Such insubordination! In any event, I wish it were otherwise, Tzehainish, believe me I do, but the right wing and the religious sector have practically become synonyms."

He got up from his chair and ferreted around behind it for the newspaper he'd hurled over his shoulder. Tzehainish giggled at the sight of Benny crawling on all fours trying to locate the scrunched-up paper, which had somehow got lodged underneath a filing cabinet. "I actually need that damn paper for a meeting later, where the hell did it get to," he muttered.

Hadas shook her head in exasperation at Benny's antics but sighed at the real issue he'd raised. This was a conversation that they had had before, and she didn't quite know which of her trusted friends and colleagues she agreed with. They were both right. She knew that her child benefits bill wasn't making her any friends in the religious world, but she desperately hoped that some of the more clear-headed religious leaders would finally agree to partner with her on it.

"I'm going to the bathroom. The two of you can carry on this fascinating conversation for a few minutes." She turned to Benny, who was now safely ensconced back on his chair. "Maybe you can have a word with Shmuel Navon? You've co-sponsored stuff with him in the past, right? You have a decent history together? Do me a favor and have a quiet word?"

"I'll try," said Benny, straightening out the newspaper on his lap. "I don't like my chances though."

"Thanks," said Hadas. "And Tzehainish – finish up the budget and email it to me when it's done. I'll be in my office. And then I want you to get in touch with Navon's aide. His name's Avi something, right? He seems a little more reasonable than his boss. Have a call with him, see if you can set up a meeting for the four of us, and we'll try to talk sense to Navon one more time."

"I'm on it," said Tzehainish.

"You're a doll, Ebony," said Hadas, with a wink.

"No problem, Ivory," grinned Tzehainish back at her.

"I'm honored that you see fit to humor an old man like me," said Benny, clasping his hands together in a namaste.

"I'm going," said Hadas. She walked a few paces toward the door, but then turned around. "And Benny: don't try to steal Tzehainish again. She is *not* going to work for you."

"Foiled again," said Benny with a shrug.

Later that afternoon, Hadas and Tzehainish were sitting with Navon and his aide, trying desperately to persuade him to be more understanding of their position. It was not going well: they had had to sit through a twenty-minute lecture about the Jewish imperative to "be fruitful and multiply," and how her bill was a direct attack on that Biblical commandment. Navon swayed back and forth in his chair, stroking his bushy, gray-flecked beard, quoting Biblical and Talmudic passages, while Hadas waited for him to come up for air.

Hadas was finally able to protest. She drew herself up in her seat and placed a folder on the table between them, pulling out various charts and reports as she spoke. "You know as well as I do that the *Charedi* community needs to lower its birthrate. These families with seven, eight, nine children, it's unsustainable economics. You suffer from overcrowding, housing shortages, unemployment... cutting child benefits for families with more than four children will still allow your communities to grow, but at a healthier rate, and in a more sustainable way. In the long run, my bill will *help* your constituency, not harm them."

"Six million Jews," boomed Navon, poking a finger in Hadas's face, his other hand brushing away the documents on the table. "Six million Jews we lost in the Holocaust. My community are the ones trying to replenish those numbers. And not just the numbers: the culture, the Jewish learning, the life that was destroyed. How *dare* you try to take this away from us? How *dare* you say this is about economics?" Navon increased the urgency of his rocking back and forth in his chair, like a teacher in yeshivah coming to the denouement of a complicated piece of Talmud, adjusting the large black yarmulka on his head. "Every new Jewish child born is a cause for celebration, a blessing, a *mitzvah*. The State of Israel should be encouraging *more* Jewish children, not less. Your bill is an insult not just to us, but to the entire Jewish people! It is an affront to Jewish history!"

"Rabbi Navon," said Hadas, trying to placate him, "please try to be reasonable. It's—"

"Not everything is about reason, young lady," snapped Navon, standing up. He put on his large black fedora hat, straightened it with a glare, and pulled his black suit together over his crumpled white shirt. "Reason has not helped the Jewish people survive for three millennia. The heart and the soul and the Torah – they have been our strength and our salvation. Reason, science, your so-called 'enlightenment'... these will lead to the Jewish people's destruction, God forbid.

I will not let that happen. Not on my watch. Your bill will not survive, and mark my words," he said, wagging his finger again at Hadas, "neither will your political career if you continue to pursue it."

And with that, Navon walked out.

"Avi..." Tzehainish appealed to his aide. "Maybe you could..."

"No can do," said Avi, shaking his head. "He's not going to budge. You need to drop it."

"Not going to happen," declared Hadas.

Avi shrugged his shoulders and jogged out of the room to catch up with his boss.

Hadas and Tzehainish trudged dejectedly out of the room.

"How dare he lecture us about Jewish history?" said Tzehainish indignantly. "My family walked to Addis Adaba for three weeks through the desert. My grandmother died of exhaustion and malnutrition on the journey. I sat with my mother in the shade of a tree while my father and brothers buried her by the side of the road. And then we carried on walking. And all because we dreamed of Jerusalem, we dreamed of Israel. He thinks that *I* don't care about the Jewish people?"

"It's impossible," sighed Hadas. "Impossible to get through to them. They use the same words as us, but they speak a different language."

They walked on in frustrated silence, heading back in the direction of Hadas's office. Rounding a corner, they passed a meeting room with a half-open door, and they saw that inside, six members of Knesset from a couple of the small Arab parties were having some kind of caucus meeting.

Hadas turned to Tzehainish and raised her eyebrows, her frustration at the previous meeting forgotten. "Shall we...?" she asked with a sly smile.

"After you, boss," her aide replied.

Hadas knocked on the door and without waiting for a reply, pushed it all the way open and walked in. *"Ahalan w'sahalan,* friends," she announced, using the Arabic greeting. "Sorry to drop on in you like this, but if you are plotting the destruction of the Zionist regime, you really ought to keep your door closed!" (Hadas was quite proud of this opening line; Omar would have approved.)

Hadas had good relations with three of the Arab MKs who were in the room. One of them, Mahmoud Zaid, was a man about her age, an Israeli Arab from the Galilee in the northern part of Israel, also in his first term in the Knesset, whom she'd interviewed a number of times in her journalism days. He beckoned her over to the table. One of his colleagues, an older MK whom Hadas knew less well, frowned at Mahmoud, and muttered something to him in Arabic.

"It's okay, Tariq," said Mahmoud. "She's not like the others. Come join us for a few minutes, Hadas. How goes it?"

Hadas walked over to the table and shook Mahmoud's hand warmly. She'd given him some advice on a bill he had worked on a few months ago, trying to get funding for road awareness training in the Israeli-Arab sector. The bill was currently buried in committee, but the collaborative experience had been a good one. Most of the Israeli-Arab MKs were usually quite radical in their attitudes toward the Jewishness of the State of Israel, and campaigned loudly that Israel should cease to be a "Jewish State" and instead become "A state of all its citizens," which Jewish Israelis interpreted as dog-whistle code for the complete dismantling of Israel's Jewish structures and roots. Mahmoud was more moderate; in one of his interviews with Hadas, he'd told her that he accepted that Israel would always have a Jewish character of some sort. "We want to be part of Israeli society, and we understand that this means speaking Hebrew and living in a country with a Jewish national character," he'd said. "If you give Arab-Israelis equal access to this country's resources, if you enable them to celebrate their Palestinian cultural and national heritage, and if you invite them into the leadership echelons of Israel with a sense of respect and dignity, then you will be surprised at how much they will be able to give. If you grant us dignity as Palestinians on Friday morning then we will wish you *Shabbat Shalom* on Friday night."

Hadas also happened to know that Mahmoud was an old friend of Omar, from their time studying at Haifa University together, and so she liked to touch base with him every so often just to see if there were any hints in his attitude to her that Omar had spilled the beans to him. But either Mahmoud was an extremely good actor, or Omar was keeping their secret as carefully as she was.

Hadas pulled up a chair and sat down at the table; Tzehainish hovered by the wall. "The truth is," she confessed, "I'm having a miserable day. I'm trying to drum up some cross-party support for my child benefits bill, but I've just come from a rather dispiriting meeting with one of the *Charedi* MKs. You've said in the past that your voters also have big families and therefore that the bill would be a problem for you too, but I wonder if there's any way you could reconsider that position?"

Mahmoud looked queryingly at the MK who had frowned when Hadas walked in, and the older man gave a slight nod. "My teacher Dr Tariq Khalid and I were actually talking about your bill earlier," said Mahmoud, making a deferential gesture to his senior colleague. "And we think there may be a way we could make some things work to all of our benefits. My road awareness bill is stuck right now, as you know. The committee member who is holding it back is a friend of yours, Benny Shoham. I don't think he's against the bill per se, but he has some kind of history with the chair of the committee, and he's dragging his feet in order to piss him off."

"That sounds like Benny," said Hadas, exchanging a knowing glance with Tzehainish. "He can sometimes let personal vendettas cloud his broader strategic judgement. I'll have a word with him. So... if I can get Benny to remove the blocks from your road bill in its committee, you'll support my benefits bill?"

"We would certainly give it renewed consideration," pronounced Mahmoud, smiling broadly and leaning back in his chair.

Hadas paused. She looked around the table. With the exception of Mahmoud and the only woman in their group, each of them was a slightly different cookie-cutter copy-paste of the other. Middle-aged, graying Israeli-Arab patriarchs, each of them with bald patches, rolled up sleeves, nicotine-stained fingers, and waistlines spilling over their pants. The Israeli-Arab community remained for the most part a traditional, largely religious society, with women usually holding home- or education-oriented jobs and men as the communal leaders. She felt as distant from these dinosaurs as she did from the *Charedi* MK she'd just left. Her values – gender equality, science, progressiveness – were alien to both of these communities.

"You'll give it renewed consideration," Hadas repeated slowly.

"Indeed," beamed Mahmoud benevolently.

"Not good enough," countered Hadas. "Now listen here. I can be a valuable partner to you, Mahmoud. I am going to be the future leader of the Left, and I intend to be the future leader of this country. I'm not like the lefties of the past who hated Arabs only slightly less than they hated the Right. I genuinely believe in making Israel a place that gives you and your community respect, equal rights, a place at the table. A shared society. If it's up to me, you'll be a cabinet minister in my government. You know me well enough to know that those are truly my beliefs."

Mahmoud nodded. "True."

She got up from the table, walked round to Mahmoud, and swung his chair round so that he was facing directly at her. "But that doesn't mean that I'm a soft touch. I know you think that I'm a pushover, that I'm a wishy-washy liberal who just wants to be nice to everyone. But make no mistake, when I make a deal with someone, I expect them to come through with their side of the deal."

A shot of adrenaline pulsed through Hadas's body, together with a sense of supreme calm and clarity about what she needed to do and say next. She leaned over him and spoke quietly, but loudly enough so that everyone in the room could hear.

"If you double-cross me, if you make a deal with me and then go back on it, then you will regret it. I will come after every shitty little road bill you ever try to push through and make sure that it gets destroyed. I will find out who your worst enemy is and give him what he needs to out-primary you. I will make sure that you end up back in the local city council where you came from, deciding what day the trash collection should be on. Do you understand, Mahmoud? A deal is a deal as far as I'm concerned. You want me to help you with Benny, I help you. But then you help me with my bill. No ifs, no buts, no I'm so sorrys, no if only I'd knowns. I come through with my side, you better come through with yours. That's what it means to be equal."

At this, Khalid interrupted her. "How dare you speak to us like that?" he sputtered. And then, turning to Mahmoud: "I told you she was trouble. Listen to the way she talks to us. She's just like the other Zionists. You might be taken in by her, but I am not. I will not stand for this. Either she leaves now, or I do."

Mahmoud started replying to his senior colleague in Arabic. But Khalid waved him away and turned back to Hadas. "You will regret this, Levinson. My ancestors have lived in this land for hundreds of years. You Jews will not tell us how many children we should have. You will learn some respect."

He stood up straight and proud, turning his back on Hadas and facing his colleagues. "I say again. Either she leaves, or I do."

Mahmoud looked at Hadas and grimaced. "I'm sorry," he said. "I think you'd better go."

"It's fine," shrugged Hadas. "You figure out your internal issues without me." She walked toward the door, and addressed Mahmoud, pointedly ignoring Khalid. "Tzehainish will now give you her cellphone number. If you want this deal, then send her a message by the end of today simply saying 'yes.' If you don't want the deal, that's fine. I'll let Benny know that he can use your little road awareness bill as a never-ending store of shit that he can throw at that committee chair that he hates so much, and by the time the bill gets out of that committee we'll all have flying cars and you won't even need roads any more. But if you do want the deal, then you come through with your side of the bargain, and you support my child benefits bill as if it's Palestinian sovereignty on the fucking Temple Mount."

And with that, Hadas opened the door and walked out.

Tzehainish hurriedly scribbled down her phone number on a piece of paper and put it on the table in front of Mahmoud.

"That's some boss you've got there," he muttered.

Tzehainish tried desperately not to grin so broadly.

Tzehainish jogged down the corridor and pulled up alongside Hadas. "God, I love it when you curse so much," she bubbled. "It's like your secret weapon! They *so* don't expect it from you, it seems so out of context with your lefty persona and your... you know... your hair and your good looks and all that, they think you're some Barbie bimbo or something, and then you open your potty mouth and it's like a neutron bomb, it's amazing!"

Hadas grinned at Tzehainish. "Ssh, keep your voice down. Don't give away all my trade secrets."

"Do you think it worked?" asked Tzehainish, almost skipping around Hadas like a schoolgirl. "Do you think they'll go for it? Maybe you went too far?"

"Let's wait and see," said Hadas. "Depends on whether Mahmoud can win that little generational struggle we just witnessed. Tariq Khalid is the old guard, and he's probably as suspicious of Mahmoud as he is of me. Anyway, let's go find Benny and tell him about the promises I've made on his behalf. No doubt I'll have to pay a price for that, that's the way it works. But it'll be worth it."

Benny Shoham was usually to be found holding court in the Knesset cafeteria, at a corner table that had been his informal fixed place for decades. He would sit at this table for hours on end some days, beckoning political friends and enemies over for coffee and meetings in the public eye, but in hushed tones: huddled conversations that were public enough for others to see who he was talking with but private enough that their contents remained secret. The rest of the time he would sit there alone, eyes scanning the room like a Terminator cyborg, carefully noting away who was talking with whom.

They found Benny at his usual table. Hadas told him of the deal she'd suggested to Mahmoud.

"Shit, Hadas," sighed Benny. "I was having so much fun messing around with that committee chair. He's such an asshole. Oh well. I shall just have to find someone else to play with."

"Sorry to spoil your party," smiled Hadas. "So, Benny, what's the quid pro quo? What can I do for you as a thank you for this favor?"

"Well now, Hadas," said Benny, rubbing his hands together in exaggerated triumph, "I wouldn't do anything as simple as tell you straight away. My mind is a political bank account, and I remember everyone's—"

"Yes, yes, yes, we know," said Hadas. She made air quotes with her fingers. "Everyone's deposits and withdrawals, blah blah blah. I've heard you say that once or twice before..."

"Quite so," said Benny with a smile and a tilt of his head. "And I will call in my favor at the time and circumstance of my choosing."

Hadas shook her head in mock exasperation. Before she could respond, though, Tzehainish's phone buzzed, and she pulled it out of her pocket. She swiped it open, took a brief look, and held it up in the air like a trophy. "It's an SMS from Mahmoud," she said, and thrust the phone in front of Hadas's face. The message consisted of a single word.

Yes.

Chapter 7

Akiva had slept fitfully and made his way back to GeneLight before the Tel Aviv rush hour. He went to check on the baby – Shira and Sivan were both there, doing the handover from one shift to another – and then went back up from the lab to his office. He sat there alone, gazing out at the Mediterranean, imagining himself soaring above it. A shiver of anticipation danced through his body and his shoulders twitched in a nervous spasm.

Soon. Another few days. Two weeks, max. It's all going according to plan.

He shut his eyes and let his dreams seep into his bones, oxygenating his blood, stretching his sinews. He saw Sivan and Shira, smiling, happy, grateful. Free from anger, free from pain.

Never again.

His mind wandered back to when he'd first learned of Yoav's plans for the project.

He remembered knocking on the door of Yoav's apartment, which was located in a quiet suburb of Jerusalem. By now, he was Dr Cohen: the previous year, he had received his doctoral degree with honors. Farbstein, the professor of the department, was nearing retirement, and Akiva was being spoken of as the likeliest candidate to replace him – a remarkable step for someone so early in his career. Akiva's research was shrouded in secrecy, but if three years ago, when he'd met Yoav on the Hebrew U campus, he had been unsure about whether or not they were ahead of the British team, he now knew that Farbstein's team – which was increasingly becoming Akiva's team, as Farbstein took more and more of a back seat – was the leading biotechnology cloning team in the world. Their work was still out of the headlines, but that suited them well.

Yoav pulled the door open, his eyes gleaming, his smile wide, his presence as immediately overwhelming as usual. Over the past three years, Akiva had spent many hours with Yoav, basking in the radiation of his personality, constantly exhilarated by his endless energy, but, like Daedalus, trying not to fly too close to the sun. Yoav, while he wasn't a scientist, had an uncanny sense of what kinds of research moves might work, what kinds of questions to explore. He'd acted as a kind of advisor and sounding board for Akiva. And, of course, a funder: by now, Akiva had received thousands of shekels from Yoav's mysterious NGO, in return for which he had to submit only the most perfunctory of annual reports. Yoav assured Akiva that his own oral presentations to the NGO's board were the only thing that mattered.

The quiet suburb where Yoav lived was one of the most expensive of Jerusalem, and the apartment itself was outfitted to a level of style and quality that far surpassed Akiva's student digs. He stood in the doorway nervously, tapping his hands against the doorjamb, unsure of whether to enter. The smell of freshly-made popcorn wafted from the kitchen and saliva seeped between his teeth in response.

"Okay, what's the big excitement? Why are you dragging me here? I thought we were meeting at the cafe down the road?"

"No TV at the cafe," said Yoav, eyes still gleaming.

"We're watching TV? I thought we were going over that grant application that we nearly finished writing last week?"

"The grant can wait. You have to watch this movie first." Yoav produced a DVD and waved it in Akiva's face.

"The grant can wait? This is a first. You're the one who's always telling me that there's no science without money. The deadline for this application is next week, and it would really help with the research plans for the next few months."

Akiva could feel his face begin to flush, an internal sauna pumping heat into his neck and cheeks, but the more he told himself to calm down, the more flushed he felt.

"Trust me. If we miss the deadline, I have a lead to some more private money that we can tap into," said Yoav.

Akiva pursed his lips and took a step back, glancing uneasily up and down the corridor of the apartment building. "I'm not happy about all this private money we've been using lately. We're a public university, we should rely only on transparent and public funding sources. I feel like I don't even know who's paying my stipend every month – it's all these mysterious private donors that you bring in."

"Look, we've been over this," said Yoav, reaching out to Akiva, putting his arm around his shoulders, pulling him into the apartment. "We're a good team. You're a scientist, I'm an investment banker. You do the science; I do the fund-raising. You get your money to do your work, end of story."

"And what do you get, Yoav?" asked Akiva, allowing himself to be guided in. His internal sauna dialed down a degree or two. "Don't get me wrong – I'm grateful. I wouldn't be where I am right now if it weren't for you. But what's in it for you?"

Yoav held up the DVD again and stopped smiling. The tone of his voice changed from friend to supervisor. "This is what's in it for me."

"Fine. You win, as usual." Akiva slumped down onto the sofa. A gnawing feeling pulsated in the pit of his stomach, the same sensation he always got when Yoav outmaneuvered him.

Yoav wandered over to the fridge, pulled out a couple of beers, grabbed the fresh popcorn, and then knelt down by the TV. He put the DVD in the slot, and pressed play. "You ever heard of this movie?" he asked. "*The Boys from Brazil.*"

Akiva gave a puzzled look. "It rings a bell. Isn't it something to do with Nazi hunters?"

Yoav nodded.

"Half-right. It's something to do with Nazi hunters. But it's something to do with us as well."

The title credits of the movie began to play. The movie was based on a 1976 book by Ira Levin. The plot imagined a group of Nazi geneticists who had preserved some of Hitler's DNA and had impregnated dozens of women around the world with embryos that were genetically identical to Hitler. The crux of the plot was that since Hitler's father had died when he was a teenage boy, the fathers of all these teenage boys also had to die, so that the genetic Hitler would have as similar an upbringing as possible to the real Hitler, raising the chance that one of these new Hitlers would develop the personality of the original, and lead the Aryan people into a Fourth Reich.

Akiva watched, transfixed. The end credits rolled, Yoav clicked off the TV and turned to Akiva.

"He was the worst, but he was neither the first nor the last. First it was the Egyptians, then the Amalekites, then the Greeks, then the Romans, then the Christians," said Yoav, counting them off on his fingers like points in a debate. "Jewish blood has been spilled throughout history like water. And now the Arabs want their turn. Now *they* want to drive the Jews into the sea. *There will always be someone who seeks to destroy us.* Imagine if we could change that."

Akiva stared at the blank TV, seeing only his own face reflected in it, not wanting to look at Yoav, not sure he could hide from Yoav the thoughts that were racing in his mind. "Yes," he said softly. "Imagine if we could change that."

Chapter 8

They'd left Benny in the cafeteria rubbing his hands, promising to come up with a despicably evil favor that he would extract from Hadas as his quid pro quo for helping with Mahmoud's committee.

"He's all talk," smiled Tzehainish, as the two of them wound their way through the maze of Knesset corridors and stairways. People bustled around them: parliamentary aides running errands for their MKs, lobbyists walking languidly through the hallways as if they owned the place, the occasional cabinet minister on his or her way to a meeting, trailed by a bevy of assistants, journalists sniffing around for the latest piece of gossip, a bunch of teenagers on a high school trip. The atmosphere was more Middle Eastern *shuk* than the quiet hum of respectability found at the Houses of Parliament or the Capitol.

"Yup," grinned Hadas back at her, waving at the same time to someone she knew who was hustling in the other direction. "He's really a terrific mentor. He's looked out for me from my first day in this crazy building."

"It's not out of altruism, you know," said Tzehainish. "It's because he genuinely believes in you and thinks you're the great young hope of the party. Of the Left. I think he wants you to be his legacy."

"Maybe," shrugged Hadas. "That's a big word to hang around someone's neck, though. And listen, let's not delude ourselves – he has an ulterior motive too. He's looking ten or fifteen years down the line at the end of his political career, and he would love to be President."

"President... of course..." said Tzehainish, slapping her forehead. The two of them rounded a corner and were blocked by a sudden exodus from one of the committee meeting rooms, representatives of NGOs scowling at the perfunctory treatment they'd just received, MKs hurrying off with cellphones pressed to their cheeks for imaginary "urgent" calls. "Why didn't I see that? Why didn't I think of that?"

"Because you're not a politician yet," said Hadas, putting her arm around her friend's shoulder. "But you will be."

The position of President of the State of Israel was a ceremonial and honorary one, with almost no actual powers, akin in certain ways to the role the Monarch plays in the United Kingdom. It was, however, an elected position, appointed every seven years by the one hundred and twenty members of Knesset.

They pushed their way through the crowd and Hadas stopped for a minute or two to exchange small talk with a couple of people. She was energized by this environment, every minute a decision point, every conversation one of potential import, every interaction a shot of caffeine to her soul.

"So," Tzehainish went on as they found themselves in some space again, "you think he's helping you so that one day, you'll bring the Labor party back into power, you'll be Prime Minister, and you'll help him become President?"

Hadas nodded. "Sure. He's the perfect candidate for President. Grand old man of politics, no scandals, worked across party lines, mostly uncontroversial. His only problem is that as long as the Right is in power, he's much less likely to get the nod. He jokes about it with me sometimes, you know. He'll say things like 'One day, you'll be PM, and I'll be President, and we can go for evening strolls together in Jerusalem,' that kind of thing. But I know it's not really a joke. The fact that Benny's never tasted real power hasn't quenched his thirst for it. I know that he acts like a big teddy bear with you and me, but he's ambitious and quite ruthless."

"Sounds like someone else I know," said Tzehainish.

Hadas grinned. "I guess that's why he likes me," she mused. "Anyway, I'm not going to get anywhere in this screwed-up building unless I'm ruthless. It's one of the lessons that Benny has drilled into me."

As they reached the door of Tzehainish's office, they bumped into Avi on his way out.

"What are you doing here?" demanded Tzehainish. "Your space is on the other side of the building."

"Oh... hi..." mumbled Avi. "I heard from Mahmoud Zaid's aide that you made quite the impression there earlier. So I'm, um, just trying to check out if there's any, you know, developments I should know about."

"That's typical," said Hadas scornfully. "You know how to co-operate with the Arabs when it suits you. Well, you can stop sniffing around here and go report back to your boss that I'm going ahead as planned. I'll get the votes I need."

She opened the door to the empty office and walked in. Tzehainish darted past Hadas and plopped down on a chair. "Just warming it up for you, boss," she grinned up at Hadas. "Can't have the 'Left's Legacy' sitting on a cold chair!"

"Let's stick to Blonde Bitch," said Hadas dryly. "I think I prefer that. Anyway – I'm getting out of here. I'll see you tomorrow."

Hadas turned to leave. "Wait," said Tzehainish. "Your mail – I picked it up earlier. There's a bunch of things – mostly business stuff, but there are a couple that look personal too."

Hadas, having made a brief stop in the bathroom to don her brunette wig, drove out of the Knesset car park and made her way through the late afternoon Jerusalem traffic toward the hotel where she'd arranged to meet Omar that evening. She drove down Agron Street, past Independence Park, before entering the Mamilla outdoor shopping mall's underground parking lot. She took the elevator to street level, and walked briskly down the swanky pedestrian street, where fancy jewelry and fashion stores basked in the shade of the adjacent Old City walls.

She turned right at the end of the mall and walked into the Mamilla Hotel: plush, boutique, exclusive. Her affair with Omar was an extremely expensive hobby. At first, she'd insisted on paying for half the hotel bill each time but had quickly realized that her meager salary paled into insignificance next to Omar's wealth. She'd allowed her feminist discomfort at having the man pay for their intimate liaisons to be over-ruled by her amusement at the political irony that their relationship inverted the economic power structure of Jewish and Arab citizens in Israel.

An hour later, Hadas and Omar were lying in bed, naked and drowsy. Omar had put the TV on quietly and was propped up against some pillows watching a stupid Israeli sitcom that he was addicted to. (When Hadas had first found out about this little secret of Omar's, she'd made fun of him for watching such dross, but he'd replied "Know thine enemy, my dear, know thine enemy" and she'd rolled her eyes and let him get on with it.) Hadas had her head on his chest, playing absent-mindedly with his chest hairs.

The sitcom hit its commercial break and Omar pressed mute. "What's on your mind, parallel universe wife?" he asked.

Hadas looked up at him. "What are we doing?" she said. "We meet in secret hotel rooms, we have sex, we talk for an hour, and then we go off to our own separate lives."

"And Italy. Don't forget Italy," said Omar. A few months ago, Hadas had attended an EU conference in Rome on water resources. Omar had drummed up some business meetings there, and they'd managed to arrange a couple of free days in both of their itineraries when they'd been able to wander anonymously through the streets and piazzas. It had been risky – Israelis travel everywhere – but they had felt like a regular couple.

"But Rome only makes it worse, Omar," sighed Hadas. "It was so heavenly, it was so..."

"Normal?" suggested Omar. "Such a reminder of what we can't be here?"

"Yes," said Hadas. "What we can't be here. Are we ever going to get to have that here, Omar?"

"I don't know," said Omar. He wiggled down the bed in order to bring his face level with Hadas's. "You know that's what I want, right? This is not some kind of Arab boy fantasy of having sex in secret with the Jewish girl." Hadas wouldn't make eye contact with him, and he gently put his finger on her chin and pulled her face back toward him. "Hadas: I'm serious. I've never felt this way about anyone. I love spending time with you, I love talking with you. I wish you could meet my friends. I wish I could meet your friends. I wish that our lives could allow that. But maybe you and I aren't destined to be normal. Not yet, anyway."

Hadas leaned forward and kissed him. She picked up the remote and un-muted it. "Watch your show, Arab boy," she said. "God forbid you should miss a scene. I'm going to check my mail – Tzehainish gave me a pile of stuff to look at."

Hadas got out of bed, naked except for the Star of David necklace that she always wore. It had been the first piece of jewelry that she'd ever bought herself, a small star of 925 silver on a simple chain that she'd found in the *shuk* as a teenager. She played with it with her fingers as she padded over to the bathroom and put on a bathrobe and slippers. Having a rich boyfriend – even a secret Arab one – did have its advantages. Hadas hadn't exactly been poor growing up, and she'd gone on vacations and stayed in hotels before, but never in expensive ones like this. The hotels she'd stayed at before meeting Omar had generally had threadbare towels and dirt in the corners; they certainly didn't have the marble bathtubs that this one did. One of her other little secrets was that, despite being one of Israel's foremost legislators and campaigners for environmental issues, she usually took a long, hot, water-wasting bath on Omar's dime. She looked greedily at the bathtub with its gold faucets and expensive hotel toiletries arranged perfectly on its edge. "Just a few more minutes, my dear," she said to the bathtub. "Work first, destruction of Israel's water resources later."

"Are you talking to the bathtub again?" shouted Omar from the bedroom.

"It's more intelligent than that crap you're watching," shouted Hadas back.

"Touché again," shot back Omar. "You Jews, you always have to have the last word with us Arabs, don't you?"

Hadas beamed, her heart dancing inside her chest. God, she was happy. It was insane how happy she was with Omar. Happiness... not something she'd had much experience with in her life until she'd met him. Her childhood had been a tight knot of stress: the only child of a mother who was so immersed in her own traumas that she'd never had time for her daughter's, and a distant father who worked long hours as a corporate lawyer and had little time for trivialities like a daughter or a family. Hadas had found an outlet from her mother's tight-lipped pain and her father's absences by becoming more and more interested in other people's lives. She'd begun her journalism career as a student writer for the high school paper, or at least that's how she framed it in her bio on the Knesset's website. In reality, the "paper" had been a series of one-page character portraits of teachers and other students that Hadas wrote anonymously at semi-regular intervals, sneaking into the teachers' lounge to photocopy her work and then sneaking into school first thing in the morning in order to distribute dozens of copies in classrooms before the other kids arrived. Her character portraits had been so spot-on, and so viciously accurate and well-observed, that she'd become known as "The Secret Sniper" in the school community.

She'd loved the anonymous celebrity of the whole thing. Eventually, she was found out – one day she got complacent and was seen by another student – but that actually made things even better, as the school principal realized what potential she had and encouraged her to tone down the viciousness but publish thoughtful interviews under her real name. That's when she got really addicted to journalism, and from then she'd trodden a well-worn path through Army Radio, via Middle Eastern Studies at Tel Aviv University, to the Haaretz newspaper and a beginning reporter's job at Channel Two news. Her ambition and her good looks had led her to an evening news co-anchor role.

Until one day, she'd woken up and decided that it wasn't enough to talk about other people making the news. She wanted to make the news herself. The easy (and often unethical) permeability between the media and the political world in Israel made it relatively easy for her to land a decent spot on the Labor party's election list. Now other journalists wrote about her, although she would sometimes make editorial suggestions. One of those suggestions had inadvertently created her new nickname. On the first year anniversary of her becoming a member of Knesset, a journalist had written a piece about her, and she'd told him about her high school jinks. Hadas had framed the interview as her path from writing about others to wanting to play her own role in creating Israel's vision and had suggested the title for the piece as "From Secret Sniper to Blonde Believer." It had been a great piece and had cemented her role as the Left's New Hope, but it had also given birth to "Blonde Bitch."

But in all these years, happiness had never really been part of her life. It was as if Hadas assumed that it just wasn't part of her equation – it was a missing variable, and she could have a perfectly efficient and useful life without it. Kind of like the old kibbutzniks, the grim-faced, unemotional generation of Israelis who just got on with it, struggling through life, overcoming war and poverty and hardship without stooping to such luxurious frivolities as laughter or humor or love. She'd had boyfriends and lovers, of course – but no-one who had touched her heart as Omar had.

She walked back out of the bathroom, and melodramatically did a sexy limbo-dance under the TV so as not to disturb Omar's line of sight. He chuckled. "Are you laughing at me or the TV?" she asked.

"I'll take the fifth on that one, I think, my dear," smirked Omar.

She giggled back, wandered over to the armchair in the corner of the room, and sat down, kicking off a slipper in Omar's direction. The slipper landed in his lap and he absent-mindedly tossed it back at her without taking his eyes off the television. Shaking her head with another contented little laugh, she emptied the bag of mail on to her lap. As Tzehainish had said, there were a bunch of official notices and items of Knesset business, most of which could be thrown straight out (not in the hotel; Hadas was careful to leave no trace that nosey maids might pick up), but one or two of which needed some thinking about. There was an invitation to a caucus meeting that might or might not be a good idea for her to attend; she'd talk it over with Tzehainish and Benny tomorrow. And there was a response to a query she'd submitted to the Defense Committee about budgets for guards in the settlements – she had no doubt that they were hiding something about the vastness of those budgets, and she'd have to look carefully at their letter to see what her next move would be. But again, that could wait till tomorrow.

There was one final letter that looked personal – her name was typed on the envelope but the envelope itself contained no signs of letterhead or provenance. She shrugged, tore it open, glanced at its brief contents, and went white.

"Omar – turn off the TV," she said.

"It's nearly fini–" Omar began, but he cut himself off as he saw Hadas's face, and immediately clicked the remote. "What? What is it?"

"We have a problem," said Hadas, and gave him the letter. It was typed on a piece of non-descript card.

I know your secret, you Blonde Bitch.
Dump your little Arab boyfriend
or I'll tell the Press.

Chapter 9

A couple of years after that night in Yoav's apartment, Dr Akiva Cohen astonished everyone at Hebrew University by announcing that he was leaving academia in order to pursue "private initiatives." He endured a gamut of reactions from his colleagues and students: shock, betrayal, anger, envy. Selling out to the private sector. Akiva cut off all contact with his former world very quickly, and that world swiftly did its very best to remove all trace of him from its department minutes, faculty seminars and co-authored papers.

Akiva and Yoav created GeneLight soon thereafter. Akiva moved to Tel Aviv and devoted himself to designing and building the facility, and beginning the scientific side of the project. They brought Shira and Sivan on board. Yoav continued to be a remarkable fund-raiser; Akiva continued to refrain from asking too many questions about the secret NGO which provided his funds.

Akiva and Yoav then took on the task of DNA acquisition.

The middle of the night. Akiva waited restlessly in his chair at GeneLight, facing the sea through the floor-to-ceiling windows. Beyond the bright lights of the cafes and hotels of the seafront, all he could see was black. He scratched an old scab on one of his hands, opening it up, making it bleed again. He sucked at the wound nervously. He practiced some breathing exercises that he'd read about recently, in through the nose, out through the mouth. It didn't help.

The middle of the afternoon. Yoav and Akiva hunched over a computer screen, with the bustling Jewish streets beneath them, engaging in extensive and friendly chats with modern Jew-haters.

It was close to one in the morning when Akiva finally heard the elevator's bing. Seconds later, Yoav walked in, wheeling one of those suit-holder suitcases that you see being dragged through airports the world over. This one had a rather unusual garment inside it, though.

> *HEINRICH: Heil Hitler. I was told that you could help me.*
> *GEST34: Heil Hitler, friend. Who can vouch for you?*
> *HEINRICH: Speak to 4RNOW and SS2000. I have done much business with them. They have met me in person. They know I am serious.*
> *GEST34: Wait.*

Several minutes went by, GEST34's cursor blinking on the screen, giving no indication of what was going on in his other windows. Akiva looked at Yoav nervously, rubbing the back of his neck. "You sure the proxy server and the VPN will hold up?" he asked.
"They're military grade," said Yoav. "As far as he knows, I'm typing this from a small town outside Dusseldorf."
"And the back story?"
Yoav shrugged nonchalantly. "I guess now we find out."

It had taken Yoav years to develop connections in the vast, shadowy underworld of Nazi memorabilia. Online auctions selling Third Reich posters, collections of original Nazi manuscripts, and all kinds of miscellaneous... junk, really, that supposedly belonged to

ALEX J SINCLAIR

*great Nazis. A pen used by Himmler. A stethoscope that Goebbels
had apparently once borrowed. Heydrich's copy of Mein Kampf,
signed by the Fuhrer himself. Much of it was fake, hoaxes created
by sick neo-Nazis or those trying to take advantage of them. But
in the inner sanctums, where dealers like GEST34 operated, there
was genuine stuff to be bought and sold.*

The cursor continued to blink.

Yoav looked bedraggled and unkempt – unusual for him, for he was usually the coolest, snappiest dresser in the room. "You look like shit," said Akiva.

"When I'm in Berlin I have to play the part of Heinrich, the lonely neo-Nazi gopher," replied Yoav. "I leave my Armani shoes at home, and don't shave or shower for three days."

"Too much information..." Akiva tried to crack a smile but couldn't hide his nerves. "You have it?"

"I have... something," murmured Yoav. "Still think it's a long shot. A uniform he apparently wore just once, while giving a speech in the Reichstag in 1942, a speech we're not even sure actually happened."

"The seller's legit, with a solid reputation," said Akiva. "The odds aren't great, finding DNA on a uniform that may or may not have touched his skin... but we need the third item for triangulation."

"Easy for you to say. I'm the one who has to go to Berlin every time to pick these items up from the PO box, making sure I'm not being tailed."

GEST34: OK. You check out, friend. What are you looking for?

*Akiva jumped from his chair and punched the air in relief. Yoav
sniffed in unruffled satisfaction and continued to type:*

58

HEINRICH: I would like one of his hairbrushes. Something that he touched, that combed through his actual hair.

GEST34: Hmm. Not a typical request. I believe I have something that may interest you. But it will not come cheap.

The suit suitcase lay on the table where Yoav had dumped it. The two colleagues, in sync, turned their eyes toward it.

"I guess we should open it," said Akiva.

"You do it," said Yoav, putting his hand on Akiva's shoulder. "I've already seen it. I want to see your face when you look at it for the first time."

Akiva walked to the table, unzipped the suitcase, and opened it up. Inside was a Nazi-leader suit, an all-black uniform complete with its red swastika armband perfectly in place.

Akiva gaped at Yoav. "Unbelievable. Incredible."

"Those are synonyms, my friend," smiled Yoav. "No need for tautology at a time like this."

Akiva ignored him and rubbed one of the sleeves between his fingers. "Looks to be in decent condition considering how old it is."

"Yup," responded Yoav. "Maybe a bit too decent condition. When I saw it I was concerned it might not be genuine. But it looks like the real thing – the fabric's old, the labels come from one of the Nazi leadership's known tailors." (The project had required Yoav to become a minor expert in German fabrics of the 1940s.) "If it's not real, it's a bloody good fake, and a near-contemporaneous fake at that."

These were Akiva's favorite moments with Yoav. He didn't have to hide his excitement, his nervousness, his anticipation. He could let Yoav see how much this meant to him. He tapped his hands on his knees and then clapped Yoav on the back eagerly. "There's only one way to find out for sure. Let's get to work!"

HEINRICH: Money will not be a problem as long as the mer-

chandise is authentic. May I ask how you have verified it?
GEST34: This is an item that comes directly from Rosa.

Akiva turned to Yoav with eyes wide. Yoav rubbed his fingers
together excitedly, blew on his hands, and then continued to type:

HEINRICH: You are certain?

'Rosa' was Rosa Krautenbacher, one of the Nazi party's loy-
al maidservants at the mountain retreat in Bavaria. It was a
known fact in the neo-Nazi underground world that when the
war ended, Rosa collected lots of little artifacts from the Bavaria
house and used their sales to create a very nice pension for herself.
Her stuff was genuine.

GEST34: Of course I am certain. You know my reputation. You
would not have come to me otherwise. And this reputation depends
on cast-iron authenticity of every item I sell. Not to mention my
health and life. At the prices I charge, if one of my customers was
to discover that something I sold was fake... well, let us just say that
our community is not very patient or forgiving in these matters.
HEINRICH: I apologize. How much will the item cost?
GEST34: This is one of my most prized collector's items. The price
is $100,000. Non-negotiable.

Yoav leaned back in his chair and locked his hands behind his
head triumphantly. The price was roughly what they had guessed.
They had the budget for it from one of the project's major donors.

The two men headed down to the lab and got to work. This was Akiva's domain, and he got to action confidently, gliding around the delicate equipment like an elite tennis player in flow, the intense thrill of scientific exploration coursing through his veins. Yoav acted as lab assistant, handing him all manner of scissors, scrapers, and collection bags from the equipment table that Akiva had set up.

"How do you know where the DNA will be?" asked Yoav, poking his head around Akiva as he focused on scraping a particularly fiddly bit of material from one of the suit's arms.

"I don't," muttered Akiva, elbowing Yoav back out of the way with unflustered control. "Just needle in a haystack stuff, really. Looking for the places where his skin might have rubbed off against the suit and left some cells. The cuffs are a good bet. Insides of the legs if he put his trousers on without wearing socks. Collar and neckline, of course. Maybe, just maybe, the top of the waist – probably not, but worth trying. I'm just scraping samples from as many of these places as possible, then we'll put them under the DNA electron microscope, and if there are any carbon-based cells there, it'll detect them and run the analysis. Then, we compare the results we get from this sample to our other two..." here Akiva pointed at a nearby computer screen. The screen's left side was filled with a series of graphics, colored boxes and graphs that Yoav didn't understand; the right side had the same templates but everything was blank. "What we want to see," went on Akiva, as he gently deposited the material into one of several petri dishes, "is that the right-hand part of the screen matches the left. The left contains the DNA results from the hair in the hairbrush that we got last year, and the cells we scraped from the lining of the gloves from the bunker. Identical DNA in both. If DNA from the suit matches, then that will mean three separate DNA samples from three separate items, bought from different dealers, with different provenances. Then we can be sure. And we need to be sure, otherwise this whole project will never work." *Otherwise, my project will never work.*

HEINRICH: We have a deal. We will wire you the money today along with our PO box in Berlin for delivery.

Yoav closed the chat program, turned off the computer, unplugged it, and also unplugged the modem to which it was connected. He moseyed over to Akiva's couch and plopped himself down on it. "Piece o' cake," he grinned.

"One down," said Akiva. He stayed sitting down, staring at the blank computer screen, cracking his knuckles. It was working. His plan was working. And Yoav suspected nothing, he was sure of it. "One down, two to go..."

It took Akiva the best part of an hour to finish his cuttings and scrapings. By the end, the suit was in tatters, and there were thirty or forty little petri dishes filled with bits of fluff and dirt and fabric and maybe, just maybe, a couple of skin cells.

"Now what?" asked Yoav.

"Now... we look for the needle."

The first several dishes came up blank. Dish number 8 indicated carbon-based materials, and Yoav and Akiva looked anxiously at the screen. The graphics and tables started getting filled in by the computer program, but it was clear, even to Yoav's untrained eye, that there were major differences between the left- and the right-hand side of the screen.

"Shit," grunted Yoav. "So, it's not his?"

Akiva waved him away with an expert hand. "Patience," he said. "Could be nothing. Could be the collector's DNA, could be someone he shook hands with, could be anything. Let's keep going."

At 3:30 am, about two thirds of the way through the samples, the computer indicated another carbon-based sample. This time the graphics on the right-hand side of the screen filled up in the same patterns as the left. Yoav looked

at the screen, unsure if he was interpreting it correctly; he looked sideways at
Akiva for confirmation. Akiva was gazing at the screen, a tear rolling down his
cheek, his head slowly nodding. After an eternity, he turned to Yoav.

"It's a match. It's number 3. We have him."

"Adolf Hitler," said Yoav, staring at the screen in wonder. "Welcome back to
the world. Do I have plans for you..."

Chapter 10

The day following the birth had passed uneventfully. The procedures that Akiva and Yoav had pre-planned years ago clicked into smooth operation: care of the child, core staff working in shifts, clean removal of the mother. As the sun began to set, you could almost taste the salty air from the warm evening breeze blowing in from the sea, even behind the cool double glazing of the GeneLight office. Tomer Kleinberg had arrived, as per Yoav's instructions. He and the rest of the staff – Akiva, Yoav, Sivan, Shira, and Neta – were gathered in Akiva's office, full of smiles, relief, the exhaustion of success, but also with a grimness and a weightedness about what lay ahead of them. Akiva had flipped the channel on the TV on the wall so that it now showed a CCTV feed of the lab; this was GeneLight's hi-tech "baby monitor" that they would use when none of the staff were actually down in the lab.

They gathered in a semi-circle around Akiva. Akiva, who had bought an expensive bottle of whiskey with Yoav's money, poured everyone a small shot glass, and they stood there, glasses in hands, expectantly.

Akiva looked round at his staff and smiled. His emotions for these people were complicated – he'd known them and worked with them for years, and he felt genuine affection for them as people, despite his lies, despite his plans, despite what he really thought of *their* plans. So his smile was real, warm, relieved; for one brief moment, simple.

"I am a man of few words, as you know. I want to thank you all, from the bottom of my heart, for your help in getting us to this moment. Each of you has played a critical role. A unique role. I thank you, and the future thanks you."

Yes, it does. My future, though, not yours.

Akiva paused. He gestured to Sivan. "I've asked Sivan to speak. She's been the driving force behind so much of our actual operational structure. I thought that it would be most appropriate for her to say something. In memory of Yosef and Meirav."

Sivan gave a short bow. "It will be my honor," she said.

Akiva smiled again. His shy persona was real, but it had suited him over the years to play it up. Better to let the others talk.

"It is now eight years, three months and fourteen days since my world was destroyed," began Sivan, speaking quietly and with firm clarity. "Since they murdered my Yosef, my strength and my salvation, my soulmate, my everything. And my beautiful, sweet, Meirav, my gorgeous baby, who I loved more than I thought it was possible to love anything, who was not even two years old when those animals sprayed bullets into her. Not a day goes by without me thinking of them, without me convulsing in pain at their absence."

Sivan paused and took a deep, agonized breath. Her colleagues waited in respectful silence for her to continue.

"The murderers of my family were caught. One was killed by our army during the apprehension operation. One remains in prison, for now. But I have no doubt that I will live to see the day when he is released. He will be released in some prisoner exchange, and he will enjoy his life again, and he and his disgusting brethren will murder more of us. Because we are civilized. Because we play by the rules."

Sivan looked around at her colleagues. She sniffed and blinked a couple of times. Shira, who was next to her, reached over and hugged her with one arm. Sivan turned and gave a grateful smile in return.

She regained her composure. "These rules make us weak," she sneered. "These rules are not the way the Middle East works. They are not the way the Arabs work. And so as long as we play by the rules of the West, by the rules of civilization, we are doomed to lose."

Sivan's colleagues remained silent. Neta gave a small nod of encouragement. Akiva watched Sivan, reining in his emotions, poker-faced as always.

"That is what Yoav understood, all those years ago. He understood that if we are to win, we need to play by the rules of the Arabs. We need a *deterrent*. But a real deterrent. A deterrent that speaks their language. For the Arabs, blood is the strongest of emotions, and revenge is the strongest of motivations. Blood and revenge. These are words that speak to them. This is the language they understand. And this is the language of deterrence that we need in order to stop them from trying to destroy us."

"Sometimes our weak leaders dip their toes into this language," scoffed Sivan. "We demolish a terrorist's house, or we put up an extra roadblock. But these barely qualify. These are Western forms of punishment, Western forms of deterrence. They do not work here in the Middle East. Yoav saw that we need to go further. We need to show the Arabs that we understand blood. That we understand vengeance. That we understand history. That we mean it when we say '*never again*.'"

Neta was nodding again. Shira stood akimbo now, next to her, with her head held high, defiantly.

"So that is what we have done here, in our secret laboratory in Tel Aviv, and what we will do in the future," snarled Sivan. "We have created a deterrence of blood and vengeance, but *on a scale that our enemies can scarcely imagine*."

"This newborn Hitler will be the first of many. The most evil man the world has ever seen, the one who gassed us, burned us, annihilated us. He will be a fitting symbol of the Jewish people's new lust for vengeance. Through him, we will show the Arabs that we now speak a different language. That we will *never* stop seeking revenge."

Sivan was raising her voice now, spitting out the words. "His name and his evil will make people sit up and pay attention. But he will only be the first. Others will come after him. Mengele, Himmler, Goebbels. We will exact our revenge on the entire Nazi leadership. And then we, or others inspired by us, will begin the Arab branch of our enterprise. We will obtain the DNA of Yasser Arafat. Of Ahmed Yassin, who founded Hamas. Of the terrorists who murdered our athletes in Munich. *We will create here a torture chamber for our worst enemies reborn.* They will live here lives of misery and humiliation, and when each comes of age, becomes recognizable as an adult, they will be unveiled and publicly punished for the crimes they committed against our people – and they will become watchwords. Every antisemite, every Islamic terrorist, every neo-Nazi, every Jew-hater in the world, will look at these reborn murderers, will look at the life of pain and suffering that they endure as a result of their sins against the Jewish People, and will think twice – will think a thousand times! – before attacking Jews. Here, by the sea, we will show the world what happens to those who try to destroy us, who think they might drive us *into* that sea. They will see what we do to their blood. We will show those who hate us that even the grave will not protect them from us. *That even death does not save you from the Jewish People's vengeance!*"

"And so, my friends, raise a glass with me to drink. We Jews say *L'chaim*, to life, when we toast. Today, those words are truer than they have ever been. We are drinking to our life. There will be no more Yosefs, no more Meiravs. No more holocausts. *Never again will Jewish blood be spilled.* Because we have created the ultimate, doomsday weapon of deterrence: vengeance. Terrible, time-defying... death-defying... *vengeance.* Vengeance will protect us. Vengeance will give us deterrence. Vengeance will give us life! Vengeance will set us free!"

Sivan stopped, out of breath, cheeks red and eyes burning with anger, and raised her glass. "To vengeance!" she declared. "To vengeance and to life!"

"To vengeance and to life!" Yoav repeated, wrapping his arm around Sivan from the other side, hugging her. The rest of them repeated the words, clinking their glasses against each other's. Akiva pasted his usual smile onto his face and joined in with the clinking and the *L'chaiming* and the satisfied looks. He knew how to play along by now. A few more weeks, and he wouldn't have to play along any longer.

Chapter 11

Hadas paced the floor of her apartment. She had a reputation for being cool as a cucumber under pressure, at school, at army radio, in her career as a journalist, and in the Knesset. But as she paced, she could hear her heart thumping, her throat was dry, and she couldn't stop picking at a hangnail on her left index finger. This was new. Someone out there knew her secret. Someone out there could destroy her.

The doorbell rang, and she sprang to open it.

"Thank God, Benny, thanks for coming so late and at such short notice."

Benny Shoham smiled slyly. "I figured it had to be some kind of serious emergency, and now that Hadas Levinson is invoking the name of God, I can see that it must be really serious! What gives?"

"Come in, shut the door after you," said Hadas, walking back into the living room. "And don't get any ideas, you dirty old man. Tzehainish will be here too in a minute."

Benny raised an eyebrow. "Even better," he said. "Me, Ebony and Ivory. I'm so glad the two of you have finally agreed to fulfil one of my dreams."

Hadas shook her head at him. "And yet another addition to my long list of 'things Benny has said that would end his career if I made them public.'"

"I'd be worried if I actually had a career any more," shrugged Benny. "I'd also be worried if I was heterosexual. You two girls will just have to be disappointed tonight."

The doorbell rang again, interrupting whatever comeback Hadas was about to say. She opened the door for Tzehainish, whose long black curls were glistening with damp from her post-evening-jog shower. "I came as soon as I could," she said. "Is it really as urgent as you implied in the text message?"

"Well, let's start with the fact that neither of you, my two closest confidantes, have ever been to my apartment before," said Hadas, gesturing around the room. "You know that I try to keep work separate from my private life. But I felt that we needed a private place for this discussion, and nowhere at work would do."

Tzehainish sat down on the sofa in Hadas's living room. Israel was such a small country that many politicians, especially those from the Left, preferred to live in Tel Aviv, not Jerusalem, the downside of their hour-or-so commute each day being outweighed by the upside of Tel Aviv's vibrant, secular lifestyle compared with the tense religious undertones of Jerusalem. Like most Israeli apartments, especially those in the middle of Tel Aviv, Hadas's was Manhattan-small, every inch of space used effectively. The furniture was mostly basic IKEA pieces, found the world over, which had served Hadas well since her years as a young journalist who had to count every penny. Sprinkled among these pieces, though, were some more recent acquisitions, splurges on high style Italian imports that were manifestations of her more recent success: a writing desk in the corner, a modern lamp on the coffee table, and next to it, a designer bowl of potpourri from which a delicate aroma of lavender wafted.

"Well," said Tzehainish. "We're here. What's so urgent and private that you had to bring us to your inner sanctum at 9:00 pm on a Thursday night?"

"As I said, you are my two closest confidantes, the two people in this shitty political swamp of ours whom I trust implicitly, who have been there for me from the beginning in the Knesset. Tzehainish, you've supported everything I've done from the side, and Benny, your mentorship from above has been invaluable in getting me to where I am now. But there is something I have been hiding from you, and now I need to tell you."

"Oh, you're not finally coming out to us, are you?" said Benny, rubbing his hands together in mock camp glee. "I knew it, I always knew it! Welcome to the club, honey!"

"Benny – enough, please." Hadas spoke now in a firm voice. "What I am going to tell you is no less explosive than if I were to be coming out of the closet – actually, it's much *less* acceptable than being gay here. If only it were that simple."

And so Hadas told them about Omar. About how they'd met three years ago, when she'd interviewed him for a piece on East Jerusalemite Palestinian identity, and they'd both felt an immediate and mutual attraction. About the series of chaste coffee dates that they'd had, on the pretense of her continuing the research on the issue with a long-read piece in mind for one of the weekend supplements. About how they'd finally leapt into the unknown, begun a romantic relationship, become lovers, just as Hadas was making the decision to leave journalism and go into politics. About the secret meetings and rendezvous (Hadas spared them the details, despite Tzehainish at this point becoming rather starstruck and inquisitive about the list of high-end hotels that Hadas nonchalantly reeled off).

And then she showed them the note.

"Shit," exclaimed Tzehainish. "Who the hell is this? Who does this creep think he is?"

"Or she," noted Hadas.

"Bullshit, this is a guy move, there's no way a woman would do this to one of her own," said Tzehainish.

Hadas frowned. She'd been burned before by other women, jealous of her quick success. She could easily conjure up the names of three or four female rivals who she imagined, despite their regular air kisses and coffee meetings, would have no qualms about throwing her under a bus.

"Unfortunately, I've learned that in politics, gender equality extends to people of both sexes being assholes," Hadas shuddered. "I'm not ruling anyone or anything out."

Until now, Benny had remained silent. He took the note from Hadas, looked at it intently, and then looked up at her.

"This is serious, Hadas. This is potentially the end of your career."

Hadas took the note back.

"That's why I wanted you here tonight, Benny. I knew that Tzehainish, you'd give me moral support and indignation and courage to fight back – and I really need all of that, believe me – but Benny, I knew you'd see the depth of the issue from a party perspective. I need your years of experience in the swamp to help me figure out what to do."

"This isn't a party issue," said Benny, rubbing his chin thoughtfully. "It's much worse than that. The party might forgive you for this. Some in it might even embrace you for it. But the country – the people – that's where your problem is. If this gets out... well, 'Blonde Bitch' is going to sound like a term of endearment in comparison to what you'll be called."

"I know," said Hadas. "That's why I've been keeping it a secret." She paused and pursed her lips. A wave of cold pulsed through her, despite the evening heat that was drifting through the living room's open windows. "*Trying* to keep it a secret, I guess. Anyway – I need your help tonight. I need you to help me figure out what to do."

Silence.

Hadas looked up at each of her two friends, but neither would make eye contact.

Silence.

"Well, this has been a lovely evening," grimaced Hadas, her friends' silence confirming her worst fears. The desperation of her situation gripped her muscles like a clamp. She straightened her blouse and turned her chin up. "Thanks for coming. See you tomorrow at work, right?"

Benny cleared his throat and finally looked up at Hadas.

"Hadas, I need to ask you a question, and I think it's probably the question that Tzehainish wants to ask you too, and before we start discussing plans, we need to know the answer to this question."

Hadas waved him away impatiently. She was one step ahead of him, she was always one step of ahead of him, despite his seniority and experience. God, he could be such a maddening old fool at times.

"There are two questions, actually, and the answers are yes, and no, respectively. So let's move on."

Benny looked puzzled. He turned to Tzehainish, who responded with an exasperated shake of her head.

"Question one," explained Tzehainish, "is do you love him? The second question is, are you prepared to give him up? And the answers are yes, and no, right, Hadas? Otherwise…" – with this, she turned to face Benny – "we wouldn't be here tonight."

Hadas looked at Benny and nodded. She was suddenly out of breath, light-headed with exhilaration. This development, terrifying as it was, had clarified her feelings for Omar in a way that she would not have thought possible. Faced so starkly with the prospect of losing him, or the price of staying with him, she now knew that come what may, she wanted a future with Omar.

Benny tipped his head toward Tzehainish and beckoned to Hadas to pass him the note again. He scrutinized it once more.

"Do you have any idea at all who might have written this?" he asked.

"No idea," sighed Hadas. "But I guess there are plenty of people in the Knesset who would be happy to see me thrown out of politics."

"The right wingers, for a start," suggested Tzehainish. "You're becoming just a little bit too much of a thorn in their side. And they don't have too many problems with playing dirty."

"And the *Shasniks*," said Benny. *Shas* was a party of traditional *Mizrachi* Jews whose parents and grandparents had migrated to Israel in the early years of the state from North Africa, Iraq, Iran and Yemen. "They see you as the reincarnation of the old, white, *Ashkenazi* elite, and they despise you for that."

"Wait," said Tzehainish, reaching out to touch Hadas on the knee. "This morning, when we got back to my office from the meeting with Mahmoud…"

"Avi Kanievsky..." frowned Hadas.

"Explain, please?" asked Benny.

"Shmuel Navon's aide. We bumped into him coming out of the office," said Tzehainish. "There was no-one else in it at the time. He had some half-baked excuse for being there... you don't think...?"

Hadas pursed her lips and furrowed her brow as she considered the notion. "Navon does hate me, that's for sure," she said. "It's like the child benefits bill is a declaration of cultural and religious war against them. But do you really think he would do something like this?"

"Believe me," jumped in Benny, leaning forward in his chair, "they have zero qualms about using the most disgusting of political tactics when it suits them, especially against secular politicians. They would see this simply as using your own depravities against yourself."

"Still," conceded Hadas, "it's only circumstantial evidence. The office was probably empty for most of the morning. Anyone in the Knesset could have slipped in and left it or got a mule to deliver it under false pretenses. And as you've noted, half the country hates me."

Silence again. Tzehainish, out of ideas for now, was smiling weakly at her, but Hadas saw a hint of pity in the smile, and she couldn't take that. She didn't mind other people hating her, arguing with her, insulting her. But pity? That was unbearable.

"Come on, Benny," said Hadas, trying to use the force of her personality to will a solution into sight. "What do you think? What's my strategy here?"

"It seems to me that you have four options," said Benny. "Option one, break up with this Omar, and try to forget the whole thing."

"Not going to happen," said Hadas firmly. Making this statement so emphatically again gave her goosebumps on her arms; her chest swelled like it was going to burst.

Hadas and Omar. That mattered more than anything.

Benny tilted his head to one side, as if weighing up whether to push Hadas on this, but then nodded and moved on.

"Option two, take the note to the police and ask them to open an investigation. Not advisable. Chances are it will leak out immediately and then the political damage will be done anyway, even if they do find the note's author. You'll have shot yourself in the foot."

Hadas only needed to ponder the thought for a split second before coming to the same conclusion.

"Agreed," said Hadas. "So no police."

"Option three," continued Benny, "is to come clean. Own the narrative. Hold a press conference, admit to the affair, try to ride it out. I don't advise this either. The writer of this note is correct in one thing: the country will not accept a major Jewish politician in a long-term romantic relationship with an Arab."

"Okay," said Hadas. "I don't like option three so much either. Option four?" she asked, desperately hoping that Benny would have one final trick up his sleeve.

"Keep doing what you're doing and hope that they're bluffing."

Hadas sighed in defeat.

"You think that's a possibility?"

Benny shrugged again, but the look on his face was resolute.

"Probably not. People in our world don't usually have a strong compassionate streak."

"So you're saying that in options two, three and four, one way or the other, my political career is over?"

Hadas shut her eyes and an image of Omar materialized in front of her, as vivid as if he were standing in the room. He raised an eyebrow and gave one of his melodramatic doffs of the imaginary cap. She giggled involuntarily and shut her eyes tighter. The image shifted, and now he was face to face with her, moving toward her, his eyes shut, a smile on his lips as he slowly brushed them against hers. Hadas took a quick intake of breath, and opened her eyes. She surveyed her two closest colleagues again, conscious that she was blushing. *He's more important. I want him* and *I want politics. But if I have to choose, I choose him. I choose him over my career. I choose him over the Knesset. I choose him over Israel.*

Tzehainish moved over to sit next to Hadas, grabbing her hand in a comforting gesture. Hadas's eyes began tearing up, and Tzehainish hugged her. Hadas hugged her back, sucking in deep, pained gasps of air as she burrowed into her friend's hair, finally letting her guard down, letting herself lean fully on Tzehainish for support. Benny remained seated, uncomfortable at this burst of female emotion in front of him, unsure how to react. Hadas extricated herself from Tzehainish's curls, brushed her friend's hair back from her face, and gave her a soft kiss of thanks on the cheek. She stood up, rubbed her eyes with her sleeve, and took a deep breath.

She knew what she had to do.

"Option four it is. If I'm going to go down, at least I'll enjoy myself for as long as I can. So we double down on the child benefits bill. If that shit Navon is behind this, then I at least want the satisfaction of knowing that I beat him. Let's get it to a vote on the floor by the end of next month."

Chapter 12

Friday afternoon. Akiva, Yoav, Sivan and Shira sat in Akiva's office. They had held regular meetings since the birth, and this was the third. So far, Sivan explained, everything had gone according to plan. The surrogate birth mother had been paid off and helped to leave the country, back to Romania. Sivan was gradually shifting gears into being a pediatrician, with the responsibility for keeping the child healthy in the years ahead.

"And the child?" asked Yoav. "Any abnormalities? Anything of concern in terms of medical cloning issues?"

"Nothing so far," said Shira. "He seems like a perfectly normal, healthy baby. We're–"

"Don't call it *he*," snapped Sivan. "Remember the protocols. We call it *it* at all times. We do not humanize it. We do not develop feelings of attachment to it."

"Sorry…" mumbled Shira. "I know, I get it, but still…"

"This is really important," scolded Sivan, straightening her back and piercing Shira with her eyes. "That baby is going to start smiling in a few weeks' time. It's going to gurgle. It's going to roll over on its back. It's going to sit up. It's going to crawl and giggle and clap its hands and do all the things that babies have been trained by evolution to do so that they develop connections with their parents. It will be cute. Do not be taken in by it. *You have to remember at all times what it is.* This is evil incarnate. Literally. This is Hitler. This is a scientific clone of the monster who murdered six million Jews. It may look like a baby, but it is not. It is the abyss. It is the devil. It is disgusting. It is an abomination."

Shira said nothing. She looked at Akiva for support, but Akiva turned toward the window, rubbing his eyes with his fingers and his ears with his thumbs. Suddenly, as if remembering something he'd been meaning to ask, he turned back.

"Yoav, what about registering the child with the authorities? Getting it an Israeli ID number and all that? It will need to be in the system, even if only to get things like vaccinations."

"It'll be taken care of," clipped Yoav.

"But how?" asked Akiva, trying to make his inquiry sound innocent. "You'll use a false name? When will we get the details for our records here?" *Careful, now. Try to get what you need, but don't let him suspect anything.*

"It will be taken care of," repeated Yoav. "You don't need to know more than that for now."

Akiva began to answer back, but Yoav waved him away.

"Let's change subjects. I want to talk about its nutrition regime. Breast milk, correct? We've spoken about that. I don't want it being fed formula."

"That's been the easy part," said Shira. "We thought we'd have to find an old-fashioned wet-nurse and have to answer all kinds of hard questions about the project. But there's been no need. They have these things called breast milk banks for mothers who can't nurse. It's quite amazing what you find on Facebook. Anyway, I had to create a convincing profile and back story, present myself as a mother dedicated to breast feeding but taking strong drugs that prevented me from doing so, and easy as pie, I've got more donations than I know what to do with. That child won't starve."

Yoav nodded with satisfaction. Akiva turned toward him with the beginnings of a puzzled look on his face, as if to ask a question, but thought better of it.

"One other issue," said Shira. "He might have a little bit of diaper rash. I'm sure it's nothing, but Sivan, I think you should take a look."

Sivan stood up. "You called it *he* again," she said.

"Oh... sorry..."

Sivan looked at her, shaking her head slowly. "Let's go down to the lab and check out this diaper rash," she said.

Without another word, she walked out of the office and called the lab elevator. Akiva, Yoav and Shira slowly got up and followed her. When the elevator arrived, she ushered them in. There were only two buttons: '20' for the office level, and 'L' for lab. She pressed L, the doors closed, and some moments later they opened again to the gleaming white lab.

Sivan briskly walked into the operating theater, which had now been transformed into a basic nursery room. The baby was asleep. It wore a white onesie, and was lying flat on its back, arms above its head in a kind of "hands-up!" style. Because it had been a C-section, its head had come out perfectly, with none of the initial squishiness that often happens in vaginal births. It had perfect skin, jet black hair, and it lay there, breathing deeply in and out with the kind of absolute calm that only newborn babies are capable of. It was an adorable baby.

Sivan looked around absent-mindedly. She shrugged her shoulders, and then dug into her pocket and pulled out her car keys.

She placed the end of the key on the baby's cheek. The baby stirred a little but stayed asleep.

She pierced her eyes at Shira again. "I am going to cause this baby pain now," she said quietly. "I am going to wake up this beautiful, peaceful baby by pressing a car key into its cheek and causing it extreme discomfort and then real, genuine hurt. The baby is going to howl. It is going to shriek. It is going to wail. And we will not comfort it. We will watch as I continue to poke the key into its flesh. We will watch as I scrape its cheek and draw blood. And we will remember. That is our core commandment as Jews. *Remember*. Remember what Amalek did to us. This is Amalek, right here, in front of us. When it giggles, do not forget that it is Amalek, the same Amalek who laughed as it sent us into the gas chambers. When it starts to toddle cutely, do not forget that it is Amalek, the same Amalek who made us walk on forced marches until we dropped dead from exhaustion and malnutrition. When it claps its hands and smiles at us, do not forget that it is Amalek, the same Amalek who machine-gunned us down into mass graves."

Akiva dug his hands deep into his pockets, locking them into place, trying to stop them shaking, trying to stop his whole body shaking. He took a deep breath. *Keep calm. Don't give yourself away. Let her do what she needs to do. Think about the big picture. The long-term picture.* He locked his eyes on the baby, picturing it with him on the plane, both of them soaring away to the future. His arms loosened just a little.

Sivan pressed the key further into the baby's skin, and now the baby did wake up. It was a standard car key, a black, rectangular-ish plastic mold on one end, complete with three buttons, one with an icon of a closed padlock, one with an icon of an open padlock, and one with an icon of a horn blaring. The actual metal key end was not sharp, with a rounded point, presumably the result of generations of Toyota engineers' endeavors to save its customers' pockets from having holes being poked through them.

But it was sharp enough.

As Sivan increased the pressure, the key slowly made more of an indent in the baby's smooth cheek skin, as if she were trying to carve out a permanent dimple. The baby began to cry.

Akiva felt his pulse quicken again. He curled his hands, still in his pockets, into tight fists, forcing the tension through his forearms and biceps into his shoulders, focusing every ounce of his concentration on keeping himself still, keeping the tight spring wound up inside him under control. His eyes moistened against his will, and he quickly blinked it away. *You can't lose it now. Deep breaths. Hold it together.*

"Its fine motor skills are not sufficiently developed to enable it to try to push the key away," noted Sivan. "It is helpless. Just like we were. I have absolute power over it. Just like it had over us. But now the tables are turned. And I will show it *precisely* the same level of mercy that it showed us. That it showed my great-aunt Frida."

She pushed the key further into the baby's flesh, and the baby began to wail Akiva let himself slip, just for a moment. "Sivan... stop... it's enough..." he stammered nervously.

Sivan ignored him and raised her voice over the baby's wails. "Babies cry for food and for diaper changes and for cuddles, but when babies cry out of real pain, it's a different sound entirely. It's a desperate sound, isn't it? A sound of terror, an impossible sound. It's a sound that is meant to waken every evolutionary nerve in our bodies. I've heard that sound. *I've heard my own baby make that sound and I will never forget it.*"

She pushed the key even further into the baby's cheek, so that it was really pushing into the baby's mouth from the outside, an indentation of half a centimeter or more. "It has no sense of time, so it doesn't know if or when this pain is going to stop. It's like this pain it feels is for eternity."

The baby's screams shrieked inside Akiva's head, begging him to make it stop, begging him to intervene. He willed himself to ignore it. He clenched his right fist even harder, and loosened his left fist in order to pinch his thigh through his trouser pocket. The pain from his leg focused him again, momentarily blocking out the crying. He was almost begging himself to keep the poker-face on. *You can't give up your secret now, not when you're so close.*

Sivan wiped at her face with her left hand, rubbing her eyes red, but keeping her right hand pressured on the baby. "The modern day Amaleks out there, the Arabs who wish to finish Hitler's work" – she was shouting now, over the baby's wails – "they will hear these cries. They will see what we are now capable of. Those murderers, those animals who gunned down my Meirav and my Yosef... let them cringe in fear at what we will do to them. We will seek revenge in this lifetime, and in the next lifetime, and in the one after that, we will never stop coming after their blood! Let them fear Jewish vengeance so much that they will never dare attack us again! Let them see that we never forget! Let no-one ever try to destroy Jews again. *Never again!*"

The baby's cries filled the room, terrible, devastating. Its body struggled

‚n whatever inchoate way it could to get away from the source ‚ut failing absolutely. Its legs kicked out in random directions, its ‚neaved. A small drop of blood seeped down the baby's cheek from ‚t the key indentation, mixing with the baby's tears, which were by now ‚owing so freely down its face that the key began to slip a little.

Tears began to flow down Sivan's cheeks now, too. She wiped them away with her free hand. "Never again, never again," Sivan shouted, her hand now trembling a little as she kept up the pressure of the key on the baby's cheek. "This is our deterrence, this is how we stop them, this is how we save ourselves, vengeance, vengeance, VENGEANCE!"

Suddenly, Sivan broke off. She yanked her hand away and span back away from the incubator, sobbing and shaking. She roared out loud at herself in frustration and whipped herself back to the incubator. She rubbed her face with her hands again, and stood there, still shaking, brandishing the key over the still-wailing baby but no longer making contact with the infant.

Avika loosened his fist, stopped pinching his thigh, and silently breathed in relief.

"I think you have made your point, Sivan," remarked Yoav dryly. "We get it. Shira gets it. Enough."

Yoav grabbed her arm firmly and twisted the key out of her hand. He pushed her arm down and away from the baby.

Sivan turned to Yoav, red in the face, still shaking, but now puzzled. Yoav stared back at her, impenetrable. "Enough," he repeated coolly.

"Enough for now," said Sivan, recovering her composure. She brusquely took the key back from Yoav and put it back in her pocket. The baby continued to cry, the noise subsiding slightly but still filling the room. "Let it feel pain. Let it cry. Let it cry for my Yosef and Meirav. If its tears save another family from going through the hell that I went through, then let it cry all night. Let it cry all its life. Let them all cry all their lives."

"Upstairs," said Yoav, gesturing with his head to the lab door. "We're done here now."

Sivan gave a short, stiff nod and began to walk back toward the elevator. Yoav and Shira followed. Akiva walked out after them but didn't get in the elevator.

"You go upstairs. I want to go over some of the files down here and maybe run a couple of blood tests on the child. Just want to make sure the hemoglobin count is stable. That was an issue in some of the animal clones. Worth keeping an eye on. I'll rejoin you guys shortly."

The elevator doors closed, and Akiva was left alone. Above the elevator were two LED floor indicators, "20" and "L", and he waited for the light on the L to click off, indicating that the elevator was on its way up. He checked his watch: he guessed that he had no more than a minute or two before they'd be back in his office, back in front of the CCTV feed. And he couldn't let them see what he needed to do now.

He ran back into the lab and stood over the incubator. The baby was sniveling, still in obvious pain from its ordeal of a few moments ago. Akiva looked anxiously over his shoulder toward the elevator once more. Satisfied that he was alone, he bent over, picked up the baby, and held it close to his chest, breathing deeply, trying to get his heart to slow down so that it would calm the baby.

"*Mein kleines Baby,*" he murmured to the infant in a soothing voice. *My little baby...*

Akiva held the baby in his arms and began to rock him.

"*Shh, shh, es ist okay, es ist okay,*" *it's okay, it's okay,* he half-sung quietly. He bent his head over and kissed the baby's forehead, and then, transferring the baby's weight to one arm, he used his other one to wipe the baby's cheek where Sivan had drawn blood. He looked at his watch. 30 seconds since the elevator doors shut.

He raised the baby a little and held him to his chest, cradling his tiny head with his hand against his heartbeat. Rocking, cradling, shushing. Crying. 45 seconds.

The baby calmed down and began to doze off. Akiva kissed him again and gently put him back into the incubator. 65 seconds.

"*Alles wird gut,*" he cooed. *Everything will be fine.* "Just a few more days, little baby. As soon as I can get you a passport. We'll be in California soon, just you and me. Everything will be fine."

All was quiet again in the lab. Akiva pulled a wet wipe out of a tub on one of the tables, moved out of sight of the camera, and wiped his face. He gave a little sniff and nodded to himself. Then he walked back over to the elevator and pressed the button.

Chapter 13

O ver the next couple of days, Hadas and Tzehainish doubled down on the child benefits bill as she'd vowed in her apartment. Tzehainish worked the phones with the parliamentary aides of supporters of the bill, and Hadas spoke with colleagues in other parties who she thought she might have a chance of talking round to it. It was a thankless task but, Hadas kept reminding Tzehainish, and really herself too, this was what legislation was about. A lot less glamorous than *The West Wing*.

It was a welcome respite from what was really uppermost in both of their minds. But by mid-morning Monday, Hadas threw her cellphone on to her desk and blew out her cheeks in exhaustion, more mental than physical.

"Let's take a break," she groaned. "Let's go find Benny."

They tried Benny's office for the sake of it, but as usual, he wasn't there; he was at his regular table in the cafeteria, holding court. When Hadas and Tzehainish got there, they saw Benny deep in quiet conversation with the Minister of Transport, an unimaginative mid-career lackey from the Likud party whom Hadas held in particularly low esteem. She and Tzehainish exchanged eye-rolls and bought themselves something to drink (mint tea for Tzehainish, who was conscientious about her caffeine intake, and a cappuccino for Hadas, who wasn't; in fact, she and Benny would sometimes get together in the late afternoon and try to one-up each other about the number of coffees they'd drunk that day). Then they went to sit at a table some distance away from Benny, waiting for the moment when he would finish with the minister.

They didn't have to wait long. The two men exchanged a handshake, and Benny sat down alone, beckoning them over.

"Hadas, Tzehainish, come into my office," he boomed, gesturing them to sit at the table opposite him.

"I see you don't call us Ebony and Ivory when you're in danger of being overheard," teased Tzehainish, slipping into a chair and putting her tea down on the table.

"I don't know what you're talking about," said Benny, smiling broadly. "That sounds totally inappropriate and very unlike me."

Hadas put her hand on Tzehainish's arm; now wasn't the time to get into this. "Have you had any insights since last night about my... personal situation, Benny?" she asked.

Benny lowered his voice.

"You must be careful, Hadas. I know that I like to hold meetings out here in public, but for the most part I'm not talking about things that could destroy my interlocutor's political career. If you want to discuss this here, we have to talk really quietly."

"Fine." Hadas lowered her voice too and leaned in a little toward Benny. "So – your thoughts?"

Benny shrugged his shoulders. "I don't think I have any further analysis other than the four options I set out last night."

Hadas deflated. She'd allowed herself to raise her hopes just a little, to believe that Benny would be able to come up with some kind of magic solution. Reality hit her again.

"Were you doing some digging just now? In your previous conversation?" pressed Tzehainish, sensing Hadas's shift of mood and urgently trying to find some idea, some chink of light, some way forward for her boss and friend.

Benny paused. He took a sip of his coffee, put the cup down, and started circling the rim of the cup with his finger, trying to squeeze out a squeak. "Not really," he said quietly, barely moving his lips. "It's very tricky. The moment I let any hint drop that there's some kind of scandal going on with Hadas, word will spread like wildfire. As we've established, you have plenty of enemies, and it'll suddenly become the new hobby of half the Knesset to find out what the scandal is and be the first one to reveal it. So I have to tread very, very carefully. I'm not optimistic about finding the culprit. Your basic options remain the same: end the affair or run the risk of being found out sooner or later."

"She's told you, she's not ending the affair," said Tzehainish. "The *relationship*," she corrected herself quickly, turning to Hadas, and giving her a look of support.

Benny exhaled a long, deep breath.

"Who would have thought that Hadas Levinson would let her heart rule her head," he sighed.

"I'm as surprised as you are," said Hadas, staring at him until he looked up from his coffee cup, forcing him into eye contact. "But this is what my heart wants, Benny."

Benny nodded gently. "What about Navon's aide? Have you thought about confronting him?"

"I spoke to him earlier," said Tzehainish. "I made up some lie, told him that a document seems to have gone missing from Hadas's desk, did he see anyone else in the office when he was there? He brushed me off, wouldn't engage. He said something like 'if anyone's doing any stealing, it's you,' and turned his back on me. I don't know. I don't trust him, that's for sure, but I don't have a sense of whether he or Navon are behind the blackmail."

"I'll keep my ear to the ground," concluded Benny. "But I have to do so with extreme caution. *And so do both of you.* The worst thing we could do would be to tip someone else off about this."

Hadas leaned over to give Benny a hug, grateful to have him in her corner. He smiled back weakly. Hadas got up to leave, Tzehainish following her.

Two minutes later, Hadas and Tzehainish were back at Tzehainish's cubicle. An envelope lay on the desk, one corner tucked under the phone. Tzehainish reached for it, but Hadas pushed her arm away. "I'll do it," she said.

The envelope contained a 4x6 photo of Hadas and Omar sitting in the Valley of the Cross together. It looked as if it had been taken from some distance away, probably with a zoom lens, but it was definitely them. Across the top of the photo was written, in big, black, thick marker, five simple capital letters: *END IT.*

Hadas's eyes darted around the room. The office was empty. There was no way of knowing when the envelope had been placed there, how, or by whom: could have been the blackmailer himself, a collaborator, or an innocent delivery sap. But someone, *someone* had been in here, in this public space, carefully and coldly placing this smoking gun where anyone could have seen it. Benny was right, they weren't going to leave her alone. Just the opposite: they were getting bolder. Closing in on her.

She took another look at the photo, and then ripped it up carefully into little pieces.

"I shall go flush these down the toilet," she muttered with a grimace. "Where this bastard belongs."

Chapter 14

As he did every Monday morning, Akiva traveled from Tel Aviv to Jerusalem to visit Yad Vashem, the Holocaust Memorial museum. He had left Tel Aviv slightly after rush hour, and it was about 10 in the morning now, but still, the last remnants of the Jerusalem commuter traffic, combined with the steep gradient of the winding highway that leads toward the city, meant that his car had slowed to a crawl.

Akiva always shared a private joke with himself as he got to the actual entrance to the city, the set of traffic lights where the highway ended and the city sprawled out in front of him.

The City of Gold, he thought to himself. *What a mess.*

And indeed, to a first-time visitor, maybe someone who had been waiting a lifetime for the moment when they would finally enter Jerusalem, the opening vista of the city is a mess. Gas stations on the side of the road. Office blocks and dilapidated residential buildings ahead of you. Beyond that first set of traffic lights, what seems like six or seven different main roads splitting off ahead of you, each one full of buses, fumes, noise. Sidewalks swarming with Ultra-Orthodox Jews in their black coats and hats, national religious Jews with their large knitted *kippot*, secular Israelis wearing tanktops and shorts, tourists with their baseball caps, all jostling for space, all jostling for hegemony.

It's my Jerusalem, each group seems to be saying. *Not yours, mine.*

The Old City, that City of Gold at which Akiva smirked, was miles away, on the other side of town. Here, it was cacophony, not prophecy, that filled the streets.

Akiva turned right and drove toward the southwestern part of the city where Yad Vashem was located. He drove past Mount Herzl, where Israel's prime ministers and presidents are buried, along with the country's largest military cemetery on its eastern slope. On the other side of the Mount Herzl, in the valley underneath its western slope, lay Yad Vashem.

Akiva bore right to the underground parking lot, and found a spot quite easily; most visitors to Yad Vashem came in tour buses, not private cars. A minute later, he emerged by foot into the entrance plaza of Yad Vashem, a gleaming open square of Jerusalem stone, bright and blinding in the morning sunshine. Akiva walked through the glass-walled entrance lobby, past tour groups seeking the restrooms, past the stairs down to the cafeteria, and out into the museum grounds.

Akiva made his way over to the indoors historical museum, the heart of Yad Vashem: a triangular tunnel, the middle section of which was set into the ground as it bore through a small hill. As Akiva walked through the entrance, he suddenly passed from the blinding brightness of the day into the darkness of the museum's opening exhibits. He wandered quickly through the series of dark, winding display rooms on either side of the triangular tunnel. He wove his way in and out of the displays, criss-crossing the central tunnel again and again, moving through the series of exhibits that documented the history of the Holocaust from the rise of the Nazis in 1933 until the end of World War II. Darkness and death surrounded him. Photos of ghettoes, mass graves, death camps. And then Akiva, slowed down slightly by a large tour group, finally reached the end of the museum, quite literally the light at the end of the tunnel, where the triangular underground passage emerged back out of the mountain into a glorious, light-filled vista of Jerusalem, a lobby area with floor-to-ceiling windows, the trees and buildings of Jerusalem bursting to life in front of his eyes. The message of the museum planners was clear: after the dark, miserable years of Diaspora and Holocaust, Israel provides the Jewish people with safety and stability – with light.

Akiva did not need to see the exhibits. He knew their pictures and their history well enough. That was not why he came to Yad Vashem every week. His ritual, instead, was to hang out at that final Jerusalem vista, gazing at the landscape in front of him, looking at the light, and thinking about the future light that he would bring to the Jewish people and to the world. In all his discomfort at what he was doing, at the money he was taking and the sacrifices he was making and the lies he was telling, this light gave him comfort.

He also loved eavesdropping attentively on what people were saying as they left the museum.

There were the teary-eyed American girls, on a free *Birthright* trip to Israel paid for by the Jewish community, with cut-off shorts and pedicured toes, who hung on the arms of the Israeli soldiers who were escorting their group. "Now I get it," they would say. "It's because of you that the Jewish people will never again have another Holocaust." Translation: "I will have sex with you tonight, and even my grandma in Florida would approve."

There were the Israeli groups of grim middle-aged friends, still young enough to remember how their parents, who survived and made it to Israel, refused to talk about what happened to their own parents, to their brothers and sisters, their friends. These Israeli visitors did not say much when they emerged from the museum's darkness. Quiet nods, tight mouths. Rarely tears.

There were the Israeli kids, the school groups. Running through the museum like it was some kind of adventure playground. They were the only happy visitors in the place, too busy being excited about Yossi's new crush on Daphna and what Miki said to the homeroom teacher the other day and when the new Noa Kirel album was going to be released to remember to be solemn and heavy-shouldered about the Holocaust. Perhaps there was some kind of pleasing irony about these *vilde chayas*, these wild, rule-less Israeli children, free at last in their own land, ignoring the Germanic cultural protocols and etiquettes of a museum visit.

Then there were the German tourists, visiting Israel to marvel at what the Jewish people had done despite their grandparents' best efforts. Akiva liked these groups the best, because they usually didn't realize that anyone around them could understand German, and so the snippets of conversation that he heard tended to be more candid, more unguarded. "*Ja*, it is terrible what we did to the Jews, but look, they are now doing the same thing to the Palestinians."

Akiva found the routine of hearing these statements repeat themselves from week to week to be calming, restorative, grounding. He wasn't much of a praying kind of person any more, and often felt uncomfortable when his colleagues – most of whom definitely *were* praying kind of people – stopped in the middle of a meeting for *minchah*, the afternoon prayer, or spoke about the religious heights they had reached at Friday night services that weekend. He had to go along with them, for appearance's sake. But for Akiva, these weekly visits to Yad Vashem were, he reflected, a kind of prayer, a moment for self-evaluation, a moment to regain inner strength for the long task ahead of him.

He closed his eyes for a while in silent meditation, then opened them once more on the Jerusalem vista. A group of Asian tourists (Chinese, he presumed – the new Chinese bourgeoisie seemed to have a fascination with Israel and were recently among its most frequent visitors) was passing by, ending their visit with suitably grave faces. Some of the Israeli middle school kids were still there, fooling around, teasing each other, still joking about Miki's comment to the homeroom teacher. A couple of the kids were playing some kind of fake sword-fighting game with a pair of chopsticks, and bumped into an elderly Chinese couple, who shrank against the wall, but did not react, as if unsure of the etiquette about criticizing Jews in this of all places. Akiva smiled at the irony again. Israeli kids eat Asian take-out that their middle-class parents buy them, they keep the chopsticks to play swordfights with their friends, and they do that in the middle of Yad Vashem, getting in the face of Chinese tourists who are visiting to see how the Germans tried to wipe these kids off the face of the earth. You couldn't make it up.

"*Pfennige* for your thoughts." He suddenly heard Yoav's voice behind him. Akiva spun around.

"What are you doing here? How did you know to find me here?" he asked, puzzled.

"It's been my job to know where you are and what you're doing for many years now, Akiva," drawled Yoav. "You think you can disappear every Monday morning and not have me wonder where you are? Not have my people follow you? Not have my people report back to me?"

A brief chill fluttered up Akiva's spine. He dismissed it.

"Report back to you? Your 'people'? What are you talking about, Yoav? Why's it your business where I go on my Monday mornings? You've been following me?"

Yoav didn't reply. They were standing a little way back from the light-filled windows, and it was dark enough that Akiva couldn't quite make out all the details on Yoav's face. But even in this half-light, there was something that he didn't recognize. There was something new in Yoav's eyes. Instead of the usual gleaming, magnetic warmth, a coldness, a clinical dispassion.

Akiva forced a smile to lighten the mood.

"Okay, so you caught me. I guess I shouldn't be surprised. Kind of an obvious place for my weekly meditation, given my line of work, right?"

Still Yoav said nothing.

Akiva laughed a short, nervous laugh. Something was not right.

"But following me, Yoav, following me? That's a bit much, isn't it? Can't a poor scientist have a few moments on his own once a week? Why are you following me?"

Yoav paused, his narrow eyes firmly on Akiva, and then responded. "I've been... making sure that nothing gets in the way of my plan."

"*Your* plan?"

"*My* plan, Akiva." Yoav nodded. "It was always my plan. You were always just the... vehicle... the functionary... the aluminum foil pan to be discarded after dinner..."

Akiva's brow was furrowed with indignation, and he was too irritated to notice the hairs on the back of his neck standing up as if in some pre-amygdalic intuition of fear.

"What the hell's got into you? How can you talk like this? 'Functionary? Foil pan?' We've been partners in this every step of the way!"

"Partners..." murmured Yoav, shaking his head dismissively. "You know, there is no German word for partner. It's just the borrowed English, *Der Partner*. Why is that, do you think, Akiva? The Germans don't like partnership, co-operation, sharing. It's all about *one*. One Reich, One Leader, One Nation, *jawohl*? Partner... once you start to think about it, even the word implies weakness. *Part*, not whole.... *Par* for the course... *Nerd*. Hah! Yes, Akiva, that's right. A partner is a *nerd* who is only *par* for the course, who only understands *part*, not the whole. And so in that sense, Akiva, you have been a true partner. Hah!"

Yoav began to laugh. A grim, thin-mouthed laugh that seemed as if it echoed from the walls of the museum, from the pictures of Nazis shooting Jews in the head, from the pictures of death marches, from the air-conditioned smell of death.

"Yoav, what's gotten into you today? You're worrying me," stammered Akiva. He'd never trusted Yoav, always seen the warmth of their relationship as something fragile, contingent on Yoav's whim. But this was something else entirely. He'd got glimpses at Yoav's power and ruthlessness over the years, but the target had always been someone else. For the first time, Akiva sensed the crosshairs were trained on his forehead.

"Yes, Akiva, I'm worrying you," sneered Yoav. "You *should* be worried!" He hissed out his words forcefully, stepping closer to Akiva, towering over him intimidatingly. "I am afraid that today is the day when I have to tell you that I have... I have not been entirely honest with you."

"What do you mean? Since when have you not been entirely honest with me?"

"Since we first met. Since before we first met." Yoav paused. He looked Akiva in the eye, his face now deadpan. There was a fleeting glimpse of fondness in his look, but a fondness tinged with pity. And then all that Akiva could see was contempt, like someone looking at a cockroach scurrying around the floor trying to escape his boot. It was the look of a man who was about to betray another man.

A wave of panic flooded through Akiva and his throat suddenly felt dry. All this time he'd been looking forward to betraying Yoav, savoring the moment in advance, rehearsing the words in his head, using the anticipation of the emotion he'd feel to get him through the long years. But now... he was starting to see that he'd missed the signs. It was the other way round. He'd made a grave mistake.

"You see, Akiva," Yoav continued, "none of this has been what you thought. When I sought you out at Hebrew U all those years ago, it wasn't what you thought. When I started finding you private money for your work, it wasn't what you thought. I had sources of funding who were waiting for someone like you. Powerful sources. Who had instructed me to find someone like you."

Akiva tried to process this new information in his head, but he couldn't make sense of it. Something was missing. The Chinese tourists, the pedicured American girls, the wild Israeli kids, all faded into the background. Akiva sensed Yoav looming in front of him, but somehow also to the side of him, even behind him. He was surrounded, almost suffocated by Yoav's presence.

"Who... instructed you...?" Akiva finally managed to spit out.

"Oh, you have no idea," said Yoav with a soft chuckle. "No idea who you've really been working for all these years. But it doesn't matter right now. What matters is that I succeeded in my mission. I found you, cultivated you, helped you. For you, it was always about the science. For me, the science was just a means to an end. The end that I always had in mind."

"What end, Yoav?" whispered Akiva. "I thought..."

Yoav shook his head with a wry sadness, calmly waiting for Akiva's mind to finally catch up with his own. "This whole vengeance thing... I never found it very convincing. You remember back when you were still at Hebrew U, that day we watched *The Boys from Brazil*... I planted the vengeance idea in your mind, because I knew that I needed you. I didn't care *why* you bought in; I cared *that* you bought in."

Akiva wracked his brain, trying to rewind through the past fifteen years of his life, revisiting every interaction he'd ever had with Yoav, replaying every scene, reinterpreting every conversation. How had he not seen this? "But you were so insistent on it... you pulled me into it, you pulled all of us into it."

Yoav shrugged and yawned. His nonchalance, even in this fraught situation, ate at the core of Akiva's self-confidence, as it always did.

"I just did what needed to be done," Yoav went on. "What I needed to do to fulfil my mission." He paused for a moment. "You know, there were so many times that I thought about opening up to you, about telling you why I'm really doing this. Why *you* were really doing this. But I knew that you wouldn't agree. You were willing to do a lot of dirty work for this mission, but this would have been a bridge too far. It's such a shame. Maybe I should have trusted you. Still, it's too late now."

"What would have been a bridge too far? What's too late now?" Akiva's chest tightened, and the dryness in his throat almost choked him as he tried to get the words out.

Yoav sighed. "That's why I'm here. To tell you. Like I said, it's not about vengeance. Never has been, for me. Well, not vengeance on an individual, anyway. Come on, Akiva, really? Punishing someone's DNA? No-one's going to buy it. They'll have you thrown away in a mental hospital and the kid in the hands of Social Services before you can blink."

Akiva's head was spinning. What Yoav was saying now was what he, Akiva, had been thinking all along. He thought he'd been playing along with Yoav's crazy idea – but Yoav had also been playing along? *Think, Akiva, think. It doesn't make any sense...*

"So why, then, Yoav? Why all these years? Why all the agony, the sacrifice? I don't understand... you cared so much about the work..."

"Yes, I cared about the work, but for different reasons, Akiva. Very different reasons. Think about it: we have brought back to life the greatest, most charismatic, most successful leader the world has ever known. A military genius, a political leader, a shaper of society. When has there ever been a leader like that?"

Yoav paused, gazed into Akiva's eyes, and took a step toward him. He put his hand on the back of Akiva's neck, and leaned forward, pulling Akiva's head toward him, twisting it so that Akiva's ear ended up right beneath his mouth.

Akiva could feel Yoav's hot breath on his ear. He tried to pull away, but Yoav kept his hand firmly pressed on his neck. Yoav whispered with a malevolent hiss into Akiva's ear: "When have *we* ever had a leader like that?"

Akiva went white. Suddenly he understood. His legs gave way and he stumbled away from Yoav, but Yoav pulled him back up, still grabbing onto Akiva's neck, his biceps straining at the weight but lifting him back on to his feet and holding his head tight again. He wasn't done. He leaned in again and spoke quietly to Akiva, enunciating each word slowly into his ear.

"You think that I have sweated over this project for my entire adult life in order to become a *glorified prison warden*? You think that I would bring back into existence the greatest political and military leader the world has ever known and let the Jewish people pass up on the opportunity to *benefit* from him?"

In a flash those replays of previous conversations became clear to Akiva. Yoav's obsession with Hitler's biography, with his single-handed creation of the Nazi party, with his military strategy. Akiva had never been interested in any of that: it was irrelevant to his intentions for the reborn Hitler. But Yoav was always fascinated by Hitler the man, the reality of Hitler, the tactics, the charisma, the style. Yoav didn't want to punish Hitler; he wanted Hitler for himself.

Yoav let go of Akiva's head derisively and flicked him away like a cigarette butt. He smiled sorrowfully at Akiva, as if to a child who's just realized that the tooth fairy doesn't exist.

Akiva's brain swirled like a whirlpool. Another tourist bumped into him, but he hardly felt it. He felt sick. It was all falling into place. Yoav's commitment to the infant having breast milk. And it wasn't just Akiva who had been discomforted by Sivan causing the baby pain, it was Yoav too, it was Yoav who had stopped her...

"This child," Yoav hissed, "will not speak *one word* of German. God forbid! God forbid that he should speak a word of that disgusting, phlegmy, Jew-hating language, that language saturated with the blood of our ancestors. This child will speak only Hebrew, only God's language. *No-one will ever know of his DNA or provenance.* He will be circumcised in the next few days, as all Jewish boys are. He will be raised by two God-fearing religious Zionists in the heart of Judea and Samaria. He will go to the best religious school and get the best tutors. He will grow up to be a sun-tanned Hebrew, hiking the land and praying in its wadis and valleys. He will love Torah, he will revel in its commandments. He will be the best kind of religious Zionist Jew: a lover of the land of Israel, a lover of Torah, a lover of God, a defender of the Jewish people. He will serve in the army. He will become an officer. His genes will work for *us* this time round. He will gather people around him like a magnet. He will go into politics and sweep all before him. Never will Israel have seen a leader like this! He will re-ignite the fire in our bellies! He will cure the malaise of skepticism and negativity that we suffer from! He will stop us from constantly apologizing for who we are! He will show the world what happens to those who seek to deny us our birthright in this land. And finally, finally, the Arab nations around us will see that we have a leader who cannot be bullied. A leader who can truly lead the Jewish people, who is not scared of condemnations in the UN or wrist-slaps from the EU."

Akiva's whole body was screaming. He'd hated the idea of what he thought GeneLight was about, but now he realized that he'd been Yoav's patsy for an even more terrible project. *What have I done... how can this be happening...*

Yoav folded his arms triumphantly over his chest and raised his voice, not so loud that others could hear, but orating as if to an invisible audience of tens, hundreds, thousands around him. "We, the Jewish people, will finally have a leader who can free us from our weakness. He will build up our army to heights it has never seen. The Six Day War will be child's play compared to the victories he will lead us in over our neighbors. And this time, there will be no Soviet winter to stop him. He will destroy the Palestinians, and the Jordanians, and the Syrians, all the Arabs around us, and the world will not even have the chance to wonder what happened. He will rule from Cairo to Damascus, from Beirut to Baghdad. He will establish around himself a Jewish empire so great and strong that it will last for all eternity."

Yoav looked pityingly at Akiva. "Vengeance was never going to set us free, my friend. I knew you were too weak to see that. Punishing one baby was the limit of your imagination. Even *that* gave you sleepless nights, for God's sake! I was always thinking much bigger. Using that baby to wreak destruction on hundreds, on thousands, on tens of thousands. That is how you bring about Jewish freedom. Strength. Might. Power. Only they will set us free. That baby will grow up to be the greatest Jewish leader in our entire history, a leader who will ensure our freedom and our supremacy. Never again will Jews be weak. *Never again.*"

Akiva's world was disintegrating around him. To be double-crossed like this, to be played, when all along he had thought that he was the player... how was it possible? What kind of terrible new reality was Yoav trying to create? Akiva shuddered at the thought. "You're insane."

Now Yoav really did laugh. "*I'm* insane? Says the man who wants to put a child in prison because of the crimes his DNA committed? *I'm* insane? I think you'll have a hard time convincing a jury of that, Akiva!"

Akiva gasped shakily at the air around him, trying to fill his lungs with courage, trembling with indignation and anger. "But... there are people who know the truth... *I* know the truth... I won't let you do this..."

Yoav nodded his head. "I know, Akiva. I know you won't let me do this. And that is why I am going to kill you."

Chapter 15

For a moment, Akiva wondered whether he should laugh it off, whether maybe Yoav was joking. But he'd never seen this look in Yoav's face before. Mustering as much assertiveness as he could, he spoke calmly back at Yoav: "You're going to kill me? Seriously? Here, in the middle of Yad Vashem?"

"Yes, here, in the middle of Yad Vashem. What better place to put an end to your life, Akiva? You have spent your career trying to resurrect Hitler, and here, in the middle of this ridiculous, navel-gazing shrine of nonsense, you are going to meet your end. A backward-looking person dying in a backward-looking temple. Like the Diaspora Jews who Hitler murdered, you are too obsessed with the past. I, on the other hand, am a Zionist. A forward-looker. For me, bringing Hitler back to life has never been about the past. Always about the future. About using *whatever means we have at our disposal* to win, to succeed, to be victorious. It's what the Jews have always done."

Yoav gave a wry, dismissive chuckle. He poked his finger at Akiva's chest, rocking him back with its force. "You think we batted an eyelid when the Egyptians' firstborns died en masse? You think we lost a minute's sleep over all the Persians we killed after we beat Haman? You think the Maccabees worried about the International Criminal Court when they reclaimed the Holy Land from the Greeks? No, we praised God for our victory each time. Whenever we've been *strong*, we've flourished. And strength comes through powerful military leadership. This boy is the greatest military leader the world has ever seen. And now, Akiva, thanks to you, *he's ours*. He's ours! You can at least die knowing that you have given the Jewish people this parting gift."

"You can't kill me here, Yoav. I think there might be one or two witnesses," said Akiva. He felt confident enough in this retort that he put his hand on his friend's shoulder and gave him a warm squeeze. *He's crazy, you've always known he's crazy. Just need to talk him down from this latest little tree. It'll be okay.* He tried to maneuver himself amicably around to Yoav's side, putting his arm all the way round his shoulder. "Come on, now. Let's go discuss this over a cup of—"

"My God, you have always been such an insufferable patronizing bastard, haven't you, Akiva?" spat Yoav through gritted teeth, pushing Akiva away. "You always thought that because you were the scientist and I was merely the money man, you were by definition the smarter one, the leader, the boss."

Akiva reached out with his hand again, but Yoav brushed it off and rubbed his own temples in exasperation. "I have spent my entire career playing along with you but now it stops. The middle of Yad Vashem is probably one of the best places in the world to shoot someone with a silencer at close range, you *dumbkopf.* Look around you! It's dark. It's crowded. It's noisy."

Yoav drew his jacket back just an inch and motioned with his head for Akiva to look. Akiva could make out the dull shine of metal even in the dark light of the museum. "How the hell did you get that past security?" Akiva gasped.

"You fool, Akiva, you have no idea who you're dealing with," smirked Yoav, moving his right arm inside his jacket to where the gun sat in its holster. "In a moment, Akiva, I am going to pretend to hug you, as people often do in this place. Then, while we are hugging, I am going to shoot you through the heart. You will feel a moment of intense, searing pain, and then nothing. You will slump to the floor. People will think you have fainted, overcome with emotion. It happens here about a dozen times a day. By the time anyone realizes that you have been shot, I will have slipped off into the shadows."

Akiva looked around nervously. Suddenly everything around him was blurry. Everything he had thought for the past two decades was wrong. He stared at

Yoav in disbelief, trying to comprehend how this man had played him all these years, and one overriding thought suddenly filled Akiva's entire being. *Not going to let this bastard win.*

One of the sword-fighting kids suddenly bumped into his legs, and Akiva had a moment of scientific clarity. He grabbed the kid's arm, wrestled the chopstick out of his grip, and before Yoav could react, he poked it with all the force he could muster at Yoav's face. The chopstick hit Yoav's cheekbone, snapped as it encountered resistance, and fell out of Akiva's hands, but he drove his hand forward with the momentum and grabbed Yoav's head with his hands, gouging his thumb into Yoav's eye. Yoav shrieked and doubled over in pain, trying to shield his face, but Akiva followed Yoav down, screwing his thumb in deeper and deeper, digging his other fingers into Yoav's temple. Yoav screwed his eye shut and shook his head, making Akiva lose his grip for a moment, but he scrabbled his hands over Yoav's face, fumbling again for the spot, and dug his thumb in once more. Yoav screamed again but Akiva didn't care. He roared with primal triumphalism from a part of him that he didn't know existed. "You're not going to win, you bastard, you're not going to win," he yelled.

Yoav fell backward and huddled over on the floor in the fetal position, hands protecting his head, rocking in pain. "What the fuck did you do, you asshole? Shit, shit, shit, my eye, what the fuck..."

Akiva watched Yoav writhing in pain on the floor, still anxious. He'd bought himself some time, but how much? The momentary high from attacking Yoav was replaced by fear flooding through his body again. *Have to get out of here.* A couple of tourists bent over Yoav to see if he was okay, and Akiva saw his chance. He bundled past the kid whose chopstick he'd grabbed and quickly began to elbow his way back through the museum, against the flow of traffic, trying to get lost in the crowds. He peered back over his shoulder. Yoav was no longer lying on the floor where he'd left him. *That means he's coming after me.* Akiva came up against a particularly tight-knit group of tourists and squeezed brusquely through them, his heart pounding not from the energy he was exerting but from the knowledge that Yoav could be literally steps behind him, could be drawing that gun any moment. He heard a thud from somewhere and jumped in fright before he realized that it was just a backpack being thrown onto the ground. He wiped the perspiration from his face and pushed ahead, finally getting to a less crowded area toward the entrance of the museum. He glanced back and saw Yoav about halfway through the central museum pathway, roughly pushing people out of his way, one hand still nursing his eye, but moving fast and gaining on him. Akiva knew that once he got out into the open, he didn't stand a chance.

Again, Akiva had a moment of clarity. The air-conditioned darkness of the museum flowed through his veins and focused him like a sniper: he needed everyone else to share his fear.

"*Mechabel!*" he shouted. *Terrorist!* "Down there, look. I heard him shout *Allahu Akhbar.* Terrorist!"

The security guard at the entrance to the museum looked up but didn't move. A few people around Akiva glanced nervously in the direction where he was pointing. But then Yoav made a mistake, his first mistake in years: he pulled out his gun and took aim at Akiva.

"Terrorist!!" This time it wasn't Akiva who shouted the word, it was an Israeli tour guide halfway between the two men. The tour guide bulldozed the small group of tourists around him onto the ground. "Down, down, everybody get down!" he shouted. Two elderly men in his group stood to the side, frozen, and the tour guide jumped up and ran into them, arms out, trying to shield them or scoop them into a corner. Yoav turned in his direction, and the metal of the gun glinted from the spotlight of a nearby exhibit. "He's got a gun!" screamed a nearby woman. Finally the security guard sprang into action, barked into his walkie-talkie, started running toward Yoav. Suddenly the entire museum was chaos. The security guard pulled out his own gun and aimed it at Yoav as he ran, but there were crowds of people in the way, shrieking, running in all directions, falling over each other, creating even more chaos. Three more guards appeared out of nowhere and ran into the museum. An alarm went off, red lights flashed from the ceiling. "Emergency. Please evacuate the building," blared a loud metallic voice. A sea of humanity surged toward Akiva and the museum's entrance. Akiva watched all this, rooted to the ground in disbelief that it was really happening, but then snapped back to himself as a flash of cold terror hit him and he realized that his life was still in the balance. He had no idea where Yoav was. He turned and dashed out of the museum with the crowds.

Akiva stumbled into the sunshine, blinded. He could hear police sirens in the distance. Someone pulling a gun in the middle of Yad Vashem: they weren't going to mess about, massive security would be here in full force within minutes. They would close off the area, and he had to get out before that happened. He ran out of the museum, into the entrance plaza, toward the underground parking lot. A shot rang out and he felt something whistle past his face, inches away. He stumbled, his left ankle gave way, he fell to the ground. His hand grazed the hot Jerusalem stone, breaking his fall, and he winced in pain at the sting. Turning, he saw in the distance, running toward him with a gun in his hand, another man who he didn't recognize. Yoav had accomplices? Yoav was part of... what? Something bigger? Who were these "sources" who gave him instructions? What the hell was going on?

No time to think. Heart pounding, Akiva stood up and limped to the doorway that led to the parking lot. His sprained ankle radiated pain throughout his body but he refused to let it stop him. *Can't let him win.* He turned his head briefly and saw that behind him, Yoav's accomplice had stopped, extended his arm, and was pointing the steel barrel directly at him. There were no more than thirty meters between them, and Akiva knew that any halfway decent ex-military Israeli would be able to take him down from that distance. The doorway was only a few steps ahead of him, but his lungs were gasping for air, his ankle was barely holding his weight, he realized he was out of time. He leaned over, dry-retching in defeat, and braced himself for the shot, for the searing fire of metal tearing through his flesh.

Suddenly the sirens got louder and a police car burst through the main entrance of the plaza and screeched to a halt, blocking the line of sight between Akiva and the man trying to kill him. Four policemen sprinted out of the car toward the museum – they hadn't even seen Akiva or the gunman. But it was enough to be a distraction. Akiva straightened himself up and staggered through the doorway, half-walked half-fell down the stairs, and tumbled into his car. He pulled the key out of his pocket but his hands were shaking so much that it fell to the floor of the car. He rummaged around underneath the seat but couldn't find it. "Come on, come on, where is it..." he muttered, conscious that every second wasted was a second closer to oblivion.

Finally his fingers scrambled upon the key's cold flat surface. Still shaking, he shoved it into the ignition and fired the car to life. He spun out of the parking space, and sped up the ramp to the parking lot exit. He swerved into the incoming lane in order to avoid the exit barrier, and drove out back into the entrance plaza. As he burst out into the sunlight again, he almost ran over the man with the gun, who had run around the police car and was heading down the parking lot ramp to intercept him. Akiva spun the steering wheel to the right in order to avoid the police car, and as his tires screeched around it, he heard another gunshot and felt shattered glass cascade into the back of his neck. Yoav's accomplice had taken a shot, hit his back windshield, but missed him. Akiva spasmed as the shattered glass around him produced another rush of adrenaline through his body. He looked anxiously in the rearview mirror and saw two things: Yoav's accomplice was taking aim again, and Yoav himself was running out of one of the emergency exits of the museum toward him, hand still over his eye, pushing his way past a group of hysterical tourists.

"Shoot him again!" shouted Yoav at the other man. "What are you waiting for? We can't let him get away!"

The accomplice lifted his arm again, and swiveled his body as he tried to get a lock on Akiva's car. But it was too late. More crowds of panicked tourists streamed out of the museum behind Yoav, and suddenly they were engulfed by the mass.

Three more police cars were now driving down the hill in the direction of Yad Vashem. Akiva drove on the other side of the road, as fast as he could without drawing attention to himself. His heart was still pounding, almost breaking out of his chest, his palms so slippery that he could barely hold the steering wheel. At the main road at the top of the hill, he turned back toward Mount Herzl and the main exit from Jerusalem. He glanced back in relief. He was safe for now. But then a cold chill wrapped its arms around his chest, squeezed him so that he couldn't breathe. *The lab. The project. Shira.*

An hour later, Akiva pulled up outside the office building in Tel Aviv. He knew he was taking a risk coming back here – if Yoav had accomplices, then maybe he'd sent people here too, to wait for him? But he had to come. Speeding down the highway on the journey from Jerusalem, he had realized what he was going to see when he got here. He knew what Yoav must have done. But he had to see it with his own eyes.

As soon as he walked out of the elevators on the twentieth floor, he knew that he was right. The gleaming silver door with the GeneLight logo was ajar – something that was expressly forbidden. He pushed it open, walked through, and crumpled in horror as he saw the blood. It was a puddle on the floor, stretching in an oblong shape from the receptionist's front desk toward him. At the top of the puddle, jutting out on the floor behind the desk, was the blood's source: a head. It was Neta's. Her brains were seeping from a gaping hole onto the parquet. Akiva fell to his knees in front of her body. As a genetic scientist, Akiva had seen blood before, but not like this. He'd never seen a dead human body. He inched forward on all fours and put a trembling finger on Neta's neck, aware that it was a pointless gesture. He inched back, his shaking arms almost giving way beneath him, and collapsed onto his side.

He buried his head in his hands, scrunching himself into the fetal position, trying to erase the sight that he'd just seen, but it was burned onto the back of his eyelids. He raised his head and croaked out in a rasping voice: "Shira... Shira...?" His voice echoed back to him and he stumbled to his feet and walked past the reception desk, stepping gingerly around Neta, suppressing a retch from the depths of his stomach and soul. The offices were empty. Not a computer, not a filing cabinet, not a notepad remained. A faint smell of gunpowder lingered in the air. Akiva quickened the pace and ran through to his own office, but it was the same. Cleared out. It was as if GeneLight had never existed. All that remained was Neta and her pool of blood.

"Shi... Shir...?" Akiva called out again, a lump catching in his throat and choking the name before he could even get it out. He ran out of the office again, to the elevator that led down to the lab. A metallic taste of terror seeped through his saliva and he swallowed bitterly. Tears blurred his vision. His hands, his legs, his whole body was shaking. The elevator took what seemed like an eternity to go from 20 to L. *Please, Yoav, not her too. Not Shira, you bastard....*

The doors opened.

Empty. Nothing. All traces of his scientific project – of his life – were gone. The test tubes, the computers, the centrifugal spinners, the animal cages, the embryo refrigerators, all gone. And of course the child was gone too.

And no sign of Shira or Sivan.

Then he saw it. It looked different down here, in the harsh artificial light. Upstairs, Neta's blood had been dark, almost black. This, though, was red. Lady Macbeth red. *The Shining* red. Almost blinding him as it reflected the ceiling lights into his face. It was coming from the door of a small office of storage cabinets, set off from one of the main laboratory rooms.

He knew what had to be in there. *Who* had to be in there. He stumbled toward the door like a zombie, suddenly on autopilot, his body acting independently from his mind, which was screaming at him to stop.

He opened the door into a picture of hell. Sivan's body was slumped on the floor with her back against a filing cabinet, her white lab cloak stained with red. Her arm dangled from her body as if by a thread, and her head was twisted to one side at an impossible angle, with a hole in it like Neta's, and with blood oozing from other parts of her body too – her hands, her chest. Next to her, Shira lay face down on the floor, her brown hair matted by blood onto her face, her left ankle deformed at almost 90 degrees to her shin. Akiva stepped forward but slipped, and tumbled onto the floor between the bodies, into their blood. It was stickier than he expected, oozing onto his hands and arms like honey. He flailed out with his arms, and knocked Sivan on top of him, her blood and brains splattering onto his clothes, her hair falling onto his face. His chest tightened, he tried to breathe, but all he could sense was a glutinous mix of Sivan's hair and blood suffocating him, drowning him. His lungs screeched in emptiness, the world began to go black around him, his arms and legs and body weighed down as Sivan's dead body smothered him. But suddenly:

"Akiva..."

It was Shira's voice, but not Shira's voice... a rasping, faint, ersatz version of her voice, but enough to snap him together, to grasp with internal hands onto a few drops of adrenaline. He pushed Sivan away, managed to get himself onto his knees, and pulled Shira toward him, turning her over, supporting her neck like a baby's. She was covered in blood too, with a deep bullet wound in her shoulder. She was pale, lips blue, shivering. He stroked her cold cheek, trying to will it to warm up, to will the blood back from the floor into her veins.

"It was... Yoav..." she whispered. "Yoav..."

"I know," he said, bending down to her face, cheek to cheek, breathing in her smell, the smell of her hair and her neck that he used to know so well, the smell that he'd missed so much for all these years. "He tried to kill me too. He betrayed us all."

"He... tortured us... broke our bones... cut into our flesh... wanted to know if we'd told anyone else... any of our friends... wanted to know who else knew..."

"I'm so sorry," whispered Akiva. "I should have known. I should have seen it..."

"What...?"

"It doesn't matter. I'm not going to let him do what he wants to do." His tears dripped onto her neck, mixing with her blood, and he burrowed himself into her neck, kissing her icy skin, caressing her head, trying to reclaim years of lost embraces in this last dying moment.

"I... can't feel anything... can't breathe... Akiva... you know... I've always..."

"I know, Shira. You don't have to say it. I'm so sorry. I wasn't honest with you. I wanted to tell you a thousand times... but I just couldn't. I couldn't bear to tell you that I was lying to you. But Shira... I've been such a fool... I want to tell you the truth now... it's not too late... Shira?"

Shira didn't respond. Her body went limp in his arms.

Akiva fell to the floor, embracing Shira, crying. He kissed her dead lips, willing her to respond, despising all those years of his idiocy at not telling her the truth, at cutting himself off from her lips, her face, her soul. He got up, and roared with anger. Anger at Yoav, anger at himself for being so naïve.

He had to get out of there, every minute that went by was another minute that Yoav or his friends might turn up. Now he could see that there was nothing they wouldn't stop at. Yoav was going to take this child and make him an Israeli Hitler. A Jewish Hitler. A Hitler who spoke Hebrew. A Hitler who studied Torah. A Hitler who would lead the Jews into a holy war against the Arabs who surrounded them. This was not how it was meant to be...

He got up. He couldn't wallow in these thoughts now – he had to get out of there. Back to the elevator, up to the offices, then back down to the street. He dug deep inside himself for the energy and conviction he'd felt before. *You're not going to die here too, Akiva. Not going to let them win.*

He took a couple of steps back toward the elevator, but stopped himself. No. Too risky. Yoav's people could be waiting for him to get out at the lobby. They might even already be upstairs in the office, waiting for him to emerge from the lab elevator. The only possibility was the emergency exit. When they'd built the lab, a city regulator had told them that they needed some kind of stairway access up to street level in case of an elevator malfunction. So at the back of the lab there was an old iron fire-door which led – Akiva assumed – up to the street. He'd never so much as opened that door, let alone used the steps. He knew that Yoav must know about it in the back of his mind somewhere, but there was just the chance that Yoav hadn't thought of it or hadn't told his people about it.

Akiva took one last look at Shira. "I love you," he said out loud, his voice echoing around the empty metallic surfaces. "I'm sorry that I never trusted you enough to tell you. Never trusted myself enough." He took a deep, unsteady breath, forcing his diaphragm to squeeze out the spasms of retching from his stomach. He ran to the door and tried to push the handle down. The handle grunted and strained, years of inertia and rust needing to be cracked apart, but eventually it gave way, and the door opened. Behind it was a set of concrete stairs leading upward, lit only by a dim emergency light.

Akiva was in terrible shape. After running up three flights of stairs, he collapsed on the concrete floor, struggling for breath. *You idiot... You'll do Yoav's work for him. Escape a murder attempt at Yad Vashem, escape being massacred in the lab, and have a coronary here on the emergency stairs!* He started giggling to himself at the absurdity of the situation, his nerves giving way to manic laughter. The laughter turned into a coughing spasm, and he gasped for breath, clutching his chest, feeling the sweat on his stomach congeal with Shira and Sivan's blood along with the dust from the stairs on the front of his shirt.

Suddenly the thought hit him that Tomer must be dead too, and this sobered him up. Tomer Kleinberg, his attorney, whose knowledge of GeneLight's inner details he'd revealed to Yoav the other day. The sickening realization hit him that by telling Yoav that Tomer knew those details, he'd basically signed Tomer's death warrant.

He got up, and started making his way more slowly. When he got to level -1, he stopped, and sat down to catch his breath again. He guessed that the emergency exit would deposit him on the street somewhere, but where? If it was the front of the building, he might as well be dead. His only hope was that it might lead out to the side or the back, where he could slink off in the shadows and somehow get away.

He slowly walked up the final flight of stairs. He reached the door – another heavy fire-door, with a horizontal push-bar. He paused and considered his options again. The image of Shira lying in his arms floated back to his consciousness. *Must keep going. For her. And for all of the others.* Pushing down on the bar, he gently opened the door and peered through the crack. The afternoon Tel Aviv heat and humidity enveloped his body, clinging to the sweat and blood. He stuck his head out and saw that he was indeed at the back of the building, by the dumpsters and industrial recycled paper bins.

He started running, dragging his legs up off the ground, sucking air into every crevice of his body, willing his muscles to do the impossible. He turned around and swore to himself, distraught at how little distance he'd put between himself and the building.

Then he heard it.

"Akiiiiivaaaaa!"

It was Yoav's voice. He turned around again and saw Yoav and two other men running toward him from the far side of the building. One of the men had his arm outstretched, and as Akiva turned to continue running, he heard a couple of shots being fired. One of the bullets hit a glass window store front to his right. The glass shattered and Akiva instinctively raised his hands to shield his face. A searing pain erupted in his right arm and he turned to see a piece of glass shrapnel about the size of a playing card stuck to his tricep. It was like someone was holding a burning knife to his skin and wouldn't stop cutting.

He shrieked in pain, doubled over to one side, his running curtailed into a limping stumble. "You're not... going... to... win..." he sputtered, too quietly for Yoav to hear, but loud enough to give himself a temporary boost. He reached around with his left hand and pulled the piece of glass out, crying out in agony once more. His shirt oozed with blood. He picked the pace back up but then heard another shot, and felt shards of concrete sprinkle down on him from somewhere close overhead.

His heart was going to explode, his ears were ringing, he could barely catch his breath. He was slowing, Yoav and his men were gaining on him. He stumbled forward onto the main road. To his left, about half a kilometer away, there was a large hotel: people, crowds, protection. He turned in its direction but it was too late. He wasn't going to make it, his legs were giving way beneath him. Yoav was a hundred meters away, ninety, eighty. His whole body dragged him down, and his eyes began to water in defeat.

Then Akiva saw it. His one chance, his only chance. Taxi. Heading toward him. Akiva staggered into the road. He knew that he must look like a street bum, dripping with sweat and blood and concrete dust and God knows what else, but he couldn't give the driver a chance to have second thoughts. "Taxi...!" he shouted. "Taxi!" He moved into the taxi's path and held out his hand. The driver had no choice but to stop, and as soon as he did, Akiva swung around, opened the door, and fell in, collapsing in a heap on the back seat. "Drive, drive!" he wheezed.

The taxi driver looked around. "Are you okay, bro'?" he asked. "You look like shit. You have money for the fare?"

Yoav was fifty meters away, forty, thirty.

"Yes, I have money, here, here," gasped Akiva, pulling out his wallet, wincing in pain from his arm, and throwing it on the driver's lap. "Just go, go, go."

The driver shrugged with that mix of arrogance and nonchalance that only Israeli taxi drivers have. "Why didn't you say so, bro'?" he asked.

The taxi sped off just moments before Yoav and his two men could get there. The one with the gun raised it to fire at the cab, but Yoav pushed his hand down. "Not here," he said. "I already have one mess to clean up at Yad Vashem, I can't afford another one now."

He watched the cab speed off into the distance. He put his hands on his knees, also out of breath.

"He has nowhere to hide," said Yoav. "He got away now, but it's only a matter of time. He must not live, and he won't."

Akiva watched Yoav disappear into the distance through the rear window. His whole body was trembling, almost like an epileptic fit as his brain started to process just how close he'd been to being killed. He shakily pulled his phone out of his pocket, sucking in deep breaths to try to calm himself down. His trembling fingers hovered over the keypad, but then he thought better of it. He turned to the driver. "Can I use your phone for one minute?" he asked.

He dialed a number, but it went to voicemail.

"It's me," he said. "I need to see you."

Chapter 16

T he drive from Tel Aviv to the settlement of Har Daniel took Yoav about an hour and a half, and led him through the entire spectrum of Israeli sociology. He left the coastline of secular Tel Aviv, with its beaches and bars, drove through the city's traffic-clogged streets of cafes and office buildings, and past its eastern suburb of B'nei Brak, Israel's largest Ultra-Orthodox community outside of Jerusalem. Here, the streets were narrower and so were the world-views: *Charedi* men in black coats and fedoras, women dressed modestly, despite the summer heat, in stockings and hair-coverings and dresses that reached from their ankles to their wrists, and each family with several small children in tow. The *Charedim* were seen by social scientists and demographers as a threat to Israel's future: how could a modern economy tolerate 20% of its population who chose not to learn Math and English at school (Talmud was more impor-tant), how could a modern country integrate citizens who did not want to be integrated?

But for Yoav, these families were part of his solution. The future Israeli leader who was now sleeping in a safe location under the watchful eyes of Yoav's people would not tolerate *Charedi* isolationism. He would inspire them, incite them, or if necessary, compel them, to buy into his new national project of strength, power and empire-building. And then their large families would only redound to Israel's benefit: these kids who he drove past now, scampering around the feet of parents dressed for the Polish shtetl, would in a generation's time be the Israeli Hitler's new footsoldiers, doubling the size of its army and providing the sheer numbers that would enable Israel to build a military force of unstoppable clout.

Buoyed by these thoughts, he continued his journey eastward into Judea and Samaria, the heartland of Biblical Israel, what the traitorous leftists called the occupied territories. Here the landscape and demographics changed. Israel's flat coastal plain was behind him, and the hills and valleys of the West Bank loomed ahead of him. He had left the densely-populated conurbation of Greater Tel Aviv and was heading into Greater Israel. There were fewer cars and more views, some of them breathtaking, as the landscape of Abraham, Isaac and Jacob glided past his windows. Hills of green, dotted with the red roofs of gleaming Israeli settlements, side by side with Palestinian villages in the valleys, with their starker, box-shaped white houses. Here was the geographic and demographic conundrum that had confounded American presidents, that the Israeli Left tore its hair over, and that the Israeli Right lied about: how could you create a two-state solution out of this patchwork quilt of Israeli and Palestinian towns? Yoav had long since moved beyond those concerns. He had faith in the future. Hitler didn't worry about what the British would say about Czechoslovakia, and his new Israeli leader wouldn't worry about what they'd say about these inconveniences either.

It was late afternoon, a few hours after his attempts on Akiva's life at Yad Vashem and outside the facility in Tel Aviv. He knew that he had to complete that part of his work shortly, but for now, it had to be put on hold: he had more important business to take care of. His destination was the *rosh yeshivah* of Har Daniel. Rabbi Aaron Denkstein was one of the Israeli settlement enterprise's most outspoken and revered leaders, courted by politicians from the Right, hated by those from the Left. Now seventy-three years old, he had run Har Daniel's yeshivah for almost thirty years, and was the acknowledged spiritual leader of an entire generation of youth from the settlements. He was the father of six, with thirty-eight grandchildren (and still counting), and already the first of what would presumably be literally hundreds of great-grandchildren.

Yoav had spent two years studying at the Har Daniel Yeshivah as a young man, as part of the usual arrangement for young religious boys, combining intensive Jewish study with army service. He'd grown close to Rabbi Denkstein and came back to visit him frequently – as did many of Har Daniel's graduates.

As Yoav drove into the settlement, he felt the embrace of homecoming from the familiar surroundings. Clean tree-lined streets, small houses with kids' plastic play houses and swing sets in the front yards, and behind every gap between the houses, the expanse of the Biblical Israel landscape in the distance, with its rolling green hills and stone terraces, dotted with other small groups of red roofs that signified milemarkers in the Jewish people's redemption of this land.

Yoav stepped out of his car and breathed in the Biblical air, filling his lungs, closing his eyes for a moment, getting a momentary high, as he always did, from the belief that the same oxygen that his forefathers had inhaled was now infusing his body.

The yeshivah itself was a large building in the middle of the town. Nondescript from the outside, save for a massive, five-meter-high metal Star of David that was emblazoned on its front edifice. The lower point of the star appeared to finish beneath the ground level, so that its two sides formed the doorway through which one entered the building. The artist who had designed the entrance to the yeshivah in this fashion had built the star so that it looked planted firmly in the ground: "Like the young men who will study here, whose Jewish roots will also be planted firmly in this land of ours," Rabbi Denkstein had said at the yeshivah's official opening ceremony in 1988.

Yoav walked through the embedded star, through the lobby area, and straight into the beit midrash, the study hall. This was the center of the yeshivah, a huge open plan room with rows and rows of desks, each piled with students' holy books in various states of disorganization. The smell of books, body odor and testosterone transported him back immediately. This room was home for Yoav as much as his parents' house growing up. Here he had made friends for life, arguing with them about minutiae in the Talmud until midnight and then stumbling back at 6:00 am the next day for morning prayers and then more studying. He wandered over to the desk that had been his, and opened the Gemara that was on the table to see who now inhabited that space. "Ariel Kackon," he read. "Ariel," he said out loud to this 19-year-old whom he'd never met but with whom he now shared some intangible bond, "you're in a great place right now. And in your lifetime, you're going to experience wonders and miracles that will make the Six Day War look like a pillow fight."

Rabbi Denkstein's study was on the second floor. Yoav walked up the stairs two by two, and knocked on the door.

"Come."

Yoav opened the door. "Shalom Rabbi," he grinned, a precocious teenager once more.

Denkstein got up from his desk, walked toward Yoav, and the two men hugged.

"It's so wonderful to see you, Yoav," he said. "It's been too long, too long."

"Well, I was waiting for you to tidy up in here a bit," winked Yoav, "but then I gave up."

"Ah! Same old Yoav!" chuckled Denkstein. "Of all my students, you were the only one who ever dared make fun of my... organizational habits, shall we say?"

The room was a mess – it was as if it was built out of books, and only books. There were no walls to be seen, just rows and rows of books, and piles of more books on every available surface. It was a sight that would not be out of place in an Oxford don's study, and indeed Denkstein had such eclectic intellectual interests that many of the books could also have felt at home in a university. There were books on Homer and Ancient Greece, on French philosophy (Descartes was one of Denkstein's particular interests), and even a section containing books by the heretics of modern science: Dawkins, Hitchens, Hawking. And, of course, there were hundreds of books that would not be found in that Oxford don's room: Torah commentaries, Talmuds, halachic response literature, the Zohar, modern Israeli legal treatises... this was why Yoav admired Denkstein so much. He was a man of the world, an intellect, someone who could stand shoulder to shoulder with the professors of Oxford, Harvard, the Sorbonne, and Hebrew University; and he was an uncompromising believer in the right of the Jewish people to the entire Land of Israel.

"How is the family, Yoav?" asked Denkstein. "All are well? I was surprised to get your message this morning – I was a little worried that there might be some emergency."

"Everyone is fine, thank God," said Yoav. "But I am here on urgent business, you were right to guess that."

"So, sit, tell me, tell me..." Denkstein had a habit of repeating two-word phrases. The students had nicknamed him *Double-'em Denkstein* (and they were pretty sure that Denkstein knew it, and played to the crowd with this verbal tic).

Denkstein sat at his desk, behind his piles of books, and Yoav took a position opposite him.

"Rabbi, I'll come straight to the point. A female acquaintance of mine has... got into trouble. She comes from a wonderful family, *dati'im*, Modern Orthodox Jews, settlers, salt of the earth, but she got a little mixed up in the wrong crowds at university. She had a secular boyfriend, and... I'm afraid to tell you, Rabbi, that she became pregnant."

Denkstein rubbed his beard, which was white with gray flecks, and just a little too wispy to look truly dignified. "Oy," he sighed. "We shouldn't know such things, shouldn't know."

Yoav crossed his legs and continued. He had planned this segment of the chess game months, years in advance. He knew the moves by heart. "She basically went into hiding, so that no-one would know about her pregnancy. Just gave birth a few days ago, Rabbi, to a baby boy. She reached out to me, since I am an old friend of her family. She cannot raise the child on her own and she wants him to be adopted, but it is important to her that the baby be adopted by the... right kind of family, if you know what I mean. I am coming to you because I thought that you might know of... maybe a couple in this area who have not been able to have children of their own, who would make a loving home for such a child, who would not want to adopt a *goyische* child from Russia or China, God forbid, who would want to adopt a child who they know comes from their world, their values... I thought perhaps that we could take this sad situation and make some good come of it."

Denkstein had tears in his eyes. He rose up from his chair, walked around the desk, and put his hands on Yoav's shoulders. "You are a fine young man, Yoav," he crooned. "You always were. This is a wonderful idea, a wonderful idea. I know just the couple for this mitzvah. They live not too far from here in a small new settlement named Nofei Itamar. Beautiful people, people with values, *talmidei chachamim*, Torah scholars, modest, committed to each other, to their community, to the land of Israel. They are both in their 40s, they got married a little late in life, and have not been able to conceive. I know them well. They have spoken about adoption, but, as you say, they have not felt fully comfortable with the whole... international adoption market thing. This, Yoav... wow, wow, wow, this would be a miracle for them. A miraculous solution."

Yoav smiled. He loved Denkstein, but he had always been a sentimental old fool. He felt a little bad about playing him in this way, but it was a necessary step. In the world to come, Denkstein would look down and be happy about the unwitting role he had played in the redemption of the Jewish people.

"Rabbi, there are three... complicating factors..." Yoav went on, putting his hand on the rabbi's arm behind his neck, but continuing to look straight ahead, manipulating Denkstein's return to his desk. "Firstly, the couple can never know who the real parents are. This young girl wants to forget the whole thing, she wants to go back to her family and her community and rebuild her life, she wants to get married, have a family of her own, live a religious life... she can't have it weighing over her head that one day this child might seek her out, might bring out into the open all the... mistakes she made in her youth. So that means that they can never know her identity, and neither can you. This must be done on the sly, no courts, no documents, nothing that the secular courts could get their dirty hands on in the future."

Denkstein walked back to his side of the desk and sat down again. "I understand," he said. "It will be for the best for the new parents too. They will actually feel better about it, knowing that the child will be fully theirs."

The rabbi nodded, smiling again at the thought of the miraculous news that he would shortly be telling this childless couple.

Bishop to a5. Yoav went on, his mind moving through his pre-planned strategic steps almost on autopilot. "Secondly: the mother must not know who the adoptive family are, but *I* must. You have my word that I will not make contact with them. But I will want to follow them and the child from afar. As I said, this young girl comes from a good family, who I have known for years, and I want to be able to look her in the eyes and say "Trust me, everything is okay.""

Denkstein rubbed his beard again. "This is more complex, Yoav," he murmured. "It is a great burden that you would be taking upon yourself, a great burden."

"Rabbi, I know. But I am prepared to take on this burden's weight. This is a double mitzvah that we are undertaking together here, you and I, and I just need this piece in place in order to do the right thing by the girl. She trusts me. She will not need more than my word."

"Then, Yoav, if that is the condition for this double mitzvah, I accept. I will give you the couple's details, and thereafter you will be able to track them from afar. Now... what is the third... how did you put it? Complicating factor?"

Queen takes pawn. So easy. "This baby was born off the grid," said Yoav. "The girl took care of herself during pregnancy, and the baby is perfectly healthy, but she had a home birth with the support of a midwife friend of hers. The baby hasn't been registered with a hospital. So you'll have to concoct a story for the authorities. Perhaps you can say that the child was left at the doorway of the yeshivah and that you don't know who the parents are. You'll think of something. You'll have to find a... sympathetic person at the local population registration office who can help you deal with the necessary bureaucracy so that the child can be registered and the couple can legally adopt him."

Denkstein waved away this third condition with his hand. Both he and Yoav knew that "a sympathetic person" was code for a former student, a good Modern Orthodox boy or girl of the settlements, someone who trusted Rabbi Denkstein and who would be willing to bend the rules or overlook missing paperwork for the sake of a greater mitzvah. "This is the easiest part, Yoav. We Religious Zionists are great believers in the State of Israel, but we also know that sometimes its secular rules must be... tweaked... for the sake of Heaven. It will be done. Just as you say, just as you say."

Yoav bent his head forward in thanks, his mind already thinking ahead to his plans and schedule for the rest of the day. This piece had fallen into place perfectly, exactly as he knew it would.

"So, Yoav, the only question that remains is: when? When do we give this miracle baby to his new and doting parents?"

"The baby is six days old today," smiled Yoav. *Rook to h8.* "I think that two days will be enough time for his parents to prepare the bris, don't you?"

Denkstein threw up his hands and laughed. "Yoav, this is wonderful, wonderful! Go, go make your arrangements, and I will cancel my afternoon class and go speak to this couple and give them the good news myself."

Yoav stood up. Denkstein walked over to him and hugged him, tears streaming down his face. "Yoav – you have given me a gift too. So much of my work is about pain and suffering: the funerals, the hard work of building the Land of Israel, the pain of army and terrorism and staving off those who wish to tear our roots away from this land. Now look at me, I am giggling like a child, I can't wait to go and tell these people that their prayers have been answered, that they will have a child, and not just any child, but a child from a religious home, a Zionist home, a child who will bring joy to them and also enable them to perform a mitzvah for this girl who they will never know!"

"There's just one final thing," stated Yoav. "The child's mother has requested that he be named David. I can't tell you why, for obvious reasons. But it would mean a lot to her if that could be his name."

Denkstein waved away his hand at Yoav again. "It will not be a problem. I will find a way to suggest it to the family. It will be done."

David. Israel's great Biblical military leader. The king who united Israel's tribes into a kingdom, who defeated Goliath, who routed the Philistines, who built up Biblical Israel into a regional empire. Yes, that was the right name for this new leader. He would carry David's name, and restore his legacy. Restore his empire. *Checkmate.*

After the narrow escape from Yoav at the destroyed GeneLight facility, Akiva had told the taxi to get the hell out of Tel Aviv without really thinking about where he was going to go and what he was going to do. The taxi driver had headed north from GeneLight's office, up toward the Tel Aviv port, and then east toward the Ayalon highway that was the main north-south artery of the city. By that stage, Akiva had taken a few deep breaths and realized that Yoav wasn't following him. He took a look at his arm and saw to his relief that, painful as the glass shard had been, it hadn't made too deep a cut, and he managed to staunch the bleeding with a couple of tissues from his pocket. Deciding that he needed to hide out for a day or two to figure out what to do next, he asked the taxi driver to drive south a couple of exits on the Ayalon, and then double back and head west, back into Tel Aviv. There were a couple of big, anonymous hotels in the south part of the beach area; Akiva had attended conferences at each of them over the years. The taxi dropped him by one of them, and he hurried inside, paid cash for a room for the night, and holed up.

Akiva staggered into the hotel room and shut the door behind him, leaning back against it and letting his legs give way beneath him as he slid to the floor in exhausted relief. He looked down at himself. He looked like he'd just crawled out of a swamp. He was caked with dried-on sweat, blood and dirt – God knows what they had thought of him at reception. He turned his palms up toward his face and almost retched as he saw them still stained with Sivan and Shira's blood. He needed to shower, but first, he needed dark and quiet. He clambered to his feet, shut the heavy hotel curtains, turned off the lights, pulled off his clothes and threw them into the corner, and buried himself under the bed covers. Akiva got into the fetal position and shut out the world.

He slept for fourteen straight hours. When he woke up, he got into the shower and started scrubbing off the evidence of yesterday's horrors, gingerly massaging the sorest parts: his ankle and his tricep. Shira's blood washed off his hands, surrounding his feet with a puddle of pink water, and he collapsed against the shower wall, crying and shaking. "Shira..." he rasped. "I'm sorry... what have I done..." Then, a burst of anger suddenly coursing through his veins, he began hitting the shower wall with his open palm. "Yoav, you bastard, you bastard!" He turned his face up into the stream and let the hot water mix with his tears.

He got out of the shower and allowed his scientific self to resurface. *Need food. Food and clean clothes.* He threw on the hotel bathrobe, got the elevator down to the gift shop, bought an overpriced pair of swimming trunks and an "I Love TLV" T-shirt, did a quick change in the nearest restroom, and then went straight into breakfast. Twenty minutes later, perfunctorily full, he returned to his room, and sat on the balcony overlooking the same Mediterranean Sea that his office at GeneLight had overlooked. He gazed out at the clear blue sea ahead of him, breathing in the view, infusing his lungs with the tangy smell of the sea air, shutting his eyes for a moment and focusing on the sounds of the beach drifting up to him: the *pak-pak-pak* of people playing beach tennis with wooden paddles, the gentle splash of the Mediterranean surf washing against the sand, the lively shrieks of horseplaying kids, the hum of diners at beachside cafes. The normality of the scene brought him peace. *And I can still bring peace to them. Focus. Think. It's a setback. But it's not over. There has to be a way.*

Two hours later, Akiva went back to the gift shop, bought a baseball cap and a pair of dark sunglasses, again using cash, and then walked out of the hotel into the bright Tel Aviv sunlight. He got on a bus to Jerusalem, and an hour later, at the Central Bus Station there, he pulled out all the cash he could from his bank account, going up to his maximum overdraft limit. He had no idea if Yoav had the ability to track his financial transactions, but he wasn't going to take any chances. Akiva now had to assume that Yoav could do all kinds of things, things that seemed like they were from the movies: gain access to his phone calls, his bank records, who knew what else. Anyway: if Yoav *was* somehow able to gain access to his bank account, he'd see a withdrawal in Jerusalem, not Tel Aviv. Akiva shrugged. Would this throw Yoav off the scent? Would he realize it was a bluff? Maybe.

Next, he went into the nearest computer shop and bought the most expensive laptop he could buy. His own laptop had obviously been destroyed or confiscated in the raid on GeneLight, and he needed access to the internet. He then walked a few blocks to the nearest cellphone shop and bought the most expensive smartphone that would work with a no-contract, anonymous SIM card.

He walked back to the Central Bus Station, allowing himself a quiet smirk that he had used GeneLight's corporate credit card to pay for these two extravagant purchases. It was a small victory, but after what Yoav had done to him over the past twenty-four hours, it was at least something.

The bus back to Tel Aviv was a quiet ride. The bus wended its way out of the city, down the hills on Jerusalem's outskirts, through curves and valleys, bridges and underpasses, making its slow way to Israel's coastal plain. The hills around Jerusalem were dotted with Jewish towns and Israeli-Arab villages, intermingled and mostly harmonious.

The gradient of the road flattened out, and the high rises of Tel Aviv began to appear on the horizon. The bus drove past Ben Gurion airport, and then continued onto the Ayalon highway, where only yesterday he had fled from Yoav in terror. Akiva's bus pulled into Tel Aviv's Central Bus Station and he hopped on a local bus back to the hotel. Once there, he unpacked and set up the computer, and began searching online for anything he could find out about Yoav Schindler.

Yoav wasn't tracking Akiva that morning; he was leaving that to his people. He had other business: bringing the baby in a brand new car seat to Rabbi Denkstein's home. Along with the car seat was a brand new diaper bag, a stroller, and a suitcase full of the finest and cutest baby clothes. Together the two men transferred the baby and all the accoutrements to Denkstein's beaten-up old car, and Denkstein drove off. Yoav followed behind him across the Biblical landscape. Twenty minutes later, they came to Nofei Itamar, an isolated settlement, and Denkstein parked his car by a small pre-fabricated house on the far end of one of the streets: the only house without plastic toys and swings and tricycles littering the front garden. Yoav, as agreed, parked a good distance away. The neighboring lot was as yet unoccupied so Yoav had a clear view as he watched Denkstein pull the car seat out, lay it down by the front door, and ring the bell. The door opened, and a man and woman opened it together. The new mother burst into tears. She picked the baby up out of the car seat and hugged him, crying, laughing, shaking. The father was weeping too, his arms around Denkstein's neck, barely able to stand, somehow being supported by this frail septuagenarian, who was also in tears, hugging him back. Then the new father broke off, turned to his wife, hugged her with their new baby boy, and as Denkstein took a step back to let the man and woman have their moment, Yoav looked on, his heart soaring with emotion at what his hands had wrought, as this new family, this new family that he had created, enjoyed its first family hug together.

He started the engine and slowly drove away. This family wouldn't know it, but they would always have a guardian angel. From now on, things would somehow always go right for them and for their baby boy. They were part of Yoav's Phase 2 – not the Phase 2 that he'd sold to Akiva, Shira and Sivan, but Yoav's real Phase 2, in which this child would get the best Torah education, attend the finest schools, be steeped in the Religious Zionist community of the Land of Israel, go to the most prestigious army unit, the best university, and finally lead Israel to redemption. Those parents down the street, still weak with tears and love and laughter and hugs, did not know that their life in the future would have a guiding hand behind the curtains, making sure that their jobs were secure, making sure that their child had the best home room teacher in the school, the best tutor, the best basketball coach, whatever he wanted; making sure that luck would always be on his side. And their life would contain yet another miracle: in the future they would go down in history as the loving, doting, proud parents of Israel's greatest ever leader.

Chapter 17

Omar Suleiman was one of East Jerusalem's most sought-after bachelors, and every Palestinian mother of a certain socio-economic class dreamed of marrying off her daughter to him. As a young man in his twenties he had dated one stunning 18-year-old after another, but since meeting Hadas he had run into a problem. He could never let it be known that he was in a relationship with a Jewish Israeli, but a close second in terms of damage to his communal position would be the rumor that he might be gay. Palestinian society was still extremely conservative, both with regard to the place of women in society and even more so with regard to sexual orientation. There were some Palestinian gay bars and social scenes under the radar (and indeed, Omar donated to a Palestinian NGO that supported them), but for the most part homosexuality was not spoken about and was seen as something undesirable. Many East Jerusalemite Palestinians, who were not Israeli citizens but whose Jerusalem residency documents enabled them to travel all over Israel, found outlets for their lifestyles in Tel Aviv, which, despite the accusations of "pink-washing" by the Israel boycotters, was one of the world's most welcoming cities for LGBT communities; Palestinian residents of the West Bank and Gaza, who were not allowed into Israel, had it much worse.

The first time Omar heard the rumor that he might be gay, he made a decision that he needed to be seen in public with beautiful Palestinian women. And so every now and then, he made sure to step out at a popular nightclub or restaurant with a suitable female partner.

On Saturday night he'd gone on a date with the latest model. Hadas knew about this social necessity, and while she wasn't exactly happy about it, she accepted it, as long as Omar's relationships with these other women never deepened beyond holding hands. His date, Sahar, had flirted with him endlessly all evening, and made her availability for further physical engagement very obvious. They'd had an awkward moment when he had dropped her back at her parents' house, and Omar was increasingly concerned that these public evenings out would calm the rumors for a while, but not indefinitely: the girls would talk, and at some point someone would realize that it couldn't be a coincidence that he'd gone out with so many beautiful women without pursuing things physically with any of them.

These thoughts were on his mind as he lit his cigarette and rested it on the ashtray in front of him. He was at a cafe in East Jerusalem, just off the main drag, Salah-A-Din street. He was meeting with Ali Fayyad, his fixer. He had known Ali for years; he'd been a floor foreman in the factory when Omar was just learning the business ropes with his father, and Omar had immediately been impressed by Ali's combination of a no-nonsense attitude toward, but also a sometimes touching level of empathy with those working around him. Soon after taking over the company, Omar had earned Ali's eternal loyalty by helping his daughter Aisha get some medical treatment in an Israeli hospital. She had had a growth in the back of her neck that had turned out to be benign, but for a while they had been worried that it might be cancerous. Because of the tumor's delicate position near the spine, the local East Jerusalem hospital doctors had not exuded confidence in their ability to remove it successfully. Omar had found out that at Tel Hashomer hospital in Tel Aviv was one of the world's experts in this kind of surgery, and had pulled strings to get the girl there, personally funding the operation privately.

He'd got to know Ali well during that period, spending time at his home, and often driving him and Aisha to and from Tel Hashomer. And he'd realized that Ali was wasted on the factory floor. From then on, Ali's official role remained in the factory, but every now and then Omar would invite him for a coffee away from work. In these conversations they would usually discuss issues with the workers' union or with clients who were negotiating difficult contracts. Ali could get people to change their minds. He didn't use violence (so Omar assumed, or liked to think), but Omar had no doubt that he used subtle threats, unspoken intimidations, and all kinds of other questionable techniques to get the job done. Ali did the dirty work that Omar needed done, and needed plausible deniability about.

Ali was also Omar's contact with Hamas.

Omar had discovered Ali's Hamas connections almost accidentally, during the period where he'd been helping Ali's daughter. He had turned up to Ali's house one afternoon a little early, ready to drive him and Aisha to Tel Hashomer for a pre-op scan, and had been surprised to find Ali in the company of three other men who were unmistakably Hamas: the bushy Islamic beards, the subtle clues in their slightly more traditional clothing, the radical political language that they used, the higher proportion of *inshallahs* in the brief conversation that he had with them.

On the way back home from the hospital, with Aisha fast asleep in the back of the car, Omar had probed Ali about these affiliations. Ali, it turned out, came from a family of Hamas activists, with several family members doing time in Israeli prisons, and even a first cousin who had been a *shahid*, a martyr, killed by the Israeli army in a house raid during the Second Intifada.

"I made the decision to follow a more conventional lifestyle," Ali had said to Omar in the car. "To get a job, to work, to keep my nose out of politics, out of the conflict. But I support my cousins in their Holy Cause. I do not commit violent acts myself, but I know that they do, and I understand why they do it. It is the only way to end the occupation, to repair the disaster that our people suffered in the *Nakba*. It is the only language that the Jews understand."

Omar stared through the windscreen, poker-faced but silent. He'd heard this kind of talk many times before, so often that he could almost write the script himself. He hated it, not just for its immorality, but also because of its strategic wrongheadedness. But it was all around him, as much part of his life and existence as the air he breathed.

"I hope I do not offend you, Omar," Ali had added quickly, turning anxiously towards his boss in the driver's seat. "I know that you are involved in peace conversations with the Israelis. I... I hope you do not think less of me for my... skepticism at your optimism."

"I do not agree with Hamas, Ali," Omar had replied evenly, keeping his eyes focused on the road ahead. "I believe that violence is wrong, and only begets more violence. I believe that terrorism is never justified. And I believe that the Jews have a right to be here, even to have a State here, alongside ours. On those issues, you and I disagree, and perhaps we will have further conversations about them in which I will try to persuade you that I am right. But I know that Hamas are patriots, I know that they want the best for the Palestinian people, just as I do. I also want to end the occupation, to enable us to establish our own Palestinian State here, with East Jerusalem as its capital."

"*Inshallah*," Ali had said.

Omar smiled and permitted himself an "*Inshallah*" in return.

Since then, over the years, there had been two or three times when Ali's contacts in Hamas had been extremely useful to Omar. Once, he had wanted to open a distribution line with a small chain of grocery stores in Jenin, and had been blocked by the head of the local *hamula*, who had wanted nothing to do with Omar, whom they saw as a "normalizer," someone who was willing to do business with Israelis. Omar had asked Ali to get involved in behind-the-scenes negotiations: this had led to the second-in-command of the Jenin Hamas cell paying a polite but firm visit to the *hamula* head one evening, after which Omar had been able to quickly strike a deal with the grocery stores. On another occasion, two workers at the factory had got into a fight, and one had broken the other's arm. Omar had had no choice but to fire them both – he would not tolerate such behavior in his factory – but he had found out, through Ali, that the one with the broken arm was a Hamas activist, and he had used Ali to make some quiet cash payments to his family to aid him in his recuperation and subsequent job search.

In these ways, and countless other small ones, Omar had been able to gain Hamas's backing for his business, even as his own peace activist work became more well known. And Ali had become an indispensable and trusted consigliere.

Ali came into the cafe and walked over to where Omar was sitting. Omar stood up, and the two men exchanged kisses, one on each cheek, as per Palestinian custom (an ironic one, Omar had often thought, given their anti-gay culture).

Ali poured himself some water, and pointed at the cigarette burning, untouched, in the ashtray. "Still pretending to smoke?" he asked.

Omar had few secrets by now from Ali (his relationship with Hadas was perhaps the only one that remained). "My friend," Omar replied, raising his trademark eyebrow, "I may make the things, but I don't have to like them. I can't appear not to smoke at all, as that would be hypocritical. So I light one, and let it burn, and nobody but you notices. Perhaps you might say that I am like the gynecologist who comes home at night to his wife. She tries to get all sexy with him, but he says, 'My God, I've been looking at vaginas all day long, I can't face touching another one right now!'"

Ali snorted his water through his nose in laughter, and started coughing uncontrollably. Omar bounced to his feet and leaned over to pound him on the back multiple times. "Don't die on me here, my friend," he grinned. "I like this cafe." He sat back in his chair and leaned back, hands behind his head, enjoying the reaction he'd provoked.

Ali regained his composure. "What other Palestinian boss would tell such a joke to his employee?" he asked. He reached over and held Omar's hands with his. "Allah has blessed you with this sense of humor, Omar, and I am grateful that you choose to share Allah's blessing with me."

Omar doffed his head in thanks, satisfied at his success in cracking Ali up, even if the "Allah" stuff wasn't quite how he would have put it. He looked around at the cafe. It was one of his usual haunts. Its indoors was smoky and tired, with cracked tables and wobbly chairs. Its saving grace was the large patio-balcony at the back, which had a glorious view of the Old City: the real Old City, the Muslim Quarter, with the Temple Mount in the background, with its narrow streets, sweaty shopkeepers sitting on the steps in front of their stores waiting for non-existent customers, Palestinian kids running freely through the alleys playing tag, and the smells of falafel and fried lamb and hummus wafting from the small windows that looked out from the crowded houses. This was the real Old Jerusalem, not the Disneyfied version that the Jews had built for themselves in the Jewish Quarter since their capture of it in 1967.

"So, boss," Ali said, snapping Omar's attention back to the table. He motioned to Omar's packet of cigarettes, and seeing Omar gesture easily at them, he took one and lit up, puffing deeply for real. "What can I do for you? What's on our agenda today?"

Omar proceeded to tell Ali the reason for their meeting this morning. A local imam, a young, up-and-coming guy with an opinion of himself that was slightly too high than his age warranted, had given a sermon the previous Friday in which he had railed about the cost of living, and had blamed, in part, East Jerusalem companies and businessmen who co-operated with the Israelis. The higher costs of doing business in the west of the city meant that these companies were forced to raise their prices for their East Jerusalem clientele. The imam had mentioned a few different companies who he accused of this activity, what the imam called "commercial normalization which leads to economic deprivation" – and one of the companies mentioned had been Omar's.

"Right, I heard about that," nodded Ali, taking another drag of the cigarette. "I don't go to that mosque, but my neighbors do, and they know that I work for you, so I got an earful from them."

"It must stop," insisted Omar softly but resolutely, looking Ali directly in the eyes. He knew when to make jokes, but also when to make his intentions crystal clear to his staff. The grins and gags from a few moments ago had vanished, and in their place was the business-like strategic clarity and drive of Omar as company manager. "I doubt it will affect sales in any serious way, but it might lead to discontent on the factory floor. And if the media pick it up, it'll be bad press, and the last thing I need right now is increased focus on the ins and outs of my business dealings."

"I will speak to the right people in the Movement," said Ali. "They'll make sure it doesn't happen again."

"Gently at first, though," cautioned Omar, making a calming gesture with his hand. "No need to escalate immediately. A quiet but firm word from the right people."

Ali paused and took another hit of nicotine, taking care to blow the smoke away from Omar. "I'll have someone make it clear how important your company is to the local economy. How everything is inter-related, and if your business is affected by his sermons, then that may well have a... direct impact on the ability of the Movement to make donations to his mosque. It will have the required effect."

"I can always trust you to come up with the right way of doing these things, my friend," smiled Omar.

"*Alhamdulillah*," said Ali. *Praise be to God.* "I am grateful for the opportunities you give me, boss." By now, they had been brought coffee, and they raised their cups to each other and drank.

"Omar," began Ali again after a pause. "There is something... a small matter... which I would like to ask your help with."

Omar spread out his hands. "My friend, whatever I can do, you know that I will."

"It is a slightly delicate situation, and not something that I would normally feel comfortable raising with you," said Ali hesitantly.

"My friend, how long have we known each other?" declared Omar, reaching over to put a hand on Ali's arm. "You know that I draw the line at giving money

133

to anything that will cause violence or harm. But apart from that, if I can help you or our people in some way, you know that I will."

"This may be... a gray area," stammered Ali. "It concerns the son of Hassan Khoury himself."

Omar raised his eyebrows. Both of them this time: surprise, not comedic effect. Hassan Khoury was one of the leaders of the military wing of Hamas in the West Bank. He was a hard-core extremist, who had been tied to a string of terrorist attacks over the past several years. He had served time in Israeli prison but had been released as part of the deal to free Gilad Shalit; in 2011 Israel had agreed to trade over 1,000 Palestinian security prisoners in return for Shalit, a young soldier who had been captured by Hamas and held in captivity in Gaza for five years.

Omar looked around the cafe and leaned forward to speak to Ali in a quieter voice. "I am not sure," he murmured, "that Hassan Khoury would be one of my biggest fans. And to be honest, the feeling is mutual. His ways are not my ways. You know that, Ali."

Ali nodded. "I am aware of this. But this is more complicated. It's about his son, his eldest son. The boy is 16. He has got himself caught up in some... criminal activities. Internal Palestinian stuff, nothing to do with the Jews. Got ideas above his station, tried to pull some extortion on a couple of stores in Nablus, and it has backfired on him. The owner of one of the stores has connections to Fatah, and they sent some thugs to break one or two of his limbs to teach him a lesson. The boy managed to evade them, but he is now scared to go outside, his family is concerned, and to be honest the situation threatens to blow up into a major Fatah-Hamas quarrel."

"Or as we Palestinians call it, Monday..." said Omar, shaking his head in exasperation.

Ali nodded again.

"But what does this have to do with me?" asked Omar, still cautious, but curious.

134

"The boy needs somewhere to hole up for a week or two while things calm down. Khoury will meet with the right people in Fatah, he will apologize on behalf of his family, make the necessary gestures and gifts, restore the honor of the store owners. It will blow over. But that will only be possible if the boy is unharmed. If he comes home with a broken arm, then Khoury will seek revenge, and then..."

"Things will escalate," completed Omar, blowing out his cheeks.

"As you say. Escalate. So. The boy needs to be hidden away until the powers-that-be sort things out. It can't be any of the usual safe houses; there are too many leaks, and he would be found easily. So I thought that maybe... the Royal Garden?"

The Royal Garden was a small hotel in Ramallah that Omar owned a stake in. He and Ali had conducted the occasional meeting there. It was one of Ramallah's nicer venues, but small and boutique. Omar loved it; he dreamed that one day he would be able to spend time there with Hadas.

Omar put his hands together and played with his fingers in a web. This was getting interesting. "Say more..."

"Perhaps you could arrange for the boy to stay in one of the rooms for a few days under a false name. Normally a hotel would want to see documents, ID, something, especially for a child checking in on his own. But if a way could be found for these requirements to be overlooked... I doubt that anyone, in either Fatah or Hamas, would think of looking for him there."

Omar considered the situation. Normally he would not touch such a scenario with a bargepole. He had no desire to get involved in a spat between Fatah and Hamas. And this Khoury fellow was a true terrorist, scary as shit. Not someone you wanted to mess with. On the other hand, this was a humanitarian issue, an intra-Palestinian issue, no terrorism involved. It was, in that respect, clean. And it would not be a bad idea for Khoury to owe Omar a favor. One never knew when such a thing would come in handy.

Omar reached over the table and extended his hand towards Ali. "It will be done," he said.

Ali shook his boss's hand and smiled broadly. "A thousand thank-yous, Omar. May Allah shine his face upon you."

"Remember," warned Omar quietly again, "I need plausible deniability on this. Khoury must know my involvement, but no-one else."

"I will take care of everything," said Ali.

Omar leaned back in his chair and downed the dregs of his coffee. Khoury owing him a favor. Yes, that would definitely be a net strategic gain. He waved at the waiter and called for the check.

Chapter 18

The yeshivah in Har Daniel was bursting at the seams. The new parents had many friends, and each came from large families (a fact that had made their failure to conceive even more painful); and Denkstein had made sure to fill any remaining space with yeshivah students. Yoav had made a generous donation to the yeshivah that would cover a beautiful festive meal after the bris. This would be a celebration that would be remembered.

Yoav stood at the back, in dark sunglasses. He could never be totally incognito in these parts, but it helped. Still, there was an endless stream of former classmates, not-quite-neighbors, and family friends who noticed him, and came over for a warm handshake or hug. There were also several people in the room who Yoav knew – knew very well, in fact – but who did not acknowledge him with anything other than a discreet nod from afar. Yoav's funders had made it clear all along that they wanted absolute protection from the nuts and bolts of the project, not just plausible deniability but barriers upon barriers between their funds and their ultimate donation. They had not been to the GeneLight lab, they did not speak with Yoav by telephone – with one exception – and face-to-face meetings were absolutely prohibited. In the future, their identities would be revealed, the People of Israel would thank them, and their names would be spoken about in the 21st century as Rothschild's was in the 20th. But for now, anonymity was crucial. Still, Yoav had not been able to resist letting them know about the bris, and they had not been able to resist coming. It was not every day that you got to be present at the circumcision of Israel's future savior.

The baby was brought in by one of his grandparents, cradled on top of a luxurious cushion, as per the custom. The crowd began singing, softly, beautifully, the traditional Jewish words that welcome a new baby boy into the Covenant of Abraham. The mohel said a few words of explanation, how honored he was to be chosen to be the one who would perform the ceremony for this wonderful family of *tzadikim*, righteous people. How fitting it was for this couple that the bris was the Covenant of Abraham, he said. Had not Abraham and Sarah waited endless years for their son? Had God not finally fulfilled his promise with them, when, despite Sarah's old age, he had performed a miracle and delivered a son to them? So too with this couple, who, as we all knew, went on the mohel, had waited endless years for their son. So too we are all here today as witnesses to their miracle, as they now transform from being a couple to being a family, as they now bring their beautiful baby boy into the Jewish people.

The new father uttered the blessings that bestowed upon the mohel the status of his designated appointee for the performance of the mitzvah of circumcision, strictly speaking the father's obligation but for centuries legally delegated in this way to the mohel. The mohel dipped his finger in the ceremonial red wine and put it in the baby's mouth; this was the traditional way of numbing the baby ever so slightly for the incision that was to follow. The crowd in the yeshivah sang a quiet melody with simple words, filling the hall with a kind of holy calm, almost meditative. And then the calm was broken by the child's cries, as the mohel made the cut.

But he was an expert, a veteran of thousands of such procedures, and within seconds he had finished the job, bandaged the baby's newly-foreskin-less penis, put on a diaper, then another slightly larger diaper for extra cushioning, swathed the baby in a blanket, and given him to his mother, who, tears streaming down her face, gave him a bottle, leaning over to kiss him, nuzzle him, rock him, occasionally looking up at her husband in disbelief, then looking back down at their son. The husband sat down next to his wife, holding her and their son in an embrace, kissing her, kissing the baby.

The baby took the bottle and quietened down, ensconced in love. The couple's tears dripped onto the baby's clothes and onto his cheeks, and the father lovingly wiped his new son's face as he guzzled.

The mohel finished off the last few ritual pronouncements of the ceremony and then the hall was filled with singing again, *mazal tov v'siman tov, siman tov v'mazal tov*, may there be good fortune and good omen to us and to all of Israel, they sang, over and over again. And then, *david melech yisrael, chai v'kayam*, David King of Israel lives and exists, they sang, as people clambered for a view of the new family, sharing their joy, crying in happiness with them.

A line of people formed to congratulate the new couple, men bear-hugging the father and women kissing and embracing the mother. A group of younger *yeshivah-bochers* began an impromptu *hora* in the middle of the hall. Denkstein tried to quieten them down so that he could give the *dvar torah* that he'd planned, a short sermon connecting these miraculous events to the weekly Torah reading, but the happiness in the room was too loud, too vocal, too overwhelming, and he was swept into the *hora*, dancing, singing, praising God for the miracle of today.

Yoav stood in the back, clapping and singing along with the crowd. *Indeed, David King of Israel lives*, he thought to himself. Shortly even he lost his inhibitions and joined the ring of dancers.

The food was brought in on beautifully-decorated buffet tables: bagels, smoked salmon, salads bursting with the colors of pomegranate and dried cranberries, quiches of every type, herring, whiskey, the works. The singing and dancing went on in parallel with the eating. The new father was press-ganged into joining the dancing, and then lifted on a chair above the crowds, arms outstretched to the heavens in thanks, cheek muscles hurting from smiling so much. The mother would not budge from her baby, continuing to feed him and rock him and embrace him.

Yoav enjoyed some of the food, shook a few more hands of old acquaintances, and edged away towards the yeshivah's exit. This had been the morning he had dreamed of for years. The project's idea – the real idea, not the fake one that he'd sold to Akiva – was audacious, it was brilliant, it was so... right... in so many ways. Jewish history was full of instances where the Jewish people had taken evil and turned it into good. Had Moses himself not been an Egyptian prince? Had Esther not been an assimilated Jew in Persia? Had Abraham not grown up as an idol-worshipper? And had not each of them saved the Jewish people in some way?

Creating a Jewish Hitler had not been Yoav's idea; he had been brought into it by someone who you didn't say no to. But Yoav's connections and his skills of persuasion had helped create the clandestine committee of supporters and funders who would support the project for the long haul. Once or twice, in those early conversations, people had recoiled from the idea, had blanched at some imagined moral problem. He had quickly talked them round.

So Yoav had collected the money, the funders, the supporters. He had just needed to find the right scientist. He'd started at the Technion, in Haifa, which was Israel's premier scientific university, looking for the best and brightest young experts in cloning technology. But pretty soon most people started telling him the same answer: the person you need isn't here in Haifa, but is down in Jerusalem. A young doctoral student named Akiva Cohen. Works in Farbstein's team. Word has it that he's one for the future.

And that led Yoav to that fateful day when he'd clinked magazines with Akiva for the first time. Yoav had planned out a long con with Akiva, and Akiva had fallen into every episode like clockwork. Friendship. Funding. The lure of a private laboratory. And then *The Boys from Brazil*. Yoav had waited for months until he had felt it was the right time to show the movie to Akiva. He'd known that Akiva wouldn't go for the Jewish Hitler idea; there was always something about him that was a little too weak, a little too careful, a little too concerned about what others might say. So Yoav had come up with another reason for bringing Hitler back to life. A different chess gambit for a different opponent, as simple as that. Akiva had fallen for it so easily, so eagerly, so unaware that he was just a pawn in a different and much larger game.

Yoav took one last look at the hall full of joyful dancing. The father had returned to his place with his wife and their new son, and the three of them sat embraced together as if by glue. Their happiness radiated out like electromagnetic waves that boosted the elation of the people in the yeshivah, each of whom danced and sang as if it were his or her own son. The place was rocking like the most electric of concerts.

Yoav inhaled a deep breath, as if trying to capture the very energy of the place in his lungs, and walked out purposefully towards his car. He checked his phone for the text message that he had been waiting for, and nodded his head in satisfaction to see that it had come in. His schedule for this day was going according to plan. Enjoy the celebration this morning, stay afterwards for a spot of lunch at the festive meal – he'd paid for it, after all. Those obligations were now complete. Now he had to pop into a local store to buy a new kettle; their old one at home had been acting up lately, probably a faulty thermostat but not worth trying to get fixed. Then he'd go home and spend some time with the kids after school.

Tomorrow, he would get round to killing Akiva.

Chapter 19

F or most people, two days without speaking anything of substance to another human soul would have been madness-inducing; for Akiva, holed up in his hotel, it was normal, and it gave him some calm and clarity. Usually his time alone consisted of working on complex scientific problems or undertaking delicate empirical experiments, mixed in with bouts of silent darkness on his sofa, in which he left the past and the present behind and immersed himself in imagined scenes of the future. His future, the world's future, was so clear to him, so real, that these daydreams about it were almost a form of self-therapy. But now it was different. The future, which usually lay before him with crystal clarity, now seemed blurred, fuzzy, a photo taken with the auto-focus not working. And then, in those moments when the picture did sharpen, it cracked like a kaleidoscope and suddenly it was Yoav's future, not his, that came into ugly focus. *No. Can't let that happen. There must be a way.*

Most of what he had found out about Yoav he already knew. Yoav was the son of a career Likud politician who had been a low-level member of Yitzchak Shamir's cabinet in the 1980s but never quite made it beyond that. He'd grown up in Jerusalem and rubbed shoulders with the princes of the old Likud party, the Meridors and the Rivlins and the Livnis – a rung or two below them in the party apparatus, but still, friends with all the movers and shakers. Old-fashioned security hawks, as eagerly elitist as the best liberal politician in looking down at the common or garden variety Israeli voter. The kind of people that Akiva's father had worked for. Maybe even the kind of people that Akiva's father would have become, if he'd lived. As that thought drifted into Akiva's mind, his chest tightened in a brief twinge of sorrow, but he quickly buried it away: he stuck it in the box deep inside of himself with all the other things he suppressed: the lies. The secrets. The hope.

Yoav had grown up in the Likud political family but never went into politics; and despite all his searching, Akiva was unable to pin down precisely what Yoav did or who he worked for. Several years ago, right before they established GeneLight, he'd married a religious woman from one of the settlements. Akiva had met Elisheva, Yoav's wife, on just a handful of occasions over the years. They didn't socialize together: Yoav had always kept his family life very separate from his GeneLight life. Akiva knew that they had four children, and that Yoav had moved from his apartment in Jerusalem to a leafy suburb of the Ofra settlement in the West Bank, neighbors with lawyers and doctors and academics, some of whom were there for the ideology, and some of whom were there because the prices were that much cheaper than Jerusalem.

Almost none of this information was new. Yoav was one of these people who knew everyone; but no-one really *knew* Yoav. This was becoming apparent to Akiva as he thought more about their relationship over these past years. Yoav was a connector. He knew everyone in the government, every *rosh yeshivah* in the territories, every mayor of every city. Akiva remembered one time when they were building the GeneLight lab underground at the offices, and they'd hit some kind of snag with a permit or something. Yoav had turned up to find Akiva and Sivan at their wits' end, banging their heads against the Israeli brick wall of apathetic bureaucratic incompetence. He took the paperwork, went into a private room to make some phone calls, and returned seven minutes later – Akiva had timed it – with a smug smile on his face. "All taken care of," he'd said. And indeed, a short while later, Akiva had received a phone call from the Tel Aviv municipality apologizing for the run-around and promising that the relevant permit would be sent by courier the next morning.

Akiva had benefited from Yoav's connectedness over the years, but now, with a flash of cold nausea that rose from his stomach into his throat, he began to realize the long-term implications of that connectedness. Yoav had already tried to kill him, and Yoav would surely try again. And he would keep trying until he succeeded. Yoav must have connections in the police force, the army, the government: there was no way that Akiva could turn to the authorities. Akiva was alone. He would never be safe again. He could trust no-one; well, with one exception. One exception...

Akiva assumed that Yoav would have destroyed not just GeneLight's physical offices but also its financial structures, and since, it pained him to admit, he'd basically lived off Yoav's largesse over the past many years, and Yoav now wanted him dead, he doubted very much that his salary would be paid on the first of the next month. The corporate credit card was working for now, or at least, it had worked the other day in Jerusalem, but presumably at some point in the near future it would get declined. So he would shortly have a major cashflow problem, which would turn into an accommodation problem.

Using his new, no-contract cellphone, Akiva made a call to one of the many quick-loan companies whose advertisements on the sides of buses and the inner pages of local newspapers regularly cajoled the Israeli public to take out loans of tens of thousands of shekels with minimal collateral. Akiva would never have considered such arrangements in the past: the interest rates were much higher than those of the banks. But one of these companies became a simple solution to his current financial plight. Within minutes, he had a 100,000 NIS loan agreed at rates that would make a mafioso blush, and the promise that he would see it in his bank account the next morning. He had no intention of paying back the money, but he'd deal with that fallout at a later date.

Three days after the events at Yad Vashem and the GeneLight offices – the day after the bris in the Har Daniel yeshivah – Akiva once more put on the baseball cap and sunglasses that he'd bought in the hotel gift shop, and set off for Jerusalem, again thinking that that might throw Yoav off his scent. Once there, he got off the bus, went straight to a nearby branch of his bank, and walked out several minutes later with a couple of stuffed envelopes: five hundred 200 NIS bills.

He got the bus back to Tel Aviv in jubilant mood, feeling that he was finally clawing his way back into the game with Yoav. Back in the hotel room, he opened his computer. He hadn't read the email since Yad Vashem; but now he finally felt able to look at it again:

From: jondoherty@newstartbayarea.com
To: akivacohen@privatemail.co.il
Subject: follow up on your request

Dear Dr Cohen,
I'm following up on our conversation a few weeks ago and your subsequent email with further details. Just to let you know that I've found a few rental properties that I think will be suitable for you and your son. I'll be happy to pick you up from your hotel when you arrive and show them to you. Do you have a precise date yet? You'd mentioned mid-to-late July as the likely timeframe.
Looking forward to hearing from you,
Jon Doherty
New Start Bay Area Realtors Inc.

Akiva read the email three times, trying to imagine that future as still viable, trying to breathe it in through the screen, the Pacific sea air tingling on his tongue, the joyful long afternoons, talking together, learning together, laughing together, seeing the fruit of his labors take shape, the quiet evenings with the California crickets chirping outside his window when he would continue his plan to change the world. Then the chill of the past two days' reality washed over him, and he deleted the email.

He stared at the screen for a minute.

His finger hovered over the touchpad, quivering back and forth in the air between hope and despair. For a moment the finger seemed somehow separate from his body, with a mind of its own, a divining rod bobbing between the arid dryness of defeat and underground waters of improbable redemption. He watched his finger make contact with the touchpad, open the trash folder, and move the email back into his inbox. He moved his finger off the computer and held it with his other hand, afraid that if he let go, some part of him would delete the email once more. He stared again at the email's subject line in his inbox and drew in a shaky, shallow breath.

Maybe, somehow, it could still happen.

That afternoon, Akiva made a mistake.

It was simple, really. Stupid. He'd gone through all this rigmarole with the trips to Jerusalem and the cash payments to the hotel and the baseball cap and sunglasses, but then he'd given in to sentimentality and gone to *Ravioli*.

Ravioli was a restaurant no bigger than a hole in the wall on Dizengoff Street, one of Tel Aviv's central thoroughfares. Its specialty, ironically, was lasagna, and its menu consisted of just six different types: lasagna with mushrooms, lasagna with eggplant, and lasagna with four cheeses, each either with or without pesto. That was it. If you didn't like lasagna, this was not the place for you, Akiva and Yoav would always joke when they ate there.

And so after his trip back from Jerusalem with those cash-stuffed envelopes, stomach rumbling, he'd gone to *Ravioli*, ordered his favorite, and had a decadent meal. For the first time since Yad Vashem, he relaxed. The well-thumbed surroundings, the aroma of pesto and tomatoes wafting from the kitchen, the delicious comfort food, the familiarity of the little restaurant...

And then it hit him. The familiarity. Of course this would be one of the places where Yoav's people would be watching.

Akiva's stomach lurched from being pleasantly full to sick with anxiety. He looked up from the little relaxed bubble he'd been sitting in. The restaurant had only a dozen or so other tables in it, and they were mostly empty. An elderly couple sat at one, and a couple of teenagers sat at another. He doubted either of these couples were connected to Yoav. But outside, surely, there had to be someone watching. Someone who had seen him walk in, checked his likeness against a photo on his phone, and was now waiting for him to leave the restaurant and walk back to his hotel, ready to stick a knife into him in the middle of a busy street...

Akiva peered at the street from where he was sitting, but the slightly grimy windows of the restaurant prevented him from seeing much detail. *Think. There must be a way. It's a problem to be solved, and you've solved harder ones than this.*

He walked over to the back of the restaurant, where the one waitress, a girl of about seventeen or eighteen with a nose ring and a T-shirt that exposed an inch or so of her midriff, was leaning against the wall tapping away on her cellphone. She half-looked up at him, but continued to focus on her cellphone. He'd paid and left a tip already, so as far as she was concerned, the need to provide him with good service was over.

"I... um... wonder if you could do me a favor," beamed Akiva, putting on the best impression he could muster of a confident, poised customer. Someone normal. Someone like Yoav.

The girl looked at him with barely-concealed disdain. "Sure," she muttered.

"I am in the middle of a rather unpleasant dispute with one of my neighbors," said Akiva. "His water pipes have been leaking into my apartment, and after months of trying to get him to do something about it, I finally hired a lawyer, who had a letter threatening court action hand-delivered to him this morning."

The teenage waitress looked at Akiva with the kind of intense disinterest that is the exclusive reserve of her demographic.

"I'm afraid that I might have spotted him outside the restaurant," went on

Akiva, oblivious, but speaking more quickly now, the words tumbling out of his mouth as his confidence began to falter. "I suspect he wants to confront me about the situation. Do you think you could possibly go take a quick look outside and see if you can see anyone who looks like they are watching the place?"

"This is the middle of Tel Aviv, you know," scoffed the girl. "There's probably like a hundred people out there on the street."

Akiva took a deep breath. *Keep going. You need to keep going.* "I know," he persisted. "But most of them are running from one place to the next. Look for someone who's... standing still. Maybe someone standing around who looks like he's waiting, or something like that?"

The girl shrugged her shoulders, gave a skeptical eyeroll, and wandered over to the restaurant door. She opened it, and went outside. There were a couple of tables out on the sidewalk and she made some kind of show of giving them a wipe, and then came back into the restaurant.

"Yeah, there's some guy there, I think," she said. "Across the street. Constantly looking over here. Either he was trying to get a glimpse of my tits as I bent over to clean the tables, or he's your neighbor."

"Or maybe both," said Akiva with a bright smile.

The waitress was not amused by this attempt at a joke, folded her arms over her chest, and looked contemptuously at Akiva.

"Sorry..." Akiva went beetroot red with embarrassment. He coughed and cleared his throat. "Anyway... thank you... erm... I wonder if there's a back entrance to the restaurant that I could possibly use?"

The girl gestured with her head toward the kitchen. "Through there," she snapped. And with that, she got her cellphone back out, and it was as if the entire last three minutes had never happened.

Akiva walked in the direction of the waitress's head-nod and pushed open the swing door that led to the kitchen. One foot in the restaurant, one foot in the kitchen, he glanced back and saw a man walk in. Somehow, he knew that this was the man who had been waiting outside the restaurant. He knew this had to be one of Yoav's men.

The man was scanning the tables of the restaurant and then his eyes hit on Akiva. Immediately the man darted forward, pushing a chair out of his way, making a beeline for Akiva. Akiva froze, his escape plan in tatters, his legs suddenly unable to move.

The man produced a flick-knife, as if from nowhere, and pushed over another chair as he got level with the teenage waitress. The chair knocked into the waitress, causing her to drop her phone. It hit the tiled floor with the telltale cracking sound that every cellphone user dreads.

"You piece of shit, that's my phone," the waitress cried, suddenly coming back to life. Yoav's accomplice, ignoring her, had moved past her and slowed down, moving menacingly toward Akiva. The waitress bent down to pick up her phone and looked at the cracked screen in disgust.

"Hey, piece of shit, I'm talking to you," she shouted. Oblivious to or not caring about the wider scene she was now in the middle of, she walked over to the man and gave him a strong push in the back. The man stumbled and spun back in surprise.

"That's going to cost me 200 shekels for a new screen," she fumed.

The assassin brandished his knife in front of her face. "Stay out of this, little girl, if you know what's good for you."

The waitress ignored the knife, flicked her hair back, and folded her arms in front of her chest. "Don't you 'little girl' me, shitface. You give me 200 shekels cash, right now, for my phone screen."

With the assassin's back turned toward the waitress, away from him, Akiva willed his legs into submission and quietly slipped into the kitchen. He looked around in desperation, assuming that the altercation over the cellphone would only give him a few seconds' grace – and there was no way he could outrun Yoav's man. *Science, science, use science. Use your brain. That's your only advantage.* His eyes hit upon an industrial size pot of water on the stove, set to a constant simmer. Before the bemused chef could react, he picked up the vat with both hands, struggling under its weight, and waddled with it over to the door. Right by the door was a table where the chef put the dishes ready to be taken out to the diners. Countless times he'd seen waiters push open the swing door with their feet, put one foot over the threshold into the kitchen, and reach over to the table to pick up the orders. Akiva put the pot of boiling water on the table, pulled the table over toward the door a bit, and then pulled the pot of water over the edge of the table so that its center of gravity was still on the table, but only just. It was balanced precariously enough that a good push by the swing door would tip it over the midriff and thighs of whoever came through.

He glanced back into the restaurant and saw the waitress continuing to harangue the assassin, who, despite what was presumably years of black ops training, was not prepared for the wrath of a teenager whose cellphone has been broken.

"My life is on this phone, you understand?" she was ranting at him, thrusting it in front of his eyes. "Look at it! It's wrecked!"

The assassin finally turned away from the waitress and sprang toward the kitchen. He barged through the swing door with his shoulder and fell right into Akiva's trap. The swing door hit the vat of water with some force, and it toppled forward all over the assassin, drenching him in boiling water from the waist down.

The man screamed in pain and began tearing at his clothes. He pulled his shirt out and began ripping his pants off, and the sight of his red scalding flesh underneath made him scream even more. He fell to the floor, shaking and writhing in agony, just as the waitress walked into the kitchen behind him to see what had happened.

"Please... cold water... I need cold water... please..." he wept.

The waitress folded her arms again. "200 shekels, shitface. Then we'll talk about cold water."

Akiva had found the exit door at the back of the kitchen. As he looked back at the small scene of devastation that he'd caused, the waitress raised her eyebrows at him and nodded in grudging approval.

He slipped out into some kind of back alley, presumably parallel to Dizengoff street, the main thoroughfare on which the restaurant stood. He assumed that, despite this brief victory, he didn't have much time. Yoav's goon would no doubt have alerted others of Akiva's presence in the restaurant.

And so Akiva started running. He was no fitter now than he had been the other day at the facility, after Yad Vashem. Within minutes, he was dripping with sweat, chest bursting in agony, breathing heavily, trying to push his legs into the air ahead of him, but being dragged back by them as the ground, as if magnetized, pulled his feet down with each step. His pace slowed to a stumbling, stooping walk. He turned down another quiet road, then another, trying to zigzag and get lost in Tel Aviv's winding backstreets. He looked back over his shoulder once, twice, three times. He seemed to be safe. For now.

What next, though? He couldn't risk going back to the hotel: if he'd been identified going into the restaurant, maybe they could figure out the direction he'd been coming from, and narrow their search to hotels in that area. His own home was out of the question, of course.

So where? He had no friends, none that he could go to in this kind of state with this kind of secret. His only real option was to go to the person for whom he'd left that voicemail from the cab after he'd run away from Yoav at GeneLight.

The journey only took a half-hour or so, and by the time he reached his destination the sun was still high in the sky. He knew that he would have to wait several hours. He wandered around the neighborhood for a bit, but felt nakedly exposed, jumping at every snapping twig, every car door slam. Eventually he went to wait back at where he needed to be. It was a mid-rise apartment building on a quiet tree-lined street with a keypad code entry for residents. He thought he remembered the code from the last time he'd been there, but apparently either his memory had given out or the code had been changed. He managed to sneak in by helping an elderly couple with their shopping, and then spent the rest of the afternoon nervously looking from the small lobby area to the street outside.

It was after 7:00 pm when he finally saw the car that he'd been looking for. It pulled up to the building and paused as the automatic barrier to the underground parking lot lifted. Akiva ran out of the lobby, opened the back door of the car, and threw himself in onto the back seat.

"Don't go in the lot," he shouted. "Drive, drive!"

The driver turned round to him in surprise. "What the hell's going on?"

"I'll explain," he sputtered. "Just move. Fast."

They drove off and Akiva peered through the back window. There didn't appear to be anyone following them. He took a deep breath and turned back to the car. "Sorry about the dramatics," he said, leaning forward through the two front seats to give the driver a kiss on the cheek. "How are you, Hadas?"

Chapter 20

Hadas emerged from Tottenham Court Road tube station into the brisk London air. Her blonde hair was bunched into a woolly pompom hat, with a few stray strands waving over her face, and she was wrapped in a warm coat. Most of the Londoners were walking around her in shirtsleeves or light jackets in this relatively mild autumn weather, but for 18-year-old Hadas, who had just the previous day arrived from a humid Tel Aviv still suffering from the remnants of the summer, it felt positively Arctic.

She headed down Oxford Street, eyes shining at the grandness of it all. The buzz of the crowds, the music blaring in brief bursts from the stores as their doors opened and closed, the smell of burgers from the fast food joints, the noises of different languages and different cultures bumping up against each other. She couldn't believe that she was in London! And she was going to make the most of this short trip. In two weeks' time, she was being inducted into the IDF, and her life would not be her own for the next two years. This vacation had been her mother's idea, a brief getaway to see a bit of the world, enjoy herself, take in a West End show or two, before returning to the next phase of her life.

She spent the day wandering in and out of clothes stores and electronics shops and cafes. She was staying at a small hotel in Bloomsbury, just around the corner from the British Museum, where she planned to camp out the whole next day. Hadas was a bookish, intelligent, slightly nerdy teenager, born at just the right time to be a Harry Potter freakette, and fascinated by all things ancient. Her good looks and incredible blonde hair helped her hide this geekishness, although for a certain segment of the male teen population around her it created a kind of double-whammy of infatuation: not only was she beautiful, but she could also talk theories about why Dumbledore insisted on trusting Snape so much. Sort of the perfect woman for an 18-year old nerd.

In the late afternoon she made her way back to the hotel, had a quick shower, and got dressed again. She'd bought herself a ticket for Les Misérables, and while the show didn't start for another couple of hours, she wanted to be there in plenty of time to soak up the atmosphere first.

It was then that she noticed the flashing red light on the hotel telephone in her room.

She picked up the phone and figured out what to dial to get to the message service. "Miss Levinson, we have a note for you down at reception. You can come and pick it up at your convenience. Have a lovely evening!" *Miss Levinson!* She loved being called that by all these Brits. It was hilarious. She couldn't remember the last time anyone – teacher, government official, police officer, *anyone* – had used her last name in Israel.

She took the elevator down to the lobby and picked up a small envelope with what felt like a piece of card inside it. She opened it and was surprised to see Hebrew script:

> *I happen to be in London at a conference this week. I would be most interested in meeting you. If the feeling is mutual, I'll be at Costa Coffee on Goodge Street this evening between 17:00 and 19:00.*

> *Akiva Cohen*

Hadas furrowed her brow. Akiva Cohen? She knew her mother's maiden name had been Cohen, and she also knew that her mother had a younger estranged brother named Akiva. She'd never met this Akiva, but surely this had to be him. Her uncle? In London? How bizarre was that? She looked at her watch; it was just after five. She had plenty of time. She shrugged to herself. *I'm in London, on my own, doing my own thing as an adult for the first time in my life. Why the hell not?*

Fifteen minutes later she walked into the coffee shop, pulled off her hat, and looked around. She had no idea what this man looked like. But as she stood in the entrance, hands on hips, unsure what to do, she saw a man in the corner look up, seem to recognize her, close his laptop, and stand up. She walked over to him tentatively. She didn't know if this stranger was going to try to hug her or kiss her or burst into tears, or what.

Luckily, he seemed equally awkward. He held out his hand, smiled, and said: "Akiva Cohen. Your uncle, in case you haven't figured that part out yet."

Hadas shook his hand. "Hadas Levinson," she replied. "So... *you* recognize *me*, even though *I* don't recognize *you*? How do you know what I look like?"

Akiva smiled apologetically. "I'll explain everything," he said. "But first things first. I'm mid-coffee here. It's not as good as Aroma back home, but it's quite acceptable. You want me to get you something...?" He gestured at the order counter.

"Not right now," murmured Hadas, sitting down a little warily in the seat opposite him.

"Okay," said Akiva. "Let me know if you change your mind." He took a sip of his own coffee and cradled the cup in both hands. "So. This is strange. I take it that you barely know of my existence, and yet I have been dreaming of this moment for some time."

Akiva studied Hadas's face, for once unselfconscious. "You're... remarkable... there is something about your face which reminds me of my mother – your grandmother – and yet also... well, my sister: your mother. You're very much like how I remember her. Of course, it's been... God, it's been over twenty years since I last spoke with her, I guess. She was about your age when she left. I was ten." Akiva's eyes began to tear up. He fussed around with the napkin dispenser on the table, pulled out half a paper-thin one-ply, then dug into the mechanism, trying to retrieve something more substantial, eventually extricating a huge pile that he deposited on the table between them. "All fingers and thumbs..." he mumbled, wiping his eyes. "I'm so sorry... I really didn't plan to get all sentimental like this... I'm sure it's the last thing you want to see here in London..."

"I... I don't really know anything about you. About my grandparents. My family." Hadas spoke quietly, looking down at the table. A few strands of blonde hair fell over her face and she made a half-hearted attempt to brush them away. "My mother is always... she gets very angry when I bring it up. She says it's too painful, that she's protecting me. She says that you're all religious fanatics and that she ran away to Tel Aviv to escape." Something switched in Hadas, and she suddenly raised her voice back to normal levels, looking up into Akiva's eyes, almost daring him to contradict her. "She says that if she'd stayed, she'd have eight children by now and be living in a settlement and oppressing Palestinians. She says that she needed to break away from her old family in order to save her future family... in order to save *me*..."

"I know," said Akiva softly, almost to himself. "I know that's what she thinks. And maybe she's right. Maybe all that is true. Maybe it would have turned out that way. But it didn't have to. I don't live in a settlement any more. And my office is in Tel Aviv, about twenty minutes from your apartment. Your mother doesn't know that."

Akiva was holding on to his coffee cup tightly, like a commuter clutching a pole in a juddering subway train. Hadas glanced down at it and leaned forward to take in its aroma. "Maybe I will have that coffee now," she remarked.

Akiva visibly relaxed and walked over to the counter, returning two minutes later with a steaming cup of coffee and a croissant.

Hadas put her face over the new cup and breathed in its fumes. The fresh cappuccino smelled like home, even from thousands of miles away. "So what happened? Why does my mother hate you so much?"

Akiva sighed. "Your mother and I grew up in a religious family. I see that you know that much?" Hadas nodded. Akiva continued: "Your mother was born first, then me seven years later. They had some difficulties conceiving between her and me, a few miscarriages. My father, your grandfather, died soon after my birth. Car crash. Shortly after that, my mother moved into one of the first settlements in the West Bank and raised us on her own. Not an easy thing in those days in the religious community. But she did it."

"This much I kind of know," said Hadas. "I've never heard it laid out so straightforwardly as this, but I've pieced it together from things my mother's said over the years." She raised her coffee cup toward Akiva's. "Clink," she grinned.

Akiva smiled uneasily, unsure how to respond, wrong-footed by Hadas's confidence and ability to adapt to this new situation. His neck began to flush with awkwardness, and he lifted his cup of coffee, using both hands to steady himself, to take a sip and recenter himself. It was a technique that Shira, who already knew him so well, had recently taught him. The thought of her brought him calm, confidence, gratitude.

"We... we lived a good, happy life at first, despite my father's death," went on Akiva. "I adored my older sister – your mother. But then things started to go wrong when your mother was a teenager. She was rather precocious, and became very politically active on the Left – the opposite of my mother, the opposite of everyone around us. She went to Tel Aviv the whole time, she stopped keeping Shabbat, she started saying all kinds of things to my mother about us oppressing the Palestinians, telling her that we lived in a settlement, that we were part of the occupation..."

"Well, I agree with all that," declared Hadas, flicking her hair back, folding her arms, her eyes examining Akiva's for agreement, argument, weakness.

"I'm sure you do," conceded Akiva, with a tip of his head. "I would expect nothing less from Miriam's daughter."

"Miriam..." pondered Hadas. "No-one ever calls her that. Only 'Mimi.' I asked her about it once and she said that Miriam was way too *dossi*, too religious." She relaxed back into her chair and considered the strange man in front of her. His awkwardness was kind of endearing, but there was a sadness there too somewhere, a closedness which reminded her of her mother.

"I guess she had to break away from everything," reflected Akiva. "My mother was mainly to blame. I only saw that many years later, when it was too late. But she made Miriam's life hell. They fought non-stop. And just as soon as your mother finished high school, she ran away from home and never looked back. I haven't spoken with her since."

Akiva paused and took another sip of coffee. He looked round the cafe as if searching for inspiration, but then brought his gaze back to Hadas, forcing himself to make eye contact (another of Shira's coaching techniques). He'd been so nervous about setting up this meeting, but it was working out so far. Part of him wished he'd told Shira about it. But he knew it was too risky. *Can't let Yoav find out about this.*

Hadas broke the croissant in half and munched on it thoughtfully, taking a moment to savor the soft pastry melting in her mouth, and wiped some of the crumbs off her lap. "My mother told me that she more or less had to fake her own death to get away from her family," she continued finally. "She ran away to India, bummed around there for a year or two, joined an ashram, did God knows what, and then eventually, when she thought that enough time had passed to be safely forgotten, she came back on the quiet. Changed her name immediately in the official population registry, did everything she could to erase any way to trace her back to her family."

"It worked," Akiva acknowledged. "As far as we knew, she stayed in India. We basically gave her up for dead, or good as. No-one in the family had any idea that she'd even returned to Israel. And certainly no-one knew that she had settled down, got married, and had a child."

"The strange thing is," considered Hadas, "that by the time I came along my mother was just so... normal. She got a job as a receptionist in a law firm, met my father, who was a young lawyer there, they got married, they had me, she went to university to get a degree. I knew that my mother had had some kind of odd childhood, and had spent a bunch of years in India, but frankly, in my circles, that wasn't that unusual. The parents who *hadn't* hung around in India were the weird ones!"

"Miriam being normal," said Akiva, shaking his head. "Amazing." He motioned to the uneaten half of Hadas's croissant that lay between them, and raised his eyebrows at her in query. She smiled warmly and pushed the plate over toward him. He beamed back at her and tore off a piece.

"And you? Do you get on with your parents?" asked Akiva, mid-chew.

"I don't know," murmured Hadas. "Mostly. Sometimes I think that I react to my mom the way she reacted to her mother. I took a summer course last year in German–"

"You speak German?" Akiva interrupted quickly.

"*Ein bisschen,*" shrugged Hadas. *A little.* "Just enough to piss off my mom, I guess. She hates it when I speak it. Drives her crazy. But I do it *because* it drives her crazy. I guess I thrive on the conflict a bit. Like my mother, I guess. Maybe I can't escape my genes."

"Don't say that," said Akiva sharply. "I believe we can always escape our genes."

"What do you mean?" asked Hadas.

Akiva let out a bit of a sigh. He scratched a finger on the table in a figure eight, going around and around. *Can't tell her too much. Can't trust anyone.* "Let's just say that I'm a big believer in nurture, and not so much in nature."

The two of them sat in silence for a few moments. Hadas looked closely at Akiva, studying his face, searching for glimpses of her mother, of herself, even, seeking familial connections to this unfamiliar stranger. Akiva looked round the room again, occasionally coming back to catch Hadas's eye with a nervous smile.

"So – how did you find me?" asked Hadas. "How did you find *out* about me, even?"

"Sheer luck, really," said Akiva, eager to get back to a conversational comfort zone. "My office is in Tel Aviv, not too far from the sea, and I had been working

159

late one evening, and went for a walk on the promenade to get some air. Your mother jogged right past me. I couldn't believe it, I thought I was seeing things. She was totally focused on her running, she had no clue – and also, I guess I look a lot more different from my 10-year-old self than she does from her 17-year-old self. Anyway – she ran past me before I could even think or react. I wasn't even 100% sure it was her."

"So she just ran off past you – what then?" Hadas leaned forward, hands on the table, mouth open in amusement, imagining the scene.

"Well, I'm a little embarrassed to say that I kind of stalked her. I figured that she must do a regular route there, at regular times, so I hung around, same time, same place, for a few days, and eventually saw her again. And that time I followed her."

"You followed her?" Hadas gave him a skeptical look. "No offence, but... you kept up her pace?"

"You clearly inherited your zeal for the truth from your mother," chuckled Akiva. "You're quite right – I'm not exactly Mr CrossFit." He patted his belly with an affectionate grimace.

"Yeah, more Mr Croiss-ant, I think," quipped Hadas good-naturedly.

Akiva laughed out loud for the first time in their meeting. "Touché." He picked up the last big chunk of untouched croissant. "Waste not, want not, eh?" he said, and stuffed it in his mouth in one go. Hadas was in mid-sip of coffee and spluttered it back into her cup in laughter, suddenly reverting to being a teenager. She grabbed a few napkins from the pile that Akiva had put on the table, wiping her mouth and covering her face in faux embarrassment. Akiva sat back and chortled again, delighted with his successful joke. It didn't happen very often.

"Anyway," he said finally, as Hadas's giggles subsided, "In answer to your rather cheeky question, I may not be a jogger, but I *am* a scientist, and scientists plan ahead. I had rented a bicycle in advance. Although I must say that even on a bike, it was a challenge for me to keep up her pace! I managed to tail her back to her apartment building. And once I had the address, it was a relatively simple bureaucratic matter to find her. The name change slowed me down for a while, of course, but I found her in the end."

Akiva wiped some crumbs off the table. He took his plastic plate and shuffled it back and forth, measuring with his hands the exact halfway point of the table. Hadas watched him in amusement, waiting for him to continue.

He carefully set the plate in place and put the knife at a precise six o'clock position on it. "Sometimes science is about brilliant minds making incredible breakthroughs, and sometimes it's just about the legwork and the data and the trial and error. This was one of those latter cases. And once I'd found her... I found out that she had a daughter."

"How long ago was this?" asked Hadas, leaning back in her chair. "How long have you... known about me?"

"A year or so," said Akiva, following her lead, leaning back, only now able to fully relax. "You see, for me, Miriam was my older sister, who I loved, admired, thought the world of – and then she disappeared from my life. Overnight. Your mother kind of broke my heart, really. I knew that she would never want to see me again, or at least, I was never brave enough to run that risk of rejection. But I don't have children of my own... I never will... and so the idea that I had a niece out there, just around the corner, living her life, well, that was quite moving for me. I've been keeping tabs on you – nothing too crazy, no 'Big Brother is watching you' kind of stuff, but finding ways to check on you discreetly. I snuck into the audience at your school graduation ceremony a few weeks ago, which was lovely – and I, um, happened to overhear you afterwards telling a group of friends about this trip. You were quite loud, I could hear you from across the room. What I did would barely qualify as spying."

Hadas smiled. "Yes, I recall being quite excited that afternoon and telling my friends about everything in excruciating detail," she said.

"Including the name of your hotel," said Akiva. "And it really does coincide with a conference that I am attending. The chance was too much to resist. And so – the note at reception, the mysterious meeting.... And here we are."

They'd both drained their cups by now. "Another one?" asked Akiva.

"Sure," replied Hadas. "I'd love one." Then, as Akiva was stretching to get up:

"Why do you say you'll never have children of your own?" Hadas grinned. "You're still young enough, and despite the belly, you're not a bad catch."

"Hah!" Akiva exclaimed, impressed at his niece's perceptiveness in honing in on the one piece of his story that demanded interpretation. *She's smart,* he thought to himself. *Intelligent, thoughtful, academically gifted* (this much he knew from his checking up on her)*, but also emotionally intelligent, a good listener, a good reader of people. She would go far.*

"Nu?" pressed Hadas. "Why no kids?"

"I guess I'm married to my work," obfuscated Akiva. "No time for anything else." It was a cop-out, and it wasn't anything like the full truth, but it would have to suffice.

Akiva bent over toward Hadas for a moment in a tone of seriousness. "Miriam must never know that we've met, you understand that, right? I don't know if she would react well to it. This must remain entirely between us. I would be delighted to see you again, to meet regularly, to get to know you – you're the only family that I have. But it would have to be a secret."

Hadas nodded. "I understand. And you're right about my mother. She can be unpredictable. We'll keep this just between the two of us. I'd like that actually. A secret uncle!"

"My colleagues at work too. They can never know about our connection. If they found out, it would make my long-term goals impossible."

"That's weird," said Hadas, creasing her brow. "Why on earth would you need to hide me from your colleagues? What long-term goals?"

Akiva paused before answering, weighing how much he wanted to reveal to this relative-stranger. *You can't. Even if she's family. Not to her, not to Shira, not to anyone. Too risky.*

"It's complicated," he said. "My work is quite secretive. I may never be able to tell you much about it. And my colleagues think that I am a Religious Zionist, like them. If they were to find out that I had family who are liberals, and that I retained a connection to them... it might make them start asking questions that I'd rather they didn't ask."

Hadas frowned, puzzled, but did not push it. Inwardly, she shrugged; if there was one thing she had learned to expect from family members, it was a modicum of weird.

Akiva relaxed again. "So what about you, Hadas? What are your plans? Army service, and then what?"

"Well, I'd like to get into journalism," Hadas said. "Maybe start at army radio, and see where that can take me."

"Journalism," echoed Akiva. "Yes, I can see that." He paused. "Maybe you should also think about politics?"

Chapter 21

"Why do you think someone might be following you?" asked Hadas, as she drove through the Tel Aviv streets. "Is this about that mysterious voicemail you left me the other day? Sorry I haven't had a chance to get back to you, it's been a bit nutty at work."

Akiva was still twisting around in the back seat, scanning the road behind them. "I'll explain. But first we need somewhere safe to talk. Not your apartment. Where can we go?"

"Hmm. Luckily for you, I've become quite the expert at finding places for secret liaisons," smiled Hadas. She hit speed dial on her phone, and after a couple of rings, Omar's voice filled the car.

"Hi my love, you're on speakerphone with Akiva, so keep it clean," said Hadas, turning to Akiva with a wink.

"Oh, good, I had been wanting to speak with your uncle," Omar's voice crackled through the phone. "Akiva, I need some advice from you on getting this mole removed from my shoulder. Isn't that right, you're a dermatologist or something? Dermatologist, physicist, geneticist... you'll have to forgive me, I do always get my science -ists mixed up..."

"Does he never stop?" asked Akiva to Hadas in exasperation. Hadas shrugged and grinned.

Akiva shook his head and made a jokey strangulation gesture at the smartphone that was mounted on the dashboard. "We need somewhere to meet, Omar," he croaked, his voice suddenly giving way. His arms began to tremble as the safety of Hadas's car drained his body of the past few hours' adrenaline. "Discreet. Ideally where I don't have to get out of the car onto the street."

"Okay," said Omar, snapping into serious mode. "I'm in Jaffa right now, just finished a meeting with some clients. I can be at the David Intercontinental in 10 minutes and get us a room there. It has an underground lot. You can park there and get an elevator straight to the room. I'll text you the room number when I've checked in."

"Fantastic," said Hadas, keeping her eyes on the road, but stealing the occasional concerned glance back at her passenger. "We'll be there soon after you."

Omar opened the door to room 1408, on the Executive Floor. "Hadas, my dear, you've changed!" he exclaimed. "The hair... the clothes... and, gracious, my dear, the stubble... you've really let yourself go, darling."

"I see that despite the protestations of all who know you, your sense of humor refuses to improve," said Akiva, his eyes suddenly moist with grateful tears. He shook Omar's hand warmly. "It's good to see you again. Thank you for helping me out here." He walked into the room and sat down on the armchair in the corner. Hadas and Omar sat on the sofa opposite him.

Akiva looked at them both for a long minute.

"I'm in trouble."

Swearing out loud into the cool blast of his car air-conditioning, Yoav hung up the phone and threw it in disgust onto the passenger seat. He'd just received word that his man at *Ravioli* had somehow let Akiva escape again. The man was shouting something down the phone about second degree burns, but Yoav didn't care. Akiva was still alive.

He drove for a few more moments and then pulled over to the side of the road. "Fuck," he muttered to himself. He picked up his phone again and dialed. He pressed call, but then immediately pressed end again. "Fuuuuuck," he said again, louder, slamming a hand on the steering wheel. He dialed the number again, this time letting it go through. Within half a ring the call was picked up.

"I understand things are progressing?" The man's voice on the other end was deep and gravelly, like a late night radio talk show host's.

"Everything is going according to plan," stated Yoav in a clipped voice. "The baby is settled with the adoptive family, and is in the perfect environment to grow up in."

"You've done well, Yoav," said the gravelly voice. "This has gone just as you imagined it, almost exactly like the picture you painted for us when we first discussed this project all those years ago. Astonishing foresight. One day Israel will recognize you for your prophecy."

"You were the prophet, sir," answered Yoav. "It was your idea to begin with. And I could not have made it happen without your support. But it's not about the recognition."

"Indeed," said Gravelly. "And Akiva? You have dealt with him?"

"Not yet..." noted Yoav, trying to make it sound matter-of-fact. "He managed to escape again. We had him cornered in this restaurant in Tel Aviv, but then–"

"I don't need to know the details," cut in the man. "This is disappointing, Yoav. You assured me you had the situation under control."

"It will be," responded Yoav.

"'It will be'?" said Gravelly. "I take it that means you know of Akiva's *precise* current whereabouts, and you are *at this moment* on your way to finish the matter off yourself?"

Yoav paused. "No," he backtracked. "We don't know where he is right now. We've lost him. Temporarily."

"Then you don't have the situation under fucking control," growled the gravelly voice. "That bumbling scientist has evaded you and your men *three times now?* You and your highly trained, *at great expense* I might add, men? Or perhaps they are not as highly trained as you have led me to believe. Or perhaps you have not spent my money as effectively as you claim. Perhaps you are underestimating Akiva's capabilities." Gravelly voice paused. "Or perhaps *I* am *over*-estimating yours."

Yoav said nothing. His hands gripped the steering wheel more tightly, the flesh on his knuckles whitening.

"I am concerned, Yoav. Concerned that he might talk. All it needs is one word from him to the press, and the whole thing is over. You have covered the tracks quite well with the child's adoption, but a nosey reporter with half a brain could uncover those tracks relatively swiftly. Our plan–"

"I'm on top of it, I promise," said Yoav quickly.

"Don't you fucking interrupt me, boy," spat the gravelly voice. "And don't you dare brush off my concerns. Just remember who you are and who I am."

"I'm sorry, sir," coughed Yoav. "I apologize for the interruption. And I certainly share those concerns."

"I'm not sure you *do* share my concerns, Yoav, because if you did, you would not be swanning around shaking people's hands at brises; instead you would be devoting every waking hour to making sure that Akiva would already be dead by now. Every minute that that man is alive and walking and with a bloody cellphone in his hands is a minute that he could snap, make a few phone calls, and bring two decades of investment and work crashing down on us. Our plan will only work if no-one has any idea about this child's genetic origin. If that ever gets out, our whole endeavor comes crashing down, and we will all have to skulk back off to our corner with our tail between our legs, and abandon this country forever to the weak, shitty little leaders that it has always had." Despite his anger, his tone of voice still sounded like a radio DJ chatting with a phone-in listener. He rarely raised his voice; he didn't need to.

Gravelly paused. "Well?"

"I will make sure that he's dead," said Yoav. "As soon as possible. He got lucky at the restaurant, but we'll redouble our efforts to find him."

"Don't wait for him to surface," said Gravelly. "Flush him out. Use Moshe."

"You're sure it's worth the risk to bring in Moshe at this stage?" asked Yoav. "We need him in place for the long run. What if–"

"There *will not be* any fucking long run if you don't get this sorted," barked Gravelly. "Use Moshe."

"Fine. I'll take care of it," agreed Yoav. "And as soon as Akiva surfaces again, we'll kill him. *I'll* kill him."

"You'd better," hissed the voice. "Update me every six hours until it's over."

Chapter 22

Hadas blew out her cheeks. "Human cloning..." she murmured. "I had no idea. I always thought you were doing something connected to the military, and that's why you could never tell me anything about your work. Now I understand your secrecy all these years. Do you know how many laws you've broken?"

"Several, I'm sure," winced Akiva. "Yoav protected us from everything."

"This Yoav, I'm pretty sure I know who he is," said Hadas. "I've seen him around the Knesset. He's some kind of lobbyist, I think. Or funder. Always whispering in the ear of some cabinet minister outside a committee meeting. I've never met him, but Benny has pointed him out to me. He's scary stuff."

"So I am beginning to discover," nodded Akiva. Goosebumps flickered through his arms and he shivered as the image of Shira dying in his arms flashed into his consciousness.

"So... what's gone wrong?" asked Hadas. "Why are we here now?"

"I'll explain," said Akiva. Forcing the truth out was already excruciating. During all the years of lies and hiding his real self, he'd always known that at some point he would have to do this. But it wasn't easy. Taking down the façade he'd built required a new kind of muscle memory, a re-oiling of long-forgotten neural networks. "But I've never told anyone what I'm about to tell you. Let me... get there in my own way."

"We're all ears," said Hadas supportively. She and Omar sat next to each other opposite Akiva, hands entwined. Since telling Akiva about their relationship a year or so ago, they'd hung out together behind closed doors a few times, and they both enjoyed the opportunity to be a normal couple with him.

"Cloning," went on Akiva, relaxing a little as he retreated into his science, into his comfort zone, "is, at its core, from a philosophical perspective, about recreating history. It's biological rebooting: a sheep, a person, doesn't matter, it's about saying 'let's hit reset, do this again, and see what happens.'"

"Rebooting history..." he repeated, savoring the words, rolling them around his mouth like fine wine, words that he'd said in his head so many times, but was now saying out loud. "Think about the way that history constrains us in this region, day in, day out. The pain of the past hangs over this region like smog. The past is our straitjacket. It weighs down on our shoulders. Sometimes we can't move because of it, we can't breathe. We talk about the massacre of Jews by Palestinians in Hebron in 1929 as if it were yesterday. The Palestinians do the same about the pain we have caused them in their past. We get history confused with sociology."

"We get history confused with sociology," repeated Hadas, squeezing Omar's hand and snuggling into his side. "I like that. Might use it in a speech in the future."

Akiva gave a thin smile. He looked through Hadas and Omar, staring into the distance beyond them. His pulse quickened as he realized that he was finally about to tell someone, finally, after all these years. "And so our hatred of the other side, our dismissal of their humanity, becomes normalized, becomes a fact of nature, a fact of life. 'Of course the Palestinians will never accept us here, of course they will never change, because they *can't* change, it's just who they *are*,' we say to ourselves. And I'm sure they say the same things about us. We've got ourselves sucked into such a miserable situation that the *immutability* of the other side is seen as a reality – an almost genetic reality."

"'Twas ever thus, and ever thus shall be," mused Omar. "It's a standard motif in the conflict resolution literature. If you look at the surveys in both Israeli and Palestinian society, shockingly high percentages believe that the other side just 'is' against them and will never change. Can never change."

"Okay – but what does this have to do with your cloning work?" asked Hadas.

Akiva took a deep, unsteady breath. This was the moment. He clicked his knuckles together nervously. A moment of self-doubt flashed before him like a strobe light. *Just say it.*

"Who is the person in all of history who has done the most harm to the Jewish people?" he asked. "Every kindergarten kid in Israel knows the answer. Adolf Hitler. The devil. Amalek. Immutable evil."

"But," continued Akiva, the words tumbling out of his mouth now more quickly, "what if Amalek... changed? Apologized? Saw the error of his ways? What if Hitler made *teshuvah*, repentance? If he publicly apologized, begged the Jewish people's forgiveness, and spent the rest of his life working for good?"

"Akiva, you can't rewrite history," said Hadas patiently. "Hitler didn't repent. And he's long dead. You can't clone him."

"You can," stated Akiva, more steadily now. "*I* can. We have acquired and verified items from which we were able to extract Hitler's DNA, and we – I – have cloned that DNA into viable embryos, and one of those embryos was born a few days ago as a living, breathing, healthy baby boy."

Hadas went white. "Akiva... You've brought Hitler back to life? Are you out of your mind? Why? Why would you do such a thing?"

A deep calm washed through Akiva's body. The sense of release flowed through his veins like an infusion of blood plasma, his cheeks reddening with confidence, his spine straightening with pride, his voice suddenly deep with self-belief. *My project. My plan. My dream.* Speaking about it made it real. He continued the script that he'd rehearsed in his head a million times.

"Why? Pressing the reset button, Hadas. Rebooting. *Redeeming the belief that people can change.* That the past doesn't define the future. We all know that Hitler did terrible things to the Jews. That he was a monster. But what if the same Hitler – *the exact genetic clone of Hitler* – could be raised to be a totally different kind of person? A kind person. Someone who likes Jews. Someone who works for peace. That's what I'm going to do. This new Hitler will grow up under my care. I will provide for him a warm, loving environment, an environment in which he is educated toward tolerance, pluralism, openness, and the importance of caring for the other. He will be a mensch. He will in due course learn about the enormity of the crimes his DNA committed, and devote *his* new life to the opposite path. He will learn about Jews and Judaism in a thoughtful, open, positive way. He will be different."

Akiva paused for a moment and took a breath. *So this is what fire in your belly feels like. This is what self-confidence feels like. This is what Yoav feels all the time.*

"Don't you see what that will do?" he urged. He had a swagger in his voice that he barely recognized but he loved how it sounded, how it made him feel. *Swagger.* Even the word sounded great. "People will see that our genes don't define us. That *our past doesn't have to define our future.* Just because someone has acted in a certain way until now doesn't mean that he is incapable of acting differently. Genes are irrelevant; it's the environment that matters. It will be the ultimate scientific proof that change is possible. *That peace is possible.* Jews will no longer be able to say 'well, Palestinians are just *like* that.' Palestinians will no longer be able to say 'well, Jews are just born that way.' They do say that, don't they Omar? I'm sure you know plenty of people who say that, right?"

Omar slowly raised his eyebrows and dipped his head just a fraction. "About this, you may be right, Akiva," he said. "Continue."

Hadas spun her head round to give Omar an incredulous look. "Surely you can't be buying this, Omar," she scoffed. "Please tell me you're not buying this."

Omar was expressionless. He stared at Akiva closely, piercing him with eyes that were used to probing business strategy, detecting whether someone was bullshitting him or not, assessing value. He kept his eyes on Akiva while responding to Hadas. "I'm not buying anything for now, my dear. Just browsing in the *shuk* while the storekeeper spins me stories about his wares. Doesn't cost anything to listen. My credit card is still in my wallet, and my wallet is still in my pocket. For now, I will just note that I agree with your uncle that many of my people believe that the Jews will never change, and that, as Akiva puts it, our past defines our future. The extremists feed upon those opinions. Those opinions are precisely why I have to hide my relationship from you just as carefully as you have to hide yours with me."

"It's paralyzing to all of us, that kind of opinion," persisted Akiva, leaning now toward Omar, grateful for a bit of an opening, a glint of support. "Not just here in Israel, but across the whole world, wherever there is conflict, wherever the pain of history weighs over people. But I'm going to break that paralysis. This child is going to *look and sound exactly* like our old enemy, the classic Hitler that we have all learned to hate. Nature – his genes – will take care of that. But nurture is going to beat nature. I will raise this Hitler to be kind. To be caring, thoughtful, philosemitic. To be mortified by what his DNA did last time round. To be determined to do better; to *be* better." He paused. "To *perfect himself*."

He drew himself up, full of confidence, gushing now like an experienced orator. "He will apologize to us, to the world. To the gay community and the Roma community too. He will prove to everyone in this region – everyone in the whole world – that *different circumstances can change how people act.* Who people are. Terrorists aren't born terrorists. Nothing is predetermined. Everything – everyone – can change. The past does not define us; the future is what you make of it. Because if *Hitler* can be kind and thoughtful and caring toward Jews, then anything is possible. He'll upend assumptions and mindsets, not just here in the Middle East, but in North and South Korea, in China and Tibet, in Russia and Ukraine, in tribal wars in Africa... everywhere. *Never again* will people believe that peace is impossible. He'll force people to look at each other differently, to look at history differently, to look at the future differently. Hitler will bring peace to the world."

Hadas stood up. "I've heard enough. You're quite mad. I can't look at you any more. I'm leaving... you can go back to your Frankenstein's lair or wherever it is you come from, but I can't listen to more of this. Omar, come, honey, let's go." She reached her hand down to his shoulder.

Omar gently brushed her hand away and didn't move. He was still staring at Akiva, deep in thought.

"Omar?" implored Hadas. "Please. Let's go. Enough."

"I don't know," murmured Omar. "I don't know. It is crazy, that's for sure. Crazy, crazy, crazy. But we live in a crazy world. I don't know..."

"Omar, please, I can't take your jokes right now," pleaded Hadas.

"I'm not sure that I'm joking, my dear," said Omar. "It is crazy, but there is something in what your uncle is saying. I have spent most of my adult life working for peace, and the vast majority of those conversations ultimately get bogged down by the weight of history. By the feeling that the other side just can't change, that they're all just... born that way."

Hadas looked deflated, suddenly sapped of all energy. She slumped back into her chair, held her hands over her eyes for a long moment, and then looked again at Omar. "Please – I don't know what you are thinking, but this can't be. I know I've brought you into this, he's my uncle, it's my family mess, but please..."

Omar turned to Hadas and held her hand. She didn't move, and he took her head gently and angled it toward his eyes. "It's a crazy idea, my darling. But is it crazier than the idea that we should be in endless conflict for all eternity? Is it crazier than the idea that Israel could annex the entire West Bank without offering citizenship to the Palestinians? Is it crazier than the idea that Hamas can drive the Jews into the sea? We live in a place where thousands of people express utterly crazy, insane, appalling ideas *every single day*, and no-one blinks an eye. I don't know if your uncle's idea could work – but I don't know that it definitely *couldn't* work."

Hadas shook her head almost imperceptibly and shut her eyes.

"I'm afraid you haven't heard the worst part yet," stammered Akiva, sucked back from his vision of the future into the wretched reality of his past couple of days. Telling Hadas and Omar had made things so real, just for a few moments, so close to the plan he'd been working on all these years. But then the pain of what Yoav had done to him, of Yoav's plan, radiated through his body again, and suddenly he could barely breathe. "Yoav doesn't know anything about this. No-one else did. All these years I was hiding my plans from Yoav, thinking that I was using him, thinking that I had the upper hand. But I was wrong. He was double-crossing me all along."

Akiva told them about what happened at Yad Vashem, about his journey back to the lab, about the few snippets that Yoav had told him about his plans when he thought he was about to kill him.

Hadas put her head in her hands. "What have you done, Akiva, what have you done..."

"Please, Hadas, not now," begged Akiva. He blinked his eyes quickly and forced air into his lungs in a series of tremulous wheezes, his confidence of a few moments ago swept away by the avalanche of his current situation. *There it goes. Back to the usual Akiva.* "It doesn't matter what you think about my project. But I need your help. Yoav *tried to kill me.* He shot at me. Twice. He barely missed me. I don't know what I'm going to do... Hadas... I'm scared..."

"You might need to be more than scared," noted Omar. He held up his smartphone and showed them the article that had just popped into his news feed.

Triple Murder in Tel Aviv, ran the headline. Underneath it: *Staff of startup company murdered at their office.* Under that: a crystal-clear photo of Akiva. And under that: *Police say company director is prime suspect.*

Chapter 23

"What the hell?" gasped Akiva. His hands began to quiver, and he swallowed some bile that seemed to have just apparated into his throat. "He's trying to kill me, and now he's framing me for murders that *he* committed. Who *is* he...? Who is he connected to...?"

"Oh, Akiva, this is some pile of shit that you've gotten yourself into," muttered Hadas. She shook her head. "Okay. Doesn't matter for now. Stay calm. Let's be clear about what needs to be done. Firstly, in the immediate short term, we have to keep you alive. That's going to be hard enough as it is. For now, I think you are probably safe. No-one saw us getting from the car to the elevator to the room, and the room is booked in Omar's name."

"My love, I don't want to get all Zionist conspiracy theory on you," mused Omar, interlocking his hands, rubbing one thumb against the other palm pensively, "but unfortunately we Palestinians have learned the hard way that it's very hard to stay untracked in this country if someone really wants to find you. What if Yoav has access to the hotel corridor security surveillance tapes? We know that he has people working for him, we now also know that he has influence over the police, and it's a small country. Wouldn't take many staff-hours to speed through the past twenty-four hours of surveillance tapes of every single major hotel."

Hadas pursed her lips and gave a brief shrug. Her mind assimilated the new data quickly and integrated it into an adjusted policy. "Maybe. Yup. Maybe. So we need to keep you on the move as well, Akiva. Different hotel every night."

Akiva gaped at her, but then nodded in acquiescence.

"Secondly, we have to find your baby," she went on. "That might be the only way to keep you alive in the long run. Without the baby, you have no leverage over Yoav, and eventually, he *will* find you and he *will* kill you. If you can somehow get the baby back, it might give you something to work with. That's a weakness you can exploit to bargain for your life. *If* you can find the baby."

The tremors in Akiva's hands subsided slightly. He took an unsteady but deep breath in. "This is why I needed to see you tonight, Hadas. I needed your coolness, your ability to ask the right questions, to see the core of the issue."

Hadas nodded. "The truth is it's a welcome distraction from... other issues in my life right now."

"Like what?" asked Akiva.

Hadas said nothing. She looked at Omar, who shrugged. "You might as well show him," he said.

Hadas reached into her briefcase and took out the blackmail note. She handed it over to Akiva with a weary gesture.

"Who did this?" demanded Akiva. "Who is this from?"

"That, Uncle Akiva, is the question. Someone who dislikes me? Someone who hates Arabs? Neither of those two criteria narrow the field down very much, I'm afraid."

"And who else knows about this?"

"Tzehainish and Benny," said Hadas. "Now you. We're working on it. They're sniffing around for me."

Akiva made as if to ask Hadas more questions, but she batted him away. "It doesn't matter for now," said Hadas, happy for the distraction from her woes. "Let's focus on your situation, not mine. There must be a way to track the child down. Even if Yoav has played with the records, he'll have to get the birth registered somehow, with some kind of formal adoption procedure. He'll want the baby to have the proper vaccinations, to have health check-ups. In order for any of that to happen, the baby will need an ID number, at least."

ALEX J SINCLAIR

"Right, that makes sense. We've said all along that the child would get an ID number. Actually, I was counting on that so that I would be able to get it a passport. To get it to America." Akiva put his face in his hands. "What an idiot I've been."

Hadas didn't contradict him. She gazed at him, poker-faced.

"But you know how many babies are born in Israel every year?" asked Akiva, looking up again, meeting Hadas's eyes, but then averting his, unable to handle her thinly-veiled disdain. "About 200,000. Even if we narrow down the search for records of birth in a one month period, that's still thousands of possible children. It will be like looking for a needle in a haystack."

"A wise man once told me that science is sometimes about the brilliant mind having the incredible breakthrough, and sometimes about the legwork, the data, the trial and error," noted Hadas with an ironic smile. "It's a tall order but it's not impossible. I'll ask Tzehainish to help with some of the legwork." At this, Akiva began to protest, but Hadas waved him down. "I know, your secret project and all. But you're past that now. I trust Tzehainish completely – and she's a brilliant researcher. If anyone can find that needle in the haystack, she can. And Benny too – we need to bring him in. He has so many connections, he knows everyone – he's like our version of Yoav. We can use him to try to figure out where Yoav is, who he is, who his people are. And I trust them both one hundred percent."

"Okay," conceded Akiva. "Of course, time is of the essence. The first months of a child's life are when he picks up the nuances of his native language. Every day that he hears Hebrew instead of German is a day we lose to those synapse connections in his brain. We need him back in a German-speaking environment and culture as soon as possible."

"There's no 'we,'" scolded Hadas sharply. "And I don't want to hear about synapse connections and German culture. I've already told you, this project of yours is madness. I don't want any part in it. But I *am* going to help save your life."

178

Chapter 24

The next morning Akiva was woken by a knock at his door.

"Room service," he heard spoken in a muffled voice.

"I... I didn't order anything," he stuttered. He got out his cellphone and stared at the screen. Should he dial the police? Hadas? Reception? Maybe it was a genuine error? He got out of bed, wincing slightly as his back creaked, and carefully edged over to the door. He rubbed his hands together, trying to dry the layer of cold sweat that was suddenly covering them. He pawed at the peephole cover with trembling fingers but it didn't budge. He put his ear to the door but heard nothing. He coughed nervously. "There must be some mistake."

"That is impossible, sir," said the voice. "I have the details here. One slice DNA, one frozen embryo, one test tube. I was told that you would be doing the mixing yourself."

"Omar!" Akiva cried out in a mixture of relief and exasperation, opening the door. "You scared the living daylights out of me."

"Sorry, Uncle," grinned Omar, waltzing into the room.

"Careful, my boy," reprimanded Akiva. "I like you very much, and I know that my niece does too, but I am not ready quite yet to see you under the *chuppah* with her."

"Well, I suppose I shall pin my hopes on the conjunction 'yet' in that sentence. Or is it an adverb? I can never remember."

"It's an adverb," said Akiva. He turned back to the bed and made a perfunctory attempt to tidy the sheets, trying to hide just how terrified he'd been a few

179

seconds ago. "What happened, you played truant from that class at Harrow?"

"I see Hadas has told you all the little secrets of my mis-spent youth."

"Anyway – why are you here?"

"Hadas's orders," clipped Omar, giving a mock salute. "And you know those are not to be messed with. Different hotel every day. So: we check out, we drive around for a bit, then we check in somewhere else. Or rather, I check in, and then I smuggle you into the room without anyone seeing. So go take a shower, get dressed, and let's get out of here. We'll stop at a cafe on the way and I'll buy you a coffee and a croissant."

"What about your business? You're not needed there?"

"It's fine. Most of my work I can do from my phone. And if output falls a little bit over the next few days, the teenagers of Israel and Palestine will just have to find other ways to kill each other. I'm sure they'll manage." Omar gestured to the bathroom. "Get moving."

Half an hour later, they were on the highway that led up the coast. "There's a small business hotel in Herzliya," noted Omar. "Hadas thought it might be a better bet than the big touristy ones in Tel Aviv and Jerusalem."

"Based on her extensive experience dealing with shadowy right-wing conspirators who have connections to the rich and powerful?" grunted Akiva with a hollow laugh.

"Point taken," conceded Omar. "You have a better suggestion?"

Akiva said nothing. He gestured at the road ahead and shrugged his shoulders. "Keep driving..."

"So," said Omar. "Hitler. Repentance. Peace. Tell me more."

"You don't think I'm crazy like Hadas does?" asked Akiva.

"I didn't say that," chuckled Omar. "Jury's still out. But I am curious. How did it start? From what Hadas has told me, you grew up as quite the right-winger, you know, father who worked for Begin, living in the settlements and all that."

"It's a long story," said Akiva. "Ironically it began through my mother. She was quite brilliant. She worked for one of the Talmud professors at Hebrew University, officially as his secretary, but really as a kind of permanent research assistant. It was in that era when it was much harder for women to break into academia, and especially in a subject like Talmud, which was such a traditional male bastion. I'm pretty convinced that she wrote most of his research for him. He won the Israel Prize at one point, and she sat there in the audience clapping."

He cracked his knuckles together nervously. *Speak, Akiva, speak. It's okay. After all these years you can finally speak.*

"Anyway, when I was about seventeen or eighteen, she went to a conference in Paris with him, on approaches to holy texts in different religions, something like that, and she took me along with her for the trip. It was the first time I'd been out of Israel. She kept me on a pretty tight leash, but one afternoon, while he was giving a paper, and she was in the auditorium helping him with his notes or whatever, I was hanging around in the lobby of the conference center, and noticed this man sitting in a corner making an extraordinarily detailed paper airplane. He had a metal ruler and scissors and was hunched over this piece of paper while he folded it and cut it and bent it and God knows what else. It's amazing, I still have this vivid visual memory of seeing him there in the corner like that... Anyway, I was quite into science by that stage, so I went over to watch, and we got talking. Turns out he was a philosopher, also at the conference, but also one of these polymaths who knows everything about everything, and he was fascinated by aerodynamics and such. He told me that he passed the time at these conferences by making paper airplanes that were as verisimilar as possible."

"And so you became an aeronautical engineer...?" asked Omar, turning to him with a cheeky grin.

"Careful, my friend," laughed Akiva. "Keep your eyes on the road. That fake charm might work on my niece, but not on me. No, the point is that he was Palestinian. He was a lecturer from Birzeit University. I must have spent twenty minutes with him talking about aerodynamics before I even realized it. He was the first Palestinian I ever met; well, the first I ever really talked to anyway. I couldn't quite believe it. He was so intelligent and delightful and friendly."

"They do say that about some of us," quipped Omar.

Akiva ignored him this time. He relaxed his knuckles and leaned back in his seat a little. This was a new experience for him – speaking about his life, his real inner life, with someone openly – but he was beginning to enjoy it. "Anyway – we had this wonderful interaction for, I don't know, an hour, an hour and a half. We talked about politics too. He was very patient with my nonsensical young religious Zionist absurdities. He didn't argue with me; he just asked me questions. A lot of questions that I couldn't answer. He made me start thinking. About my preconceptions. About history, about life."

"But your mother – she didn't suspect anything?" asked Omar.

"You want to get into the slow lane," said Akiva, pointing ahead. "The Herzliya exit's coming up. And I still want that coffee and croissant that you promised me, so let's look for a cafe when we get off the highway, okay?"

Omar slowed down and switched lanes.

"Anyway," went on Akiva, "there was nothing to suspect at first. It wasn't like the Conversion of Paul on the road to Damascus. That conversation had a massive impact on me, but only on my thinking, and only gradually. I still carried on the same religious nationalist path for many years, outwardly at least. I did the typical army service and yeshivah combination, remained part of the community, and all that. But inside, and in private, I did all kinds of thinking. And I changed. But I never told anyone."

"You hadn't 'come out' yet," Omar said with another grin.

Akiva nodded eagerly, smiling back, thrilled at how Omar seemed to understand him, understand what he'd never been able to say to anyone for all these years. "Yes, that's really what it was. I was in the closet. Totally. But that was crucial. As far as the Likud universe knew, I was still Akiva Cohen, son of the legendary Naftali Cohen. I wore a *kippah* every day *on* my head, but *inside* my head I was somewhere else entirely. And there's no way Yoav would have invested in me if he knew what I really thought. Who I really was."

"You mean, a leftie? A peacenik?"

"I don't know," mused Akiva, turning to look out of the window. Tall office buildings sailed past them, intermingled with roadside strip malls, the occasional glimpse of the sea glinting in the distance between them. "I don't really like those political labels. Left, right, up, down, I don't know what they mean any more."

"So what then?" asked Omar. "How do you define yourself?"

Akiva smiled wistfully. Omar was a good listener, and an attentive questioner. Behind the jokes, Akiva could see, was a sharp, strategic mind, thoughtful and insightful. *No wonder Hadas loves him.* He rolled his tongue around his mouth, searching for the words. "Remember that you're the first person I've had this conversation with... well, ever, really." *And it feels so good.* "So I can't say that I have a well-articulated answer. But I guess I think of myself as an idealist, a realist, and a scientist, in equal parts. I'm an idealist because I think that people can change. That the future can be different. That part came to me after my conversation with the professor from Birzeit."

"I can relate to idealism," nodded Omar, as he pulled the car over to the exit ramp from the highway. At the top of the ramp, there was a traffic light, and Omar turned to Akiva to face him head on. With sadness in his voice, he said quietly: "And I know that in this part of the world, being an idealist puts you against the mainstream."

Akiva was momentarily jolted out of his internal revery as he considered Omar's mini-revelation back at him. The idea that others had similar experiences to him, that he had... allies...? was that the right word...? touched an unknown, deep-seated part of him. The lights went green, and Omar turned back to the road. Akiva continued to talk, suddenly more aware that he was talking *with* Omar, as opposed to just himself. This was what Shira had always wanted from him, he realized with a flash of anguish. But he'd never been able to give that to her. And now she was gone. Her image floated into his mind but he forced it out, trying to focus on Omar.

"But that's why I'm a realist too," Akiva went on, raising his voice a little too loud, using his own volume to drown out everything else he was feeling. "I think that it's *hard* to get people to change. I don't think my experience with that professor in Paris was typical. In order to change deeply, most people need something else, something bigger, something that makes more noise, something that will jolt them out of the straitjacket of their history, something that will confront them with clear proof of the possibility of change."

"A jolt like rebooting Hitler as a repentant philosemite?" asked Omar.

"Precisely," agreed Akiva enthusiastically. *Maybe I'm not crazy.* "And above all, I'm a scientist. Because ultimately, I believe that science, technology, human ingenuity, what have you... these are the things that can solve our problems. I believe that science can provide the answers. Scien*tists* can provide the answers. Be it famine, disease, climate change, poverty..."

"Or intractable, age-old conflicts," added Omar.

"Quite. Intractable, age-old conflicts," said Akiva. He turned to look at Omar, the perennial tightness in his chest loosening, that elusive oxygen of self-confidence pumping through his veins for once. "Lots of people have tried to solve the Israeli-Palestinian conflict: politicians, diplomats, philosophers, religious leaders, businesspeople... but not scientists. Not until now. Not until me."

"And you kept all these thoughts hidden inside you for your entire adult life," noted Omar, shaking his head in quiet awe at what he'd heard. "It's astonishing. Brave. Tragic, actually."

Akiva was silent, moved by Omar's acuity. He pointed at a large cafe on the side of the road, one of the national chains. Omar slowed down and turned into the parking lot. He found a space, but kept the engine on with the AC running.

"And why California?" asked Omar, honing in again on the right question to ask. "Why America? Why not Germany, or Austria?"

"I figured it would be good if he speaks German first, but English a close second," murmured Akiva. "You know, for when he needs to communicate to the world when he's older. I scouted out the Bay Area last year. There are plenty of quiet, out of the way, anonymous suburbs. They have very liberal laws on home-schooling there. I'll be able to raise him with love, home-school him in German, teach him to be a mensch. I'll work from home – I'll be able to make enough money from editing science papers online and other bits of consulting work from my computer. I have it all planned out."

"You *had* it all planned out," corrected Omar. "Seems your friend Yoav had other plans all along."

"Yup," sighed Akiva. He shrugged his shoulders wearily. "Let's focus on the good for now. This place does a great *pain au chocolat*. And a large cappuccino too, please."

"On it," said Omar, and got out of the car and trotted over to the cafe entrance.

❖

Akiva remained in the car, AC running to keep out the mid-morning summer heat. He turned on the radio, flipping channels until he came across a news item about the ongoing murder investigation. They'd found out – or, Akiva guessed, been fed by Yoav – about his father's connection to Menachem Begin, and that was giving the story a bit of extra media frisson.

Suddenly there was a rap on the window. Akiva turned round, expecting to see Omar with his coffee, but it was a young woman wearing a baby in a sling over her chest. Akiva turned off the radio and opened the window.

"You really shouldn't just sit here with the engine running like that," she said, leaning down into the window. "It's terribly bad for the environment, not to mention the fumes that my baby has to breathe in as we walk past. If you're hot, go sit in the cafe."

Akiva gave her a thin smile. "I'm so sorry, you're right of course. I'm just waiting for my friend to get us some coffee from inside. It'll be just another minute."

With that, he pressed the button to raise the window. The window nudged the woman's chin as it went up and she recoiled. "How rude!" she exclaimed, and pressed her face toward the window to continue her rebuke.

And then Akiva saw her stop.

And look at him.

And look at him differently.

And back off.

"Shit," muttered Akiva to himself, his heart suddenly jumping into his throat. He picked up his phone and dialed Omar, fingers trembling so much that he could barely get the numbers right. "Come on, come on," he murmured as the phone rang. He could see the woman walking quickly toward the cafe, taking her phone out, awkwardly shifting her baby to one side as she began to dial.

Finally Omar picked up. "Patience, patience," he said. "I'm nearly at the front of the queue."

"Forget the coffee," said Akiva. "Someone's recognized me. We have to get out of here now, now, now!"

Chapter 25

"What...? Okay. On my way," said Omar.

Akiva shifted himself over to the driver's seat, reversed out of the parking space and pulled up outside the cafe just as Omar exited it. Omar jumped in and they sped off.

"Look behind us," shouted Akiva over the loud revs of the engine, drumming his fingers on the steering wheel, his heart pounding again, the temporary tranquility of his conversation with Omar shattered by the persisting dangers of his present reality. "Woman with a baby in a sling. Is she watching us?"

"Where, where, where?" panted Omar, twisting around and scanning through the back windshield as they pulled out of the lot. "Ah, I see her... no, I think we're in luck, she was facing the cafe as you pulled around and she's now looking at where the car was parked... I don't think she's seen us."

"Hope you're right," muttered Akiva in a tight voice. A brief but appalling thought flitted through his mind: *Am I going to be on the run forever?* He pulled the car onto the street and headed away from the cafe. Suddenly the siren of a police car burst into life.

"There!" exclaimed Omar, pointing to a side street ahead of them. The police car was pulling out of the side street onto the main road, driving toward them in the direction of the cafe that they'd just left. It sped past them. A minute later they heard another siren, unclear from where.

"Do you think she got the number plate of the car while you were parked?" asked Omar.

"Don't know." Akiva hesitated. "Don't think so." He scrunched his forehead as he tried to replay the scene in his mind, blocking out the steps with his hands. "She backed away from me, I think she turned around and walked back to the cafe... then I drove off... so I don't think so..."

"Good," said Omar. He put his hand on Akiva's shoulder and gave him a brief kneading massage. "Keep driving. Keep calm. Nice and normal, stay under the speed limit. But still, I think we should get out of Herzliya. They'll start checking the local hotels. Head back to the highway. Let's get back to Tel Aviv."

Akiva made a couple of turns to head back to the highway entrance.

"Shit," he gasped, nudging Omar and pointing ahead. "It looks like they're checking cars up there."

About a hundred meters in front of them, a police car had parked at a perpendicular in the middle of the road, creating an impromptu roadblock that forced the traffic into a bottlenecked one-lane crawl. Two officers stood by the car, paying close attention to each passing car.

"We're screwed," said Akiva. "There's no way to turn off the road before we get to them." The world was closing in on him again. He couldn't breathe, it was as if Yoav was in the car with him, somehow wrapping his hands around his neck and slowly strangling the life out of him...

There were no more than twenty-five or thirty cars ahead of them. The traffic inched forward as each car was checked by the policemen and waved on. Twenty... nineteen... eighteen...

Omar wasn't giving up so fast. He was looking in every direction, shifting his body almost 360 degrees, craning his neck. Akiva rested his head on the steering wheel in defeat, but Omar remained focused on finding a solution to the task at hand, oblivious to the pressure of the situation. "What's that building over there?" he burst out suddenly, pointing through the front windshield. "A little way beyond the roadblock."

Akiva lifted his head up from the steering wheel wearily. "Looks like a furniture store," he said. "Yeah, I think it's Sofas Ltd. I seem to recall they have a branch here."

"Call Hadas on your phone," said Omar. "Put her on speakerphone so that she can hear me."

Fifteen cars ahead of them.

"What's up?" answered Hadas.

"Stop whatever you're doing, listen to me, and then make a call to the police saying the exact same thing," reeled off Omar. "No time to explain."

He pulled out his own phone and dialed the police, his hands rock solid, as if making a routine business call.

Thirteen cars. Omar licked his lips as the call was answered.

"Yes, hello," said Omar, "I believe I've just seen that man who's wanted for the murders in Tel Aviv. Akiva something-or-other. I'm at Sofas Ltd in Herzliya and I just saw him run in and head to the back of the shop. He ran right past me, I'm certain it's him, I've been following it on the news all day. Terrible story."

Omar paused, listening.

"Yes, I'm absolutely sure. I'm looking at his photo on the internet again right now, it was definitely him."

Omar hung up his phone and spoke into Akiva's speakerphone. "Hadas, right now, right now, call the police, same story. Sofas Ltd, Herzliya. They might ignore one as a crank call but if they get another one, they might just take it seriously."

"On it," said Hadas, and hung up.

There were nine cars ahead of them. Eight. Seven.

"How do you know they'll call these ones in?" faltered Akiva. "They might just send another patrol car there."

"I don't know anything," shrugged Omar. "I hope they'll put out a general call, these guys will figure out they're right around the corner from the sofa shop, and they'll want to zip over there and take the credit for arresting you."

"If they take the calls seriously. And if there's no-one closer."

Six cars. Five. Four.

Akiva's anxiety filled the car, infecting Omar too. "Come on, come on, come on," he muttered. He leaned forward, almost touching his head to the windshield. "Hadas must have made the call by now. Come on, come on, put two and two together, put out the alert, come on..."

There were three cars ahead of them. Directly in front of them was a white Toyota, and in front of that was a gray Kia. One of the policemen stood in front of it to make it slow right down and the other one peered into the driver's window.

"Good, good," exhorted Omar. "Someone must look a bit like you up there. Buys us a few more seconds. Come on, come on."

But then they let the gray car go, and the Toyota in front of them began moving forward.

"We're out of time," croaked Akiva. He turned to the left and right one more time, trying to will an escape route into existence. Nothing. He took his foot off the brake. The car began to inch forward toward the roadblock. Akiva struggled for breath as Yoav's virtual hands closed over his windpipe. *It's over.*

Omar continued to lean forward, gazing at the furniture shop ahead of them, gripping the dashboard. "Come on, come on..."

Suddenly one of the policeman bent his ear to the walkie-talkie that was strapped to his shoulder and shouted something at his colleague, gesturing wildly in the direction of the sofa shop in the near distance. They ran away from the Toyota back to their patrol car, hurled themselves in, and screeched away, leaving burnt rubber tracks on the road and a cloud of dust behind them. The Toyota moved forward, clearing the way for Akiva to put his foot on the gas, overtake it, and zip down the exit ramp to the highway.

"Thank you," rasped Akiva to Omar, gripping the steering wheel tightly to avoid the convulsions that were pulsing through the rest of his body. "I don't know how you came up with that, but thank you."

Omar banged his head three times back against the headrest in relief and gave a roar of delight, the pent-up adrenaline suddenly flooding every pore. He got out his phone and redialed Hadas. "It worked. We're clear. We're on the road back to Tel Aviv. I'll explain later. Although let's just say that your uncle's going to need to borrow that wig of yours at this rate."

He listened for a moment, said "fine," and hung up.

He turned to Akiva. "New plan. I'll check you in to one of the hotels on the sea front. You rest up there for the day. Stay out of sight. Then this evening we meet Benny and Tzehainish at Hadas's apartment. Try to get ahead of this thing."

The Central Police Station was drenched with late afternoon Jerusalem light. Inside, in the ice-cold air-conditioning of the top floor's offices, Yoav shook the Police Commissioner's hand. "A terrible business," he tutted. "Thank you for placing it as your highest priority. It is of paramount importance to the Cause that we apprehend Cohen as soon as possible."

"I won't ask questions, because I know that you can't give me answers," said the Commissioner. "If you tell me it's for the Cause, that is all I need to know."

"Anything I can do to help you bring him to justice, you call me."

"Thank you, Yoav," said the Commissioner. "I have my best people on it. We'll find him."

Yoav's phone buzzed with a text message. He glanced down at it. *Target located*, it said.

Yoav smiled again at the Commissioner and squeezed his shoulder with his left hand. "Good to see you, Moshe," said Yoav. "Regards to your wife and kids."

"And mine to yours. We'll get the families together again soon."

Yoav walked out of the building into the afternoon sunlight and stretched his arms out, tilting his head to the sky, enjoying the warmth of the sun on his face. He found a quiet spot underneath a street awning, phoned the sender of the text message, and listened for a minute, nodding in satisfaction. He then hung up and dialed the man with the gravelly voice.

"I have good news," he said, trying to hide the relief from his voice. "We got a sighting of him at a cafe in Herzliya a few hours ago. Lost him there, Moshe's local idiots chased some kind of red herring at a nearby store, but we got enough of a description of the car from the woman at the cafe for my people to be able to go over the traffic camera footage afterwards and locate and track it. It made its way to Tel Aviv and parked at one of the hotels there. He's using a fake name, but we're pretty sure we've identified his room. He's not in the room right now, but as soon as he gets back, we'll be waiting for him. *I'll* be waiting for him."

"Don't fuck it up this time," said Gravelly. "My patience is running thin."

"I have it–" said Yoav. But the line was already dead.

The twilight breeze of Tel Aviv wafted through the windows of Hadas's apartment, infusing the room with the smell and sounds of the cool evening sea. Hadas, Akiva, Omar, Tzehainish and Benny sat around Hadas's coffee table. Hadas introduced Omar to Benny, who shook his hand formally, and to Tzehainish, who gave a schoolgirlish grin from ear to ear, and then did the same with Akiva, who was wearing his baseball cap and dark sunglasses.

"Your uncle?" blurted Tzehainish incredulously. "You never mentioned anything to me about an uncle..."

"It's a long story," said Hadas. "Screwed-up family history. Not for now."

"So what's the urgency?" Tzehainish asked. "Why are we meeting like this again? Have you received another blackmail threat?"

"No, this is something else," said Hadas. "This is about Akiva." And with that, she gestured to him to remove his hat and glasses.

"What the hell?" shouted Benny, jumping to his feet. "This is the guy who's all over the papers. The murderer. Hadas, what is going on?"

"He's innocent," said Hadas quickly. "That's the first thing you need to know. Sit down, Benny. You have my word, he is innocent. He's being framed for the whole thing, and it's *his* life that is actually at risk. I have some things to tell you about my Uncle Akiva. Just hear me out."

She went over as many of the details as she thought she needed.

"And that brings us to the current situation," finished Hadas. "I believe we need to locate this baby and retake possession of it. I imagine you must be feeling a whole mix of emotions right now. I know that I do. Maybe you think that my uncle is crazy. Maybe you think that *I've* gone crazy for standing by him. I wouldn't blame you. But I'm asking you as my closest friends and colleagues to help me in this short-term task. What to do with this child in the long term – we can talk about that afterwards, we'll get social workers involved, the courts, we'll figure all that out. I'm not interested in the genetics, in whether or not this child could actually grow up to become a Jewish Hitler. But I want to know what other resources and connections are part of Yoav's long-term plan, how deep this conspiracy goes. And we need to retrieve this baby. Otherwise, Yoav won't stop until he kills my uncle."

"And perhaps us too, now," said Tzehainish quietly. "I am flattered that you have sought out my help tonight, Hadas, but in bringing me here – in bringing us here – you may have endangered our lives. If Yoav is watching Akiva, that means he could be watching you, and now watching us. And if Yoav is prepared to murder Akiva to keep his long-term plan viable, then he will not think twice about adding us to his list too."

Hadas was silent. She had not considered this. "I'm... I'm so sorry..." she mumbled. "You may be right. I don't know what to say..."

Hadas gazed at each of her friends in turn, trying to silently apologize, but realizing that what she'd done was irrevocable.

Akiva broke the silence. "It's my fault," he said. "Don't blame Hadas. I brought her into this mess, and that means I brought you into it too." He looked at each of them in turn. More lives that he was ruining as a result of his dream. *It has to be worth it.* "I'm so sorry."

"It doesn't matter," Tzehainish declared, sitting back and folding her arms across her chest. "It's done. It's history. I'd have come anyway. We all would." She looked at Benny, seeking confirmation.

Benny raised his eyebrows and shrugged. He said nothing.

Hadas began to lay out the plans that she had been formulating. Akiva would continue to lie low, for obvious reasons. Tzehainish would start investigating birth and adoption records in the West Bank over the past several days. It was likely that Yoav would be trying to cover up the tracks of what he'd done, but she should look for anything that looked remotely suspicious or out of order. Meanwhile, she, Hadas, would speak to a contact she had in the police department and see if they had come up with anything in their investigation into the incident at Yad Vashem. Again, she imagined that there would be a cover-up, but perhaps she could get some clues, some wisp of information that would help them get to Yoav. And finally, Benny would use his political connections with colleagues on the Right to see if he could sniff out anything at all about Yoav's funders and supporters. Maybe, just maybe, if the three of them divvied up the investigation in this manner, they'd be able to triangulate some information that could be helpful.

"Don't you think we should just go to the police?" said Tzehainish. "If Akiva can prove his innocence, he should do that. Besides, we have laws in this country, and Yoav has clearly broken them. Let's put the system to work against him."

Akiva shook his head. "I don't think we have any idea how powerful and connected Yoav is. We can't trust the authorities until we have more of a sense of who we're really dealing with and how high up he reaches. Look, we know that Yoav has somehow got the police thinking that I'm the suspect. The moment we go to the police, I'll be arrested, and... well... it would be easy as pie for Yoav to get to me then."

"I have to agree with Akiva," said Hadas. Her leadership instincts were in full gear by now, bringing the whole force of her personality to bear on the situation. To take control. "Going to the police would be signing his death warrant. And

I can't have the police involved either. Or the press. The publicity would be terrible. My role – our role – in this whole mess must remain secret."

Tzehainish nodded her assent, and said that she would get to work on the records first thing in the morning.

"What about you, Benny?" said Hadas. "Enough with the silent treatment. Are you willing to help? Do you think Akiva's crazy? Do you think I'm crazy?"

Benny rubbed his chin and clicked his tongue against his lips, as if choosing his words for maximum effect. "I'm afraid I do think you're crazy, Hadas," he chided. "I don't know what else to conclude. Cloning Hitler? Bringing him up like a *boy scout* so that he can say how terribly sorry he is? And this will suddenly change the Middle East and the world as we know it? Yes, I think you've gone quite mad. When you told me about your deal with Mahmoud the other day, I was afraid that your relationship with Omar was somehow clouding your judgement, but this takes the cake. This is insanity."

"I don't blame you for thinking that," shrugged Hadas. "Maybe it is insanity. But you have to see that my uncle's life is in danger now, and I can't just sit back and do nothing."

Benny sighed and shook his head.

Hadas turned to Tzehainish and put a hand on her arm. "What about you? You think this is crazier than a bunch of white Jews in 1991 sitting round a table and saying, I have an idea, let's secretly send thirty-five jumbo jets and cargo planes to airlift thousands of Ethiopian Jews to Israel over the space of twenty-four hours? Israel's finest moments have always been through ideas that would have been considered crazy at the time. This might be no different."

Tzehainish didn't answer. She was gazing into space, brow furrowed.

"Tzehainish?" Hadas prompted, squeezing her arm. "Are you listening to anything I'm saying? Please tell me what you think!"

Tzehainish, still with a puzzled look on her face, turned to Benny. "You just said you thought that Hadas's relationship with Omar was clouding her judgement in her conversation with Mahmoud," she said slowly.

"Don't change the subject," snapped Benny. "The child benefits bill pales into insignificance compared to this madcap scheme. You're her bosom buddy, maybe you can talk some sense into her…"

Hadas sighed and got up as if to stretch her legs toward the kitchen, but Tzehainish grabbed her by the elbow and tugged her back down.

"You only told Benny and me about Omar the day *after* that meeting with Mahmoud," she said.

Hadas stopped in her tracks.

"I only told you and Benny about Omar the day *after* that meeting," she repeated quietly, slowly, as if unjumbling the words like a puzzle to see if their significance was really what Tzehainish was implying.

"Benny," said Hadas, her voice breaking a little, one part of her mind a few paces ahead but unwilling to spell it out to the rest of her. "Benny… how is it possible that you would be thinking about Omar *before* I'd actually told you about him?"

Benny shrugged his shoulders. "I must be mis-remembering the order of things," he said with a nervous laugh. "Have pity on an old man like me, memory failing him, mind like swiss cheese…"

"You don't mis-remember things," jumped in Tzehainish indignantly. "'My mind is a political bank account that remembers everyone's deposits and with-drawals,' is how you always put it, I believe. I smell bullshit here, Benny. Hadas, I think–"

"I can handle this myself," interjected Hadas coolly. She turned to Benny. "I smell bullshit too, Benny." She got up from the sofa, walked over to him, and stood akimbo in front of him. There were tears in her blue eyes but behind them was a piercing look of accusation.

"I'll ask you again, Benny," she challenged, voice no longer cracking. "How is it possible that you would be thinking about Omar *before* I'd actually told you about him?"

Benny said nothing.

Hadas moved even closer to him and pushed him in the shoulder. "How is it fucking possible, Benny, that you would be thinking about Omar before–"

"Fine," said Benny with a scowl, pushing her arm away. "Your little friend has caught me out. It was me. Yes, it was me, Hadas. I found out about this relationship of yours and I didn't want it to ruin your career. Better *I* scare you into cutting it off than someone else finding out. If it had been someone who really wanted to do you damage, they wouldn't have played around with silly little blackmail notes and photos, they'd have gone straight to the press. But yes, it was me. I wanted to shock some sense into you."

Hadas stood her ground opposite Benny, shaking her head. "I can't believe it," she whispered, almost to herself.

"Oh, don't be so bloody naïve," snapped Benny. "You think I was going to let you throw your career away? You are our party's great hope for the future. Our *country's* great hope. I have personally invested countless hours of mentoring, and more political capital than I care to think about, in helping you get to where you are today. If this relationship of yours gets out, *your political career is finished*. You think I was going to stand by while the Left's best hope in a generation fucked things up for herself and for the rest of us by having a stupid fling with a fucking Arab? You think I was going to let that happen? Let that happen to you, to the party? To the country? You should thank me, Hadas. You should thank me for being the friend who tried to talk sense into you, who tried to save you from yourself."

"You piece of shit," snarled Tzehainish. "Who the hell are you to decide what she does with her life?"

"Tzehainish!" shouted Hadas. "I told you, I can handle this myself." She turned to Benny and spoke to him with a restrained fury that came from the depths of her being: "Your whole political life you've been preaching co-existence between Israelis and Palestinians. Your whole life. So what – it was all for show? It was all fake?"

"Again with the naivete," scoffed Benny. "Co-existence doesn't mean fucking each other. Co-existence doesn't mean marrying each other. Are you crazy? It just means not killing each other. It means smiling nicely at each other across the board room or in the park. We're not actually going to be friends with these people, Hadas. They are Arabs and we are Jews. Chalk and cheese. Oil and water..."

"...Ebony and ivory?" interjected Tzehainish again, leaning back on the sofa in disgust. This time Hadas let her friend's interruption go by, and she remained standing over Benny, arms on hips, shaking her head in quiet disdain.

"I think you'd better go," Hadas fumed. "You'd better go, and you'd better not breathe a word of any of this to anyone, ever. You may think I'm insane, Benny, but I know plenty of your dirty political secrets. They may not be big ugly secrets like mine, but I bet I know enough of your petty betrayals and underhand tricks that I could destroy so many of your political relationships that your career would be over and you'll end up living out your retirement in the Big Brother house, not the President's."

Benny shrugged. "Fine. I'll go. I'll swear myself to secrecy. But mark my words, Hadas, you stop this insanity. Both of these men" – here he pointed first at Omar, then at Akiva – "are symptoms of your madness. It will end in disaster for you. You mark my words, and stop this nonsense – both of these nonsenses – before it's too late."

He walked out, slamming the door shut.

Chapter 26

O mar yawned and stood up. "Well, this has been a delightful evening, rather more messianic and apocalyptic than my usual feet-up-in-front-of-the-telly fare, but variety is the spice of life, I suppose. Nevertheless, those teenagers just *will not* kill themselves, so I do have to go to work in the morning. And unlike the rest of you, I appear to have no role in this exciting investigation."

"My car's parked in a lot not far from Akiva's hotel," said Tzehainish. "I took a walk on the beach this afternoon and came by cab rather than try to find parking on the street here."

Hadas was still seething from the interaction with Benny. "Wait a minute," she said. Holding her head up straight, she took a deep yoga breath, all the way through her lungs to her diaphragm, letting the oxygen flow through her entire body, pushing out the anger, pushing out the irritation, recentering. The bastard wasn't worth it. She emerged from her moment of meditation with renewed focus and clarity. "Here's what we'll do. Omar, can you take a taxi back home? I'll borrow your car tonight, I'll take Tzehainish to her car and Akiva back to his hotel, and then tomorrow I can drive your car to Jerusalem and transfer Akiva to a hotel there. I'll leave the car somewhere for you with the keys locked inside it, and you can pick it up with your spare set."

Omar gave a mock salute. "An operation planned with military precision. No wonder you Jews won the Six Day War."

"How do you put up with him?" Akiva asked Hadas in exasperation.

Hadas shrugged and giggled. "I don't know. I guess someone has to."

Tzehainish stood up, walked over to Omar, and gave him a kiss on the cheek. "I think he's just fine." She turned to Hadas. "I approve of him. He's good for you. You have my blessing, boss."

"Oh, I *do* like *her*," purred Omar.

Hadas rolled her eyes (but inside, was secretly pleased, relieved, even hopeful; if Tzehainish felt that way, maybe others would too?) "Okay, lovefest over. Come. Let's get going. It's late, and we have a lot to do tomorrow. Just give me two minutes to put my disguise back on."

Hadas shortly emerged from the bathroom as a shades-wearing brunette again, and the four of them left the apartment and made their way downstairs. Omar ordered a taxi using an app on his phone, which arrived within a couple of minutes. Before he got in, he turned to Tzehainish, and kissed her on the cheek. "I reciprocate both the kiss and the sentiment, my dear. Hadas told me that you are a friend as well as an aide, and I see that very clearly now. Thank you for standing by her." He then turned to Hadas, held her by both hands, and kissed her on the lips for a long while, longer than he'd ever done in public. Saying nothing further, he got into the cab.

The three of them stood there for a moment, seeing Omar off, and then Hadas jingled his keys. Minutes later, they were in the car, driving through Tel Aviv toward the beachfront hotel where Akiva had checked in earlier.

The hotel sat at the southern end of the Tel Aviv beach. The promenade opposite the hotel ran parallel to the sea, where gorgeous views of the Mediterranean and spray from the waves crashing onto the rocks mingled with the hum of Tel Aviv life. Even at this late hour, it was bustling with joggers, couples out on romantic moonlit walks, and, of course, the obligatory cyclists and electric scooters.

They were about a hundred meters from the hotel, with the sea on their right, when Tzehainish tapped Hadas on the shoulder and pointed out the lot where her car was parked.

"That's fine," said Akiva. "I'll walk from here. I could do with a bit of sea air before I go to bed. Goodnight all. Hadas, let's speak in the morning."

He got out of the car and began to stroll through the parking lot toward the hotel. Tzehainish gave Hadas a hug from behind, got out of the car, and ambled over to her own. Hadas sat for a moment, car idling, shifting her gaze between the two of them. She saw Tzehainish's car start up, and watched her fiddle with the radio, and then looked back at Akiva.

Suddenly she saw someone move out of the shadows behind Akiva. A man wearing all black, who began to walk quickly toward Akiva. Akiva was still a little way away from the hotel, walking past a row of parked cars. He'd moved away from the busy promenade of joggers and was on his own. He was stopping every now and then to look over at the sea and up at the stars, seemingly lost in thought, and the man in black was making swift progress toward him, now just meters away.

Then Hadas saw the glint of metal in his hand.

The man in black was now no more than twenty meters from Akiva, and closing fast. Akiva was walking past a section of the parking lot jammed tight with electric scooters, bicycles and motorbikes. A part of Hadas's brain that she didn't even know existed sized up the situation in a split second. She put the car into gear and sped forward. The car mounted the sidewalk and kept accelerating. She was vaguely aware of people screaming and running to her right, joggers and cyclists seeing a car speeding on the sidewalk toward them and drawing the obvious conclusion that this was a terrorist attack. But she kept the car straight, away from the joggers, still accelerating, at 30 or 40 kmh by now, heading toward the bunch of scooters and bikes.

Akiva had just walked past the scooter/bike section, and the man in black was still in it, and that's exactly what that unknown part of Hadas's brain had perceived about two seconds ago. She slammed the car into the scooters and suddenly the air was filled with the screech of metal, as the bikes crashed into each other, domino style. Hadas kept her foot on the gas and piled through the bikes, pushing them forward like a snowplow. Her right side mirror broke off, and the window beside her on her left got shattered as a motorbike's handle slammed into the car, spraying glass all over her. She shrieked out loud in shock, but managed to instinctively duck away from the glass, grabbing the steering wheel even more tightly as she braced her body away from the open window and kept driving through the bikes, pushing them between Akiva and the man in black.

This all happened in the tiniest of moments. The man in black, who had been mere seconds from his target, had managed to dive away from being hit by the bikes, but he now had a mountain of crushed metal and rubber between him and Akiva. His pathway was blocked.

Hadas found her voice and screamed through the shattered window on her left. "Akiva! Run! He's trying to kill you! Run!"

Akiva stood frozen, stunned.

"Go, go, go!" shouted Hadas again.

The man in black, knife still in hand, was slowly trying to clamber over the heap of bikes. Akiva suddenly snapped back to life and saw what was happening. He backed away from the parking lot and stumbled from the curb onto the main road, and darted clumsily through the late night traffic to get the other side of the street where the hotel was.

The man in black finally made it through the heap of bikes. The moonlight caught his face. Hadas gasped in recognition. *Yoav.*

Yoav glided across the road, slaloming through the oncoming traffic, in pursuit of Akiva.

Akiva hobbled past the main lobby entrance of the hotel and into the banquet hall, where a large wedding party was taking place. Hundreds of guests milled around, drinks and canapes in hand, slapping old friends on the back and air-kissing elderly relatives whom they hadn't seen in years. Sweating, heart pounding, half-looking behind him, kicking himself for breaking cover and exposing himself in the open air, Akiva lurched through the throngs of guests, desperately trying to find safety, to put as many people as possible between him and Yoav.

Yoav arrived at the entrance of the banquet hall and looked inside. He had seen Akiva go in, but now he saw no sign of him. Too many people.

"Shit," said Yoav under his breath. Even if he could locate Akiva in the crowd, it was too risky to kill him here. Too hard to make a clean getaway. Somehow Akiva had escaped him again. Yoav had killed, or had had others kill, at least a dozen people in the past, with relative ease. But somehow, Akiva continued to evade him. He put the knife away in his pocket and turned back to the sea front.

Hadas had seen Yoav run after Akiva, stop at the entrance to the hotel, and turn back. Now she realized with a chill that she too might be in danger. She tried to reverse the car, but it was tangled up in a mess of bikes and scooters, and it was slow going. Then, to her horror, she saw Yoav cross the road back toward her.

"Oh no, no, no," she muttered, twisting the steering wheel from side to side. She moved the car forward again, then backward, trying to grind it free from whatever was getting it stuck. One of the tires burst with a boom, but she kept going, backward, forward, screeching metal and burning rubber all around her.

It was no good. Yoav was jogging toward her. Hadas looked at him in terror. Her lungs constricted, suddenly desperate for oxygen but unable to take it in, like a deep sea diver with the bends. In seconds he would be upon her, and then she would either be dead, or, at best, he would discover who she was underneath her disguise and make the connection between her and Akiva. She saw him pull the knife back out from his pocket and draw level with the car.

"Come on, come on, please, please move," she pleaded with the car. She was in reverse, engine straining, desperately trying to back out of the pile of bikes, but something was blocking the car. "Please, move, move damn you..."

Yoav put his head through the shattered window and she recoiled from him in alarm, twisting her body as far to the other side of the car as she could, her foot still desperately pumping on the gas pedal, her hands still gripping the steering wheel.

"So, Akiva's grand savior. And who are you, pray tell?" Yoav said calmly. He reached inside to grab her. His fingers were centimeters away from her head – but then suddenly something freed up behind her and the car jerked backward, making Yoav spin away from it. The car sputtered back in reverse. Yoav ran toward it again, but it was too late. The car was now free from the pile of bikes and Hadas, still shaking with fear, slammed her foot flat down on the gas, straining back on the steering wheel, as if physically trying to help the car to put more distance between her and Yoav. She clattered backward off the sidewalk onto the main road, braked, put the gear into drive, and then sped off into the distance. She hunched her shoulders over the steering wheel and let out a primal scream of victory and relief, keeping her foot on the gas, speeding away down the beach road, praying that Yoav wouldn't have time to get a look at her license plate.

She was lucky. It was dark enough that Yoav couldn't get a good look, and he stood there, lips pursed, as she sped off into the distance toward Jaffa.

"Akiva Cohen, you are a lucky motherfucker and an annoying motherfucker," Yoav spat. "But you are going to be a dead motherfucker before too long. You're just delaying the inevitable."

He aimed a frustrated kick at a motorbike that was lying in a mangled heap at his feet. He shook his head. And then he walked off back to where he'd parked his car.

Hadas was by now in the middle of Jaffa, and, seeing that Yoav hadn't followed her, realized that she was safe for now. She was breathing heavily, her stomach was twisting with nausea, adrenaline was pumping through her veins, but her head suddenly clarified. A chance had now presented itself, a chance to get a foothold in this chain of events and begin to make things work in their favor. She pulled over, picked up her phone, willing her fingers to stop trembling, and dialed Tzehainish. She picked up immediately.

"What the hell just happened?" gasped Tzehainish.

"That w-was Y-Yoav." Hadas flinched at her own voice, so distorted by shakiness that she barely recognized herself. "The one who Akiva told us about earlier. He was trying to kill him again. The thing with the bikes and scooters – it was the only thing I could think of doing."

"Holy shit, it was incredible, Hadas! *You* were incredible. I was just sitting in the car trying to find some decent music and suddenly I see this crazy scene play out, like, right in front of my eyes, I couldn't believe it!"

"Tell me what's going on right now," said Hadas. "What is Yoav doing?"

"He looks like he's giving up. He's walking off... I think toward some other cars... wait, he just got his keys out and beeped his car open. He's not too far from me, he's getting into his car..."

"Listen," implored Hadas, clenching every muscle in her body to force herself to stop shaking and pull herself together. "This is our chance. He hasn't seen you, he doesn't know you exist, you're not even on his radar screen right now. You have to follow him. Find out where he goes. We know his official address, but we don't know where the child is – maybe, just maybe, if you follow him now, he might not go straight home, you might get some kind of clue."

Tzehainish gave the briefest of pauses, and Hadas immediately regretted asking her friend to put herself in danger. But before she could speak again, Tzehainish responded. "Got it. I'll let you know what I find."

Hadas took another deep, unsteady breath. "But... do it carefully, keep your distance. Remember he's a professional. Don't let him spot you."

Tzehainish's voice came back quickly this time, matter-of-factly, her bravado masking the anxiety underneath. "You seem to have forgotten my resume, boss. I did a training course for the Mossad during my army service. They gave us a bit of instruction in this kind of thing. I'm not exactly James Bond, but it's nighttime, there aren't many cars on the road, and I'll be able to follow him from a safe enough distance. I'll have my headlights in his back, so I'll be able to see him but he won't be able to see me too clearly. I'll be okay."

"Good luck," said Hadas. "But please be careful. He will not hesitate to kill you if he discovers you, that much is clear."

A longer pause this time. "I know." And with that, Tzehainish hung up. She watched as Yoav started his car and drove off, waited a few seconds, and then drove off after him.

Hadas lay her head back against the headrest, shut her eyes, and breathed a few long, deep breaths, finally gaining some calm. She opened her eyes, got out of the car, and took a walk around it to survey the situation. It was a mess. The side mirror, the broken window, the tire, half the paintwork scratched off, both front and back fenders hanging on by a thread, a huge dent in one of the rear passenger doors. She pulled out her phone, quietly impressed with herself that her hands had stopped shaking. In a minute, she would call Akiva and tell him what had happened. But before she spoke to Akiva, she needed to hear Omar's voice.

Omar picked up immediately; he was still in his taxi on the way back to Jerusalem.

"Honey," said Hadas, "You know you were saying the other day that you were thinking of getting a new car...?"

Chapter 27

Tzehainish followed Yoav north through Tel Aviv toward the Ayalon highway, and from there to Road 5 that led eastward toward the West Bank. She had predicted that this would be his route, and even though she lost him once as she got stuck at a red light, she managed to catch up with him.

As they got onto Road 5, the traffic thinned out, and Tzehainish was able to stay some distance behind Yoav, keeping him in her line of sight, hoping that as far as he was concerned, her car would be just an anonymous set of headlights in the distance behind him.

Yoav turned off Road 5 onto Road 60, the main north-south highway of the West Bank. This road was a smaller one, one lane in each direction for the most part, and the traffic was even lighter. In the normal scheme of things, Tzehainish would never have dreamt of driving on this road, of coming this far into the West Bank. She did everything she could to avoid places like Ofra, one of the larger settlement towns in the northern part of the West Bank, where Akiva had mentioned that Yoav lived, and where by now Tzehainish could see that he was heading. Her hopes of a breakthrough were fading; Akiva already knew Yoav's home address, and so if that was where he was going, she wouldn't find out anything new tonight.

Yoav was still fuming to himself about Akiva's dumb luck in evading him again.

He turned on a calming classical music station, and told himself again that it was just a slight delay, just a matter of time until Akiva would be dead and there would be no further traces of the birth origins of Israel's future leader and savior. He looked at the digital clock on his car's dashboard.

Then he looked in the rearview mirror.

About twenty kilometers before Ofra, Tzehainish saw Yoav's car ahead of her slow down and turn off the main road. Slowing down too, she took the same turn-off and followed Yoav at what she hoped was a safe distance.

The turn-off led to a dirt road that wound up a hill, twisting and turning in the darkness. There were no street lights, and apart from her car's headlights, it was pitch black everywhere. Tzehainish drove on, staying as close to Yoav as she dared, keeping his brakelights in her line of vision, losing them as he went round bends, speeding up to catch sight of them again.

As she went round another blind turn, she saw Yoav's car slow down to a snail's pace ahead of her and pull slightly to the side of the road.

"Shit, shit, shit," she muttered to herself. Her heart fluttered with a sudden flash of deep vulnerability. *I have no idea where the hell I am. And no-one has any idea that I am here.* The words that she'd spoken to Hadas a couple of hours ago reverberated in her head. "If Yoav is prepared to murder Akiva to keep his long-term plan viable, then he will not think twice about adding us to his list too..."

Tzehainish slowed down her car too, hoping that Yoav might carry on. But he stayed put. She put the car into neutral, idling about fifty meters behind him. His car engine was still on. Tzehainish peered through her windscreen, but it was too dark to make out what Yoav was doing.

She looked around to see if she had space to swing the car around and escape back down the hill. "No time..." she muttered to herself again. Trapped.

Tzehainish waited, hands on the steering wheel, foot ready to hit the gas. She licked her lips but found no moisture. Yoav's exhaust gently spewed fumes into the cool night air like the breath of a bull preparing to charge at a matador. What was he going to do? Speed down and ram her off the road? She wasn't even sure that he was in the car still: maybe he'd left it running as a decoy, and he was at this moment sidling down the road with a knife or gun...

Have to get out of here. She shook her head and put the car into gear. "Shit, shit, shit." The steering wheel was slippery with sweat from her palms, and she gripped it tighter. She slammed her foot on the gas and the car jerked forward toward Yoav. She wriggled down in the seat, trying to get her head under the window, to give him less of a target. Barely able to see ahead of her, she sped up the hill, pushing her car faster, forcing her head down low. She gave an involuntary scream as she got level with Yoav's car, her tires sprinkling it with pebbles from the road.

She was past Yoav's car. She wriggled back up the seat, put her front beams on, and continued driving up the hill as quickly as she dared, hoping to outrun Yoav. She skidded on a sharp bend in the road, and her stomach jumped into her mouth as she realized that she was in as much danger of driving over the steep edge of the hilltop road as she was of being caught by Yoav. Heart pounding, she looked back in her rearview mirror for signs of Yoav's headlights behind her.

Nothing.

He didn't seem to be following her. Maybe he'd radioed an accomplice to wait for her on the road ahead? She peered ahead of her into the darkness.

Tzehainish slowed down again and pulled over by the side of the road, turning her lights off. She waited, her heart still thumping, craning her head ahead and behind her to see where the threat would come from.

A few minutes went by with nothing disturbing the silent night around her. Her breathing began to slow, and she began to shiver as the adrenaline drained out of her system. Maybe she was safe after all. Perhaps Yoav had stopped to make a phone call, or even to take a leak? But that made no sense; they weren't more than twenty minutes from his home, and he could have pulled over on the side of the main highway for either of those purposes. And now they weren't even going in the direction of Ofra; God knows where this winding side road actually led to.

"Shit," she said out loud to herself again. She did a three-point turn in the middle of the pitch black road, and then began driving slowly back in the other direction, toward the lay-by where Yoav had pulled in, ready to accelerate rapidly again if she needed to.

She got there and Yoav was gone.

She drove on for a bit, wanting to make sure that she had the right place, but soon she came back down to the main road. No sign of Yoav. She turned the car back up the hill, and pulled into the lay-by where Yoav had stopped. She turned off her car and gazed across the valley. All she could see was darkness. There were a few lights in the distance of some small settlement, but that was it.

"So why, Mr Schindler," said Tzehainish, again out loud to herself, "did you stop here? What is so important about that view that you were looking at, I wonder?"

Tzehainish drove back to her apartment in Tel Aviv, slept a few hours, packed some sandwiches, fruit, and water, and got in her car again to head back to the lay-by the next morning. On her way, she stopped at a camping store and bought a pair of powerful binoculars.

Seeing the lay-by in daylight left her none the wiser. There was nothing there. She trained her binoculars across the hill, where she'd seen the twinkling lights the previous night, and saw a small settlement, a bunch of pre-fab houses glistening with morning dew. She drove up the hill a little bit further and found that the road double-backed on itself, allowing her to park the car on another lay-by that overlooked where Yoav had stopped.

"I guess this is my office for the day," she said to herself.

The truth was, it was a very convenient office. She opened her laptop, connected to her phone's hotspot, and spent most of the time doing what she would have done that day in the Knesset – answering emails and putting the finishing touches to some minor legislation that Hadas was involved with in the coming weeks. She listened to a couple of podcasts, put on some music, and interspersed her car-office time by getting out every now and then to stretch her legs up and down the side of the road. Every few minutes, she got the binoculars back out and trained them on the lay-by below her and the settlement across the valley.

The area was deserted; she counted a grand total of fourteen cars that went past her during the day. It was an utterly beautiful area. The hills rolled in the distance ahead of her, their ancient stone terraces glinting in the sun; the air was clear and silent; the wind rustled in the olive trees that dotted the landscape around her. Here, in the heart of Samaria, in the land where Abraham wandered, where Saul met David, where the northern tribes of Israel established their shrines and kingdoms, Tzehainish couldn't help but empathize with the communities who were her political rivals, and in many ways rivals for the future face and direction of the State of Israel in general. Cognitively, she knew that Greater Israel was a mirage, a trap, a massive radioactive magnet that twisted your values out of shape the closer you drew to it: the settlements were a grievous historical error that Israel had made, embedded so deep in the heart of Palestinian population centers, and unless something changed soon, they would bring disaster upon the Jewish people and the State of Israel. But emotionally, spending the day in that Biblical air let Tzehainish see something that she hadn't previously recognized: there was indeed magic in this place. Magic that we might have to leave behind with sadness; but magic nevertheless.

Then, in the middle of the afternoon, she spotted him. She was scanning the area across the valley with the binoculars and saw his car drive up to the entrance of the little settlement. At least, she thought it was his car; she couldn't make out the license plate, but it was the same color, same make. It had to be Yoav.

Tzehainish located herself on Google Maps and tried to figure out what the village in the distance was, but there was nothing marked on the phone. She wasn't surprised; so many of these little illegal-to-begin-with settlements just popped up on a hilltop, and they didn't make it onto the official maps until after the completion of the court process to legalize them retroactively (a process which invariably succeeded). But she could figure out roughly where the settlement was on the map interface, and was able to get Google to set up a route navigation to the "unknown pinned position" she'd indicated. Twenty-three minutes.

She started up her car and allowed Google's velvet smooth voice to navigate her into the heart of Nofei Itamar.

Chapter 28

L ike a nicotine addict who has been told that he must wait twenty years until his next cigarette, Yoav needed to breathe secondhand smoke every now and then. His secondhand smoke was being near the boy's home. Since transferring the baby to his new parents a couple of days ago, he had stopped every evening, on his way home, to look out at Nofei Itamar from the lay-by across the valley. At night you could make out the handful of shining lights of the homes of the settlement, and Yoav had figured out which one was the home of the baby and his family. Gazing out at the lights, oblivious to anything else around him – including Tzehainish – he imagined the scene inside the house. The pious mother and father, surrounding their new son with Jewish prayer and religious rituals. The volumes of Bible, Talmud and commentaries on the bookshelves that would be the scenery with which Israel's future leader would grow up. The songs around the shabbat table, the *shiurim*, study classes, that his father would hold, bouncing his son on his knee while he discussed the Torah's weekly reading... the new Hitler would have a solid Jewish background to match his political genius and military might; and, of course, the funds and political backing that Yoav and his colleagues would make sure the Jewish Hitler would be surrounded by. It was an irresistible combination. A combination that would lead to a new Israeli empire that would wreak destruction on its Arab neighbors and rule the region for a thousand years. Yoav watched the lights and let his soul gently sink into these visions of the future, like soaking in a hot bathtub. Even after just a few days, it had become a ritual for him. Almost like a daily prayer.

But he'd felt increasingly drawn to the settlement itself like a magnet. Twice he'd driven up to the entrance and turned around at the last minute. He had to get even closer. Closer to the house. Closer to the source of the nicotine. He just needed a waft, a taste, a glimpse. That would satisfy his cravings for now.

Yoav nodded at the guard as he drove through the still-makeshift entrance of the settlement. The dust of the unpaved road swirled around the car's tires, even at its slow pace down the main street toward the baby's house.

He'd sworn to himself that the parents would never meet him. It was too risky. If they started asking questions about the role that Yoav had played in the adoption, there was no way of knowing how that would play out. He couldn't take that chance. He had to remain anonymous. But he was desperate to see the child, as desperate as if it were his own flesh and blood who was being taken care of in this small pre-fab with its unkempt yard.

He pulled up some distance away, noticing several empty lots around the family's house. This couple were clearly one of the first to move in here: true Zionists, true pioneers, he thought to himself approvingly. He wound down the window and put an anxious hand out into the hot air.

Maybe it was a mistake coming here at this time of day. She won't take the baby out for a stroll in this heat. Next time I need to come in the early evening.

Next time... Yoav realized that this would be his life from now on. The project wasn't over; there was still much political work to do in order to prepare the ground for Israel's great leader. But the pace would be entirely different. Busy mornings in the Knesset, the Supreme Court, Army Headquarters, making sure that the Cause's footsoldiers were entrenched in every domain of public leadership; and then slow afternoons trying to catch a glimpse of the child running out of his kindergarten. He and Akiva had embarked on a project to defy time itself, and yet, in a sly and devastating irony, time itself now had the upper hand. *You will have to wait, my friend*, it hissed mockingly at Yoav. *You may be able to bring the dead back to life, but you cannot speed up the future. Before this child can lead Israel to its redemption, he will have to learn to crawl, to*

walk, pee in the toilet, learn to read, get acne, play soccer, do his high school exams...
all of these things must come first, and I, Time, I alone will make them happen.
You will have to wait for me.

The coming decades stretched ahead of Yoav like a prison sentence. In his
head he had developed a kind of advent calendar, each morning crossing off one
more day, one more slow, painfully slow day on the road toward redemption.

And Yoav also knew that he would be an old man by the time the fruits of his
work would begin to have a public impact. How old would this child be before
he was ready to lead Israel? Hitler had been forty-three when he'd taken control
of the Reichstag in 1933. Yoav couldn't wait another forty-three years. How old
would the Jewish Hitler have to be before he could take control of the reins of
state? Thirty? Was that realistic, was that even possible? Could this new Israeli
version, with Yoav's help behind the scenes, get to that level at that young age?
Deep down, Yoav's most troubling fear was that he would not live to see the day
when this Jewish Hitler would lead the people of Israel to their final victory.
Like Moses on Mount Nebo, he would see the promised land but not make it
in.

He pulled his attention back to the house in front of him. And then a minor
miracle happened. The door of the house opened, and the child's mother awkwardly backed out of it. As she turned around, Yoav saw that she was holding
a basket of wet clothes, presumably just removed from the washing machine;
but more importantly, she was wearing the baby in a sling, swaddled against her
breasts above the laundry basket.

She hobbled over to the clothes horse, which was standing in the sun a few
paces away from the house, and started hanging the clothes. She was singing
softly as she did it, and every now and then took a break from the laundry,
straightened her back, and rocked side to side for a few moments, rubbing the
baby's body through the sling.

Yoav was transfixed. It was like a scene from a nursery rhyme, a glimpse of
heaven, a sight of a simple but glorious quotidian. She was so happy. Even

from inside his car, twenty meters away, Yoav could feel the rays of love and tenderness and just utter, utter joy exuding from the woman. He nodded with satisfaction as he saw her put the laundry down again for a moment, pull the baby toward her and give him a kiss. Hitler had had a strong relationship with his mother, and he wanted this baby to have the same. At some point down the line, when the boy reached twelve, he would have to decide whether the boy's father should be killed, so that this child's nurture would mirror Hitler's. Yoav shrugged inwardly. There was plenty of time for him to make that decision.

He continued to gaze at the mother and her child, relieved that she was so engrossed in what she was doing that she hadn't noticed the stranger in the car gawking at her. He made a mental note to himself that the family probably didn't have a tumble dryer – this was fine during the summer, on a day like this, but in the winter months it would be a pain not having one. He would find a way for one to be donated to them. Denkstein would know how to organize this.

He took a deep breath, as if trying to inhale the beauty of this scene one last time before he left; one last hit of secondhand smoke before heading off for another day without it. He took a final look, and then quietly backed the car down the street a couple of houses, did a three-point turn, and drove out of the settlement, paying no attention to the young religious Ethiopian woman who was driving past in the opposite direction.

Along with her sandwiches and binoculars, Tzehainish had brought with her some other supplies for a day of sleuthing in the West Bank. She was wearing a long, flowing skirt and had a colorful head scarf wrapped around her hair. She looked the image of a nice, young, married Modern Orthodox woman.

As she pulled the car up to the soldier guarding the gate, she wound down the window and leaned out of it. "Morning," she smiled. "I heard amazing things about this new settlement, and I wanted to come and have a drive around. My husband and I are thinking about moving here. Okay with you?"

The soldier barely looked in her direction and waved her through. She parked her car not too far from where Yoav had just been. Unlike Yoav, Tzehainish didn't know where she was going or what exactly she was looking for. There were about twenty small houses laid out in an L-shape that was intended, presumably, to be the beginnings of the first streets of the new settlement. The road was gravel and unpaved, and the houses were pre-fab blocks that had been built in a factory elsewhere, brought here on trailers, and dumped in makeshift fashion. Each pre-fab sat in the middle of a little garden or yard, most of them still full of wild plants and bushes, but one or two, whose owners had apparently been a little more diligent in their first weeks in the settlement, showing signs of some tending and tilling.

Many of the yards had kids' toys strewn in them: tricycles and plastic cars and mini-climbing frames. Tzehainish was buoyed. This might still be a needle in a haystack, but it was a much smaller haystack.

A young woman of about her age was walking in her direction, pushing a stroller in front of her and holding a dog on a leash with the other hand. Tzehainish wandered toward her, smiling, and gave her the same story that she'd given the guard.

"And where are you living now?" asked the woman.

"Petach Tikvah," answered Tzehainish – this was a large, anonymous town in the center of Israel, and there was little chance of her being asked if she knew anyone there. "But, please God, we'll be moving out here to Samaria soon." *I may not be religious, but I know how to talk the talk.*

"With God's help," the woman smiled back at her.

"So tell me," said Tzehainish, "What kinds of people live here in the settlement?"

"Oh, all sorts," said the woman. "Mostly professionals who commute to Jerusalem or Tel Aviv: we have a couple of accountants, a few teachers, I think there's a guy who just moved in who's a lawyer, that's always handy! My neighbor does PR for a local winery, her husband is a graphic designer... so pretty much everything, really, thank God." The woman paused and adjusted something on the stroller. "All religious, of course," she added quickly.

"Thank God," echoed Tzehainish. "And... mostly young families, I guess? We don't have any children yet, but..." here Tzehainish lowered her voice for dramatic effect, "We're planning on starting soon!"

"With God's help," crooned the woman, gesturing with her eyes up to the sky. "Yes, all young families, lots of little kids running around. In fact just the other day we got one more! There was one couple who didn't have children, it was a terrible story, lovely couple, but for whatever reason she never managed to get pregnant. And then suddenly, last week, they managed to adopt a little baby boy, it was the most wonderful thing. You should see them now, they are so over the moon, thank God. Such a miracle!"

Tzehainish's pulse quickened. "What a wonderful story," she beamed. "Where do they live? I'd love to go wish them a mazal tov while I'm here, see if I can perform a little mitzvah and help the mother for five minutes."

"What a lovely gesture," said the woman, clutching her hands to her chest. "They're at that house on the corner."

Two minutes later, Tzehainish was knocking at the door. The door opened, and she gave her story for the third time that morning, adding that she'd been told by a neighbor about the great miracle that had happened to her and her husband. The middle-aged mother was friendly and bubbly and invited Tzehainish in.

"I've just put him down for a nap, but he's not asleep yet. Would you like to see him?" she asked.

"I would love to see him," breathed Tzehainish. The mother led her into a small bedroom, newly-painted with baby blue pastels and colorful pictures all over the walls. In the corner of the room was a crib, in which a one-week-old baby was lying.

Tzehainish looked down at the baby. *Could it be...?*

"Would you like to hold him?" asked the mother. "Never too early to start practicing, you know!"

"Would I like to hold him?" murmured Tzehainish. She paused. Something inside her wanted to scream and run out of this room and out of this house as quickly as she could, but she held it in. She knew what the correct answer had to be. "I would love to hold him!"

The mother picked up the child and handed her to Tzehainish. She held the baby, rocking him gently in her arms. The infant looked up at her. It had clear, piercing blue eyes, like the sky, like the sea. Tzehainish gazed at them and something deep inside her felt a pull of gravity into them. Her head spun as if eddying into a whirlpool, being sucked greedily into the baby's eyes like a crumbling star into a black hole. She blinked and snapped herself back. For a moment she considered trying to run out with the baby – perhaps she could push the mother out of the way, get to her car... but no, it was impossible. The mother would shriek, the neighbors would hear, the guard would stop her...

She gave the baby back to the mother and smiled. "He's very cute," she said. "Very cute."

"Thank God," said the mother, beaming.

"Thank God," repeated Tzehainish.

Two hours later, she was in her car driving back to Tel Aviv. She called Hadas on the Bluetooth.

"Hadas," she said, "I've found the baby."

Chapter 29

Hadas looked at Akiva and mouthed almost the same words: "She's found the baby." Then, back on the phone to Tzehainish: "Where? Wait, I'm with Akiva. I'm putting you on speakerphone."

Tzehainish continued: "In the middle of the West Bank. A small illegal settlement not far from Ofra. I'll send you a pin of the exact location. The child seems to have been adopted by a childless couple who are connected to Yoav's old yeshivah. I met the mother, I wandered round the neighborhood and spoke to a couple of other neighbors. Found out that there was a bris in Har Daniel a few days ago, so I went there too, pretending to be the wife of a friend of one of the students, and found a secretary there with a big mouth who filled in more details. Apparently the food for the bris was donated by a 'delightful yeshivah alumnus,' one Yoav Schindler, would you believe. Zipped to the local Interior Ministry branch, did some digging around there, the adoption records are all in order, but the child's biological parents are listed as unknown. It's got to be the one."

"Great," said Hadas, giving Akiva a clenched fist of victory. "Amazing work. As usual. I owe you one."

"You owe me more than one," said Tzehainish. "I've been masquerading as a religious settler in the middle of Palestine the whole day."

"I always knew you had it in you," grinned Hadas. "Listen – go home. You've endangered yourself enough already. I won't have you exposed for whatever happens now. I am forever grateful, Tzehainish."

Hadas hung up, and looked at Akiva.

"So," she mused, rubbing her hands together, re-energized. "Now we know where they are. How do we get to them? How do we get the child back?"

Akiva was slumped in bed, on top of the comforter, surfing mindlessly on his laptop. He closed it and slung it carelessly to one side, unmoved by Hadas's enthusiasm. "That's the difficult part. I've thought through every angle, but I'm out of ideas."

"I'll do it," said Hadas, jumping up to her feet and starting to pace excitedly. "I don't know how, but I'll do it."

"Out of the question. If you get caught, your career is over. I can't let that happen. I won't have that on my conscience."

Hadas frowned and slowed her pace a bit, brow furrowed as she calculated the different options. "You're right. But you can't do it either. The moment you come out of hiding, Yoav will try to kill you again. And if you set one foot in that settlement, it'll be like you're lighting a flare and shouting to him 'over here, over here.' You can't be involved in this stage."

"Speaking of which – what am I going to do about Yoav? You said that getting the child back would give me leverage, but I'm not so sure. He'll keep coming after me. I won't be able to hide from him forever. He'll find me and the baby in California, or anywhere else we go... and then..." Akiva put his face in his hands. Every time he thought about the threat to his life, it singed every nerve in his body, constricted every muscle.

A depressing silence hung between them. A conversation between two chambermaids drifted past from the hotel corridor.

"Unless..." murmured Hadas, stopping in her tracks and rubbing her temples. "Unless... Yoav could somehow think that the baby had *died*... if he thought that the baby was dead, then the project would be over, come what may, and you might just be able to disappear..."

"But I want that baby alive."

"Yes, I know you do... but Yoav has to think it's dead..."

Hadas's voice tailed off and her face went white.

"What?" said Akiva.

Hadas didn't respond. The idea that had just come to her was insane, dangerous, incredibly risky – but it might be the only way. The pieces weren't quite all in place, though... unless... *yes, that might work...*

"What?" Akiva asked again.

Hadas took a deep breath. "I know how it could get done. You wait here. I'll call you. I need to speak with Omar."

The journey from Omar's office in East Jerusalem to the Valley of the Cross by the Knesset took twenty minutes, and most of that was spent stuck in traffic. Some days it would literally have been quicker to walk. The geographical distance between these two peoples, he often thought to himself, was so small, and yet the psychological distance was so vast. He had heard it said that New York was not a city but a collection of villages. Well, in that case, Omar thought to himself, Jerusalem was not a city, it was a collection of universes. And in some parts of Jerusalem you just had to cross the street to enter a different universe.

And so he drove out from Salah-A-Din street, past the American Colony Hotel, the grand old lady of Palestinian tourism, the accommodation of choice for countless Arab and Western-Arabist VIPs over the decades. From there, he turned onto the main Bar-Lev road, which ran parallel to the old pre-1967 border: the Green Line. To his left, the universe of Arab East Jerusalem. To his right, the universe of the Ultra-Orthodox Meah Shearim. From Palestinian hustle and bustle to 18th century Poland in a few steps. He continued driving, leaving the Old City walls behind him, suddenly entering yet another universe: modern West Jerusalem, a burger bar on every corner. Somehow, his philanthropy and his political activism would bring all these universes into dialogue and fruitful co-existence. The alternative – the continuation of the present's fragmentation and disintegration – was too terrifying to bear.

He parked his car at the Israel Museum and walked a few minutes through the footpaths of the Valley of the Cross. Hadas's message had been cryptic, but he trusted her that the words "I need you. 1 hour. Usual place." were to be taken quite literally.

They embraced. For once, Hadas didn't cut it short as she usually did in public. She held on to him, pressing her face into his neck, breathing him in, locking her hands around his back as if to straitjacket him. She didn't want to let him go, couldn't let him go. It was as if his being part of this situation had made their relationship more real, and that, coupled with what she knew she was about to ask of him, was turning her love for him into something more than just abstract love: into true interdependency, partnership, shared dreams, shared life. Before she knew it, she'd grabbed Omar's face in both her hands and was kissing him all over, his lips, his eyes, his cheeks.

"Steady on, old girl!" Omar's British persona defaulted into place. "PDA and all that, you know. Not cricket. Can't let the *hoi polloi* find out about your little bit of Lawrence of Arabia on the side, can we?" It was silly, this whole British exaggeration, he knew it, but Hadas found it funny, and he loved that she found it funny. He loved making her laugh. Making Hadas laugh was quite simply the most incredible thing he'd ever experienced, and he wanted to spend his life doing it.

"I don't care. Today, I don't care," said Hadas, not letting go, continuing to kiss him and pull his face towards her.

Omar switched to Arabic. "*Ana bahebek, ya malaki.*" *I love you, my angel.*

Their kisses gave way to smiles, the smiles back to kisses.

They finally disengaged, and Hadas wiped her face. Omar looked quizzically at her. "Let's sit," she said. "Tzehainish has found the baby. But there's something I need your help with now."

Neither Hadas nor Omar noticed the person with the binoculars watching them from a distance.

Chapter 30

Almost twenty-four hours later, Omar made an even shorter journey from East Jerusalem, to a hotel that stood at the beginning of King David street, only a few meters from the walls of the Old City.

Omar always dressed to kill, but when he made these trips to West Jerusalem hotels, he made even more of an effort. If the security guard at the hotel entrance thought he was a guest, or a well-appointed visitor coming to spend money in the hotel's lobby cafe, then he'd glide through. The problems began when he was asked for his *te'udat z'hut* – his ID document. This immediately revealed that he was an East Jerusalem Palestinian, and that meant he was in for an extended conversation with the guard, the guard's supervisor, and the hotel manager.

"We're sure you understand, sir, that the security of our guests has to be our highest priority."

"We hope you don't mind co-operating as we scan you with a handheld metal detector."

"We'd like to ask you to kindly remove your shoes so that we can examine them."

"Do you know how much these shoes cost?" Omar always wanted to say. But he never did. It was just easier and quicker to swallow your pride, let them do their thing, let them be convinced that you weren't a terrorist, and then walk into the hotel, up to the room, take off those expensive shoes and clothes, and make love to your beautiful Jewish Israeli Member of Knesset girlfriend.

On this occasion, though, the guard wasn't interested in him, and he walked straight past.

"Ironic," Omar thought to himself, "Given that today, for the first time ever, I *am* actually entering this hotel with terrorist business on my mind..."

After meeting Hadas the previous day, Omar had got to work. He had called Ali and told him that a situation had arisen that might enable Hassan Khoury to pay him back the favor sooner than had been expected. He would meet with Ali soon and explain everything, but in the meantime, Ali should clear his schedule for the next day or two.

Once inside the hotel, Omar ambled over to the elevators, and double-checked the SMS that he'd received from Hadas:

Citadel. 14:00. Room 347.

He knocked on the door, and after a short pause, it opened. Akiva grasped Omar's arm gratefully and beckoned him into the room. Hadas moved the hotel room desk and chair over to end of the bed, creating three seats in rough parallel. She sat herself in the chair. Akiva and Omar sat next to each other, semi-uncomfortably, on the bed. Hadas booted her laptop and positioned it so that all three of them could see it. She opened up Google Maps, and played with the mouse until she had the zoom that she wanted.

"Let's get straight to it," she said briskly. "Here's the settlement where the child is located. It's so new and so illegal that it doesn't even appear on Google Maps or anything else official. But it's here, on this part of the hilltop by Beit Furik. That's the Palestinian village nearby. There's a dirt track that leads there from the main road. That's the only way in or out."

"What about the army?" asked Akiva, peering anxiously at the screen. "Do they patrol the area? They could cause us problems too."

Hadas shook her head. She'd anticipated the question, anticipated Akiva's nervousness, anticipated how to respond. She was doing what she did best: leading. "Minimal. Guard at the entrance. Apart from that, nothing."

"So the IDF knows about an illegal settlement and collaborates with the settlers to keep it secret..." mused Omar.

"Not the first time, not the tenth time, and not the last time," said Hadas.

Omar folded his arms and sniffed loudly. "Those sons of..."

Hadas put her hand on Omar's knee. "Enough," she said. "We're not doing politics now. We're doing action." She had the steely look in her eye again, and Omar snapped back to focus.

Hadas turned to Akiva. "We're going to retrieve the baby under the pretense of a terrorist attack."

"A *what*?" sputtered Akiva.

"It's simple and effective," noted Omar dryly. "What would arouse less suspicion than a Palestinian terrorist attack on an isolated Jewish settlement in the middle of the West Bank? It happens all the time."

Akiva shook his head in incredulity. "And you think *I'm* crazy?"

Omar raised his trademark eyebrow. "I do want to point out that this was not my idea, but rather that of my Jewish Israeli parallel universe wife."

Hadas explained the plan that she'd come up with. Omar would get in touch with what he called his "colleagues of colleagues" in the West Bank. Omar knew that this meant Hassan Khoury, but he had not revealed that name to Hadas; even she would find it beyond the pale to think that one of Hamas's most wanted terrorists was now their accomplice. Omar would tell Khoury, through Ali and his intermediaries, that he had discovered a terrible tragedy had taken place: a Palestinian baby had been abandoned by its mother who, fearing that she did not have the means to support him, had left the newborn on the doorstep of a health clinic in West Jerusalem. This baby had been taken in by the Israeli authorities and put up for adoption, and was now being raised by religious Jewish settlers in the West Bank. The mother, regretting her actions, had sought out Omar, as a well-known leader of the Jerusalem Palestinian community, to ask for his help in getting the child back. Omar would tell Ali that he did not want to get lawyers and courts involved, as that process could take years, and the mother wanted her baby back now, while it was still an infant, not in three or four years as a religious, Jewish, Hebrew-speaking toddler – that would be unthinkable.

Omar would suggest the following plan to Ali, who would pass it on to Hassan Khoury: have a couple of Khoury's men infiltrate the settlement and kidnap the baby under the pretense of a terrorist attack. They would then pass on the baby to Omar, who would, unbeknownst to them, transfer it back to Akiva.

"This sounds... incredibly risky," said Akiva, nervously grinding his knuckles together. "What if these people get connected back to you? To us?"

Omar got up off the edge of the bed and paced around the room, hands in his pockets. He rubbed his tongue around the inside of his mouth, ruminating on how to phrase his answer. "As you know, Akiva, I have always tried to straddle many worlds. I work tirelessly for peace and co-existence, I have done business with Israelis my entire life, and I have many Israeli friends. But I have always made sure to remain deeply connected to the Palestinian community, and not just to the secular left-leaning Israelified branches of it. I am not a terrorist, do not condone terrorism, and fervently wish that one day we will see two states here, side by side, with peace, prosperity and freedom for both peoples, but I also deeply believe in my people. *I love my people.* And I am... forgiving... of those who allow the frustrating, painful, absolute bloody *shittiness* of the Occupation to lead them into... dark corners. And so, yes, I joke about my 'colleagues of colleagues,' but that is a reality."

He paused, aware that what he was about to say would be difficult for Hadas to hear. He bent down to the mini-bar, pulled out a can of Coke, popped the tab, and took a long swig, searching for the most difficult of words, the hardest thing he'd ever had to say to Hadas. "I have contacts with people... who have contacts with people... who would seek to kill both of you for being Israelis. For being Jews, perhaps. One day, people like me will need to lead my people into a détente with Jewish Israelis. I'll only be able to do that if I have bona fides in my community. As unpleasant as that is, as morally compromised as that is, it's the reality." He gazed at Akiva, unable to make eye contact with Hadas, wondering how what he'd said would play out in her head. Wondering if this would be too much for her.

Akiva wiggled back on the bed, taking advantage of the space that Omar had left. "What you've said is hard to take in. But I'm the last person in this room who should be criticizing someone else for living a double life." He paused. He could sense a tense silence from Hadas, a silence that he needed to fill. "Go on, Omar. You still haven't answered my question. Can your connection through these 'colleagues of colleagues' be traced?"

Omar took another swig of Coke, stalling for time again. He took a deep breath. "My contact is extraordinarily discreet. I trust him fully. I have done all kinds of things in the past – perhaps never going quite as far as this, but in business terms, things that have asked people to betray their clans, to risk their livelihoods, to do things that, if discovered, would lead to them being rejected by everyone they love. I will not tell my contact any more details than he needs to know, and when he speaks to *his* contacts, he will not reveal that anything comes from me. I am quite safe. And therefore so are you."

Another long silence prevailed, as Hadas and Akiva digested what Omar had said. Hadas spasmed with emotional agony. This was all her plan, her idea, she'd put Omar in this position, but still, hearing Omar say this kind of thing so openly was a new experience. She trembled with a sudden need to hug him, to feel the real Omar against her body, the Omar she knew, not this Omar who spoke of terrorists and Occupation and dark corners. But she stayed seated, outwardly calm, professional. Leaderly.

Eventually Akiva spoke up again. "The baby's adoptive parents – they're an innocent couple – they must be unharmed. This is clear, yes?"

Omar finished the Coke and threw it in the trash. "They will have to be, um, roughed up a bit," he grimaced. "The attack will have to look authentic. But the terrorists will be given strict instructions to retrieve the baby, and leave the parents alive. They will follow these orders."

An appalling insight overcame Akiva with crushing force. "They'll be alive, but they'll be devastated, won't they?" he said, his voice cracking. He shut his eyes. The words were too awful to contemplate, too awful to say, but he had to say them. "They will have lost their new baby. Their life will never be the same again."

"I know," choked Hadas, as the full impact of the shocking idea she'd come up with began to carve itself into her consciousness. "But I can't see any other way of doing it. If the baby remains with its parents, you will forever remain a threat to Yoav's project, and he will not stop trying to kill you, and at some point, he *will* succeed. The only way we can save your life is to get that baby back." She sighed painfully, alienated by the words she had just heard herself articulate, words her head knew to be true, but words that corroded something deep in her heart. Omar reached over to her and held her hand in support.

Akiva cupped his face, and then looked up again. "But the whole of Israel is going to be up in arms about this kidnapped baby. I can just imagine the headlines. We don't want a repeat of 2014."

In 2014, three Israeli boys had been kidnapped while hitch-hiking in the West Bank. It was later found out that they'd been murdered almost immediately, but until their bodies were found, the whole of Israel was in uproar about it, with campaigns to find the kidnappers and "bring our boys back home." The event had been one of the major precipitators of Operation Protective Edge and the war between Israel and Gaza.

"You're right to ask the question," said Hadas, elbowing her internal concerns to the side and refocusing on the needs of the moment. "The public – and even more so, Yoav – need to believe that the baby was *killed*, not kidnapped, so that there will be no attempt to find it, and so that Yoav will abandon his efforts to kill you. We have a plan for how to do that. What works in our favor is that we know that Yoav used all kinds of fake documents and certificates. Tzehainish's digging has revealed that the child is registered with the population registry, but not yet fully registered with the health authorities. So there aren't clear records of its blood type, or anything else that could identify it forensically."

Akiva furrowed his brow. "I'm not following you. Why does that matter? The baby will be missing, and enough neighbors and friends will know that they had a new baby. Adopted or not, on the grid or not, there will still be an outcry."

Hadas looked at Akiva and held his gaze. "The baby will not be missing," she said.

"I don't understand."

"There will be a body, found a few hours later in a field near the settlement. It will not be your Hitler baby's body, but there will be a body. The body of a newborn baby. Butchered and burned beyond recognition."

"Another baby... what baby? I don't get it."

Omar cleared his throat and began pacing again. "The advantage of our little, um, cover story for my colleagues is that it's based on a real and known phenomenon: Arab babies abandoned by their mothers after birth. Teenage girls who get into trouble, or rape victims, or incest victims. They hide their pregnancies, don't want people to know that their honor has been destroyed, somehow manage to give birth on their own. Often neither the mother nor baby survive. But sometimes they do, and then the mother gets rid of the baby somehow. Babies like this are found outside hospitals, on street corners, outside churches or mosques, every few weeks. Usually, by the time they're found, the babies are already dead. It's a dirty open secret in our community. It's a terrible phenomenon. It breaks my heart. I fund an NGO that seeks to educate about this problem in our community. But... one of these abandoned dead babies can serve a larger purpose. My people will keep their ears peeled for a newborn baby who has been abandoned and did not survive. They'll take possession of the body, take it with them, and, once they have... um... 'our baby'... they will take the dead Palestinian baby's body to a field near the settlement, butcher it, and burn it there. There will be an outcry, and yes, the parents will be utterly devastated forever. That is certainly a sin... a crime... an indelible stain on our consciences that we will all have to live with for the rest of our lives. But it will cover our tracks. It will save your life. Yoav will think the baby is dead."

Akiva put his head in his hands and said nothing. Hadas and Omar exchanged glances. Omar made as if to say something, but Hadas almost imperceptibly shook her head. They waited.

Akiva finally lifted his head up, his body sapped of energy, his eyes bleary. His whole torso contorted in pain. A tear ran down his cheek. He shook his head. "What am I doing...?" he whispered. "What am I becoming...?" *It's not worth it any more. It's not worth the pain.*

Hadas put her hand on his knee and squeezed. "Uncle," she said softly. "It's the only way. We will all have to live with it. We will have to bear the guilt. It's the only way to save our lives, to save our plan."

Akiva looked up at Hadas through his tears. "'*Our*' plan?"

Hadas looked at Akiva for a long time but said nothing.

She squeezed Akiva's knee again. "*Your* plan. *Our* lives. Let's just focus on that for now."

Chapter 31

H adas and Omar would go about their regular business until Omar got the call. Nothing could begin until a suitable abandoned Palestinian newborn baby could be found. Once that happened, everything would be set in motion. The two Palestinian terrorists would take the dead baby and, after nightfall, drive in a stolen Israeli vehicle to Nofei Itamar. They would quietly cut through the settlement's perimeter fence, break into the family's house, rough up the parents, kidnap the baby, and drive off. They would then find a nearby field and do the necessary actions on the dead, abandoned Palestinian baby, making it easy enough to be found by passers-by in the morning light. Omar's contact (Ali, whose name or precise connection to him Omar would still not reveal to Hadas) would then meet the terrorists on a quiet road nearby, take the baby, pay them off, and then drive to another pre-arranged quiet spot where Omar would be waiting. Omar would take the baby, and drive back to Jerusalem (he'd got himself a rental car while he looked for a new one to replace the one that Hadas had trashed the other day); with his permanent Jerusalem residency ID, there would be no problem getting through the checkpoint, and he'd just pass off the baby as his own. Once in Jerusalem, he'd liaise with Hadas and Akiva, who would take possession of the baby.

"And then you get the hell out of the country, Akiva," said Hadas. "You take the baby, and go far, far away. Yoav will think the baby is dead. Even if his tentacles do have international reach, he won't have any reason to seek you out any more. As far as he will be concerned, his plan will be over. Maybe he'll have suspicions that you were somehow connected to the terrorist attack – it will be a pretty big coincidence, after all – but he'll have no proof, no baby, and no reason to go after you. But you'll still need to lie low for many, many years."

Omar and Hadas had gone over the plan a dozen times, and it seemed watertight. Sitting with Akiva now in another hotel room, they went over each detail with him: perhaps his fresh eyes would see something they had overlooked.

"I can't... it's not right... I still feel terrible about this couple – the adoptive parents," moaned Akiva. He rubbed his eyes roughly, creating a kaleidoscope of black and red and blue, willing the colors to coalesce into a different picture, a different way of doing it. "We're going to ruin their lives. They waited all this time for a baby, they finally got one, and now they're going to think it was murdered. It's too awful for words."

Hadas didn't respond. Omar stayed silent in the corner, looking out of the window at the lights of Jerusalem outside.

Akiva looked at Hadas for a long time through his bloodshot eyes. He shook his head gently. "I've always been so proud of you. I remember the bold, confident, happy-go-lucky girl who I met in London all those years ago. I remember how this girl grew into a soldier, a journalist, a public figure, a politician. All the while I was so happy to be connected to you, so moved to be your secret uncle. And here we are. We sit in a hotel room, with disposable cups of coffee at our table, collaborating with terrorists, planning to destroy the lives of innocent people, as if we were discussing the tactics of a soccer team or the strategy of a political campaign."

"Enough, Akiva!" Hadas banged her fist on the table, and one of the coffee cups spilled a little from the vibration. She looked at Akiva with barely-concealed fury. *Why the hell couldn't he see what needed to be done? It was shit, but it was necessary. It was the way to get the result they needed.* "This *is* a political campaign. You set this in motion the moment you agreed to collaborate with Yoav. And the moment you told me about this project of yours, you turned me into a collaborator too. So yes, this is a political campaign, but it's also a military

233

campaign, *because our lives are at stake*, so now is the time for strength, Akiva. This is a shitty situation, but there is a way out, a way back to our normal lives, a way back to the plan – to *your* plan – and there are steps that need to be taken in order to get there. So enough! Yes, these Palestinian terrorists who we don't know are going to beat up two people who have done nothing wrong, they are going to make this poor couple think that their child has been murdered, this wretched couple who have waited all their lives for a child, and who are now going to be utterly devastated when that miracle is cruelly taken away from them, and all of this is going to happen because Yoav has *forced* us into this situation, Akiva, because this is the only way we can *save your life*. And save my life too, probably. I can live with that, Akiva. You need to be able to live with it too."

Akiva pulled his shirt up over his face, breathing in his fading deodorant, burrowing into a moment of silence. He pulled it down again and ruffled his hands through some wisps of hair. "I know you're right. I can't stand it, I can barely breathe because of it, but I accept that you are right. Okay. So what now? We wait? Any day now you'll get the call, Omar?"

"Any day now," said Omar. "Until then, we wait."

Chapter 32

The waiting time was surreal. Hadas went back to her work in the Knesset, mostly remaining cloistered in her own small private office, studiously avoiding Benny, and giving hushed updates to Tzehainish. The child benefits bill was making progress and she had finally found some partners in the Ultra-Orthodox party who seemed willing to work with her; perhaps she'd have to compromise on one or two aspects of the bill, but its prospects of passing had never seemed higher. A week ago, this would have filled Hadas with joy, but now, she had to fake that joy while her insides were in turmoil. Every time the phone rang, she jumped. Most of the time, though, it was Akiva.

"So how is today's hotel?"

"Pretty much the same as the last one. Still no news?"

"No news. Stay holed up in the room. No going out on the street, no taking any chances."

"Until our new terrorist friends spring into action..."

"Akiva, stop," said Hadas. "You can't think about that."

Akiva sighed heavily, his breath hissing through the phone line. "So you keep telling me. 'We just have to do what needs to be done.' The ends justify the means, right?" He gave a mirthless chuckle. "Yoav would approve."

"You have to fight fire with fire," said Hadas. "The moment you show weakness, Yoav will exploit it, and you'll be dead."

Akiva's tension flooded through the phone. The click-click-click of his shoes on the parquet as he paced, the tap-tap-tap of his fingers on the window, the line crackling with the scratching of his hands as he tried to scrape the nerves out of his hair. "So I have to *become* Yoav in order to beat Yoav?" asked Akiva. "Is it worth it? What will that do to me if I go down that road? Once I do that, can I turn back?"

"Maybe. I don't know. Maybe you can do it temporarily. Become Yoav, win this fight, and then get back to being Akiva for the longer battle."

Hadas moved the phone from one ear to the other. She looked at the pile of parliamentary papers strewn on her desk, papers that represented her future, a future that her relationship with Akiva was now putting in jeopardy. "You're the one who believes that people can change," she persisted. "That the past doesn't define us. So maybe this is the moment *you* need to change. Become ruthless. Win. Then change back."

"I'm beginning to wonder if I've been wrong about all the nature and nurture stuff. Maybe change isn't so easy."

"Look... I have to go," said Hadas. "I'll call you if I have any updates."

Akiva continued to speak into the empty phone line. "Maybe... maybe I'll always be Akiva..."

Omar had the easiest time of the three of them. The situation with Hassan Khoury's son had calmed, and the boy had moved back home. Omar had made sure that a rumor about his role in the events, and his help for Hamas's leader, was leaked, and this had done wonders to his credibility in some quarters. As he did his occasional factory tours in the days after the leak, he enjoyed the warm handshakes and new-found looks of admiration from some of the middle managers who had previously been a bit standoffish. No-one said anything up front, of course, and Omar certainly made no mention of the rumors, but he did pop one or two more *Alhamdulillahs* into his conversations than usual.

"And they said I wasn't a good enough actor for the lead role in the Christmas

Play at Harrow," he murmured to himself.

Omar was patient. He and Ali spoke every day, but strictly about business. Omar knew that once Ali had set things in motion, it would happen in due course. "*Sumud*," he said to Hadas in one of their phone conversations, while she was telling him how antsy she was. "It's the Arabic word for patience. Our "colleagues" use it to talk about how they need *sumud* to wait for the time when the Jewish presence here will finally be eradicated. They think in terms of years, decades even. All you need, my dear, is just a tad of *sumud* for a few more days. Just a spoonful of *sumud*. Ah, my dear, it's just like Julie Andrews sang, remember? Oh just a spoonful of *sumud* makes the Zionists go down, the Zionists go down, the..."

But Hadas had already hung up on him.

"I'm going to need more staff," said Yoav.

"I am beginning to wonder whether the issue is the need for more staff," said Gravelly Voice. "Or perhaps it is the *senior staff* of this operation that needs refreshing."

"Sir, I know this is taking longer than we expected but the way forward is clear. Perhaps if we could meet together I could explain the–"

"We don't meet face to face," interrupted Gravelly. "Ever. You know that. I need plausible deniability. Those have been our operating procedures since day one. No face to face meetings, phone calls always on a secure line. I know very well what you look like, and you know very well what I look like. That is enough."

"Of course," said Yoav quickly. "I didn't mean to–"

"For what purpose do you desire more staff?" interrupted Gravelly again.

"Since the other night in Tel Aviv, he's disappeared," said Yoav. "He's staying in hotels, but every time we pick up a lead, when we go to check it out, he's no longer there. I assume he's moving from location to location every day. He's... smarter than I thought. But it's a small country, and there are only so many hotels. More if you count the AirBnBs, but still, we're talking about a few hundred sites total. Thirty extra staff, plus my core team of ten, each person visits, say, twenty sites per day, that gives us eyes on every single accommodation in the country, every day. We can quiz staff with Akiva's photo, and in most places we'll be able to set up a small spy cam or two in public areas. It's just a numbers game now. Percentages. With thirty extra staff I can guarantee that we'll locate him."

"And where do you suggest I procure these thirty people? I'm not an employment agency, and we are talking about people with a very particular set of skills and a need for absolute discretion."

"I thought... I thought you could have a word with... you know... your..."

"The Prime Minister?" said Gravelly. "You want me to bring *the Prime Minister of Israel* into this mess? To risk that kind of exposure? As far as he's concerned this is just a small, isolated murder enquiry that is providing the press with its weekly feeding frenzy. If he, or anyone around him, gets a whiff of my involvement, they will very quickly start asking difficult questions that I really have no desire to answer."

"Make up a story," persisted Yoav. Even with someone like Gravelly Voice, he knew how to be persuasive, how to force his ending on the chess game. "Hang it on Akiva's father. You know, want to end it quickly so that the Party isn't damaged by the publicity, something like that."

Gravelly paused. "It's a plausible line, I suppose." Another pause. "Fine. I'll make it happen. But I will frame it as a demand to support the police in their work. Nobody reports to you directly. You get all the information and surveillance data via Moshe."

"Thank you," said Yoav, hiding the relief from his voice. "You won't regret it."

"I already do," said Gravelly. "Make sure that *you* don't regret it as well."

◈

Two days later, the cool East Jerusalem early morning air flooded through the window of Omar's bedroom as his phone blared. Groggy from the rude awakening, he reached across instinctively for Hadas, but she wasn't there. Of course... she was never there in the mornings. Every morning he woke up missing her presence, aching to feel her warm body next to his. The pang of her absence snapped him into consciousness with a jolt and he answered the phone. It was Ali.

"Yes, my friend," said Omar into the phone. He listened for a few more moments, and then responded: "Correct. The place where we agreed. And the sum that we agreed. I'll see you there when it's over. But remember: just you, and you alone. You are the go-between. It is good for me to be associated with Hamas, but not with the people on the front lines. In this regard, Ali, you are both my PR man and my alibi, and I have paid you well for this complex position over the years. *Please allow me to continue to treat you with this kindness.*"

Omar meant these last words as... not a threat, exactly, but a reminder of the hierarchy between him and Ali. He listened as Ali protested his undying loyalty to him and his guarantee of discretion.

"Good," said Omar. "So just you. No-one else can know about this. Ever."

He listened again, and nodded into the phone. "*Aiwa, habibi.*" *Indeed, my friend.* "I wish us many future collaborations together."

He ended the phone call, and lay back down, head ensconced in his luxurious pillow, staring at the ceiling, suddenly shivering with loneliness.

Then he called Hadas. "We're on. They'll be on their way there this evening, as soon as it's dark. Tell your uncle."

"Are you okay, love?" asked Hadas. "No jokes about packages being delivered or goods in transit?"

"No jokes now," said Omar. "Even I can't find this funny."

239

By early afternoon the summer sun was beating down, magnified by the build-ings' Jerusalem stone, searing the air. A few hours after Omar received his call, Yoav received one too. He listened intently for a minute or so. Then: "Excellent work. Which hotel?"

-"And you're sure he's there now?"

-"And you have no idea who they are? These two others who are with him?"

Yoav furrowed his brow. *Who on earth could be helping Akiva? What had he missed?*

-"Your man who reported this to you – okay, sorry, woman – has she reported it as a confirmed identification?"

-"Excellent. Get back to her. Tell her that it's a false ID. Not the right guy, she should keep looking. And that's how you file it."

-"I don't give a shit about your procedures, Moshe. Figure something out."

-"Good. You keep going, keep searching, as if he's still missing. Keep your people on the job."

-"Until I say so. Yes, all of them."

-"Thank you, Moshe. Well done. I won't forget this and neither will my boss."

Yoav hung up, and then briskly dialed another number. Things were falling back into place.

"I have a positive ID on his location. One of the Jerusalem hotels. I'll text you the address. Apparently he's with two other unknowns. No, I've no clue. Doesn't matter, whoever they are they're expendable too. But I don't want to touch them in the hotel. Stay on them. Put a spy cam in the corridor so you see exactly when they leave. We'll take them out on the road."

Yoav hung up. He would wait to call Gravelly until it was over. It wouldn't be long now.

The day's heat had given way to a cool Jerusalem evening, the air sweet with the aromas of *knafeh* and *baklava* from the street stalls. The tense silence in Akiva's hotel room was broken only by the occasional sounds of the city drifting upwards through the plated glass. Akiva lay on the sofa, occasionally putting on his ear plugs and eye mask and descending into his own inner world for a few minutes (he had had no choice but to let Omar and Hadas in on this emotional need of his), then sitting up again, looking at Hadas and Omar, and then burying his head in his hands. Hadas paced. Omar gazed out of the window, motionless and emotionless.

Akiva's digital watch beeped 7:00 pm. He looked down at it, then looked up from his reverie. "You're sure they understand the plan, Omar?"

"They know, they know," said Omar, not moving his gaze. "Be patient. They can't just waltz in like they're UPS. If they get caught trying to get into the settlement, then this whole thing falls apart, so let's just trust them to... do their job... As soon as I get the call from them, I will head off to meet my contact. The plan is a good plan, let's just stick to it."

At around 7:30 the call came in. Omar listened intently, occasionally interrupting to ask some questions in Arabic. Suddenly he looked concerned, and his voice was raised, with a tinge of panic in it.

Akiva got off the bed and stood by Hadas, silently seeking explanation, but receiving only a shake of the head.

"Something's wrong," she whispered. She tapped Omar on the arm, but he gestured her away, speaking slowly and earnestly into the phone. Finally, he took the phone away from his ear, pressed end, and carefully put it back in his front right trouser pocket. He continued looking out of the window and then leaned his forehead against it, hands pressed against the glass, like an Ultra-Orthodox Jew at the Western Wall.

Hadas moved towards him and grabbed his shoulder. "What? What is it?"

Omar still said nothing. He shrugged off Hadas's hand and turned to face her. His lips were quivering and his eyes were suddenly bloodshot.

She reached out and held his hands with hers. "Omar? What's the matter? I've never seen you like this before. Talk to me."

"It's gone wrong," rasped Omar. "Terribly wrong. The terrorists infiltrated the settlement and got into the house. But... it seems that while they were roughing up the parents, the father fought back more... assertively... than they were expecting. It's hard for me to piece together the details from what he told me just now, but the bottom line is that they've... they've..."

"No," said Hadas. "No. Don't say it. Please don't say it."

Omar couldn't make eye contact with either Akiva or Hadas. "They've killed the parents."

Chapter 33

"Oh my God," shuddered Hadas, putting her hand to her mouth. "Oh my God oh my God oh my God..."

Akiva collapsed to the floor. "I... I can't..." He tried to breathe in but his body wouldn't respond to him, his lungs couldn't suck in air, his throat tightened as if throttled by an assassin's hands. He tried to pull himself up to a seated position, but he was shaking and sweating and his hands grasped at thin air.

Omar reached down to help him but Akiva scrambled up and began flailing his arms at him. "You told me they would be unharmed! Did you know? Were you lying to me? You've turned me into a murderer!" Akiva was shouting at Omar now, pushing him back to the wall of the room. "What have you done, Omar, what you have done!"

Omar raised his hands to his face, defending himself from Akiva's attacks. "I wasn't lying," he shouted back over Akiva's cries. "I give you my word, I wasn't lying, I thought it would be okay, I told them that they should just rough them up to make it look realistic, I gave explicit instructions that they were to be left alive! I was assured this would be the case! I've been lied to as well!" He spun away from Akiva, pushing him onto the bed, and then collapsed back against the wall, legs giving way beneath him. "I've turned myself into a murderer too, you think I like that? You think I wanted that? It's everything I've spent my whole life struggling against! And I wouldn't even be in this bloody mess if it weren't for you!"

Akiva sat on the bed, breathing heavily but motionless. Finally, he managed to grate out some words: "We've killed innocent people... *I've* killed innocent people..." His cheeks were hot with tears. "What have we become? What have I done? This project was meant to be about bringing an end to killing, not turning us into murderers too. It's not just Yoav I've turned into, I've turned into Hitler himself. I've brought him back to life, I've outwitted time, I've outwitted God himself, and now as some kind of cosmic irony, I've turned into Hitler."

Hadas sat on the bed next to him, and tears were running down her cheeks too. "I'm so sorry, Uncle. It was my idea. I thought... I thought..." She reached over to hug him, but he shook her away.

"Don't touch me, I'm Hitler, I'm Hitler, I'm Hitler!" he shouted. He fell backward onto the bed. "I'm Hitler, I'm Hitler..." he mumbled to himself. He turned over and stuffed his face into the pillow.

Omar, still slumped on the floor against the wall, cleared his throat. "I'm afraid there's more," he said. "One of the terrorists appears to have been injured in the fracas, fallen over, and broken his ankle. He is in agonizing pain and can't move. They can't get out of the house."

No-one spoke. Hadas stood up and began to pace again. Akiva remained in position on the bed, catatonic. Finally he sat up and leaned heavily against the bedstead, shivering, holding his stomach to keep it from retching.

"It's over... it's over."

"It's not over," snapped Hadas. She stood halfway between Omar, who was now sitting against the wall, head in hands, and Akiva, quivering on the bed. She put her hands on her hips and surveyed them both. She rubbed the tears from her cheeks and brushed her hair back. Closing her eyes, she dug into the deepest layers of herself for calm, clarity, leadership. Ruthlessness if necessary, and it was necessary now. She opened her eyes with renewed focus. "Let's examine the situation. We have been party to a terrible act. We will have to deal with our guilt in that act afterwards. But right now, the terrorists are in the house, and can't get out, or at least, not without help. We need to get them and the baby out of there. It is now..." – she looked at her watch – "7:45 pm, and every minute that goes by increases the chances of them being caught. So we don't have much time. Akiva, Omar: am I missing anything? The analysis is correct?"

Akiva shrugged his shoulders and half-nodded. Omar looked up from his slump, gazing intently at Hadas. He knew what she was about to say.

"We'll have to go there ourselves."

Omar nodded. "I believe you are right, my dear. I see no other way."

Akiva was silent for a moment, breathing shallow breaths. Eventually he managed to stammer out some words: "I have become Yoav, I have become Hitler, and now I have to become an Arab terrorist. How will I ever be able to talk with people about peace? How will I live with myself after this?"

Hadas sat down next to him again on the bed, and this time he did not push her away. "You can't do this now, Uncle Akiva," she whispered. "You can't have this conversation with yourself. Afterwards, fine. You can go see a therapist, you'll do what you need to do. Right now, there is a situation that is threatening to escalate out of control and engulf us all. We need to act."

Akiva's shivering got even worse. His whole body began to convulse in shock. "I can't... I can't do this. I'm not built for this. I'm a man of peace. I'm not Yoav. I can't change."

Hadas's patience began to fray. She grabbed Akiva by both shoulders and shook him. "I don't care if you think you're built for it or not," she blasted. "Sometimes you just have to act, Akiva. Do you realize what is going to happen if those terrorists get caught there in Nofei Itamar? You think there's any way that it will not get connected to Omar, to me, to you? Forget your project, forget my career, forget Omar's business – *we will all end up in fucking prison*, Akiva. *Life in prison.* Abetting terrorists? Collaborating with Hamas? Accessories to murder? Israelis aren't very forgiving about that kind of thing. So don't sit there whining about your morals. *Our lives and our futures are at stake now.* Pull yourself the fuck together and let's get there, get done what we need to get done, and then get back to work. Shit, if you can't handle this, how did you think you were going to be able to handle the abuse you're going to get when you finally unveil your little Hitler to the world? You need to grow a fucking backbone, uncle. Plus some other body parts that I won't name out of niecely modesty."

Akiva stared at her, stunned to attention. "I've never heard you curse like that before..."

"Yeah, well maybe I've been too starstruck by you for too many years and was too busy playing the part of the dutiful niece. But you can ask Tzehainish – I curse all the fucking time in the office."

Omar piped up: "I can also attest to that particular aspect of my dear Hadas's character," he said, smiling again, suddenly enjoying this delicious display from his viewing point. "I'm not saying I approve, of course: at Harrow we were taught that swearing was to be strictly reserved for playing rugby and watching pornography."

"Oh, for fuck's sake, Omar, my love, enough already with the Harrow shit," thundered Hadas. "You were there for two fucking years almost two decades ago. Get over it!" She looked at them both in exasperation. She knew what needed to be said, what needed to be done. She always did. "We are in the Middle East. We have got ourselves sucked into an almighty pile of shit. We have done something *unforgiveable*. Absolutely unforgiveable. But if we don't act now, our lives as we know them are going to be over. We still have a chance to save this situation, and save our lives, but we need cool minds and clear actions."

Omar nodded, jolted back into seriousness, and looked at Akiva. "That's my girl," he said. "That's why she's going to be Prime Minister one day."

Akiva took a deep breath. "I think I will have to agree with you, Omar. Okay. I don't like it, but I'm with you, Hadas. Lead us."

Hadas took a breath too. "We go there ourselves," she repeated. "We leave now, we'll be there in twenty minutes. We take Omar's rental car. We'll get into the settlement as Jews. I know how to flirt with and sweet talk soldiers if any of them starts to look too closely at Omar. We'll get to the house, we take the baby, we smuggle both of Omar's fucking... one-legged terrorists... out of there in the trunk of the car, we dump them, one of them does the business with the

Palestinian baby, and then we sail home back to Jerusalem as planned. It's the same plan as before, but this time we are going to be there to witness the dirty work. There's no other way."

Five minutes later, the three of them were in the car, heading out of Jerusalem. The hills of the West Bank began to rise toward them in the darkness.

Chapter 34

Yoav picked up the phone.

"They're on the move," his man on the other end of the line said. "They've left the hotel and they're on the road. I'm tailing them."

"Which direction are they heading?"

"They just left Jerusalem. Headed toward Samaria."

"Shit," said Yoav. *Surely they couldn't have figured out where... but how?*

He paused for a moment before replying, clicking his tongue, calculating the chess moves he needed to make. "I can't take any chances. Stop them. I don't care how, just get them off the road. Make it look like an accident. Kill them if you can, but if that's not possible, I at least want them immobile for the next few hours while I take care of things."

Yoav hung up. He would need to do a rapid relocation. He'd need an excuse to tell Denkstein and the family, and a new site to take them to. "Shit," he said again with a scowl. He picked up the phone and dialed the man with the gravelly voice.

Omar drove at pace through the evening traffic, honking occasionally, weaving in and out of the lanes.

Hadas reached forward from the back seat and put a hand on his neck, giving him a brief massage. "Careful. Stay beneath the speed limit, don't do anything illegal. The last thing we need right now is to get pulled over by a cop."

Omar took a hand off the steering wheel and reached behind to squeeze hers. "Don't worry, my love. Anyway, when we get into the West Bank you should take over the driving. Just in case we go through any checkpoints."

"Fine. Pull over when we get off the–"

Hadas couldn't finish her sentence. A car suddenly pulled alongside them and smashed into them from the side. They were thrown to the right, toward the hard shoulder, as the other car continued to drive with diagonal thrust, pushing them off the road.

"I can't control it!" yelled Omar. He dragged his body against the steering wheel in the other direction, but he was no match for the professional he was up against. The car veered off the highway and slammed into an earth mound on the side of the road. It tilted on its side, almost turning over, and then careened over the top of the earth mound and came to a crashing halt facing down at a 45 degree angle on the other side.

Yoav's man slowed down, pulled over, and looked back at the damage he'd caused. It had been a simple task, one that someone with his training could have done in his sleep. Seeing the steam rising from the car's engine, and the airbags bulging from the car's windows, he nodded in satisfaction, continued driving, and called his boss.

"No problem. They won't be going anywhere tonight."

"Any witnesses?"

"A few cars some distance behind me. But it's dark, there was a pretty big gap between them and me. They may have seen it, but there's no possibility of anyone IDing my plates. It's clean."

"Are they alive?" asked Yoav.

The man craned his neck back toward the crash site. "Probably," he shrugged.

"No direct collision with anything, looks like a soft landing. Sorry."

"You think you can finish it now?"

"Negative. Too risky. I'd have to back up, leave my car on the side of the road... too many variables. But they're immobile for the time being."

"Okay. Get out of there and I'll update you later tonight. Maybe we can finish the whole thing before morning."

Yoav hung up and got ready to head to Nofei Itamar.

Silence. Except for the hiss of steam escaping from the engine and the noise of the traffic from the main road.

Hadas blinked her eyes, seeing stars, trying to gain focus. "Omar... Akiva...? Are you okay...?"

"I think so," gasped Akiva from the front passenger seat. "I'm... I'm stuck... can't move a muscle because of this airbag..."

"Omar?"

Nothing.

"Omar?" repeated Hadas, louder.

Silence.

"Omar... please, please, no, please, Omar..." Hadas was crying now, trying to reach through the airbag that had deployed in the back seat, clawing it away desperately with her hands, stretching toward the front where she could see Omar's head pinned between the front airbag and the head support of his seat.

Omar's head moved and he made a croaking moan.

"Oh thank God," breathed Hadas, still scrambling to make contact with him, to touch him. "Omar... can you hear me? Are you okay?"

"I've been better, my dear," said Omar groggily, trying to maneuver his head away from the airbag. "But I think I'm in one piece."

Hadas managed to get the door open and squeezed herself out of the car, half-rolling, half-falling onto the ground beneath her. She ran around the car to open Omar's door and pulled it open. He stumbled out of the car into her arms and they fell down together in a clumsy embrace.

She wiped some dirt off his face and kissed him. "Can you stand?"

"I'm fine, I'm fine," said Omar, getting carefully to his feet. "Go help Akiva."

Hadas limped to the other side of the car and helped Akiva out too. He staggered out of the car and grabbed his back in a twinge of pain. "What happened?" he asked.

"It must be Yoav's people," said Hadas. "No way that was an accident."

"So they were following us? They know where we are?"

Hadas shrugged. "I don't have any other explanation."

"That means they can guess where we were heading... which means..." Akiva slumped to the ground.

Hadas cast a look over the car and put her hands on her hips. "It means that we are stuck here on the side of the road, and as every minute goes by, the chances of us getting to the settlement before Yoav diminish."

Akiva peered his head up over toward the main road. "Can we hitch-hike there?"

"You think the three of us will get a ride together? To that exact village in the middle of nowhere? Even if we could, our chances of anonymity disappear," said Hadas.

Akiva picked a few blades of grass and threw them into the air aimlessly. "So we're out of options." He put his hands behind him, leaned back and sniffed, gazing at the steam still hissing from the car's engine.

"Shush!" said Omar suddenly. He had been carefully shaking himself down and rubbing his neck where the seatbelt had pressed into it, but he now dove toward Akiva and Hadas, trying to push them behind the car. "There's someone with a flashlight."

Akiva and Hadas looked at where Omar was pointing. There it was, a cell-phone flashlight probably, and holding it, the silhouette of a man stumbling over the earth toward them. The three of them knelt down behind the car. They heard the man's voice drifting toward them, mixed in with the sounds of the steam and the traffic. "Hey... you there..."

"There's no way he won't find us," whispered Akiva.

"Just shush," hissed Hadas. "I'm thinking." She frowned. "Wait a minute... I recognize that voice."

The flashlight came round the side of the car, blinding them, and each of them covered their eyes with their hands. The man lowered the flashlight and shook his head ruefully.

"I did tell you this would end in disaster," said Benny Shoham.

Chapter 35

"Benny! What the... do you have anything to do with this?" Hadas spluttered, scrambling onto her knees in anger.

Benny took a couple of delicate steps forward on the uneven terrain. "Now I'm offended," he said. "I may have resorted to fake blackmail to try to get you to see sense, but I would draw the line at hurting you. No, I don't have anything to do with this. I just saw what happened and wanted to make sure you were okay."

"You saw what happened?" challenged Hadas, unconvinced. "What, you were just here by coincidence?"

Benny stumbled a few more steps forward and proffered an arm down to help Hadas up. "I was here, Hadas, because I have been following you around these past few days. Since our meeting the other night, I have been extremely worried about you, about what you might do. I've been cancelling all my appointments and keeping an eye on you, hoping that I might get another chance to stop you before you do something crazy."

"But... I was so careful..." mumbled Hadas. She hesitated, but then reached up and grabbed Benny's arm, levering herself to her feet.

"Well, that's what you thought about your secret little dates with Omar, and we know how that turned out, don't we?" said Benny. "Every time you've left the Knesset I've been right on your tail, by foot and by car, and you didn't notice once. Don't quit your day job, that's all I can say. Your friend Yoav and his buddies seem to have had no trouble finding you too, as is apparent from that rather interesting bumper car exhibition just now. Anyway, the most important thing is, are you all okay? I haven't phoned for an ambulance, I wanted to make sure there were no two-headed babies in the car before I called in anything official."

Akiva stood up gingerly. "No two-headed babies. Not in the car, nor anywhere else."

"And where might the three of you lovely people" – here Benny nodded at Omar too, who returned the gesture coldly, still sitting on the grass – "be heading so late at night?"

"You don't want to know," scowled Hadas. "And it doesn't matter, now, anyway. It appears that Yoav has derailed our plans, quite literally. He's won."

"Wait," said Akiva, turning to Hadas and lowering his voice. "Maybe... maybe there's still a way... if we could... use his car...?" He gestured at Benny with his eyes.

Akiva didn't wait for Hadas to respond. He took a step toward Benny and grabbed him by the shoulder, suddenly re-energized. "We need to borrow your car. Just for an hour or two. It's... it's critically important. I know... I know what you think of me, what you think of my ideas, but unless we get back on the road in the next few minutes, Yoav will have moved the child, and our lives will be back in mortal danger."

"Now look here," declared Benny, taking a step back. "I've told you already what I think of this nonsense. I've been following you in order to *stop* you from doing anything stupid, not help you on your way. The best thing that I can do for you right now is to take you back in my car to the nearest police station and bring the authorities into this. It's–"

"Benny," interrupted Hadas. "Please. Akiva is right. We are *this* close to being able to gain an advantage, to being able to gain some leverage over Yoav. But we are also this close to being in real, serious trouble. The police won't be able to protect us. Even you can see that from everything that's happened. You know what Yoav's capable of. Help us." She walked over to him and held his hands in hers. "Please."

Benny stared at Hadas for a long moment. He shook his head in exasperation. "You're insane," he muttered. "All three of you. But fine. Fine. Take my car. I'll call a cab home."

Hadas reached up to Benny and gave him a warm hug. "I won't forget this. I'll make it up to you. I promise."

Benny shook his head again and pursed his lips.

"Okay, let's go, let's go," said Akiva, even more animated, clapping his hands, herding the others like a sheepdog, not wanting to give Benny a chance to change his mind. "Every minute counts." Benny gave his keys to him, and the three of them clambered over the earthen mound back to the main road where Benny had pulled over.

"Just be careful, okay?" Benny shouted over at them.

But they were already out of earshot.

There was little traffic. They arrived at the settlement and got past its security gate without a problem; Omar pretended to be asleep in the back of the car, and Hadas and Akiva were clearly Jewish, and therefore not a threat. The security guard waved them through and they drove toward the couple's house, following the directions that Tzehainish had given them.

They parked in the front yard and quietly got out of the car. It was pitch black; the settlement didn't have street lights yet. The sky above them was a breathtaking planetarium of stars, the air was quiet and fresh, and crickets chirped as if on a Disney soundtrack. The silhouettes of the hills of Biblical Israel loomed in the distance all around them. *It's beautiful*, thought Hadas to herself, momentarily captivated by the setting, its quiet wonder jarring with the churning of her stomach and the tightness of her breath.

She noticed that her daydreams had resulted in her falling a little behind

Akiva and Omar, who were just entering through the house's front door. She walked briskly to catch up with them.

When she got into the house, the scene was calm but devastating. Sprawled on the floor, dead, limbs tangled, were the couple. A pool of blood seeped around the husband's head, and from the wife's chest. In a corner of the room, incongruously, was a car seat, placed gently on the floor, and in it the baby lay sleeping peacefully. Next to the car seat was a duffel bag, containing, Hadas assumed with a grimace, the dead Palestinian baby that the terrorists had brought with them.

Akiva clutched his hands to his stomach. "I think I'm going to puke."

Hadas grabbed him roughly by the shoulder. "You can't puke. We mustn't even touch anything here. Not a fingerprint, nothing. This has to look like the actions of lone terrorists, not a whole committee. If you feel sick, Akiva, step outside for a minute."

She turned to Omar. "Where are your friends?"

Omar gestured behind him. "Baby's room. Just took a quick glance. His ankle looks pretty shitty, all swollen."

Akiva took a step toward the dead couple on the floor, as if sleep-walking. "I can't... I can't take my eyes off them. It's like... they're dead, but their blood is crying out to me. Accusing me."

Hadas pulled him back. "Accusing all of us," she said. "But we can't dwell on that now. We're in this now, we're in the middle of it, whether you like it or not, and we have to finish it. We are *going* to finish it."

Akiva nodded.

Hadas pointed to the front door. "Go get some fresh air. Don't touch anything. Hang out by the car. We'll go deal with our klutzy terrorist, get him ready to transfer into the car trunk."

She walked briskly past Omar, noting the clean and house-proud kitchen, the bookshelves full of Bibles and Talmuds, with row upon row of *Congratulations!* baby cards displayed in front of them, the simple modesty of these ordinary, good-hearted people to whom Yoav had given a miracle. The joy in the house still reverberated in its walls.

A door ahead of her was painted light baby blue, with a cute cartoon of a baby boy in a diaper smiling and waving, speech bubble coming out of his mouth saying "David's room." She walked in.

If the scene that had greeted Hadas as she entered the house had been one of calm devastation, here it was one of chaos. A Palestinian dressed in dark blue tattered jeans and a black T-shirt, keffiyah wrapped around his neck, was lying on the floor, writhing in agony. The jeans were rolled up to mid-calf on his right leg, sock pulled down around its sneaker, and Hadas could see, even from where she stood, that the joint of his ankle was puffed up like a tennis ball. The other Palestinian sat in the corner of the room, gazing into space. Baby toys were strewn around the floor, the baby's crib was overturned with one of its walls smashed off its hinges, and a chest of drawers, full of brand new baby clothes and socklets and diapers, had also been flung onto the floor, contents spilled. There were blood streaks on the floor, presumably from one of the parents who had put up a fight here. The front room had looked eerily normal; this place truly looked like the site of an attack.

The Palestinian sitting down in the corner suddenly noticed Hadas. *Kus emek*, he said, *Motherfucker*, and started scrambling to his feet. Hadas saw the gun in his hand and realized that she probably looked like a neighbor come to see what was going on – a neighbor who would have to be killed too.

"Wait," she said, "I'm with–" but it was too late to get any more words out. The terrorist was on his feet and the gun was pointing at her.

Suddenly Omar burst into the room. "Stop," he said in Arabic. "She's with me."

The terrorist paused, unsure what to make of this. "She's an Arab?" he asked Omar. "She sounded like a Jew."

Omar walked over to the terrorist and pushed his arm away from pointing at Hadas. "It doesn't matter who she is. She's a friend of mine. She is not your concern."

The terrorist moved his arm back toward Hadas, not quite pointing at her, but not lowering his aim either. "You," he said in Arabic, nodding at Hadas. "What is your name?"

Hadas knew enough Arabic to understand what was going on. She didn't answer.

"I told you," said Omar, "She's with me. I am here to get you out of here, and she is helping. Do you want to get out of here, or not?"

The terrorist now turned to Omar and pointed his gun directly at Omar's head. "I don't know you," he scowled. "I know Ali. Ali is the one who is going to pay me for this mission. Where is Ali?"

Omar spoke quietly and calmly. "Ali is a colleague of mine. I am the one who asked Ali to set this mission up. I am the money, and if you kill me, you will not get your money. I am also a very powerful man in our community, and if you kill me, a thousand vendettas will rain down upon you and your family for the rest of your life. So I am asking you again, in fact, I am *telling* you, put your gun down."

The terrorist kept his gun pointed at Omar. "And who is she?"

Omar paused. "She is an American. She is a sympathizer with our cause who is helping me with this mission. I tell you again, she is here to help."

"But she spoke Hebrew when she came in the room."

"She lives in Israel on a tourist visa, and she has learned the language of the Zionists. But she is one of us."

The terrorist lowered his gun arm, still suspicious. Omar gestured to Hadas to go and check out the Palestinian on the floor. She moved warily over to him, and carefully got down on her knees by his ankle. She gave it a small press, and the man winced with pain. Hadas turned back to Omar and shook her head. She said, this time in English, with her best attempt at an American accent, "He can't walk."

She crawled over to the man's upper body and put a hand on his forehead.

"He's clammy." She put her finger on his neck to take his pulse, and then several things happened in quick succession.

Hadas's Star of David necklace was usually left tucked in, underneath her clothes, but as she bent over the Palestinian terrorist's neck to take his pulse, gravity made it slip out, and the Star of David dangled in front of the Palestinian's face.

The terrorist grabbed the necklace and yanked it toward his eyes. "*Yehud!*" he shouted. *Jew!* "She's a Jew!" He suddenly grabbed Hadas by the neck and started to choke her.

Hadas, caught by surprise, tried to bat his arms away, but his upper body strength was too much for her. She began to weaken and fell to the floor beside him, and the terrorist, despite his limited mobility, managed to maneuver himself half on top of her, tightening his grip.

The other terrorist had been watching these events in a stupor, unsure of what on earth was going on. But now he snapped out of it, raised his gun again, and pushed past Omar, moving across the room to help his colleague. Omar lunged out at him, got one arm across his body, and with his other arm he pulled the terrorist's hand holding the gun upward, away from Hadas. The terrorist fired off a shot which, muffled by the gun's silencer, still made a loud crack in the small room. The bullet went into the ceiling, sprinkling them all with pieces of plaster and cement.

"His ankle," shouted Omar. "Go for his ankle!"

Hadas, barely conscious, started kicking with her feet. She felt herself connect with a knee, with a shin, with one of his feet, but not the bad one... she was feeling lightheaded, feeling herself fade away, but she summoned all her remaining strength to give one last kick.

She connected with the terrorist's broken ankle and he doubled over in pain, letting go of his grip on Hadas and rolling away. Hadas struggled to her knees, gasping for breath, and crawled over toward the terrorist's feet. She reached out and grasped around for something that felt hard. Her hands came across a little plastic toy truck with blue wheels and a yellow roof. She grabbed it, lifted it, and slammed it down hard on the terrorist's bad ankle. He screamed in agony, and she slammed it down again and again.

The other terrorist wriggled free of Omar's clutches and raised his arm to shoot. He aimed his gun at Hadas, but Omar slammed into his back, pushing him off balance.

Another shot thudded out. Omar and the terrorist tumbled onto the floor together. The gun slipped from the terrorist's hands.

Omar lifted his head and saw Hadas was covered in blood. "You fucker," he shouted at the terrorist who he had slammed into, and started punching him in the head. "You fucker, you fucker, you fucker, you've killed her..."

"Omar–" Hadas scrambled to her feet, gasping to get the words out. "It's not me, it's not my blood – he's shot the other one. Omar, he missed me, he missed me."

Omar looked up again at Hadas, and then at the other terrorist on the ground, and saw that she was right. Blood was spurting from his chest. Omar's bodyslam into his accomplice had put off his aim and caused him to kill his partner instead.

But as Omar hesitated, taking in the scene around him, the terrorist who he'd been punching saw his opportunity. He wriggled away from Omar, hands clawing toward the gun that lay inches away on the floor.

Omar pulled him back, and tried to pin him down away from where the gun lay, but the terrorist was too strong for him. He pushed Omar half off him and once more started crawling to the gun. Omar grabbed him, this time by one of his arms, but the terrorist shook him off again. He spun onto his back and kicked Omar's torso, slamming him into the wall and freeing himself from Omar's grasp.

Omar slumped to the floor by the wall, clutching his stomach as he tried to catch his breath.

"You are a traitor to your people," the terrorist spat at Omar. "You are a lover of Jew dogs and a Zionist collaborator. You help our enemy, our enemy who brought the *Nakba* upon our people, whose army murdered my brother, whose government strangles our movements, whose people denies our freedom. You dishonor every martyr who has died in the fight to liberate our people from the Zionist occupation. I am going to kill your Jew bitch girlfriend in front of your eyes and then I will kill you." He turned back around, got onto all fours, and reached out for the gun.

But the gun wasn't there. It had been there on the floor, inches away from him, but now it was gone. Confused, thinking that perhaps he'd lost his bearings on the floor, the terrorist looked to the left and to the right, but couldn't see the gun.

"You're looking in the wrong direction," said Hadas. "Try looking up instead."

She stood above him, gun in hand, the other terrorist's blood spattered on her blouse and her face and her hair. She pointed the gun at the terrorist shakily. He scrambled to his feet but she kept her distance, gun trained on him.

"I want you to know," she croaked, "that I believe in peace between our two peoples. I want to share this land with you. I want you to have the Palestine that you dream of, side by side with Israel."

"You are a Zionist colonizer Jew bitch," spat the terrorist. "My people will not rest until you drink the water of the sea."

The terrorist sprang toward her. She pulled the trigger. Another shot rang out and the terrorist crumpled to the floor.

There was silence.

"Note to self," said Omar, clambering to his feet and rubbing his chest gingerly. "Never call Hadas a Zionist colonizer Jew bitch. Apparently she doesn't take kindly to it."

Hadas started crying, the tension suddenly draining out of her and leaving the enormity of what she'd done in its place. She ran to Omar and they hugged each other tightly, faces buried in each other necks, both now crying, shaking, laughing.

They finally broke apart. The blood that had been all over Hadas was now smeared over Omar too. They surveyed each other and the scene around them. It looked like something from a horror movie. The floor was covered in blood, and they too were covered in blood and tears, clothing torn, eyes still wild.

"Let's just make sure that they're both really dead," said Omar. One by one, Hadas kept the gun trained on each terrorist's head while Omar knelt beside them and felt for a pulse. Satisfied, he stood up, and went to embrace her again.

"For one moment there, I thought I'd lost you."

The door opened and Akiva walked in. "What's been keeping you?" he said, as he opened the door, and then "Holy shit!" as he saw the scene in front of him.

"Change of plan," said Omar dryly. "We're not taking our colleagues back with us. They'll be staying here..."

"We'll have to rethink the narrative that we leave here," said Hadas. "How are we going to make this look like a terrorist attack gone wrong? None of it will make any sense to the army."

"Never mind that for now," said Akiva. "Yoav's here."

Chapter 36

"Y ou're sure it's him?" asked Hadas.

Akiva nodded grimly. "Just saw his car pull up. It's definitely him."

"Maybe we can get out through a window or a back door?"

"No," said Akiva. *Enough.* "He has tried to kill me, he has made me run for my life and hide like a mouse. He has made me endanger *your* careers and *your* lives. And he has made me do some terrible things tonight. Things that will haunt me for the rest of my life. It's time to face him. One way or the other, this stops here and now."

Akiva walked back out to the living room and stood by the front door. The cool Biblical air wafted through the crack between the door and the jamb, and chilled his flushed cheeks. He spotted his reflection in the window, the darkness outside turning it into a mirror, and suddenly he was back in Yoav's apartment, staring into the television screen, a different mirror from a different time. *Finally. Finally I am going to tell you the truth, Yoav. Finally you are going to know the real me.* He put his hands on his hips and lifted his head high.

Hadas and Omar followed Akiva into the living room. Hadas picked up the car seat which held the baby, who was still fast asleep, oblivious to what was going on around him, and took it to another back room, presumably the parents'. She gently placed the car seat down by the foot of the bed and turned the lights off.

She returned to the living room. Omar had sat down on the sofa, arm draped lazily over its back, beckoning her to join him. She gave a quick shake of the head and stood by the opposite wall, leaning back on it with hands in her pockets. She didn't know how these next few minutes would play out, but she presumed it was better to have Yoav a little off kilter, not quite sure where to look; she would be out of his line of sight as he walked in. Akiva opened the latch of the front door, left it slightly ajar, and then stepped back to stand in the center of the room, facing the front door, hands still on hips, standing over the corpses of the dead adoptive parents.

The front door opened and Yoav entered. He looked at Akiva, and then glanced down at the dead bodies. And then he smiled. "Akiva!" he boomed with exaggerated ebullience. "*You* did *this*? I'm amazed. I'm impressed. I didn't know you had it in you. And they say you can't teach an old dog new tricks..." Yoav scratched his head dramatically. "Well, I can't deny that it puts a little bump in my plan, and I'll have to figure out how the fuck to explain this to Denkstein. But if you think that this changes anything..."

Akiva had been standing between Yoav and Omar, blocking his view, and he now moved slightly out of the way.

Yoav beamed even more magnanimously. "Ah-hah! And you must be one of Akiva's little friends who my people have been telling me about. One of his little help-mates scurrying around with him like a cockroach from hotel to hotel. Quite the frequent traveler." Yoav gave a theatrical bow. "And who might you be, pray tell? Please, introduce yourself to me!"

Omar shrugged his shoulders and spoke back to Yoav with a heavy Arabic accent: "No speak Hebrew."

Yoav raised his eyebrows in genuine surprise. "An Arab? That makes sense. I guess you didn't really have it in you after all. I suppose you pulled him in to do this little piece of dirty work," he said, gesturing at the corpses on the floor. "But Akiva, an Arab? Where on earth did you find a filthy Arab terrorist lowlife like this? Well, well, well, you are full of surprises. I'm almost sorry that I'm finally going to get to kill you tonight. At least I'll have the comfort of knowing that there's one less Arab on God's earth as well."

"You're not killing anyone tonight, Yoav," said Hadas from behind him. He spun around. She was pointing a gun at him. The gun that she'd used to kill the terrorist in the baby's bedroom. She pointed with her other arm to the armchair next to the sofa. "Sit."

Yoav didn't move. He tried to retain his bravado, but his voice cracked a bit. For the first time, he was unnerved. "And a female accomplice too? The one from the car the other night, if I'm not mistaken, who nearly got me trampled by that pile of motorbikes. Gosh, Akiva seems to have made all sorts of new friends lately. So who are you? You're Jewish, that's for sure. A little research student that Akiva has picked up? His cleaning lady? Long lost relative?"

"Remarkably good guess," commented Akiva. Yoav whipped his head toward him, his brow furrowed in confusion. He turned back to Hadas and stared at her intently.

"But there's something familiar about the face... I can't place you, but I've seen you before, I know it..."

Hadas kept the gun trained on Yoav with her right hand. With her left hand, she reached up to her wig and pulled it off. Her blonde hair was tied in a bun, and she quickly undid it, letting it fall over her shoulders. "Hadas Levinson," she declared with a fake smile, flashing her teeth but with contempt in her eyes. "I would say it's nice to meet you, but my political career has been built around telling the truth, not lying."

"What the fuck is this, Akiva?" growled Yoav. "What the fuck is this bitch doing here?"

"The bitch asked you to sit," noted Omar, now back to his perfect unaccented Hebrew. "I *do* suggest you follow her recommendation. She gets terribly angry when you refuse her."

Yoav spun back to look again at Omar. He was totally off balance now. What was going in here?

Hadas took a step toward him and held the gun with both hands, aiming it at his face. "Sit down, you piece of shit."

Yoav slowly sat down on the armchair which Hadas had pointed at.

"Gun," she said. "I assume you have one."

Yoav slowly pulled a gun from his jacket pocket and placed it on the floor.

"Remove the chamber," snapped Hadas. "I may be a bitch but I'm not an idiot."

Yoav sighed melodramatically, bent down, and clicked the chamber out of the gun. He kicked the empty weapon toward the corpses in the middle of the room and slid the chamber in the other direction to the wall. Hadas nodded in satisfaction.

"Well, Akiva, I do salute you," Yoav drawled, bravado back in place. "For the first time ever since I've known you, you have me totally baffled. So come on, tell me. What are you doing with this socialist bitch and with this Arab? Don't tell me you've joined the peace camp!"

Akiva looked at Yoav and smiled. *Finally.* His arms were shaking, but with the excitement of victory, not with fear. *Finally.*

He held his head up high. Drew in a large breath. "Yoav... I've always been in the peace camp."

Yoav paused. "Impossible..."

"For me, it's always been about peace," Akiva went on. "Since before you first met me. All along. Your extensive background checks on me found out all about my immediate family history, my religious mother, my dead Likud hero father, but they missed two important details. Firstly, that I did indeed have a long lost relative – I see you recognize my niece Hadas? Yes, my niece. I won't bore you with the details. That mistake was forgivable, I guess, because even *I* didn't know of her existence back then. But the part where you really screwed up? You found out everything about my parents, but nothing about *me.* You assumed that because I was the great Naftali Cohen's son, I was a religious nationalist too? You didn't see that I was a scientist, a *true* scientist, someone who believes that knowledge and learning and technology should work for the benefit of humankind, of *all* humankind. Not to seek revenge, not to get one-up on another person or people. But to make the whole world a better place, for everyone. To make peace."

"I don't understand," stammered Yoav, his voice faltering. "Your work at GeneLight. You were as obsessed with the vengeance thing as the rest of them…"

Akiva's hands stopped shaking. *Finally.* "You saw what you wanted to see, Yoav. Mostly I just smiled and nodded at the nonsense you spouted. So you made assumptions about me. And that suited me fine. I kept my head down, I focused on getting the science right, I focused on my own long-term plan, and let you think what I needed you to think."

Akiva paused. Here was the sentence he'd been wanting to say, been planning on saying. At last he was going to say it.

"I used you, Yoav."

His face broke into a smile, into a wide grin of relief and joy, he was almost giggling, but he controlled himself and said it again. "I used you. You thought you were using me, but I was using you. All along."

Yoav was silent.

"And now," crowed Akiva, "I'm going to tell you what this was really about. What *your* life's work is going to lead to. What Hadas and Omar are going to do for the Jews and the Palestinians who live in this land. Oh yes – I forgot – how rude of me – I haven't yet introduced you to Omar, have I? Omar, my future nephew."

Omar opened his mouth as if to make a wisecrack, but thought better of it.

Akiva continued, in full flow now, his confidence and bravado rising in direct proportion to how Yoav's was visibly falling. "Omar, my future nephew, the future husband of future Prime Minister Hadas Levinson, who will bring their peoples together as they see the possibilities for a different future, right, Hadas?"

Hadas smiled. "Right, Uncle Akiva. Omar and me. A different future." For a moment it was just the two of them in the room together. In unison, they nodded at each other.

Akiva licked his lips, taking his time. This felt so good. *Finally.* "This reborn Hitler is going to bring peace, Yoav. Not war, not a mighty Jewish empire, not the miserable, disgusting, racist future that you want. I'm going to raise this new Hitler with love. With compassion. With warmth. To be different, to be a force for good. To apologize. To show people that anything is possible. That peace is possible."

Suddenly, from the back room, came the sound of a baby crying. The normal cry of a normal baby, waking in the middle of the night, hungry for breast or bottle.

Yoav raised his eyebrows at Akiva. "It's your baby now. You'd better go take care of him. He's probably hungry."

"In a minute. I'm not done yet. There's more I want you to hear."

Hadas lowered the gun momentarily. "Akiva, it's a tiny newborn, it needs to eat. Let me–"

But Hadas didn't have chance to finish her sentence. Yoav had seen her lower the gun, and he suddenly pounced toward her, barreling his shoulder into her, pushing her to the floor. The gun fell out of her hands and skidded towards the kitchen, coming to a halt on the floor several meters away.

Omar was the first to react. He jumped up from the couch, pushed past Akiva, and ran toward the gun. He bent down to pick it up, but Yoav was right behind him and managed to push him out of the way before he could get a grasp. Hadas was on the floor at the other side of the room, winded, struggling to her feet; Akiva stood motionless in the middle of the room, unsure of how to react.

Omar's fingers were inches away from getting a grip on the gun, but Yoav beat him to it. He grabbed Omar's arms, pinned them behind his back, and half-kneed, half-kicked him so that he lost his balance and also fell to the floor.

Yoav picked up the gun.

"Now, you leftist fuckers, order has been restored," Yoav swaggered triumphantly. "And now, I'm going to kill each one of you. Two self-hating leftist

Jews and one Arab piece of shit. What a happy night this will be. When that baby over there is the king of Israel, I'll tell him about this night, and he'll laugh in joy. Because when I kill the three of you now, it's nothing compared to the bloodbath he will bring upon the leftists and the Arabs when he grows up."

Yoav stood between Hadas and Omar, with Akiva at about 90 degrees in the middle, and he swiveled from one to the other, training the gun on each of them in turn. "Who shall I kill first, that's the question... toughest thing I've had to decide all night..." He turned to Hadas and nodded his head gently in delicious anticipation. "Oh, yes, I think that a bullet in the head of the Blonde Bitch will be just the way to begin the fun and games."

He raised his gun towards Hadas.

"No...!" shouted Akiva, and dived at Yoav just as the shot rang out. The bullet slammed into Akiva's torso but his momentum kept him moving in Yoav's direction. As he fell to the floor, he somehow kicked his legs out and tangled them with Yoav's, and Yoav, caught off balance, fell to the floor with him.

Gasping with pain, Akiva rolled onto Yoav and prised the gun away from him. He managed to get onto his knees, straddling Yoav's chest, gun in hand. He tried to aim the gun at Yoav, but his hands were shaking, energy sapping out of his body. He looked down at his own chest and saw the blood pouring out of a gaping hole in his stomach. Pain ripped through his body, his vision was blurry, his hands began to lose their grip on the gun. Suddenly the image of Shira flashed across him, her blood pouring out of her as his poured out of him, and with a roar of anger he forced his fingers to regain their strength. Shuddering violently with his last few drops of adrenaline, he got the gun under control and pointed it at Yoav.

Akiva opened his mouth but all he could get out was a whisper.

"This... is for... peace..."

Akiva's final act before his death was to shoot Yoav in the head.

He turned around to get one last look at Hadas and then fell to his side, his blood now mixing freely with the blood that was seeping out of Yoav.

Silence. The baby in the other room, temporarily muted in shock by the sound of the struggle, began crying again.

Chapter 37

For a long time, neither Hadas nor Omar moved. They stared at the two new corpses who had now joined the baby's parents on the floor of the living room. Akiva and Yoav, having spent most of their adult lives entwined in a web of lies each with the other, now lay entwined on the floor.

Hadas fell to the ground by Akiva's head. She stroked his hair and closed his eyes.

"Thank you, Uncle," she whispered. "Thank you for saving my life."

Omar came over to her and leaned down toward her. "I'm so sorry," he said. "I'm so, so sorry. But we have to get out of here. Every minute that we remain here puts us in more danger of being discovered. Yoav may have told his people that he was coming here – we just don't know – we have to get out of here."

Hadas gave a long, deep sigh, still stroking Akiva's head. Then she stood up and fell into Omar's arms. Now he stroked *her* hair, as she quietly wept into his shoulder.

Omar kissed her neck, but then pulled her head up. "We have to go, my love."

"I know," she said. "But we have to carry Akiva to the car. I'm not leaving him here. This scene is a media shit-storm, and I will not have his good name dragged into it. They will call him a terrorist sympathizer, a murderer, a monster. I will not have that be how he is remembered. He was a man of peace. He can't stay here."

"But his blood is all over the place," said Omar. "The police will know there was another person here."

Hadas broke off from her embrace and looked down again at Akiva's body. "I don't care. He has no police record, so they won't be able to match the DNA from the blood here with anything in their databases. They'll never know who it was. The army'll go and turn over all the Palestinian villages in the area like they always do, and assume that it's just a third unknown terrorist. I will figure out how to dispose of his body. I have no idea right now, but I will figure it out. On my terms. On his terms. But I am not leaving him here."

Omar held up his hands and nodded. The two of them lifted Akiva up, through the living room, out of the front door. They had intended the trunk of the car to contain a Palestinian terrorist with a broken ankle, but now it contained Akiva's body.

Hadas walked back into the house; Omar followed. She looked around, as if appraising the place like a realtor. "The army won't have the faintest idea what's gone on here. Two dead terrorists in the bedroom, three dead Jews in the living room, anonymous dead newborn in a duffel bag, the blood from someone else's body that's been dragged out of the door... it'll be a feeding frenzy for the press. No matter. It will be what it will be. As long as Akiva isn't part of it." She turned to Omar. "We should leave. Get the baby. I brought some baby milk formula in the diaper bag" – she gestured to the couch where she had flung it when they first came into the house – "maybe we give him a bit of food to shut him up, and then we move."

Ten minutes later, they were driving out of the settlement, back toward civilization.

As Omar drove over a rough patch of road, the car's jolts woke the baby up and he began crying again. Hadas twisted round in her seat toward the baby.

"*Beruhige dich!*" *Calm down,* she tutted in exasperation. The baby cried even louder. Hadas leaned behind to the back of the car, and rummaged through the diaper bag until she found a pacifier. She put it in the baby's mouth, and rubbed his tummy. The baby's tiny body filled her palm as he heaved with infant tears. She continued to rub, and slowly the baby quieted down and gave a little gurgle. She kept her palm on the baby as his belly began to move in and out more rhythmically and deeply, his crystal blue eyes fixed on Hadas's, pulling her in, demanding attention, until he slowly closed them and fell back into a deep newborn sleep.

"You're going to have to learn German," she said to Omar, still gazing at the baby. "He needs to speak German. That's what Akiva wanted."

Omar pulled over to the side of the road. He put the car in park and turned to face Hadas, pulling her face back toward him. He put her hand in his.

"Perhaps, my dear, it might be better if he spoke Hebrew."

Hadas paused. A brief nod of understanding. A wry smile. She leaned over and gave Omar a tender kiss. "And Arabic," she said.

"Hebrew and Arabic it is," said Omar.

"What about us?" asked Hadas. "We won't be able to keep things secret if we're raising a child."

"Well, my dear, you know what Wordsworth said about secrets," said Omar with a grin.

Hadas shook her head in exasperation – but it was a comforting, familiar exasperation, an exasperation that held the promise of the future. She leaned over and kissed him again.

Omar put the car into gear. He wiped a tear from his eyes and started driving back to Jerusalem.

Acknowledgements

Starting to write a first novel in your 40s (and finishing it in your 50s!) is a somewhat unconventional and sometimes terrifying thing to do. I would like to thank the following people for helping me along the way:

Ofra Backenroth, Batami Gold, Jonathan Kessler (to whom I owe the Faulkner epigraph), Lyla Margalit (to whom I owe a facepalm revision that dramatically improved the plot), Daniel Moses (to whom I owe the idea of physical proximity but psychological distance in chapter 29), and Miriam Shaviv, who all read parts or all of my early drafts and gave me encouragement and feedback.

Jethro Berkman, Barry Holtz, Floy Kaminski, Rachel Korazim, Bobbi Kwall, Jean-Marc Liling, Abby Pitkowsky, Cindy Reich, Alex Stein, and Michael Wegier, who all made various introductions and connections for me.

Amin Khalef for the Arabic; Micki Rubinstein for the German.

Sue Lascelles for her editorial work on an early draft.

The two literary agents who gave me extensive and helpful feedback on early drafts, even though they ultimately chose not to represent me. Their loss. I'm not bitter!

I hope that this novel, as well as being a compelling and exciting read, raises uncomfortable but important questions about how trauma, history and religious extremism affect Israeli society and the Israeli-Palestinian conflict. My wife Peri and I made the decision to raise our children in that milieu; a decision that has for the most part been wonderful, despite the specters of Yoav and his worldview that permeate much of our society from within, and – without fatuous and inaccurate equivalencies – the pain of terrorism from without. I therefore dedicate this book to our children, Eshel, Aviv, and Melilah, in the hope that the Middle East of their future will be the one that Akiva dreamt of.

About the Author

Alex J Sinclair is an educational consultant and an adjunct lecturer at the Hebrew University of Jerusalem. He has written and spoken widely on Jewish education, Israel-Diaspora relations, and Israeli politics, in both academic and popular contexts. He has worked or consulted for a variety of Jewish educational and communal institutions in North America, Europe and Israel. His first book, published in 2013, *Loving the Real Israel: An Educational Agenda for Liberal Zionism*, was a finalist for the National Jewish Book Award. He holds an M.A. (Oxon) and M.St. from Balliol College, Oxford, and a Ph.D. from Hebrew University. He and his wife run a hotel for their three children in Modi'in, Israel.

Made in the USA
Coppell, TX
17 June 2024

33630297R00166